HUNTERS OF THE SHADOWS

By

Mark Haeuser

The characters and events in this book are fictitious. Any similarity to real persons, living or dead, is coincidental and not intended by the author.

crystaldreamspub.com
P.O. Box 698   Dover, TN 37058

Visit our website at:
www.crystaldreamspub.com

DEDICATION

In our world there are three distinct types of people. There are those who are wolves, those who are sheep and then there are a small number of those who are shepherds.
The shepherds shoulder the terrible task of protecting the sheep from the wolves. Thank God such men and women exist. They are out there in the shadows confronting those who would prey on the innocent.
This book is dedicated to those brave men and women.

ONE

Sarande, Albania 1624:

Creed snapped awake finding himself stripped from the waist up and lying in a pentagram drawn with chalk on a polished oak table. He glanced from side to side seeing no one; he was alone except for hundreds of burning candles that flickered in the breeze from the open window. He felt the cool caress of the Adriatic Sea and it refreshed him, cooling the sweat from his face. Blinking, he realized that it was night and he tried to recall the events that had brought him here to this room lying in a witch's circle of power.

It came back to him slowly and he reached for his neck; feeling along the artery, he let out a sigh of relief, realizing that he had not been bitten!

Sitting up, his head swam as the last effects of the drug he had been given began to fade and he focused around the room, looking for enemies in the

1

candlelight.

His eyes locked onto his weapons; still sheathed in his thick leather belt, they hung from the back of a heavy chair, draped over his leather coat-the coat made from the skins of two werewolves he had killed over two hundred years ago in Hungary. He felt relief as he saw the two enchanted silver tipped knives of his people, but why would they leave them where he could get to them? It didn't make sense but it also did not make sense that he still lived.

It came back now in flashes. Minions of Rasmere, a vampire by birth and head of a growing empire, had attacked him.

He dropped from the table feeling weak as the drug fled his system; they had attacked him as he left the inn descending upon him in the alley like locusts. He had put up a brief fight, almost escaping, before they held him down and the white-haired witch blew magic dust into his face.

Rasmere himself had not been there but Creed knew his people. Rasmere was Nosferatu, a blood vampire, and he was building a great army of the undead.

Slowly, using the edge of the table on which they had intended to kill him, he stood and stumbled across the room to the chair where his blades waited in the tooled leather sheaths. He swiped his long hair away from his face, retying it in the topknot style he was accustomed to. His cotton shirt was lying in a heap on the floor and he slipped it on tying the thong that held it together in a loose knot as he tucked it into his thick leather pants. With swift deft movements, he removed the belt from the chair quickly cinching it around his narrow waist.

He tried to hurry, remembering that Takada was out there alone, but his fingers still trembled as he belted his sword and tossed his jacket over his broad shoulders.

He padded to the door, thrust it open quickly and stepped into the hallway, his boot heels tapping a rhythm on the wooden floor.

Drawing his Toledo rapier, he started down the stairs keeping a watchful eye on his surroundings. He didn't need the vampire's minions jumping him again, especially in his weakened condition. He reached the bottom of the staircase and saw the curtains full of night air as they quivered from the sea breezes.

From the table in the dining room, light glinted on steel-his pistols!

He moved quickly giving up stealth for speed. He picked up and checked each double-barreled flintlock seeing they were still loaded. As he thrust them into his belt, he spied the leather case on the table, his powder and shot next to the spot the pistols had laid. Hefting it he could tell it was still laden with silver ball and powder and he placed it over his right shoulder opposite the rapier.

Creed frowned. He had to find Takada as soon as he could. The Japanese warrior was not ready to face someone as strong as Rasmere alone. He bolted from the house noting how the clouds obscured the moonlight only allowing it to peek through from time to time.

"Magic!" He spat as he sprinted down the hill

3

overlooking the town.

Someone had gone to a lot of work to bring him here from the alley and he wanted to know why.

As he ran, side-stepping the rocks and bushes that littered the dark hillside, he remembered the silver haired witch who had used her magic powder on him and realized he had never seen her before. That fact didn't bother him; it was the fact that he had never known a blood vampire to associate with a witch and that did send shivers up his spine!

He pushed the thought aside in his worry about Takada, his Japanese Ronin, who had traveled at his side these last fifty years battling the undead.

He had met the stalwart Japanese warrior by accident as he trailed a bloodthirsty follower of the vampire Ergoth into the mountains of Tibet.

He stopped for something to eat and to warm up in a small inn before climbing higher up the mountain trail. There, while he ate, Takada had walked in. Creed and the warrior locked eyes immediately. The Hunters of the undead could sense each other as well as they could sense their enemies. Takada sat down slowly, regarding the European Gypsy, who obviously did not belong in this part of the world. Not that a Japanese Samurai did either. At once they recognized each other for what they were, Hunters of the Shadows, pursuers of the undead.

They joined as partners climbing the mountain and finding the follower of Ergoth, a vampire who had once been human. He was not like his master, a trueborn; instead, he had been turned from his human form to the world of the Vampire. They had cornered him in a cave as he sought food, any animal with the blood he needed to recover his strength. When they dropped upon him, he was ill from the pains of hunger. The kill had been swift and, for the vampire, merciful as the razor sharp sword of Takada had separated the demon's head from his body.

Later, Creed questioned Takada about the enchantment of the Japanese blade, which killed the undead as easy as his own blades that were blessed of Gypsy magic. Takada had explained that a smith, who had claimed the Gods guided his hand instructing him in the design, had made the blade. He had told the Gypsy that the sword was covered in symbols of great power whispered to him by the gods of Earth, Wind and Fire. For Creed, it was not the strange designs in the sword that meant anything to him but the ease with which the sword had driven through the vampire's body.

The two men had formed a strong partnership as they traveled, following the trails of the undead as they came upon them. The hunt never slowed as the numbers of the vampire continued to grow spreading their sickness across the world.

It had been Rasmere, one of the most powerful True Bloods, who they had trailed here to this small country across the Adriatic Sea.

Creed sprinted into town passing down the almost deserted streets filled this time of night with drunks, whores, thieves and the undead!

Darting into an alley someone stepped from a doorway in front of him demanding money. Creed lowered a shoulder and plowed through the stranger. He heard the man's grunt as he struck the stone wall but he didn't stop long enough to look. His first concern was Takada not some street thief. He exited the alley and saw the lights of the Dark Raven tavern ahead.

Several drunken soldiers stood outside the front door. They were arguing with an equal number of drunken sailors while the tavern whores tried to keep them apart. Creed pushed through them knocking a sailor on his back as he slipped into the brightly lit tavern. It too was full of drunken men fighting, singing or puking as they drank the cheap liquor.

The dark haired bartender nodded as he saw the face of the Gypsy shouldering to the bar.

"Is Miranda here?" Creed asked tossing the man a gold coin.

He looked about the bar and then motioned with his head upstairs.

"She's busy," he explained.

Creed nodded. He understood that but this afternoon, she had been with Takada and he hoped she would know where he had gone. He pushed through the crowd heading for the stairs. The large Greek, Olus, blocked his way.

"Sorry Creed no one goes upstairs," he said shaking his head.

Creed smiled back as he looked up into the giant's eyes.

"I have to, Olus, Takada is missing and, I believe, in danger. Miranda, well you know how it is with them, I am sure she knows where he went." Creed held out his open hand.

Olus glanced over the Gypsy's shoulder at the bartender who shook his head no. He looked at Creed with an understanding gesture.

"Are you sure Takada is in danger?" he whispered as he leaned forward.

Creed nodded. "Yes I must find him or he may be killed."

The giant glanced from the watching bartender to the Gypsy who had become his friend; he leaned down so the barkeep couldn't see his face.

"If I allow you up there I will be fired," he explained. "So you must knock me out." His eyes met Creed's as he added. "You must."

Creed closed his eyes and nodded.

Suddenly his hands shot up reaching around the Greek's neck pulling it down as his knee shot up into the giant's chin. Olus' head snapped back and he fell against the wall, unmoving.

"Sorry." Creed whispered as he stepped over his friend's body and bolted up the stairs to the second level.

He hurried down the dimly lit hallway stopping at door number 4, Miranda's room. He knocked lightly and stepped back his hands resting on his pistols as he heard movement from inside the room.

"Who is it?" It was Miranda's voice through the door.

"Creed," he answered.

The bolt was thrown and the whore poked her head out as she held the door closed behind her.

Her dark hair was messed and her makeup smeared as she shot him a nasty look.

"I am with someone," she whispered. "How did

you get up here anyway?"

She peered down the hall behind him.

He shook his head. "Don't worry," he started as the smell from inside the room assaulted his senses. It was the familiar aroma of decay and charred flesh.

"Step aside!" The Gypsy ordered as he forced his way past her and into the room, drawing his right-hand blade.

There in the corner he stood, dressed only in his undergarments, trying to hide the sacred knife he had been given. Creed was across the room in a flash, faster then a normal human as he gripped the man's throat in a squeeze and pinned him to the wall.

"Creed!" Miranda yelled as she hurried across to him. "What are you doing?" She screamed, her large breasts toppling from her robe as she tried to pull his arms away.

Her attempts were futile. Creed's muscles felt like they had turned to iron under the coat. He looked down at her through eyes filled with hate as he asked through tight lips.

"Do you know who he is, *what* he is?"

The Gypsy's eyes frightened her. "No," she admitted backing away a few steps, shaking her head, as the usually gentle Creed had become some kind of a crazed animal.

He looked up at the pale young man. "Tell her."

"I don't know what you are talking about," the man begged as he tried to breathe.

Creed released the man's throat grabbed the hand holding the knife and twisted back the white wrist at a very unusual angle.

"Let it go," Creed snarled. "I will break your arm and there is nothing your master can do about it."

Miranda looked from the knife to the Gypsy, her eyes wide in horror.

"What are you talking about Creed? He is a customer, nothing else."

The man attempted to explain his actions. "I was afraid. I grabbed the knife to protect myself," he begged, as he was bent almost over backward trying to relieve the pressure of the hold. Desperate, he reached outward sending his mind into Creed's to use his power. To his surprise, he found the Gypsy's mind closed like a steel door.

"Do not use your feeble powers on me," Creed warned as he completed the hold snapping the limb at the joint.

With a scream of pain, the man slumped against the wall dropping the knife from his lifeless fingers. Creed stepped forward slapping the man hard enough to knock him to the rug.

"No!" Miranda cried out as Creed stepped forward kicking the man in the stomach.

With a groan her customer rolled to the floor, face down and Creed stepped over him.

"Tell her the damn truth!" He ordered as he grabbed the man dragging him up from the floor by his hair. Wrapping his powerful arm around the man's neck, he placed his enchanted blade in the stranger's ear.

"One last time," he whispered. "Tell her!"

"Okay, okay!" The man yelled in defeat trying

to break away from the Gypsy who should not have been able to restrain one as he so easily. "I am a Vampire, a disciple of Rasmere," he confessed.

Miranda stepped back, gasping as she crossed herself. "Oh my God." she whispered trying to find her voice.

In Creed's grasp, the stranger shot her a hate filled look. "You are lucky the Hunter showed up, whore, because God could not have helped you!" he spat.

Creed chuckled as he shoved the knife deep into the vampire's brain sending the undead back to Satan. He shoved the body away from him as it began to decay in seconds while they watched.

"Oh, God help me I did not know." Miranda whispered, unable to tear her eyes from the corpse that soon was no more then a rotten skeleton.

Creed walked over to where the vampire had dropped the jewel-handled knife. "He was a young vampire," Creed explained as he poured wine into a cup.

"He was human once but his master turned him, within the last twenty years I would say." He drank, trying to get the odor of the undead from his senses.

Miranda looked at him as he re-sheathed his blade and placed the vampire weapon into a coat pocket.

"I do not know what to say." She whimpered as her mouth twitched and her hands began to shake.

"Here sit down," he directed handing her some wine.

"How did you know?" she asked looking at him. He shook his head. "I didn't. I came here because I believe his master, Rasmere, may try to kill Takada. I need to know where he went tonight."

Her eyes narrowed and then spread wide in fear as her hand shot to her mouth. "He was going to the docks, to meet you," she gasped, her voice filling with fear.

Placing the wine cup on the table he nodded. "I must go there. Did he say which dock?"

"The one with the ship sailing for Spain," she answered, and fearfully she asked. "Is it a trap?"

Double-checking the charges in his pistols he nodded.

"Yes, as I am sure was this," he pointed to the dry skeleton on the floor. "I must go."

He headed for the door but she caught his shoulder before he left the room.

"Thank you," she said. "Please save him; we are in love."

Creed answered her with a nod as he hurried along the hallway. Running down the staircase, he tossed several coins to Olus who was icing his cheek at the bar.

"Here have a few drinks on me," he yelled as he passed.

The big Greek smiled. "I will, Creed. Thanks."

The bartender however, yelled something ugly as the Gypsy ran from the front door past the soldiers who still argued with the sailors.

He sprinted down the spray-covered docks smelling the fish guts that the fishermen had not removed today as they cleaned their catch.

"Where are you Takada?" he whispered, sprinting as fast as the conditions would allow.

Down at the end of dock five sat the ship waiting the morning tides to set sail for Spain. Slowing, he sensed them in the dark around him watching.

"Humans," he told himself, knowing they would be Rasmere's minions, human scum eaters who lived to serve their master's every wish. They knew that if the master favored them, they would become vampires themselves.

Creed slowed to a walk drawing his rapier. He didn't need the enchanted knives to kill human minions.

With a soft ruffle of air, they rushed him coming from every dark corner. He spun the steel of his blade. It flashed in the moonlight as it ripped through the guts of his first attacker!

Ducking, he felt the feathered end of an arrow as it passed by his head whistling into the dock's planks. He crouched as he jerked free his left pistol, firing under his arm just as the bowman aimed a second arrow at him. The flash from the flintlock was blinding in the shadows of the dock but the silver ball hit its mark, burrowing deeply into the bowman's chest. Cocking the pistol's second barrel, he fired again, striking a woman who swung an ax at him.

From his side a sword wielding man screamed as he rushed in, swinging wildly. Creed slapped aside the man's strike and then blocked a second downward blow. He spun slashing the attacker's thigh deeply sending the man to the ground with a shriek of agony.

Hurtling past the swordsman, he delivered the killing blow as he stepped back into the shadow of the warehouse. That was the last of them for now and he took a deep breath trying to steady his nerves.

Quickly he retrieved his pistol, reloading the barrels as he watched around the dock for another attack. When none came, he cocked the weapon keeping it and the sword out as he slid open the warehouse door.

Birds flew from the rafters' overhead as he stepped in seeing nothing as the sparse moonlight from the windows provided the only illumination.

The familiar smell of the undead found its way to his nose and he knew he had found them, somewhere here in this dark building. On his toes he crept through the warehouse coming to a set of stairs, he stopped, debating if he wanted to climb them, as a pain filled scream filled the air!

"Upstairs." He decided quickly.

He pushed himself as he hurried up the staircase two and three steps at a time until he reached the second floor. He stopped. His eyes focused on a door across the floor. Through the linen drapes, he could see shadows and flickering lights. Again, a scream rang out into the warehouse and now Creed was sure; it was Takada!

Slipping his rapier off he placed it against the railing of the stairs as he pulled both pistols, cocking them. He crept forward, tensing his powerful legs and kicking open the door. The door shattered into pieces as Creed stepped through into a nightmare!

Takada lay on a large wooden table in the center of the room. He was covered in blood and four pale white vampires in black cloaks huddled over him, bathing in his blood.

The valiant warrior tried to raise his head. He looked through glazed eyes while out from the shadows a fifth vampire appeared.

Creed saw the red robe stained in Takada's blood as it ran from the monster's incisor teeth.

"Darius Creeed." The thing hissed, stepping around the table as it wiped blood from its chin and licked it with a dark red tongue. "It hasss been a long time Creeeed."

Creed glanced at Takada. He had been ripped from his waist to his throat. Creed's nostrils flared as he met Rasmere's glazed eyes. The Nosferatu was drunk with blood, and the Gypsy knew now was when he would be the most powerful.

"Not long enough Rasmere." Creed answered, as hate filled his voice.

The Vampire Lord stepped closer bringing his face into the candlelight; he had changed over the years, his face becoming more canine like. Creed also noticed the Lord's skin; it was so milky white it appeared translucent and the eyes, Rasmere's eyes, had become a pale bluish white. They did not reflect the light in the room as the Lord stood smiling at his most hated enemy.

"You have grown more powerful." Creed admitted with a nod, seeing the signs. Pure Blood or not only a very powerful vampire had that milky skin and telltale unusual eye coloring.

Rasmere shrugged slightly. "The hunting has been good, Creeed." He answered, removing the cowl of his robe flipping it back onto his shoulders.

Creed saw the final sign of power, the heavy white streaked hair.

He looked past the Lord to the lesser vampires who now satisfied their own hungers from the opened body of his friend.

"What do you look for Creeed? This?" Rasmere held Takada's sword in his clawed fingers.

The Gypsy felt the bile rising in his throat as his grip tightened on the pistols.

"Return it to me." He ordered but Rasmere shook his head.

"No, Gypsssy. It iss a tool for killing my kinnnd. I willl seee it gets a good home."

His smile widened allowing more blood to drip from his open mouth.

Creed shoved the pistols forward. "You will die then!" He promised as he fired one barrel from the weapon in his right hand.

The vampire moved his head as the silver ball sped at him; it missed crashing into the far wall instead. With a look of contempt, Rasmere turned back to Creed.

"I will be going now, Gypsy. If you survive, which I believe is possible, I will see you again."

He disappeared back into the shadows motioning to his underlings who climbed from the table.

Creed tensed as they flashed their blood-covered fangs, dead eyes staring at him as they crept forward swinging their claws. He raised the pistol firing the second barrel into the closest demon knocking it backward with a flutter of black robes.

He twisted and dropped the useless weapon as another vampire dove at him clawed hands slashing. Loud screeching sounds erupted, chilling his insides, as the demon's iron like claws raked down his coat unable to penetrate the enchanted werewolf hide.

Stunned the demon stepped away unbelieving that his claws had no effect. Creed spun kicking the attacker in the chest knocking it back into the other two. He switched his second gun to his right hand firing both barrels into the rolling flopping vampire on top of the pile. Discarding that weapon, he pulled his long bladed knives weaving an arc of death as he closed in on the two rolling survivors.

One jumped to its feet showing sharp incisor teeth as it crouched to spring. Creed was too fast, though as he kicked straight into the demon's chest. The strike rocked the creature knocking the robed figure back over the table where Takada's body rested.

Creed avoided the clawed hand of the vampire at his feet sweeping the blow past with one knife as he sliced back with the other. The silver tipped weapon bit across the creature's throat, the precious metal reacting to the vampires system; it fell shaking to the floor as the smoke of death began to flame from the wound.

The last vampire sprang from behind the table trying for the door of the room. Creed flipped the blade in his right hand exchanging the handle for the tip. He tossed it at the retreating demon catching the vampire square between the shoulders as it reached the doorway. The demon fell backwards into the room as it also began to decay in the smoke of a demon's death.

Creed looked about, Rasmere was gone and only four smoking skeletons remained in the room. The smell choked and gagged him as it filled the small room.

Creed picked up his pistols, reloading them while he looked over the dead Samurai. He had not been bitten; they had simply opened him up and drank his blood as he died slowly. It was a cruel death for such a warrior. It pained the Gypsy that there was nothing he could do for his friend; it would be too hard to explain later.

He took some of his powder from the loading flask dumping it over a pile of debris in the corner.

"Fire will cleanse this place of terror." He whispered taking a candle from the table and tossing it into the powder.

By the time Creed walked from the warehouse, fire was already engulfing the upper room where Takada lay among the remains of the undead!

TWO

New York City, present day:

He walked down the crowded streets a scowl on his brooding face as pain raced through his enflamed body. Around him, a soft snow fell while crowds of workers headed home to the security of their families.

Not one noticed the pale, sweating Gypsy as he stumbled among them trying to find the old woman's shop. He gripped his left side feeling the wetness of his blood soaked shirt. He had been torn open badly in the fight this morning across the river in New Jersey. He needed treatment before the poison of the vampire claws ran too deeply into his body; otherwise, it would kill him slowly and painfully.

The cold breeze mixing with the wetness of the snow as it fell against his face cooled him for now but it wouldn't much longer. He needed help and the only one capable of that kind of help would be the old woman.

Standing amid the hurrying crowd, he saw the red outline of the worn sign.

'Fortune Telling and Palm Reading.'

Relief flooded through his fever-wracked body; he had found her!

Pushing through the crowd, he made it to the shop's door against which he leaned, heavily breathing for a moment. It took great effort but he raised his hand and knocked.

From inside someone turned up the light and the face of a young dark haired woman pulled aside the shade over the door, peering out.

"We are closed," she said through the glass.

He swallowed hard as he shook his head.

"I must come in," he explained. "I must see Lela."

At the sound of the old Gypsy's name, the young woman unbolted the door.

"How do you know my grandmother's name, stranger?" she asked with a frown on her pretty face.

Creed almost lost his balance growing more feverish. "Please I must step in."

His pain filled eyes met her gaze.

She chewed her lip. "It is a dangerous thing to allow strangers in after business hours." she said, hesitating, but then motioned with her head. "Okay come in."

He came close to falling as he straightened

bracing himself away from the door.

"You are hurt?" she asked, her face suddenly filled with concern.

"Yes but it is just a scratch." He limped to a chair in the center of the room. Stiffly he removed his jacket hearing her gasp as she saw the blood soaked shirt and hand he held to his side.

"That is not a scratch," she scolded as she leaned down to remove his shirt.

"Don't," he warned catching her hand. "The old woman must do it; there are dangers." He could feel the strength fading from his body as the warmth of the room soaked into him.

"It is okay, Darius, she has the calling," the old worn but familiar voice said from the other side of the room.

Creed looked up focusing his eyes on the familiar face.

"Lela," he murmured, feeling his head growing heavier.

Leaning heavily on her cane the old Gypsy woman walked unsteadily across the floor. "You have been hurt again?" she asked. Her eyes searched the deep ragged tear in his side as the younger woman tore his shirt away.

Feeling weak, he nodded. "Yes I found a lair in Jersey and killed the two inhabitants; I didn't sense the third one until he almost ripped me wide open." He winced as the young Gypsy probed the deep wound.

"I will need the salts," she said, standing with her fingers full of his blood.

"Slaves?" Lela asked sitting slowly and stiffly

across the table from him.

He nodded. "Yes, a Master, a True Blood, had turned them." He met her gaze as he said it and they shared a serious moment.

"You know what that means." He pointed out as the younger woman returned with a basket full of salves and powders.

Lela shook her head sadly. "There is a True Blood here somewhere and he is building a following," she sighed, appearing older suddenly. She watched as the young woman removed two jars of the powders mixing the contents onto a colored rag.

"Add a bit more of the sulfur," the old woman suggested.

"The infection has been in him a long time; it will help draw it out."

The younger woman nodded as she followed the other's suggestion. After the mix was adjusted, she folded the rag over several times so that it held the medicine in it. Next, she dampened it with red wine and dabbed it gently against Creed's wound.

It had an immediate cooling effect, like putting Cortisone salve on a bad case of poison Ivy, and Creed felt some of the tension leave his body.

Lela pointed to the young Gypsy. "This is my granddaughter, Creed, a Gypsy Witch like her grandmother." Lela smiled with a look of pride.

"Not like her mother then, I take it?" The girl's work was paying off; he felt his body cooling down and his vision clearing.

Lela motioned with her hand. "No, not like Tessy." She shook her head. "Running away with

21

that investment banker, I am glad her father is dead."

She rolled her eyes. "Pass over that bottle of wine, dear."

Creed handed the bottle to the old woman and she placed a glass on the table, filling it.

"You will need some too," she pointed with the glass to Creed. "For when she stitches that nasty wound."

Creed grunted. "You never allowed me to get drunk when you used to sew me up." he pointed out.

Lela smirked a little. "I have softened some in my old age. Besides, at first you told me not too." She sipped the wine chuckling.

Creed looked down at the dark haired brown-eyed girl who concentrated as she cleaned the wound making sure she didn't miss anything that would cause infection later. She was quiet as they talked and avoided his eyes.

"And what about you, Darius, getting slow in your old age?" Lela teased. "I remember when no vampire could get the best of the great Darius Creed, fabled Hunter of the Gypsy people."

Creed grunted. "Maybe," he sighed. "Something blocked me from sensing that third vampire," he shook his head. "I don't know what though." Before they could discuss it further, the young woman stood.

"I am ready to salve it and stitch you up Mr. Creed." she told him. "It will hurt when the salve goes into the wound." She explained and he nodded with a smile.

"It is okay," he replied. "I have had it before."

And then he added. "And call me Creed, or Darius, calling a Gypsy mister is something like sacrilege."

She blushed slightly as she nodded removing the top from a tube of thick yellow salve.

"You have taken Selena's voice away," Lela chuckled. "It is her first time doctoring Gypsy royalty."

With a sly look, she sipped more wine from her glass.

The girl didn't pretend to notice her grandmother as she laid several ample amounts of salve in his side. The burning started immediately and he had to grimace to keep from calling out or cursing.

Lela took out another empty glass. "How long since you have taken the potions?" She asked looking into his eyes, searching for signs of aging.

"About twenty years."

She grunted reaching into Selena's basket removing four small vials of caramel colored liquid.

"I will mix them after she stitches the wound. They will help speed the healing."

He nodded, watching the wizened old enchantress as she poured wine into the glass. With a practiced eye, she administered four drops from one bottle and six from the second.

"The youth and health mixture." she explained. "Next the strength and coordination mix."

She took the second set of bottles and placed eight drops from each into the wine. With a taunting smile, she added one extra drop from the last bottle.

23

"Since you are getting old, one extra drop for enhanced speed of reflex."

Darius couldn't help but shake his head with a smile. "You have always been so good to me," he commented with a hint of sarcasm.

She smirked stirring the mix into the wine. "I am getting old, Darius, and very tired. Maybe the next time you come I will not be here."

She pointed a finger at Selena. "She will be in charge of this shop after I am gone."

Selena blushed as she threaded her needle preparing to stitch the wound. Darius looked from the potion filled wine to Lela.

"Maybe you could drink some and stay around a while," he offered. "It has been done before."

She nodded in reply. "No I have spent my life aiding those of you who battle the evil of the undead. I have had enough; actually, I am surprised that it does not drive you crazy. You have been at it for so long."

Darius shrugged but did not answer.

Lela sipped from her own wineglass. "No my time is gone, Gypsy Prince; it is time for someone young and strong to take up the fight." she smiled at her granddaughter. "I have trained her well, Darius; she will be a strong ally to you in the years to come. She is stronger then I ever was, more powerful."

This caught Creed's attention; Lela was legend among the Gypsy people for her abilities.

Selena inserted the needle starting the first stitch.

"That is promising," he said without a hint that he had felt the needle.

Lela stood slowly holding onto her cane as she reached one more time into the basket of powders. She selected something that looked like a green sugar cube but slightly larger.

"When she is done, Selena will feed you and run a hot tub put this in it and soak that wound for about fifteen minutes."

She placed it on the table in front of him. Pausing, she stood over him a minute, reaching out with her hand touching his face.

"It has been my pleasure to serve you over the last eighty years Gypsy Prince." she said as a tear appeared in her left eye. "Go with God and the next time you are in the old country, place a flower on my mother and father's grave for me. Tell them I never made it back but my heart has never left them."

He nodded up to her as she turned and walked slowly across the floor to the doorway leading to the rest of the house. Pushing the curtain aside, she stopped. She turned her head but did not speak; she simply smiled at him as she had so many times before.

"Thank you for my life." She whispered and then headed through the curtain and into her room where she closed the door softly behind herself.

Creed settled his head back in the hot water washing dirt, grime and blood from his long hair. The powers of the cube Lela had given him soaked into his skin and up through his nostrils clearing his soul as well as his body. He sat back, his head resting on the tub, as he watched the thick muscles of his upper body grow tighter and larger as the Gypsy potion worked its powers on his body.

He had drunk it as soon as Selena finished her work and before eating the fine meal she prepared for him. It was the powers of the two potions that gave him the speed and strength needed to match the undead.

He thought of how time passed so quickly after seeing the aging Lela tonight and her telling him she was retiring from the business-if the killing of vampires could be called that. He took a deep breath and closed his weary eyes; even with the potions, he needed to rest as well as eat and drink regularly but tonight he was especially worn out.

Lela, he smiled remembering her years ago. Boy had she been a wild one as a child always running barefoot through the Elbe river valley ready to meet him as he returned to his native Bohemia to rest.

Her father, Demetrius, had been his good friend and neighbored the lands he owned where his estate sat nestled below the Sudetes Mountains. Demetrius and his lovely wife, Irlene, had two daughters, Lela and Iilia, who were twelve and fourteen years old the summer Darius left for Scotland to investigate rumors of a coven of vampire Druids.

While there, he received an urgent message from Demetrius stating that there was something evil in the region and they needed their Prince back home.

It was the end of the Second World War and following the years of death came a breed of vampire that had grown powerful sating itsself across the battlefields.

When Creed returned home it was such a demon that he found haunting the nights of the valley. He at first was in awe of the creature, no vampire would seek out the Gypsies as a target; they were the last of the peoples to remember the old ways.

But this demon was young having been only twenty when his Nosferatu master, Creed's old enemy, Rasmere, turned him.

The vampire was blood crazy wandering the battlefields of Europe gorging himself on the dead and dying. By the time he stumbled into the Czechoslovakian region of Bohemia, he had lost fear of anything or anyone.

He had set upon the Gypsies reeking vengeance on the vampires natural human enemies. One night, Darius and Demetrius set a trap using a young powerful Gypsy Witch. They knew if the vampire struck, she could ward him off until Darius could deliver the killing stroke. Creed never knew what happened but for some reason the vampire never took the bait and they all went home.

Darius accompanied the young witch to her home making sure she was safe before he started to drive for his own house. Halfway home, a feeling hit him, he had to get to the house of his friend Demetrius!

He wheeled into the yard of the small farm to find the bodies of Demetrius and Irlene lying just outside their doorstep. His friend had two empty pistols in his hand; he had put up a fight before he died.

Creed examined them finding their necks

broken but they had not been bitten. It was a loud scream from the barn that had sent him at a sprint into the building. There, the monster was bent over the body of the fourteen-year-old Iilia, lapping her lifeblood into his greedy mouth from the hole torn in her throat. Backed into the horse manger, her little hands gripping her fathers big silver cross, stood the valiant Lela, shaking as she watched her sister's murder.

Creed still remembered the way the demon had turned slowly, looking up from the little girl's dead body, blood dripping from its mouth. There had been a look of sadistic lust in the demon's eyes that far surpassed anything Creed had ever seen.

The thing had stood dropping Iilia lifeless to the floor as it smiled, knowing Creed couldn't get to Lela faster then it could.

With a low growl rising from his throat, the bastard of Rasmere had smiled at Creed in arrogance. It locked its gaze with his as it held a blood-covered finger in front of its tongue licking slowly like a child would a lollipop. Then it had turned lunging at the small-frightened child, Lela had held up the cross as she screamed for uncle Darius, but it slapped it aside in disdain. As the monster that had killed her family made his final move for her, the child dodged, running past the vampire before it could react.

She ran to Darius who shoved her behind his werewolf hide coat as he drew his blades. Hate and fury grew within the Gypsy until he trembled.

"You cannooot sssave her."

The demon had laughed as it walked forward

flexing its claws.

Creed had not answered. He didn't tell the thing that he was a Hunter, someone who had killed and fought pure bloods in his day. No, he did not warn the demon because for the first time in his life he wanted to kill for revenge not because it was his heritage!

The vampire charged him as Lela screamed. With a flash of the silver blades, Creed met the charge, his fury behind each blow backed by his great strength and speed. The vampire's claws screeched and bounced off the werewolf hide as his blades swept them aside. With a powerful sidekick, Darius knocked the demon through the barn wall. He tensed, waiting, as the demon flew back through the hole his body had created, rushing Creed a second time.

The Gypsy slashed as the vampire flew into him both knives cutting deeply through the demon's chest. The blows would have killed most demons but this one had grown very powerful through the consumption of so much blood over the last few years.

It stepped back from Creed, surprise in its eyes, as it looked at the gaping bloodless wounds in its chest. Creed kicked again, a powerful sidekick that tossed the vampire back onto a pitchfork placed in a rack next to the horse stall. It poked through the demon's chest pinning him there, the vampire roared in pain and anger as Creed stepped over to him.

"Send my regards to Satan." He said as he spun back slashing the monster's throat. It sent the vampire's head toppling to the straw covered floor.

Creed took Lela to the young witch's house where she drank a sleeping potion and, after crying for hours, went to sleep. He went back to the farm alone and buried the bodies of his friend and his dead friend's family.

The sun was rising as he went to the barn and took the smoky carcass of the vampire to a sacred Gypsy shrine built long ago in the valley by the Celts. There he asked for the forgiveness of Demetrius, his wife and their little girl; he had failed them by arriving too late to save their lives. He used coal oil to burn the vampire's body to ashes, which he buried, beneath the shrine. The gods of the Celts would keep the undead from ever walking the earth again.

He went to the small inn at the far end of the valley and started to drink. The Gypsy people of the valley had heard what had happened and they gave the Hunter a wide berth.

For two days, he grew drunker and angrier by the hour. He wouldn't speak but to order more wine and many were beginning to wonder if their prince had lost his mind. It was noon of the third day when he looked up and saw Lela standing with the witch Selma.

"Uncle Darius, please come home with us?" She begged as she extended her small hand to his callused one.

He had gone with them back to Selma's where he sobered up and slept for a full day. He then took Lela to her families resting place, a grove of trees that bordered their adjoining lands.

He sat up in the tub cupping his hands and pouring more water over his head. He had taken Lela back fifteen years ago when Selma died. They had paid their respects to the witch who had trained Lela in the ways of Gypsy magic and they had visited her parent's grave.

That night, as the aging Lela slept in his estate guestroom, he had driven out to the Celtic shrine. As the moon rose over the mountains, he checked the spot where the vampire was buried. The ground was undisturbed and Creed knew the monster was still imprisoned.

He stood from the tub, drying off; he couldn't save the others but he had made sure that Lela had lived a normal life. It was the only thing that had kept him from losing his mind at times. He wrapped the towel around his waist feeling his wet hair as it lay about his shoulders. He had saved Lela; it had been enough.

THREE

He stood looking across the dark city as the snow still fell lazily to the street. It was quieter out there now. A couple hurried by holding hands, walking huddled together. Someone else walked by leading a dog on a leash.

A light tap on the open door of the bedroom made him turn his head slowly.

"May I come in?" It was Selena dressed in a long shirt, fresh from her own bath, her long black hair still damp.

"Yes." He turned back to the window, his muscular arms crossed over his chest.

She walked in looking over the broad shoulders and narrow waist covered only in the cotton bath towel. She sat down gently on the edge of the bed, leaning on the footboard.

"I would like to talk if you don't mind?" she asked politely. "If you don't want to it is okay."

He shook his head and smiled as he watched two young boys throwing snowballs below.

"No, I would welcome it. What would you like to know?"

She took a deep breath. "Grandma calls you a prince, a Gypsy Prince."

He nodded in answer.

She studied his back, so strong and powerful and so full of scars.

"I did not know there was such a thing anymore."

He shrugged as below a taxi picked up an old man who held a newspaper over his head against the snow.

"What else has she told you?" he asked, curious as to how much she knew.

She dampened her lips with her tongue, something about him made her nervous, excited and scared all at the same time.

"She has told me you are over a thousand years old, a Prince of the Gypsy people and that you hunt vampires." she paused. "She also told me you are a legend among our people, what they call a Hunter of the Shadows."

He turned now meeting her dark brown eyes. "I haven't heard that term in a very long time," he smiled. "Lela remembers the old stories well."

Selena nodded slightly. "She has told them to me all my life, always reminding me never to forget them."

He nodded in agreement and turned around leaning against the windowsill.

She trembled at the muscular shoulders, arms

and chest.

"He is like a dream," she thought, feeling her insides flip.

She had read a book by a western author about the Gypsy people and he had cited scientific studies done on Gypsies describing their characteristics as a race.

The study had reached the conclusion that the typical Gypsy was slightly taller then the European average, with legs comparatively long in relation to the torso; their heads tended to be long and narrow. They had black hair, smallish ears, wide eyes with heavily pigmented irises and long narrow straight noses. Then the authors of the report went on to award them a highly favorable place in human aesthetics. The men were very fine to look at and the women very beautiful. Their swarthy complexion, jet black hair, straight well formed nose, white teeth, dark brown wide open eyes, whether wide open or languid in expression, the general suppleness of their deportment and the harmony of their movements place them high above many European peoples as regards physical beauty.

Right here in the dimly lit room, Selena agreed with every word as she looked upon Creed. The only blemish to his beauty was the number of scars he wore attesting to his years of combat against the undead. The brown color of his hair also seemed to be out of place.

"How does a Gypsy Prince become a warrior against the undead?" she wondered out loud.

"It is a long story," Creed started with a sigh.

"I was born in the year 1164 AD, my mother

34

was descended from the original Celtic tribes who settled in Bohemia some time around 300 BC. That is where I get my brown hair and temper," he chuckled.

"My father was Kshatriyas, a sect of superb warriors who made up the second caste in Hindu society. They were a mixture of the legendary Jat and Rajput warriors of India. He had made his way to Bohemia after the defeat of his forces in a war in Persia and stayed after marrying my mother. They were the beginning of the Gypsy peoples in that area. Father was given the title of King for some reason I don't remember and I was forever branded a Prince." He shrugged as she listened entranced.

"My father's people had spent centuries fighting the undead of their world and as other races forgot or chose to coexist with the monsters, we continued to fight them. It is my heritage and my responsibility to the human race." He stood thinking a minute. "Does it make sense to you?"

She nodded. "I think so, but it is a lot to swallow," she admitted.

"I know," he agreed. "But it is the truth." Then he extended his hand. "Lela says you have the power in you; read it for yourself."

She stood slowly taking his hand in hers. "You have so many scars," She observed, shaking her head as she turned his palm closer to the light. "My God your lifeline goes on forever; you have lived a very long life."

She traced along other lines.

"A life filled with violence and pain, pain caused by the suffering of others. Loved ones that are no longer alive."

She brushed back a wisp of hair from her face and started to trace more lines. A soft gasp parted her lips. "Oh my God." she whispered softly.

"What?" he asked quietly, knowing better then to rush a telling.

She looked up at him through dark brown eyes. "It says our lives will be closely entwined."

Creed nodded. "As my life was with Lela after I saved her from death."

She shook her head slowly as she pointed a long painted fingernail at one short small line intersecting with an old dagger wound. "This one says we will be together," she took a deep breath. "Starting tonight."

She was trembling as she dropped his hand color rising in her cheeks.

Creed grunted and turned back to the window. Things happened for a reason, but this? He heard fabric hitting the floor behind him as the potions in his system heightened his senses.

Soft footsteps approached him from behind and soon he felt her large firm breasts against his back as her arms circled his waist.

"I fear what I see in the future, Darius Creed," she whispered as her lips brushed his muscled shoulder. "Events of great power are about to begin, including us both. I do not know the world of shadows as you do, I am afraid."

He turned facing her his own dark brown eyes glowing in the half-light.

"You do not have to do this, Selena; there are always choices." He smelled the light scent of her perfume mixed with the soap she had bathed with.

He looked down on her dark soft skin, his eyes stopping a moment admiring her well-formed breasts; the dark nipples erect as she stood allowing his gaze. It was as if she had become alive under his practiced eye, no longer the shy young woman that had tended his wound earlier.

She raised her fingers tracing down his chest and stomach with the long nails, slowly enticing him.

"I know," she answered. "But to not follow what has been foretold is to tempt disaster," she warned looking into his eyes.

He nodded; she was correct about that fact.

She stepped closer to him, her body warm against his. She reached up brushing her lips to his. Creed returned her kiss, a long sensual kiss. Their tongues met and circled as he pulled her tight against him. His head began to swim; she was intoxicating. His stomach filled with the tingling sensation of a lust he had not felt for a very long time and he felt himself becoming hard under the towel. Selena sensed it and she reached down with her left hand and removed the towel as her right ran through his long hair. She pulled back from him her body moving as her lips parted with her soft moans. Through half open eyes, she wet her lips with her tongue softly and seductively. Watching his face, she dropped the towel to the floor as she traced a line around his hips with a long fingernail. He felt himself take a deep breath as she dropped her hand to his manhood. Her deft hands manipulated him until he felt the desire run through his body

37

stopping behind his eyes pounding there like a serious migraine.

"We are to be together, Darius, the palm, your palm, does not lie."

He was overcome by her; he no longer had the power to resist and simply nodded in answer.

She took his hand leading him to the bed where she pushed him down softly onto the comforter.

"Let me please you, Prince of the Gypsies," she purred so seductively he shivered in excitement. She leaned over him allowing her long dark locks to fall over him as she kissed his chest working her way down his belly.

Creed swallowed hard, feeling the kisses firing his desire as the blood pounded through him. She dropped her head lower, her hot wet mouth going where her hand was covering him with its softness. He couldn't help the gasp that escaped his throat as she used her hand and her mouth, manipulating him, driving him to a frenzy of unbridled lust. His muscles bunched across his body as flames of desire emanated from his groin spreading through him until he clutched the sheets under him in a death grip.

"Selena!" he whispered in passion.

She stopped suddenly, rising up over him as she straddled his body and lowered herself onto his swollen member. Her lips parted softly as she moaned when he entered her. His scarred callused hands found her hips, guiding her movements. She tore them away pinning them back over his head as she moved her hips up and down sending him into such deep ecstasy he wondered if she was real or a dream. There was little question as she moaned above him moving faster until he had to bite his lip; he wanted to share their orgasm together.

When it happened they were one, tightly locked together as their bodies shuddered in splendid release. Breathing deeply, Creed looked up at her seeing the sweat on her breasts as she regained her own breath and opened her eyes looking into his.

"I have waited for you," she whispered looking down on him. "All of my life I knew you would come for me, Darius Creed, last of the Shadow Hunters, Prince of the Gypsies."

She leaned down kissing him softly.

He felt her soft supple lips against his and for the first time in so very long, he languished in it.

Creed rose from the bed as next to him Selena still slept deeply, she rolled, moaning softly, as he stood pulling on his thick leather pants and boots. Looking down on her, he felt his heart staying next to her under the covers, remembering what she was he thought maybe he had been drugged. He shrugged that notion off; no, it had been too real for the reading not to be valid.

He stepped from the room closing the door softly; the smell of coffee brewed in the old way assaulted his brain as he padded down the stairs into the kitchen.

Sitting at the table sipping from a steaming cup Lela smiled as he entered.

"I am now happy," she said placing the cup on the table.

Creed walked to the far chair. "You look younger this morning," he observed as he sat, helping himself to the pot filling the cup that sat there before him.

He sipped. "You remember the old ways," he smiled enjoying the best coffee he had consumed for over a hundred years.

Lela nodded. "Yes, on special occasions, otherwise it is Sanka instant," she answered, a glint of mischief in her eyes.

He chuckled, rolling his eyes. "Times have changed."

He sat back and looked at her. "You do look younger, actually pretty good for 4:00 A.M.," he pointed out with an amused look on his usually serious face.

She chuckled deep in her chest. "I am much better then I was."

Creed met her playful look. "You set me up," he countered. "You knew about Selena from the beginning and all this time you never told me."

She picked up her coffee cup.

"Selena is a special one Darius, a Hunter like you."

At his questioning look, she added. "The signs are there Gypsy Prince. Do not doubt me, rather open your heart; tell me what it felt like to be with her," she paused waiting for his answer.

"You already know," he stated simply. "You always knew and you raised her under my nose secretly."

It sounded like an accusation and he regretted it came out that way.

Lela however didn't seem to notice. "It had to be so, Darius. I couldn't chance one of the Purebloods finding out; they would have hunted her before she was strong enough," Lela motioned with her cane. "How many possible Hunters have been murdered that way?" she asked knowing the answer.

Creed lowered his eyes looking into the coffee cup in his hand.

"She reminds me of Marisa," he said quietly. "No one has ever done that, make me feel like that again, maybe hurt me."

Lela nodded her head; she remembered the stories of the woman who Creed had first loved so long ago.

"Yes Marisa," she agreed. "How many times when I was a child did you mention her? The flaming red hair and sea deep green eyes, a warrior like yourself, talented in weapons and deadly in battle," she shook her head. "She was the love of your life and she was murdered by Rasmere."

Creed stood, taking his cup, and leaned against the sink. "It was actually some of the followers he had turned," he said, feeling the loss of her still deep inside. "But, yes, he is the one who will pay some day, for her as well as others," Creed vowed.

"Selena has been trained as a Hunter; she is also an enchantress capable of giving you what you need to continue the fight," she sighed. "I am not going to die for a long time, the stars say so but everyday we grow less and less. She needs to go with you, Darius, when you leave, she will be your doctor, your companion, your lover and, if the stars are

41

truthful, the mother of a child, a new Prince of the Gypsies."

She paused a far away look entering her eyes. "The next great Hunter of the Shadows."

Creed met her gaze, "Or she could be dead," he added seriously.

Lela shrugged. "It is the way of things, is it not?" she asked cocking her right eyebrow. "You taught me that."

Creed had to agree. "Yes I did, didn't I?"

They shared a short laugh between them.

Creed shook his head. "Demetrius would be proud knowing that some day his family may produce a Hunter," he swirled his cup as he remembered his friend in silent homage.

"I am tired," he drained the cup setting it down. "I think I will go back to sleep."

An amused look crossed Lela's face. "How long has it been, Uncle, since you have slept the night away?"

Creed shook his head. "I can't remember," he admitted.

The old witch chuckled again. "She was made for you, Darius, intended for you since her birth; don't let it pass you by."

Creed looked up at the ceiling. "I wont," he promised. "You were right; she is different."

It was hard for him to admit.

He was about to leave the kitchen but she grabbed his arm.

"There is one more thing," her tone became serious and he stopped, frowning.

She pulled something wrapped in cloth from

under the table.

"The ball of Asmus," Creed whispered as he glanced at her in amazement.

She nodded. "It has cleared and is usable again," she informed him.

Creed sat back down slowly, his eyes on the crystal ball of the greatest Gypsy sorcerer of all time.

"It has cleared?" he asked incredulous.

"There is something you must see," she said. "It has been there for two months, since the ball cleared."

He watched as she moved her hands about circling the crystal as she summoned her powers. Smoky flames appeared in the ball, swirling about until they settled, revealing the ivory handled sword within.

"Takada's katana!" Creed hissed staring wide eyed at Lela.

She nodded in answer. "It is here, Darius, in the states waiting for you."

He felt the anger rising in him. "Where?" he asked simply.

"Wisconsin, a sword collector in a small town," she answered.

"We will leave in the morning." He announced as he walked from the room and up the stairs to where Selena lay sleeping.

Lela chuckled. "There is one more surprise for you, Uncle," she said to herself. "You will see later."

She sipped from her coffee cup content for now.

Creed slid back under the covers and almost immediately, Selena was next to him opening her sleepy eyes.

"You left," she said quietly. "I woke up and you were gone."

She searched his eyes with her own seeing the things only a Gypsy Witch could.

He smiled back to her. "We will leave tomorrow," he told her gently as if they had been together for years.

She nodded back without argument as she reached up to kiss him.

"I love you Darius Creed," she said softly resting her head on his muscled chest. "I accept without fear what will come."

He curled his fingers playing with her hair. "You will need to, Selena, because there is no room for fear in this business."

"Some day you will love me also," she said out of nowhere as if he had interrupted her.

Creed looked down at her as she raised her head looking back at him, his face grew serious.

"I love you too Selena," he whispered watching the smile form across her face.

She ran her hand back down his stomach to his thighs gently running the fingernails of her hand up his groin.

"Make love to me again," she whispered as his body responded to her touch.

Creed nodded. "For a very long time," he whispered into her ear as he ran his tongue up her neck.

"I promise this time no one will take you from me," he added. "Not even Rasmere."

Caught in her own rising passion Selena didn't even hear him as her body ached for his touch.

FOUR

Jacob Reid whistled to himself while he finished vacuuming the worn-out floor carpet of his Dojang. He turned the old Kirby off and walked over to the weapons rack, readjusting the assorted authentic martial arts weaponry.

"There that's much better," he told himself as he heard the door chime, denoting that someone had walked in.

Frowning he checked his watch; it was well after closing time and he was sure the last of the black belt students had locked up. He placed the vacuum back into the closet amid the old sparring pads and the unbroken boards he stored for testing. At his feet, his pet cats mingled about rubbing against his feet or frolicking with each other.

"Come on guys," he invited. "Let us go and see our visitor."

He walked out of the sparring room and through

46

the small weight room to the front office.

Standing there facing the window was a longhaired man wearing a beat up old leather duster.

"May I help you?" he asked, stepping behind his desk.

The stranger turned slowly a smile playing easily across his lips.

"You are Jake Reid?" he asked, extending a scarred and callused hand.

Jake nodded in answer as he took the man's hand shaking it.

"Yes I am."

The stranger returned a short nod. "My name is Darius Creed," he paused a bit and then added. "It has come to my attention that you are a collector of rare and valuable Japanese swords."

Jake returned the nod.

"Yes, are you a collector?" He asked feeling something strange about this man, a funny feeling he couldn't pin down.

The stranger turned away again glancing at the sidewalk outside through the large windows; he gave Jake the feeling of a man who knew he was being watched.

The man named Creed turned facing him his hands folded behind his back.

"I have also heard that recently you acquired a special sword, the handle inlaid with mother of pearl and a series of Japanese characters running along the blade filled with gold?" he paused as Taz, the cat Jake had adopted out of a city alley, ran into the room instantly rubbing against the stranger's boots.

"Now that is funny?" Jake observed.

"Excuse me?" the stranger said as he bent down scratching the alley cat between the ears.

"He has never approached anyone that I know of much less allowed himself to be petted," Jake explained.

Creed smiled picking up the cat holding him snugly on one arm as he scratched its neck.

"My people have a very long history with animals," he answered. "But the sword Mr. Reid, do you have it?"

His tone was polite but Jake could see the stranger's eyes screamed of anxiety.

He nodded. "Yes Mr. Creed, make yourself comfortable and I'll get it." He left the room going to the back of the school somewhere.

Creed looked back out of the window as the cat named Taz started to growl, a deep warning growl emanating from the alley cat's throat. Creed glanced down seeing the concern in the feline's green eyes.

"Yes," he whispered soothingly. "I know they are there but thank you, valiant one."

Creed stroked the cat's ears as the animal watched the dark shadows outside from his arms.

Long ago, Gypsies had formed secret bonds with the animals they lived alongside and a cat such as the alley born one he now held still remembered the secret bond.

It had warned him of the six initiates who hid outside waiting for him. He didn't know who had sent them, but he could smell their odor-odor of humans who would do whatever they had to for their Nosferatu master. They prayed to be found worthy and that some day the vampire would turn them with his bite.

Creed could hear the returning Reid and he whispered to the alley cat.

"I have to put you down now, warrior, but stay close in case I need you," The cat flicked its tail. It understood.

Reid carried a sword covered in cloth in his hands.

"So you know swords?" he asked unfolding the cloth.

Creed stepped forward, his breath quickening as it was unwrapped; it had been so long but it was Takada's sword!

Reid handed it to him carefully.

"Be careful it is still very sharp, we have tried to translate the Japanese characters but it seems very, very old."

Creed felt his fingers flex involuntarily as he reached for the katana.

"You will not translate it," he remarked while stepping back and swinging the blade casually in several blurring circles.

He transferred the grip wheeling the sword in an underhand stroke coming to rest with it alongside his arm, point towards his shoulder.

"Wow you have used a sword before," Reid commended. "I have never seen anyone so fast."

Creed relaxed from the stance he had slid into as Taz, the cat, growled loudly from the filing cabinet he had crawled onto. Creed spun to the window seeing the six black clad figures that now stood in the street, wicked looking knives in their hands.

"What in the hell are they doing?" Reid asked.

Creed met his gaze. "I'll explain later, can you use this?" he asked quickly extending the sword to the martial arts instructor.

"Of course," Reid answered taking the sword. To his surprise, Creed pulled two of his own long bladed knives from under the battered coat.

"I don't have time to explain," Creed turned to the window. "But this is real Jake. Fight like your life depended on it!"

Across the street the six pale faced men started to sprint for the window.

"Here they come," he whispered in warning.

As a unit, the initiates jumped impacting the glass window as they burst through it sending shards of glass everywhere.

Creed ducked covering his head with his coat allowing the werewolf hide to protect him. They were all around him swinging their knives searching for his blood. Creed countered, his magnificent speed and strength no match for the still very human initiates. He drove his blades through two of them in seconds while he back kicked a third over the karate school's desk.

Out of the corner of his eye, he saw Reid strike the head from one of the attackers and then drop to a knee slicing through the guts of a second!

An initiate jumped on the Gypsy's back circling Creed's throat with a skinny arm trying to gain a chokehold. The combat hardened Gypsy reacted, tossing the man down over his shoulder. As the pale attacker hit the floor Creed drove his knives through the would-be killer's sternum.

Something moved in front of him and as he looked up the last initiate kicked him under his jaw. Creed felt his teeth slam together as he was tossed hard onto his back. With a sneer, the initiate stepped closer his knife ready for the Gypsy's blood, blood that would gain him respect in his master's eyes.

"Creed! Look out!" Reid called out from across the room unable to react in time.

It was at that moment that, with an angry growl, the alley cat sprang over the top of the sprawling Gypsy onto the face of the initiate, teeth and claws flailing!

Creed scrambled to his feet as the assassin screamed in pain under the onslaught of the feline.

"Now!" The Gypsy directed and Taz sprang away from the initiate who stumbled about one eye gone and the other horribly slashed open.

Creed spun throwing his great strength into a mighty spinning back kick, it tossed the black clad man out of the office door and into the weight room where Reid dispatched him with a well-aimed sword stroke.

Jake stumbled into the office, Takada's sword dripping human blood. "Who in the hell are you and what in the goddamn hell is this all about?" he demanded.

Creed stepped over to where Taz lay licking his claws on the desk.

"Thank you, warrior," he said as he scratched the cat's ears.

The Gypsy looked up at the martial arts instructor. "It will take a while. Is their somewhere I could buy you a meal?"

They sat towards the rear of the diner, the Gypsy eating diced ham and eggs and sipping coffee as he tried to explain to the wide-eyed Reid.

"So you are telling me that vampires exist, you are a Gypsy who hunts vampires and that the sword I have belonged to a samurai who died in 1624 AD at the hands of one of these Vampire Lords?"

Creed looked up from his plate nodding. "Exactly." He picked up his cup and sipped from it.

Jake sat back regarding the Gypsy.

"And besides that, the guys we fought, and should I add killed, are trying to get some vampire master to bite them by killing us. Of course, let us not forget the part about how the cat knew they were coming and saved you because of some age-old pact you share with animals," he shook his head.

"Yes," Creed answered. "You see it is not so hard to believe."

He picked up his fork.

Jake wiped his eyes as he shook his head. "I can hardly wait to hear what you may tell me next." He rolled his eyes.

Creed stuffed toast into his mouth. "There is something you must do for me," he started. "I need you to come with me tonight to meet with someone."

Jake shrugged. "I would say no but hell this is more fun then the circus."

Creed smiled. "Good. There is something I must

find out."

He stopped talking as he finished his meal.

They went to a secluded house at the edge of town along the hillside and Creed knocked lightly on the door.

Quickly a man answered inviting them in. Without introductions, Creed led Jake to a basement room where several glass flasks cooked on a small stove. Jake walked over, looking into one seeing a bubbling thick brown liquid that reminded him of syrup.

"What is this?" he asked.

Creed tossed off his old leather coat laying it on a small bed.

"Special herbs," He answered as he slipped a leather harness from his shoulders, hanging from the back upside down were the fabulous blades he had used in the fight.

Jake sat down in a wooden chair. "So who am I to meet?" he asked resting the old sword across his knees.

Creed removed his cotton shirt and Jake felt his breath catch in his throat. He had not realized the muscular bulk of this man.

Creed walked to the sink, washing his face and allowing the water to run over his long hair. As he stood drying his hair and face with a towel, he stretched.

"I want you to meet Selena; she is my lover and a Gypsy with special talents in the secret arts. There is something I can't shrug off about you, Mr. Reid, and only she can confirm it."

He pulled back the hair from the sides of his head tying it in a topknot as he shook the rest over his muscled shoulders.

The door from upstairs opened and down the steps walked a beautiful dark skinned woman.

Jake looked at her, drinking in her beauty, as he would have a cold beer. She was dressed in leather pants tucked into knee high boots. A white fluffy shirt covered what appeared to be an ample but firm set of breasts and was held to her waist by a broad leather belt that contained a jeweled stiletto. Her jet black hair hung loosely about her face falling hallway down her back, bit it was her dark eyes that pierced into his soul as she looked upon him. It was only after she turned her concerned eyes to Creed that Jake noticed his cat Taz in her arms.

"There was trouble?" she asked, her voice reminding Jake of a soft bubbling stream.

Creed nodded. "We were attacked by six slave initiates," he answered. "But you already knew that didn't you."

She nodded back with a smile as she stroked the alley cat.

"Taz, as he has been named, told me about it," she walked over to him.

"You are unhurt I take it." Her eyes searched his body.

"Yes," he answered softly. "Thanks to Jake here and especially to Taz. He saved me from serious injury when he sprang to the rescue."

Creed reached out scratching the cat's ears in thanks.

54

"I am grateful you protected him," Selena whispered into the animal's ear. The cat purred loudly in response. Placing him down on the bed, she turned to Jake.

"And thank you too, sir," she added.

Jake looked at the alley cat. "How did he get here?" he asked, becoming a bit overwhelmed by all of this.

Selena smiled. "He has come to join the fight," she answered. "He is one of the chosen and has been waiting to fulfill his destiny."

The way she explained it, Jake should have known all along.

The martial arts instructor just nodded. "Of course," he answered. "Silly of me to ask."

She appeared puzzled by his tone but Creed chuckled.

"Our new friend is still wondering if he should believe or should he run away now."

Selena smiled knowingly. "I see." she replied gently, walking over to him.

"May I?" she extended her hand to the sword.

"Why not?" he exclaimed, handing it to her.

She stepped back into the center of the room closing her eyes for a few seconds and when she opened them, she looked over to Creed.

"The power is still in the weapon," she told him. "But I also feel the aura of the samurai Takada still locked into the steel."

Creed nodded back but did not speak as she slid the ancient sword from its case.

"There is so much power here," she commented sliding the sword back into its home.

"Are you sure?" she asked Creed.

He nodded. "I feel it clearly," he answered. "Don't you also?"

Lowering her eyes, she nodded agreeing. "Yes my Prince."

Creed pointed at Jake. "Test him, Selena," he instructed. "We need to be sure."

She bowed slightly with a nod of her head, "As you wish."

Jake sat on the wooden chair in the center of the room with Takada's sword firmly in his hand as Selena drew the old symbols of the Gypsies on the floor around him.

As she worked, she sang softly in a language he couldn't recognize while Creed and the cat, Taz, watched from the bed.

"Any words of wisdom here?" he nervously asked the Gypsy.

Creed shook his head sending light glinting from the silver earrings he wore.

"Nothing really, if you are the one you will know what to do," he replied.

Jake took a deep breath. "Lets hope I am whatever you think I should be."

"Ready yourself." Selena said as she stood. Her voice grew stronger and her song became a rhythmic chant!

He found himself in a smoke filled tunnel, candles and incense burned all around him and he clutched the sword in his hands. Ahead he could see a greater light that emanated from what appeared to be a hollowed out area in the rock. He walked slowly forward aware that he felt no fear, only curiosity, as he entered the cave-like room. He stopped as his eyes fell on the man who sat alone on the throne-like chair that had been carved out of the solid rock.

"Come forward, Jacob Reid," The stranger invited, his voice warm and friendly.

Jake narrowed his eyes as he held the sword in front of him and, searching the smoke that moved about the room, walked slowly ahead.

"Who are you?" Jake asked.

He was strange looking, like no man Reid had ever seen before.

The man smiled. "My name is not important, Jacob Reid; no one alive would remember it in your world, except, of course, Creed. What I am is more important to you however; I am the combination of many men. At one time, we ran the Earth battling the forces of evil keeping them at bay so humans could live safely. I am part Shaolin monk, part Egyptian priest, part Hindu holy man and several others. My kind have slowly departed the world called Earth but to our dismay the denizens of evil continue to prosper."

The nameless stranger glanced at the sword.

"Ah, the sword of Takada, forged in a mighty monsoon by a smith guided by the old Japanese gods themselves. It is powerful weapon in the battle against the undead."

Jake looked down. As if in answer to the

stranger's words, the gold filled characters on the sword's blade began to glow in an unholy light.

"It senses this place," the stranger said. "It feels our power and knows it is home."

From a crack in the rock, a mysterious wind blew more smoke into the room.

The stranger raised an eyebrow. "Do you wish to appear?"

Jake looked around wondering to whom he was talking.

Suddenly the smoke became solid and nearby stood a well-built Japanese warrior.

"This is Takada," the stranger relayed.

"He has come to see for himself that the sword has been brought back from the undead."

The spirit called Takada stepped forward his eyes welded to the sword Jake held.

"You are the liberator of my sword?" he asked in heavily accented English.

Jake kind of smiled. "Well, if you call spending several thousand dollars liberation, I guess so."

Takada stepped forward his hands reaching for the blade. "I am grateful. May I touch it?" Respectfully, he searched Jake's eyes.

Jake nodded. "Sure, I guess it was rightfully yours anyway." He handed it over, stepping back in case the Japanese did a Creed and started swinging the blade around.

He looked up at the old man who gave him an approving nod.

"He has waited for a thousand years, Jacob Reid. Thank you."

Takada stepped over to a far corner of the cave

where he started to draw in his chi. Breathing deeply he began to concentrate.

What followed next Jake would never be able to explain, in words at least, to another human. The Japanese warrior launched into a sword kata like the martial arts instructor had never seen before.

The blade moved in wide sweeping arcs of power, flashing in the dim light of the room as it spun and whirled. It was magical how the warrior became one with the weapon and Jake found his breath coming in short gasps as a light sweat broke out on his body. As suddenly as it began, Takada was done, the echo of his Kiup still ringing through the rock tunnels.

With a bow, the Japanese Samurai handed the weapon back to Jake. "Thank you," he said and Jake noticed Takada was not breathing hard.

"You are welcome," He replied with a bow of his own, realizing something dramatic had just occurred between this man and the blade.

Takada stepped over next to the seated stranger and stood there his eyes on Jake.

"There is a test you must complete, Jacob Reid," the stranger began. "I cannot tell you what it is; all I can do is show you the way. Once you accept the path, however, you will be on your own."

He nodded at Jake who knew that what they were not telling him he really didn't want to know.

"I am getting used to this," he admitted. "So show me this path and let's get it over with."

He placed the katana in his belt in the traditional manner and waited.

Takada met his eyes with a slight smile and

bowed in respect as the old man smirked.

"You are brave Jacob Reid for a modern man. It is refreshing in this day and age."

The nameless stranger stood waving his hand at a section of the rock wall.

Before Jake's eyes, the rock became smoke and a tunnel appeared.

"This is the path Jacob Reid good luck I am not allowed to interfere further."

With a swallow, Jake nodded as he flexed his sweaty hands.

He gave the two men a thumbs-up and stepped down the tunnel, with a sound of grating rock the smoke wall solidified behind him.

"Oh shit!" he swore under his breath.

"Sure, Creed say's come along meet someone, then he sends me here and this old guy says walk the path whatever happened to the word, No, Jake?" he asked himself as he slowly walked down the hallway.

Ahead he saw another room filled with bluish thick smoke and in the center, on a pedestal, there was a very old casket. Raising an eyebrow, Jake approached.

"Too late to go back now," He figured as he slipped his fingers under the heavy lid.

To his amazement, the lid lifted easily away revealing the decaying body of a man. Suddenly the smoke around him began to swirl and thicken.

"Oh shit, here we go again," He said as he stepped back watching the smoke surround the corpse.

He stood stunned as the eyes of the corpse

snapped open and it sat straight up slowly turning its eyeless sockets to him!

"This is weird," Jake admitted stepping back as he watched the thing climb from the casket.

It stepped to the cold stone floor revealing huge incisor teeth as it turned towards Jake.

"Oh I see tough ghoul huh?"

He watched as in reply the thing stepped close to him taking a swing with a clawed hand as it snarled!

Jake ducked the first blow feeling the arm just miss his head.

"Take this!" he shouted back as he front kicked the monster in the lower abdomen. His foot felt like he had kicked the rock wall as he pulled it back gingerly setting it on the floor.

"That hurt," He admitted as the monster swung again this time knocking him from his feet and across the cave where he impacted the rock wall. He felt himself blacking out and could hear the shuffling feet of the monster coming for him as he tried to struggle up from his knees.

He gasped for air as suddenly bright light flashed behind his eyes across his brain!

He could see the other room, the stranger and Takada locked in a serious state of deep concentration, and then the stranger's face was in his head. The old man filled his mind as wraithlike images swam about behind him; images of battle, of wars fought in far away desolate places.

Through the swimming images came the voice of the stranger.

"Concentrate, Jacob Reid; open yourself and

accept the memories of all the great warriors who have come before you," the voice was calm and reassuring.

"The thing before you, Jacob Reid, is the essence of the undead, once a great Vampire Lord of unbelievable power. As you are, he will kill you; he is too strong for a human. But if you open your heart and mind, recall the heritage of your ancestors, embrace it and become one of them, you can win!"

Jake saw them, images of the great nomadic warriors of his German heritage, powerful fearless men who fought great battles against the legions of Satan's undead warriors.

The stranger's voice was back. "Grasp the sword, Jacob Reid; it will show you the way to your blood heritage!"

Through the haze of his mind, Jake wrapped his right hand over the pearl handled weapon at his side; slowly he looked up as four pairs of heavy leather boots stood before him. He met the eyes of four wizened barbarian warriors; the largest of them reached down, extending his scarred sword-callused hand.

"Come, brother," he invited with a deep grizzled voice. "Stand among us, the ancestors of your bloodline; we are at your side, brother; we will always be there to fight beside you."

Jake took the hand feeling power course through him and into his very soul. He felt as if he would explode as pure strength and hundreds of years of combat experience flooded his mind causing his blood to pound!

He stood among the warriors who reached for him, placing their hands on his shoulder.

"Welcome, brother," they said as one voice. "Fight not for yourself, brother, but for us all!"

Another flash of blinding light tore through his brain and he opened his eyes.

Jake was back in the cave, the vampire monster still stalking him. With an inner strength he had never known before, Jake stood slowly, looking directly into the eyeless sockets of the monster, as he drew the katana.

"Come on, you smelly bastard!" He snarled, feeling fear leave his body as the power of a thousand dead warriors steadied his hand.

Jake stepped into a stance without wondering where this new found fighting knowledge came from. He knew; it came from the renewed memories of his warrior ancestors.

The monster charged too close for Jake to use the sword. Out of reflex, he struck the charging vampire in the chest with a palm heel strike. The Demon Lord screamed with inhuman pain as it was thrown across the floor of the old tomb. Jake, however, looked at his open palm in surprise and then at the distance the blow had driven the attacker.

"Holy shit!" he whispered, and then with a smile, he looked up to the ceiling of the tomb.

"Thank you, ancestors!"

Unafraid he gripped the sword in both hands.

He prepared as the demon launched its way across the tomb, flying as it bared its teeth, snarling!

Jake swung the sword with a concentration he

had never been able to muster before, slicing through the center of the vampire as it flew over him.

In two parts, the dying demon flew to the rock floor screaming a final time in death as it began to disintegrate into smoke. Jake turned as the door reappeared behind him and he stepped back through into the room where the old stranger waited for him.

"Come here, Jacob Reid," the stranger beckoned.

Sheathing the sword, Jake responded. "Yes."

"You have passed the test, Jacob Reid; go now, return to the world of men and remember what has happened here," He raised his hand as Jake felt himself becoming smoke.

"Hey, you never did tell me your name," he reminded.

The stranger smiled. "I am Asmus, Jacob Reid."

Instantly, Jake was back in the basement with Creed and Selena.

"He is back with us," she announced. "He has passed the test."

Creed stood from the bed. "It is time to go back to work then," he said as Jake, covered in sweat, opened his eyes.

"Congratulations." The Gypsy handed him a glass of cold water. "Drink now."

Jake took the glass as he looked up at the two Gypsies. "I was wrong," he gasped, feeling light headed. "This beats the circus all to hell!"

FIVE

Jake exited the shower, reaching for a towel that
the woman of the house had placed out for him.
Creed had explained they were part of an intricate
support system.

As he toweled off his hair, he caught a peek of
himself in the mirror. He had grown leaner, more
muscular like Creed. There was a lot more to this
whole Hunter thing than he had originally figured.
He had to make sure to thank the family where they
were staying. Creed had explained to him about
how there were safe houses planted across the world
where the Hunters could go.

He explained that whenever you needed a place
to rest, get a meal or just lick your wounds, you
could utilize these houses. Creed also told him
about the secret potions and herbs needed to
maintain the heightened powers a Hunter needed.

The Gypsy explained how the strength, speed

and other abilities gained through the use of these potions would allow him to meet the vampire on an equal plain.

"Our enemies," Creed had told him, "are basically the vampire and their human minions. Vampires are divided into the True Bloods, vampires who were born vampires, and the Turned. To become Turned, a human must catch the eye or the interest of a Vampire Lord; the lord then bites the intended, drinking as much blood as necessary to kill them. The intended must die to be reborn again as a vampire." This Creed stressed.

"Common vampire literature would have you believe one bite is enough; that is false. To be a full-blown Vampire Lord, they must either be a True Blood, for it is their birthright to be a lord, or a Turned. If you are a Turned vampire, you must build yourself to a certain level of power by consuming huge amounts of blood. Most often, the great lords are born during times of great wars when they can wander the battlefield and feed themselves into a frenzy of blood lust. Somehow, when they reach a certain point of blood saturation, they lose all semblance of human being and take that step beyond."

Jake had raised an eyebrow at this point.

"How many of these lords are there?" he asked.

Creed was sharpening his blades and added oil to the stones as he shrugged.

"There are twelve very powerful True Bloods; they sit on the world council. There are maybe two or three hundred more. Later we will give you a list of them; you must know each by name and description. As far as Turned Lords and underling vampires, there could be thousands."

This had caused Jake to curse silently.

"Seems you are slightly outnumbered," he commented.

Creed chuckled at that statement. "We always have been. You see it takes a special kind of human to become a Hunter," Creed paused as if he was choosing his words carefully. "We do not make the choice; it is made for us before birth and then if you can survive the test of Asmus, your destiny is fulfilled."

He began to sharpen his knives again.

"So what about these minions like the ones who attacked us and broke my windows?" Jake asked.

Creed checked the edge on the knife, nodding in satisfaction. "They are humans who want to be vampires, don't ask me why; they are fanatics who strive to gain the special favor of their Lord or master. You see, an underling vampire that hasn't met the requirements of becoming a lord still can turn other humans, becoming their master. It has been known to happen that these underlings are given the title of Lord if they gather a large enough following of slaves and human minions. Of course, usually the True Blood that gives them the title also demands an oath of allegiance thus gaining the added numbers for his own army. It is kind of like the feudal system used in Europe during the dark ages."

He sheathed the blade as Jake nodded in understanding.

"They are a hell of a lot more structured than

man has ever given them credit for. Bram Stoker never mentioned any of this in *Dracula*," he observed.

Creed started on his second blade. "No, he did not; however he was closer then most at what he guessed was true. He was so close that I know the True Bloods once discussed having him removed."

Jake frowned. "Removed? You mean killed right?"

Creed nodded. "Yes, killed," he stated simply. "You see prior to Stoker writing the novel about the Transylvanian Lord, the real vampires had existed to the mainstream world as only legends. They at first overreacted, becoming afraid their secret lives were all over and they had been discovered. Of course, Stoker wasn't killed by the Lords who finally decided he was harmless."

Jake nodded back in answer. "I see."

He was beginning to get an understanding of the vampire mind. "It must have been pretty funny, though, to see the look on their arrogant faces when at first they thought someone knew about them."

"It was," the Gypsy remembered with a smile.

Jake noticed the silver earrings Creed wore, two in each ear lobe and one near the top in the cartilage of his left ear.

"You like earrings?"

Creed looked up at him. "Actually, yes, and if I were you, I would get some too," he pointed out examining his second blade.

Jake held up his hands. "I don't wear jewelry."

Creed chuckled. "Once I stepped into a whole coven of vampires and their minions, must have been fifteen of the demons in there. Well one had gotten onto my back and tried to bite me but he couldn't get past the silver earrings I wore; they saved my life. Do what you want, but it is an extra precaution."

The Gypsy sheathed his second blade and excused himself from the basement, saying something about firepower.

Jake decided to take a shower, since he was alone for a while. He walked out of the bathroom as Selena walked down the stairs.

"I have some clothes for you," she said. "They should be close to fitting, but try them on anyway."

She handed him a pair of the thick leather pants like Creed wore and a pair of leather boots.

Jake took a look at the pants. "They really are not my style," he admitted, but the boots were pretty cool, so he took them.

She thrust the pants at him. "Put these on too, Jacob Reid; style is not important when a vampire rakes his claws across your thighs."

This stopped Jake in his tracks as a memory from somewhere inside him stirred.

"Of course," he nodded. "Leather protects better then anything else."

She dipped her head slightly. "You must start thinking like that at all times now, Jacob Reid, or you will be dead."

It was a statement of fact and not intended to be a threat.

Taking the pants, he went into the bathroom, trying them on; they fit well, then he slid on the boots.

"How do I look?" he asked holding his arms out to his sides.

"Not half bad," Creed said standing on the staircase. "I have a few more things for you, though."

Selena looked him over. "He is no Gypsy, but he will pass," she teased with a smile.

Creed placed a wooden box down on the small table, as well as a gym bag of equipment.

"I just received these a while ago," Creed explained as he opened the cover of the polished wooden box.

Inside Jake could see four revolvers.

"These weapons have been made just for us."

Creed handed two to Jake along with three speed loaders of extra rounds.

Jake opened the cylinder looking the weapon over.

"Colt Python .357 Magnum, very nice," he commented.

Creed agreed. "Yes the best revolver for the job."

He handed two boxes of bullets to Jake. "We use an especially loaded 125 grain silver bullet designed to be lethal on all of the undead we might be up against."

He reached into the bag and handed Jake a double shoulder holster.

"Use this to carry them in."

Jake slipped into the holster rig and seated the weapons.

"Comfortable."

Creed smiled as he pulled out a coat that

matched his. "This should fit and take good care of it; werewolf hide is getting harder to come by."

Jake raised an eyebrow. "Werewolf hide?" he asked holding the jacket in front of him. "You must be kidding; why not wear a bulletproof vest?"

Creed looked up pointing to the jacket. "Trust me, that jacket will stop vampire claws; a bullet proof Kevlar vest will not. The jacket is also protection against edged weapons and has been known to stop low power bullets; don't ask me how I know."

Jake still looked skeptical, but he did try on the jacket.

"Hey it fits." He made several blocks and punches in the air.

Creed nodded. "That is good, because when you are out of a safe house you should always wear it. You can never tell when they will pop up."

Selena walked to Jake, holding a glass of colored water in her hands.

"When you visited Asmus, he gave you a gift," she handed the water to him. "Your body will now accept the potions of youth and of strength. Asmus gave it, but only the potions can keep it at its peak."

Jake held the glass up. "Here's to ya," he said as he drained the contents.

"Hmm tastes like cinnamon," he said handing the empty glass back.

A knock on the door of the basement drew their attention as the owner of the house walked down the stairway.

"Excuse me, my Prince." He addressed Creed with a slight bow. "There is a call for you."

Creed nodded as he put down his weapons.

"Thank you, Mika, I will be right up."

He pointed to Jake's coat. "There is a place inside, a hidden pocket to sheath the sword in. It will conceal the weapon while you are in public." Before he left, Creed nodded to Selena.

"Keep filling him in; I will be right back."

She nodded. "Yes Darius."

Jake studied her with a raised eyebrow.

"Did the old guy call him a Prince?"

Selena nodded. "Yes, Darius is the last of his line, the last of the true Gypsy royal family."

Jake chuckled as he looked up at the door Creed had walked through.

"I'll be damned," He whispered, loading his revolvers.

Creed put the phone to his ear. "Yes."

Over the line, a distressed voice spoke back.

"Darius, I am so glad I have found you. It is Bishop Danowski," Creed felt himself frown.

"It is a long way from the Vatican to this humble home," he answered. "It has been a long time, my old friend."

From across the sea the Bishop wiped sweat from his forehead.

"You know I would not call you unless it was dire," he said making sure no one else was around to hear.

Creed rolled his neck as he took a deep breath. "I know. What is it, Paul, that makes you seek me out after so many years?"

"An old student of mine has written asking help in a very mysterious matter. It would seem that a family in his parish has asked him for help; their daughter is sick. Medical doctors have been unable to cure her so far and the family came to him asking for a miracle. He went to the girl, one of the family's two daughters. As he was sitting with her he saw them, two small puncture wounds in the neck," the Bishop paused. "My student is a believer of the old ways Darius; he remembers his heritage. He wrote me here asking for help. He believes she is in the power of a vampire." It came out as a hiss from the aging Bishop.

"Her symptoms?" Creed asked and then added. "What do the medical doctors say?"

He could hear the crumpling of paper across the phone line.

"It says she appears anemic as if suffering from a blood disease. She is weak, very thirsty and complains of sensitivity to bright light. The medical doctors are completely baffled; they have run test after test with no result and have not detected the bite marks."

Creed shook his head. "That doesn't surprise me depending on the time he has bitten her last and when the vampire feeds from her. Normally they will heal in three to four hours but if she is close to being turned, if he is only leaving enough blood to keep her alive for the right time, she will heal faster."

The Bishop grunted in agreement. "Of course, as she becomes less human and more vampire."

There was a quiet moment on the line.

"He is close to her," Creed reasoned. "He can feed on her at will. The day your student saw the marks, he had been there and had fed."

Danowski's voice cracked a bit. "My student, Father Joseph Pellowski, needs your help." It was a plea from the old bishop. "If I was young and strong enough I would come."

The line between them buzzed for a minute.

"Where is he?" Creed asked.

It was a cold night in the San Francisco suburb as Father Pellowski closed up the soup kitchen. Putting his keys away, he began the walk back to the Church.

He pulled his coat closer around himself as the wind struggled to get inside his clothing; he shivered, slightly worried, about the homeless tonight.

Thirty-eight degrees in California was cold to these people and living in a cardboard box did little to keep out the wind. He hurried along as suddenly he felt a presence, someone following him down the cold windy street.

Stopping, he turned quickly but could see no one; puzzled he shook his head.

"You're getting paranoid, Father," he told himself but he still picked up his stride a notch.

Then he heard it on the wind, the clap, clap of leather boots on the sidewalk.

Turning again he saw a figure behind him, a figure who had not been there before. The man walked slowly his hands thrust into the pockets of a long leather coat a dark watch cap covering his head. Father Joseph stopped standing in a well-lit store entrance as the man walked right past him without meeting the priest's eyes and continued down the block.

Father Joseph sighed to himself, feeling a bit foolish as he stepped from the storefront walking for the church. He turned down the alley that he used as a short cut to the church, lost in his thoughts as a cigarette glowed brightly from a doorway.

"Father Pellowski," a rough voice called out.

Dark figures appeared as they stepped from the dark.

Father Joseph stopped frowning as three men appeared in his path; behind him, two others appeared.

"What do you men want?" he asked, apprehensive.

"We know you got some real expensive stuff in that church, Father, and we want it," the man with the cigarette said.

The priest held up his hands. "Gentlemen, what the church has, it shares with all. Come to the soup kitchen tomorrow; stay at the mission," he offered. "You can warm up and eat decent food."

This caused a hearty chuckle from the men around him.

"I told you, Stan," someone chuckled. "The damn church won't help us at all."

The speaker held a piece of pipe in his hand and gave the priest a menacing look.

Father Joseph now noticed they held some sort of weapon in their hands.

"Look men, this is not necessary," he tried to negotiate without pleading.

Stan stepped closer sticking a dirty finger in the priest's face. "We will decide that priest!" he snapped and Joseph smelled liquor on his breath.

From behind the priest, someone smacked something metal against a trashcan.

"Let's beat the hell out of him and take his keys, Stan. Come on, its getting cold."

Joseph tried to talk reason one more time. "Do not do this gentlemen. I am a man of God."

Stan stamped out his cigarette blowing smoke from his lungs. "What will God do for you now, priest?" he asked. "Get me those keys, boys," he ordered with a jerk of his thumb.

Father Joseph crouched, priest or no, he wouldn't fold up for them.

"He wants to fight," someone snickered as the attackers started to swing their weapons.

As they crouched to attack, a noise came from the end of the alley. A loud clap, clap of leather boots could be heard hitting cement.

"What the hell?" Stan yelled as the men turned to look at the lone figure that approached from the dark street.

He appeared from the shadows, slowly, his hands tucked into the pockets of his long coat and a dark watch cap on his head.

"What in the hell do you want?" Stan demanded.

The stranger stepped under a security light and Father Joseph saw he was dark haired with a dark mustache.

"I need the Father, fellas, so step aside and let us pass."

It wasn't an order, just a statement, as if the stranger didn't expect to be challenged.

Stan stepped past Father Joseph. "Get fucked!" he threatened pointing a dirty finger at the newcomer. "We are going to get something from this Priest, dude, and if you don't get out of here you'll be next!"

The stranger held his hands in front of him. "Okay, I will give you guys one more chance to leave so I can go about my business with the good father here."

Stan frowned. "Listen, dipshit, there are five of us here."

The stranger glanced around. "One, two, three; you're right, there are. You know a week ago I would have thought about leaving but I am a changed man," The stranger smiled.

"Oh yeah?" Stan said raising the pipe. "Now, you are a dead man!"

He swung the pipe at the stranger's head.

In a blur, the stranger caught Stan's wrist as he fired a powerful roundhouse kick into his chest; it picked Stan up into the air several feet. The pipe dropped from his hand with a clang, as the stranger swiveled his hips a bit and followed up with a hook kick to the attackers chin. Stan dropped to the cold alleyway, unconscious.

From behind the stranger, a second thug saw his chance and rushed the newcomer's unprotected back. Again, with inhuman speed, the stranger turned slightly kicking backward into the attacker's chest. It was a solid impact with the stranger's leg reaching full extension. The second attacker was thrown across the alley into the brick wall.

With a yell, a thug armed with a two by four studded with nails charged, swinging the weapon at the stranger's head.

Father Joseph watched, open mouthed, as the stranger braced himself, blocking the strike while he caught the thug's wrist. The stranger spun under the outstretched arm as he twisted the limb in a circle. Combining the leverage of the wristlock with the unbalanced attack of the thug, the stranger sent the man flying into the air. The heavy work boots of the attacker were still high in the air as his shoulders hit the ground.

The stranger released his hold on the man's arm as he turned to face the last thug.

"I want nothing of this!" the vagrant cried out, holding his hands open and up in front of him.

The stranger pointed to the end of the alley. "Leave then," he advised, a hint of warning in his voice.

"That was unbelievable!" Father Joseph observed as he released the breath he didn't realize he had been holding.

The stranger looked over at him, a friendly smile on his face.

"Jacob Reid," he said extending a gloved hand.

Father Joseph shook his head with amazement. "I can't believe what I just saw?" he exclaimed.

Jake took the priest by the arm directing him gently towards the alley exit.

"We should be going," he urged. "Time is

short."

With a nod of his head, the priest allowed himself to be led by Jake from the area of the fight.

It was a short walk from the alley to the church where the priest unlocked the door and they entered. Father Joseph stopped quickly in surprise as from the half lit interior he could see a woman slowly lighting candles in the front corner as a man in a long leather coat stood before the alter.

"Can I help you?" he asked walking forward before Jake could explain.

The woman cocked her head regarding him as she blew out the match in her hand. Father Joseph found himself noticing the seductive curves of her lips as the candle smoke faded.

Turning away from the lovely woman, he watched the man who turned slowly around, his hands behind his back.

Long brown hair tied back from the top and sides of his head revealed a pair of dark serious eyes that ran over the priest. Father Joseph saw twinkling silver rings in the stranger's ears and a friendly smile that played at the sides of his mouth. The dark eyes did not go with the soft smile, he decided. He was broad shouldered and looked well built but when he moved, it was with the grace of a prowling tiger. "Can I help you?" he asked again.

"My name is Darius Creed, Father Joseph, and I believe we are here to help you," the stranger answered, his smile wide and welcoming.

Over red wine and spaghetti Father Joseph, who

asked to be called Father Joe, explained his problem.

"There is a girl, a teenager really, who is very sick. Her parents are wealthy owners of a family vineyard a few miles outside the city."

He paused dipping sauce on his garlic toast. "They have wasted no expense on her illness, calling in every specialist they could find."

Sipping from his glass, Creed frowned. "And what exactly did the doctors say?"

Father Joe wrapped his noodles around his fork. "They don't know for sure," he shrugged. "They have hinted everything from a rare African blood disease to HIV."

He placed the noodles in his mouth savoring the rich sauce.

Creed grunted to himself. He had heard these types of diagnosis before.

Selena sipped her wine slowly placing the glass on the table. "What caused them to ask you for help?"

Father Joe paused from his supper. "Mrs. Toscanno is a devout Catholic and also Sicilian; she was raised there. She had a dream of a shadowy face stalking her daughter through a mist-covered forest," He paused shrugging. "She called me saying that in her country, the people don't overlook such powerful dreams."

Creed agreed with that statement. "The Sicilians are very superstitious about certain things."

Father Joe nodded. "She wanted me to examine the child, stating that the dream depicted a demon pursuing her daughter. She wanted an exorcism."

Jake dropped his fork on an empty plate. "Do you do that kind of thing?" he asked refilling his wine cup.

Father Joe motioned slightly with his head. "There are priests who are still doing the ceremony; my mentor Bishop Danowski passed the knowledge onto me."

"Like in the movie where the girl twists her head?" Jake asked sitting forward.

Father Joe shook his head. "I have not done one as of yet but something like that."

Jake sat back. "Cool," he whispered.

Selena was obviously lost in thought. "It would be close to being true; somehow she has been pre-warned about her daughter's danger," she said quietly looking to Creed.

"We must hurry; usually when such dreams occur, the danger occurs shortly after the loved one receives the warning," she warned.

Creed agreed, he sat back pushing his plate away as he sipped his wine.

"Selena is right," he advised Father Joe. "We must get to her soon. I would suggest first thing tomorrow morning."

He looked at his watch. It was past midnight.

"I am supposed to see her tomorrow for her confession and communion. I will take you then."

The old woman that acted as cook and housekeeper for the church came to clear the dishes from the table.

As Creed stood, she glanced at his face and suddenly bowed saying something in a low voice using a language Father Joe did not understand.

Creed paused, looking deeply into the woman's eyes with his own; then he returned her slight bow answering in the same strange language.

She stood erect, a renewed vigor about her as she continued her work and Creed stepped from the room.

Father Joe looked at Jake and then Selena with a frown. "What was that all about and what did she say to him?" he asked.

Jake shrugged. "Ask Selena." He stood and followed Creed.

The priest turned to the young woman who nodded with her head, "She was born Gypsy," she answered. "She asked for his forgiveness that she had not recognized her Prince earlier. She was explaining that she had not followed the old ways for a long time here in America. The language is a very old form of Romany with a heavy German dialect."

Father Joe smiled as he grunted softly. "I'll be, I never knew," he admitted. "What did Creed tell her back?"

"He forgave her, explaining that we all do what we have to, and then he told her to go with God."

Father Joe shook his head in wonder. "The Bishop told me that he was some sort of Gypsy Prince," Father Joe said. "But I wasn't sure such a thing even existed anymore."

Selena looked at him her gaze challenging. "He is real, priest; believe it."

Her voice was not full of malice; instead, it was as if a teacher had cautioned her student.

Father Joe received it in that way. "I hope he is

what Bishop Danowski said he was," he answered. "Because I am afraid to save this girl, he will have to be."

Selena didn't shrink from his gaze; instead, she met it, welcoming the challenge he had put before them.

"You will see, Priest," she smiled. "You will see."

There was an unspoken promise in her voice.

Creed stood on the porch where Father Joe and his fellow priests lived, watching the church across the street.

Jake walked out of the house noticing the Gypsy stood with his coat open and his hands clasped behind his back as if the biting cold didn't bother him. He also noticed Taz was perched on Creed's left shoulder as the Gypsy's long hair blew around them both.

"Feel free to join us," he invited without turning.

Jake stepped over beside him, realizing the Gypsy had said 'us' as if the cat was human.

"What are you up too?" he asked noticing the cat's tail was twitching slowly as if it was ready to pounce on something.

"I want to show you something," Creed said. "Actually to teach you something about yourself. When you made it through the test of Asmus, you realized you had changed correct?"

He didn't turn to Jake as he explained but continued to study something in the dark.

Jake thought a minute. "Yes, I am stronger, faster and my senses are much more acute. That meal tonight, it was as if I could taste each and every spice in the sauce."

Creed nodded. "Take a deep breath and hold it, allow it to siphon through your body to your brain and tell me what you smell."

Jake shrugged. "Okay."

He took a deep breath filling his lungs with the frigid air. "Nothing but the usual smells of the city," he said as he could feel the air spreading through his body as if becoming one with him.

"Wait," he whispered detecting something strange, feeling evil in the air. "I smell a faint odor of spoiled fruit mixing with the odor of old socks. Something tells me to be wary of this odor."

At his side, Creed chuckled. "That was good Jacob, what you are detecting is the smell that follows the human minions of a Vampire Lord. It clings to them like cheap perfume; there is someone out there in the dark watching this house. You know how to detect them now, by smell, and the deep feeling of warning from your soul."

On his shoulder, Taz growled low in his throat.

"What is the cat saying?" Jake asked with a frown.

Creed looked from the alley cat to Jake with a smile. "He says there is a lot for you to learn and he senses a big fight coming soon. He hopes you survive it; he liked you as a master."

Jake looked at the cat. "Well thank you too," he answered, slightly sarcastically.

The cat turned its head towards Jake with a

slightly perturbed look on its face.

"What?" Jake asked the green eyes.

Taz turned back away from Jake his eyes now focusing some where across the dark street.

"Should I go out and find this guy?" Jake asked, feeling the cat had just blown him off.

Creed shook his head. "No, I find it hard to believe that whoever is watching this house knows we are here. If we were to make contact now we may be hurting ourselves later."

He paused thinking a minute, "No, instead we will send the ultimate Hunter to keep an eye on our unseen friend," He picked Taz from his shoulder gently. "Go, my friend, but return by sun-up. We will need your abilities at the Toscanno house."

He kneeled, allowing the agile feline to leap lightly to the porch boards.

The two men stood watching the cat disappear down the dark street.

"The little warrior will take care of our friend out there without being discovered," Creed said as he turned reaching for the door of the house.

Jake stopped him a minute. "You keep calling the cat a warrior. What is that all about?" he asked curious.

Creed turned to look at him, his earrings shining in the light of the porch.

"He is the direct descendent of the great warrior cats of Egyptian temples. His bloodline has battled evil since before the pyramids were built. Combat against demons to protect the human race is his birthright forged over thousands of years. So you see, Jacob, he is a warrior, as important to this great fight as any of us and only death itself will stop the valor that races through his proud heart."

Creed stepped into the house as Jake felt compelled to look back to the place he had last seen the cat.

"Jesus," he whispered to himself before he followed the Gypsy in out of the cold.

SIX

Father Joe led them from the car up the polished marble walkway to the large wooden door of the massive house.

"Nice pad," Jake whispered as the priest knocked lightly on the door.

"Remember," Creed instructed at his side. "We are operating on the belief that the vampire is someone close to her; watch for that person."

Jake nodded. "I'm wired in, Creed, don't worry."

Taz followed close on their heels slipping into the well-groomed bushes; he was assigned to secure the grounds.

The door opened slowly and a well-dressed black man stood there.

"Yes?" he asked politely but his eyes ran over the two Gypsies and the martial arts instructor with a hint of disapproval.

Father Joe smiled. "We're here to see Miss Toscanno, Wilfred," he explained. "These friends are here to help me."

With a nod, Wilfred stepped back. "Of course, Father Joseph, please come in."

They walked into a large entryway their boots echoing off the expensive tile floor.

"Madam Toscanno is waiting with two of the doctors in Miss Angela's room," he informed them. "I will take you there."

Stiffly he walked ahead of them.

Jake looked at Creed and Selena, rocking his head back and forth while he mouthed the words, "I will take you there"

Wilfred led them up the long winding staircase and down a hallway to where hushed voices could be heard in a far room. Wilfred swung the door open.

"The Priest is here, madam," he announced as Father Joe stepped into the room followed by the Gypsies.

Jake stayed at the door watching the others like a security guard.

"Father! Thank God you're here."

A stunningly beautiful older woman stepped away from the two men she had been talking too. They were posted along the bedside of a young lady who was the carbon copy of her mother.

Father Joe took her hands. "Amelia," he responded softly. "I have brought help."

She nodded but her concern was for her daughter.

"She is worse and the doctors have no answers," she said with pleading in her voice as she searched his eyes.

Selena stepped past them. "They cannot help her," The Gypsy Witch advised as she walked to the bedside of the ill Angela.

Kneeling down she felt the girl's face and neck paying special attention to the area of the artery.

"What is she doing?" one of the doctors challenged. "There is nothing medicine can do for her; she continues to weaken."

Selena quickly found the faded point where the vampire had been using his incisor teeth on the girl.

She looked up at the two medical doctors. "There is something you can do gentlemen." She reached into her bag and pulled out a small vial of greenish powder.

"She will need to be given blood plasma in about two or three hours. Can you arrange that?" she asked meeting their gaze.

They hesitated, looking at Mrs. Toscanno.

"Whatever she needs," the older woman urged.

Father Joe also appealed to the two doctors. "She knows what she is doing."

The older of the two gave a slight shrug.

"Okay, for the Toscanno family we will get blood in Angela's type. We have done what we can. You have been told that the transfusion will do no good; her body is not responding."

Selena, undaunted, stood as she opened the green vial. "With this her body will respond in three to four hours."

She looked from the doctors to Amelia Toscanno. "I will need red wine, about half a glass full."

Mrs. Toscanno nodded. "You shall have it."

She rang a small bell and soon Wilfred was back in the room.

"A glass of red wine please," she ordered and soon the butler was gone.

Creed stepped over to Selena's side. "You stay with her until she comes around," he directed. "If there is any sign of something wrong, you call me."

She nodded back to him. "I will," she promised.

Creed stepped over to the doorway where Jake stood relaxed against the wall.

"You stay here with Selena and the girl. It is your job to guard them from the undead. He will return believe me."

Jake nodded. "What about you?"

Creed motioned with his head to the hallway. "I want a look around. The most important part of being a warrior is to know the battlefield beforehand." He paused for a moment. "While we are here, no matter what you hear from the outside of this room, do not leave it at any time. Do you understand?"

Jake nodded back. "Of course."

Creed stepped from the room as Wilfred walked past him with the glass of wine. The Gypsy walked down the polished floor hearing the light tapping of his boot heels on the wood.

He folded his arms behind his back careful not to reveal the weapons he wore as he walked lightly.

He could smell the odor of the vampire still lingering in the house.

"You will be back," he told himself as a dark haired young face peeked around a corner at him.

"Well hello there young lady," he leaned down smiling softly. "Who might you be?"

The girl met his gaze. "I am Andrea and this is my house," she said defiantly but still hugging the wall she half stood behind. "I should be asking who are you?" she pointed out.

Creed chuckled as he slowly nodded. "You do have a point there."

He dropped to a kneeling position so he could talk to her eye to eye.

"My name is Darius and I am a Gypsy," he explained. "My friends and I are here to help your sister Angela."

The girl stepped back from the wall and rounded the corner slowly.

"Can you tell fortunes?" she asked raising an eyebrow.

He shook his head with a sad expression. "No I can't. I was not given that ability as a child," he shrugged. "I do other things."

Andrea looked at him, a puzzled frown on her face.

"Mommy and Daddy told me that the Gypsies steal little children," she said. "But you don't look mean, Mr. Darius." She pointed at his ears. "You wear earrings like momma."

Creed couldn't control his smile as it grew wider. "Yes I do, little one. When I was born, only men wore earrings; it was a way to show one's wealth in the world," he informed her.

She nodded. "Daddy has a car called a Roll's; he says the same thing about that."

"I will have to meet your daddy," he said and she nodded again.

"He will be home this afternoon; he's worried about Angela too."

A thought came to Creed. "Has there been anyone your sister has been seeing, a stranger maybe that started to come around before she got sick?"

Andrea nodded. "She has this boyfriend. His name is Derrick but he scares me," she suddenly had a serious look on her face. "He gives me bad dreams at night."

Creed's eyes narrowed instinctively. "Why does he do that?"

She shook her head. "I don't know but one night I dreamed he was taking Angela away to a dark place."

"Does Derrick come by often?" He asked.

"It's a secret," she answered immediately. "I am not supposed to tell; Angela made me promise."

She met his eyes searching for his answer.

He smiled again trying to reassure her. "It's okay," he assured her softly. "It will help to make her better if you tell."

She paused and he could tell she was deciding.

Finally, she blurted out. "He comes to see her at

night and she leaves her window open."

Creed stood reaching for her hand. "I see. Come with me, little one. I have a friend you must meet."

She took his rough callused hand.

"Okay Darius."

They walked slowly back to Angela's room.

Creed walked into the room with the little girl.

"Andrea," Mrs. Toscanno said with a start. "You aren't bothering our guests are you?"

The little girl looked up. "No momma. I was just talking with Mr. Darius."

Creed smiled at the older woman. "No, she is fine, but I must talk with you alone."

Amelia nodded. "Yes of course, Mr. Creed," She held firmly to Father Joe's hand. "Can Father Joseph come also?"

Creed nodded. "Yes, is there some place where we can talk?"

Amelia wiped her tired eyes. "Yes, in the study downstairs."

"I will meet you down there in a few minutes," he assured them as Father Joe took Amelia's hand gently.

When they had left the room, Creed led Andrea over to where Selena was pouring the wine potion slowly into Angela's mouth.

"Talk to her; she has information I believe that you will be able to assess."

"Yes Darius," she answered, placing the empty wine cup down as she took Andrea's hand.

Creed walked over to the window and looked

out two stories down.

Jake joined him. "Quite a drop," he observed and Creed leaned down, seeing a black scuffmark on the sill.

"Not for someone," he pointed out.

Jake examined the mark. "Black boot heels," he whispered.

Creed nodded. "If I don't catch him in the gardens he will come through this window after dark. It will be your chance at him then."

The martial arts master returned the look.

"I will be ready," he promised.

Amelia Toscanno looked up as Creed walked into the study, escorted there by Wilfred.

"Father Joseph has told me about you," she started. "In Sicily the Gypsies are to be feared, they are known as thieves and confidence men."

If Creed heard her words, they had no meaning for him.

"I am here at the request of Father Joseph, Mrs. Toscanno. My friends and I will do whatever it takes to send your daughter along to a speedy recovery."

She nodded. "I would be in your debt, Mr. Creed."

Creed smiled. "Please either address me as Creed or Darius after all I am a Gypsy and the word mister doesn't fit."

He walked to the window placing his hands behind his back.

"Does you daughter have a boyfriend named

94

Derrick?" he asked without turning to her.

Frowning she looked from Father Joe to the back of the man in the scarred leather coat.

"Angela is seeing a boy named Derrick," she answered puzzled.

Through the door, tossing a briefcase onto a leather chair walked Theodore Toscanno.

"What is going on here?" he demanded, looking at the priest and his wife.

At the window, Creed turned slowly his eyes regarding the wine maker.

"Who are these people?" He demanded again.

Father Joseph stepped over to Theodore's side. "They are here to help Angela Ted," he explained softly.

Theodore looked to Amelia. "I met Doctor Benton leaving the house just now. He said there was a woman in here feeding our daughter magic potions," he raised an eyebrow in question.

Amelia nodded. "Yes I asked Father Joseph for help trying to save our daughter. He assures me that they know what they are doing."

She held her ground firmly under his gaze.

"Amelia we discussed this before," he shook his head sadly. "She needs a specialist; my secretary spent the whole morning calling around. We will find one soon."

He came to her taking her in his arms.

She looked up at him meeting his gaze. "The doctors have not been able to help her. I had to try something else, no matter how foolish it may sound."

Creed, his eyes narrowed as he watched the

couple, took a deep breath catching their attention.

"You waste your time, Mr. Toscanno. There is no specialist out there for your daughter," he stated flatly.

Turning back to the window, he could feel the winemaker's eyes on his back.

"I didn't catch your name or title.

Again, Creed turned back from the window walking to where a collection of liquor bottles sat on a small polished wooden table.

"May I?" he asked.

Amelia nodded. "Of course, Darius."

She answered and then turning to her husband she continued. "This is Darius Creed; he is a friend of Bishop Danowski and he is here to help Angela."

Theodore watched as the longhaired stranger with the silver earrings and the battered coat carefully poured a glass of wine. He sipped it slowly enjoying its rich taste.

"Yours?" Darius asked motioning with the glass towards the winemaker.

"Yes," Theodore answered. "From last year."

Creed nodded as he finished the drink. "Very good."

He placed the glass back on the table.

"As I was saying, there is nothing a medical doctor can do for your daughter, Mr. Toscanno."

"Call me Ted," he offered as he left his wife's arms and helped himself to a glass of whiskey from the table.

Creed nodded. "Angela is a victim of evil Ted, age old evil from before the memory of men. Selena has given her a potion that will start to contradict the damage that has already been done. If these doctors of yours do give her plasma, it will speed the process dramatically and by this evening she will ask for food and drink. We will have to see she gets plenty of both."

The couple nodded.

"Whatever it takes Darius," Amelia assured.

Father Joe cleared his voice. "You were asking, before Ted showed up, about a boyfriend?"

Creed nodded. "Yes, about a boy named Derrick," he looked at the couple.

Ted sipping his drink nodded in answer. "Derrick Crandel, a young man from Angela's school, his family owns a large manufacturing plant in the city."

Amelia sat down on the sofa.

"Yes a rather nice young man," she added. "They have been dating recently."

Creed grunted to himself, deciding to keep Andrea's secret for now.

"Is he expected to come by this evening?" he asked instead.

Ted and Amelia both shrugged. "I'm not sure," Ted said. "He has sent cards and flowers but he has not been by for several days."

Creed resisted the smile he felt forming on his mouth, he had been here more then that.

"If he shows up, I want to speak with him," he directed.

Ted shook his head. "We will let you know," he said and with a frown, he asked. "What kind of evil are you talking about here? Is she possessed, like my wife thought?"

97

"I will allow Father Joe to answer that," the Gypsy said and then he motioned to the priest.

"Can I see you a moment in the hall?"

"Of course," Father Joe answered. "I will be right back."

He excused himself from the couple and followed the Gypsy into the hall.

"So you pawn the explanation off on the priest, hey?" he asked with a smile on his lips.

Creed turned to face him. "Do you know this Derrick Crandel?"

"No, I am not familiar with him," the priest answered. "You think he is involved?" he asked raising an eyebrow.

Creed rolled his shoulders loosening his neck. "I think he is the vampire, Father, and he will be here tonight," he answered seriously. "Have you ever battled one before?"

Father Joe shook his head a funny look crossing his face. "No what will I need?"

Creed shrugged. "You will stay with Selena and Jake to protect the girl. If this kid is a vampire, he will try to separate us from her so he can get to her. Do you have a silver cross?"

Father Joe nodded raising the bag he had brought.

"Yes, silver cross, holy water, garlic and a blessed rosary sent from Rome," he smiled. "All the things the Bishop taught me I would need some day."

Creed chuckled. "He was right and, after this is

over, I will have to tell you about some of the great battles we had in the past. Yes, keep those things close by tonight; you will need them when he appears, and remember, he may look like a teenager but he will be a monster," the Gypsy cautioned.

He spun about to walk away as the Priest stopped him.

"How much should I tell the Toscannos?" he asked.

"As much as they will believe," Creed answered and was quickly gone.

Creed walked about the house hearing the voices of the doctors as they hurried back in with the precious plasma that would speed Angela's recovery. They had been in time, he was sure of that, and with the wine-spiked powdered herbs Selena had given her, Angela would come around soon. He was wrapped deep in thought when he walked into the kitchen of the house where Wilfred sat eating a sandwich and talking in hushed tones to an elderly black woman, dressed as a cook.

"Hello," he greeted as friendly as he could.

The butler looked up at the Gypsy, his eyes still not friendly.

"Hello," he answered as the woman reached over slapping him playfully on the arm.

"Wilfred," she scolded. "He doesn't look all that dangerous."

She stood, "Excuse this old fool mister, can I get you something to eat or drink?" she smiled friendly and welcoming.

Creed shook his head. "My name is Darius Creed, ma'am, and no, I am fine," He leaned lightly on the counter.

She sat back down. "Wilfred was just telling me that you and some friends of the Father were here to help save poor little Angela."

She poured coffee from a pot into her mug.

"Poor little girl, so sick," She sipped from her mug.

Creed crossed his muscular arms across his chest in front of him. "She is going to get better, ma'am."

"Call me Clara," she interjected with a shake of her finger.

Creed nodded. "Fair enough, Clara. Angela is going to wake up in several hours and she will want to eat. It is very important that she eat foods full of protein, to thicken her blood back to normal."

Clara waved her hand. "No problem, Mr. Creed, I have all of her favorites here."

Creed ran his hand over his eyes. "How long have you two known Angela?"

Wilfred placed his sandwich on the plate before him. "We have known her since she was born, Mr. Creed," it was the first time he had addressed the Gypsy.

Creed felt his eyes narrowing as he looked into Wilfred's gaze.

"Is there something about me that you don't care for Wilfred?" he asked.

The butler picked up the glass of milk from beside his plate. "There have been strange things happening here in the last few months, sir, and I have a feeling your being here will make it worse," he shook his head as from across the table, Clara chuckled at him.

"Oh come now Wilfred," she admonished.

Creed held up his hand. "No, Clara, let him speak; a man who listens to his senses is always a valuable ally," he explained.

This caused the old cook to laugh as she sipped her coffee. "He ain't no help, just a silly old man," she chuckled.

Wilfred just stared back at her. "I see things," he defended himself.

Creed settled against the sink, relaxing.

"What have you seen, Wilfred?" Creed asked interested. He needed to find out what the situation was here and he had a feeling that Wilfred knew.

"The boy, Derrick, comes here almost each night," he started between bites of his lunch. "Sneaks in the back way across the gardens and climbs the shrubbery onto the porch. Then he shimmies up the rain gutters to her room, sneaking in."

Creed agreed. "We figured that much, how long does he stay?"

Wilfred shrugged. "Depends, sometimes all night, sometimes only an hour or so. Now I know that Angela is sixteen and all, but I don't agree with what is going on up there," the butler shook his head.

"What would you say is going on up there?" Creed asked wanting to hear more of the butler's theory.

Wilfred drank some more milk. "Well I would

say they are up there sinning if you ask me," he stated adding a short nod at Clara. "Been going on ever since she started to hang around with those strange kids from the city," he shrugged. "Weird phone calls, coming home all hours of the night and wearing those funny clothes."

Creed propped himself up from the counter.

"After you finish, how about showing me these clothes you are referring to."

Wilfred drained his glass. "I would be happy to, about time someone listened to old Wilfred," he said flashing Clara a look.

"Did you ever tell Mr. or Mrs. Toscanno about these fears of yours?" the Gypsy asked.

Wilfred shook his head. "They think those girls can do no wrong, Mr. Creed. I learned long ago not to interfere."

He slipped on his black jacket, preparing to leave, and Creed gave old Clara a wink.

"You be ready with that food, Clara, she will want it by late afternoon, early evening."

The cook waved back. "I will," she assured him as they left the kitchen.

"Well I'll be!"

Doctor Benton scratched his head as minutes after the plasma had been transferred into Angela's body, her color deepened and her breathing grew stronger.

"What did you give her?" he asked the pretty young woman who sat nearby in a chair.

Selena looked up pausing from her work. "It is

an old remedy for her affliction, combining powdered herbs and garlic. It recovers the bodies ability to utilize its own blood for survival." She explained while she added a small amount of red colored powder to the serum she was working on.

The second doctor, younger then the first, removed his glasses chewing on the stem.

"But what did it treat?" he asked. "What was attacking her body?" Confusion covered his face.

Selena placed the mixture in a bowl grinding the contents together.

"She has been bitten by a vampire," she started her explanation. "The bite of the demon drains her lifeblood, feeding the monster's thirst as it deposits a nameless poison into her system."

As she checked the mix, Benton chuckled.

"Vampires! Nonsense. I don't believe this," he shook his head.

Jake looked over from the window. "Stick around for a while, Doc, you'll believe in more than that by the time the night is over."

The younger doctor sat down next to Selena. "My name is Preston Robards," he introduced himself.

She nodded back with a slight bow. "I am Selena."

"What is this about vampires?" he asked apparently curious.

Selena placed the powdered mixture in a separate vial and capped it.

"The vampire bites its victim," she began. "Its fangs leave behind a trace of a poison that makes the victim more easily controlled by him; it also marks the victim as the property of that vampire. The victim then becomes a slave and is to be left alone by the others; he or she has been claimed. The vampire has two choices; it can drain the victim dry of blood and kill them in one bite or over a period of time."

"What is the difference?" Preston asked.

Selena sat back brushing the long trusses of her black hair away from her face. "The longer they take to claim their victim, the more strongly the slave-master bond becomes."

However, Benton was skeptical. "So Dracula exists?" Sarcasm dripped from each word. "She had a blood disease, something we have not yet discovered. For some reason the powder you gave Angela worked," he tried to explain it to Preston.

The younger doctor was too immersed in what the beautiful Gypsy woman was saying than to hear his co-workers little speech.

Jake, however, shook his head as he sat down in a chair located near the corner of the bedroom.

"I ain't kidding you, doctor. Just wait, this whole thing will get better," he assured Benton.

The doctor rubbed his eyes; he was too tired to talk about this weird stuff right now.

"I am going to the next room and close my eyes for a while." He stretched, pulling on his coat. "Call me if she changes."

He walked from the room yawning.

Preston answered with a slight wave of his hand still staring at Selena, entranced in her beauty.

"After this is over, could we get together for a drink?" the young doctor asked.

Jake an amused look on his face sat back waiting for the answer Selena would give.

The Gypsy woman looked up from her powders and gave the young doctor a soft smile.

"Thank you for the offer," she replied. "But I am already spoken for; I have found my prince."

Preston felt his mouth drop; he was rarely turned down by a woman.

"Oh I see," he answered and then looking to Jake, he shrugged. "Sorry."

Jake rocked back in the chair chuckling. "Oh it isn't me Doc, its Creed; he's the Gypsy Prince," the martial artist informed him.

"The mean looking fella with the long hair and earrings," Preston whispered to himself turning white. "Oh just great." He placed his head in his hands.

Selena gently placed her hand on his. "Don't worry he wont be mad at you for just asking," she soothed him.

The doctor nodded as the color came slowly back to his face.

Behind them though, Jake had to grind it in a bit. "You had better hope he doesn't!" he chuckled.

The young doctor looked at Jake's smile and quickly grew pale again.

Selena scolded the martial arts master. "Jake leave him alone," and then looking at Preston she shook her head. "Its okay."

Her voice sounded soothing but Preston still felt his stomach turn.

"This is what I am talking about," Wilfred said as he opened a closet full of clothes.

Creed recoiled as the smell of the undead assailed his senses, he found himself on one knee trying to recover from the odor.

"Are you okay sir?" Wilfred asked looking down on him.

Creed took a deep breath trying to clear his senses as he slowly stood; he had not been assaulted like that by simple odor for over a thousand years! He looked up with a nod. "Yes I will be fine," he answered feeling his strength return.

"What happened?" the stunned butler asked.

Creed stood steadying himself. "There is very strong magic at work here," he replied. "Magic of the undead."

Creed walked to the closet shuffling among the clothes inside. "All black and filled with their scent."

He paused before looking tc the butler.

"She has recently begun to wear these right?" he asked.

Wilfred nodded. "Yes, within the last few months."

Creed raised an eyebrow. "Since she started to date our Mr. Crandel; it fits quite nicely doesn't it?"

He chuckled at the butler who nodded wide-eyed in agreement. Creed stepped back satisfied from the closet.

"We are about to enter a war Wilfred," he warned. "With the undead!"

SEVEN

The sun was down as the two doctors, Jake and Selena watched over Angela.

The girl had awakened some time after 5:00 asking for food.

She had eaten and drank for the first time in a week; Selena made sure she only drank the hearty wine her father made.

The doctors, as well as her parents, had been worried about the alcohol but Selena explained that it helped the body speed up the process.

Darius had outlined a simple plan; Jake and Selena, accompanied by Father Joe, would stand guard in Angela's room. He would roam the grounds hoping to intercept the vampire while the doctors; Mr. and Mrs. Toscanno and Wilfred, along with Clara, would lock themselves in the study.

The Gypsy had made it clear that Jake would face whatever attacked the girl while the priest and

Selena would be there only if needed.

At 10:00, he had wished them luck and kissed Selena goodbye as he walked to the gardens alone.

In the cool night air, the Gypsy looked at the clear night sky and the bright stars. How many times had he done this-stood alone against the demons that caused other men nightmares, waiting for them to come out of the night? He had lost track hundreds of years ago and right now it seemed pointless to think about them, but he did anyway.

The vampires had changed; in past times, they were simply bloodthirsty killers. In this new age, though, they were power hungry, wanting to build armies and control worlds. Deep inside, Darius longed for the old days when things were simpler and the demons were easier to understand.

Wilfred had told him that the boy named Derrick always came from the gardens sneaking through the well-trimmed rose bushes. The Gypsy made his way over to them smelling their odor in the soft breeze of the night as he strained every sense trying to detect the vampire.

"So far so good," he told himself as he settled down to wait.

The strong odor of their unclean souls warned him far ahead of time that they were on their way. He checked his watch, ten minutes to midnight, the witching hour!

Creed stood rolling his neck and shoulders,

feeling the weight of his weapons in their leather holsters. He was ready for them.

Slowly, as their scent grew stronger, he watched as clouds began to move across the moon reducing the natural light of the nighttime. They were using all of the tricks they could muster to hide themselves from prying eyes but to the Hunter they could never hide their odor.

Creed could also tell by the strength of the unholy smell that there would be a small group approaching him. He stepped back a bit into the trimmed bushes that ran around the outside of the garden and waited. It is an old man who learns to study his opposition before joining battle.

The Gypsy stifled a chuckle; it had been Napoleon who had told him that one liner just prior to becoming emperor of France and Creed often wondered if he had forgot it at Waterloo. The winds shifted but did little to cleanse his nostrils of the lingering filthy smell of the vampire.

"They are close now," he told himself.

Clouds parted allowing thin slivers of moonlight to illuminate the grounds around him as the gentle night breezes swirled, sending his hair playing about his shoulders.

He watched as they began to materialize from the misty trees around the property, black clad figures dressed in a mixture of leather and fabric.

They appeared to drift as they walked closer, the wind picking up swirling the fog as well as the robes they wore.

They were twenty steps away when Creed stepped out from the bushes blocking their path to the house.

For a minute it seemed as if all life stopped as Hunter met vampire.

"Dariusss Creeed," the young one, whom Creed sensed would be the true form of Derrick Crandel, greeted him. He was tall and wiry with dark black hair and a thin matching mustache.

"It would seem," the Gypsy nodded back, "that you know me. I find it curious, because I do not know you," he said, planting himself steadily while staying loose on the balls of his feet.

The vampire that was Derrick Crandel smiled darkly as the clouds shifted and the moonlight gleamed off of the silver earrings Creed wore.

"Of courssse, we know you Hunter."

He waved to the creatures behind him.

Creed felt the eyes of the four vampires in front of him and their ten human slaves turn his way.

"Should I be honored?" he asked, crossing his arms in front of his chest.

Crandel widened his smile showing blood stained incisors. The bloody fangs as well as the watery look in his eyes told Creed he had just fed.

"Of course we all knooow you Creeed," the demon answered his voice thick as he relished the fresh blood from his last meal warming his stomach. "They sssay a vampire cannot be truly great among his peeerss until he has facced a Hunter and survived. We are even luckier then mossst asss it isss said you are the greatest of all." He nodded to his companions who murmured in agreement.

Creed chuckled with a toss of his head sending

his hair flying about his shoulders as his earrings twinkled. "My face will be the last thing some of you see."

Crandel shook his head. "Our Masster willl be honored byyy our deathsss," he pointed out.

"Who is your lord Crandel?" the Gypsy asked. "Is it my old friend Rasmere?" He raised an eyebrow waiting for the answer.

Crandel tossed his head back showing the bloodstained teeth again as he laughed in the hollow tone of the vampire.

"That old foool hides back in some Bavarian castle, gypsssy," he spat his voice full of loathing. "He isss not fit to polish the bootss of our Massster!"

From behind the young vampire, the others joined in the laughter.

This caused Creed to narrow his eyes as he regarded the arrogant brood before him. "I have hunted Rasmere for most of my life young pup," he said slowly. "He is powerful beyond the grasp of someone as young as you. To talk about him like this is suicide in your world."

The words fell on deaf ears as they laughed harder.

Crandel shook his head as tears rolled down his cheeks. "He wasss powerful, Gypsy, but the movement going on here right now in thiss country is laying many of the ooold True Bloods at our feet. The future belongs to the young, Hunter, and my lord commandsss legionss, thousssands who are ready to claim our place in the order of thingssss."

Creed had heard words like this before; they had

111

rolled so freely from a man named Paul Joseph Goebbels as he had began the work of a youthful Nazi party.

Creed shook his head sadly. "You're blood drunk," he stated. "Have you ever met Rasmere?"

The young vampire chuckled. "To hell with himmm, Gypssy," he whispered. "We arrre what thisss iss about; we are the future!"

"How does Angela Toscanno fit into that future?" Creed asked.

Crandel shrugged. "We neeed her familiesss wealth to help us finance," he answered simply. "They have millionsss; it will be oursss."

The vampire's claws opened and closed as he spoke.

Creed nodded slowly. "There is just one problem with your idea," he replied slowly.

Crandel frowned. "What isss that?"

"You have to get past me."

Crandel raised a hand. "No problem."

From the wood line, on command, six large Doberman attack dogs sprinted, their eyes set on Creed!

The Gypsy tensed as the first one lunged for him, reaching down with his left arm he gave it to the dog. The trained Doberman snapped its jaws around the coat-covered arm trying to sink its teeth in. The animal grew frustrated as it realized that its teeth could not penetrate the man's sleeve.

Creed reached under his coat with his right hand pulling the Colt Python .357-magnum revolver. He placed it into the area between the animal's eyes and pulled the trigger as another leapt for him. With the grace of his Gypsy heritage and the inhuman speed of Selena's potions, he spun, lashing out with a powerful sidekick that caught the animal flush in the chest in mid air. The dog was tossed back into the rose bushes, whimpering in pain as it tried to breathe through its crushed chest.

Creed fired the revolver four more times putting down two more of the attacking dogs. He spun, looking for the last animal, only ten feet away, tensing to spring at his unprotected side. He was about to try and roll away from the attack as from the garden the green-eyed alley cat attacked!

Taz was on target landing across the Doberman's snout his sharp teeth and scraping claws tearing most of the dog's eyes and nose away with the first flurry.

"Get himmm!" Creed heard the high-pitched voice of Crandel as he ordered his followers to attack.

"Kill the Gypsy!"

Ten human slaves of the vampire's master flung themselves on him!

"Come," Crandel signaled his fellow vampires. "Let us feed on the girl and be gone."

They were away from the fight in seconds, heading for Angela's room!

Gunshots rolled across the grounds of the Toscanno estate. Jake saw the flashes from the window of Angela's room.

"It has started," he warned Father Joe and Selena.

The priest nodded in answer, pulling a bottle of holy water, his rosary and a silver cross from his bag.

"I have been waiting for years to fight the undead evil of this world," he whispered. "God, give me the strength."

Jake noticed Selena had placed herself on the foot of the girl's bed and appeared to be in a sort of trance as she chanted something he didn't understand.

"Get ready, Priest. I can smell them; they are close."

He drew his katana from inside his coat with his right hand as he filled the left with a revolver.

Boot heels echoed in the hall outside of the bedroom and Jake tensed as suddenly from behind him the window blew inward showering them with glass!

Jake turned firing a couple of quick shots at the black clothed figure that burst into the room. Its claws were extended, reaching for him as its mouth opened wide in a serpent like hiss, showing sharp white fangs. Jake felt the revolver tossed from his hand as a clawed hand swiped at his arm striking the werewolf hide coat. The claws bounced harmlessly off the leather but the impact of the blow was enough to disarm him. Jake leaped forward impacting with a solid jumping front kick to the monster's chest. The vampire was driven backward, losing its balance and falling out of the window it had attacked through. Jake heard the sound of snapping wood as from behind him the room door flew open and in charged a young looking vampire with blood-covered teeth.

He stopped as two more followed. "Take himmm," the young one ordered.

"Die!" A knife-wielding woman screamed as she lunged from his side swinging wildly.

Creed tossed two attackers off his broad back emptying the last rounds of his revolver into the nearest as he kicked a third in the knee cap, collapsing the limb. The woman fell to the ground, screaming, while the Gypsy spun heel kicking the fourth attacker sending him flying to the side.

He twisted away from a pair of hands as they sought his throat. Ducking to a knee, he covered himself with the coat as from all sides blows rained upon him. Cursing, he tore the second revolver from under his arm and stood, throwing at least two of the attackers from his back. He whipped the coat back away from his head and stuck the Colt into the nearest black leather covered chest. He pulled the trigger seeing the stunned human face as the man was blown back away from him, his clothes on fire. Keeping the weapon close to his side, he fended off the reaching clawing hands as he kicked another man back away from him.

The woman came back at him, her blade swinging wildly.

He tried to avoid the blade but too many other hands were still grabbing for him pinning him and making it hard to move, the sharp hunting knife slid under his coat scraping the flesh of his ribs! Creed knew there was too much adrenaline in his system for him to feel the pain of the wound but he could easily feel the wetness from the blood.

The woman stepped back, her eyes wide in excitement at the Gypsy's blood on her shiny blade.

"I have done it!" she screamed. "The Lord will reward me for this!" She held the bloody knife in front of her.

"Finish it!" someone urged at Creed's side. "Kill him!"

Creed felt strong arms pulling his back away from his body, allowing her a free target at him.

Creed relaxed not resisting the men who held him.

"I will be Lord Pakur's favorite for this!"

With a gleam in her eye, she lunged with the knife towards Creed's stomach.

The Gypsy braced himself and with a slight swivel of his hips shot his right foot upward. The powerful kick connected with the woman's chin. Teeth met and splintered driven by the heavy boot of the Gypsy, her jaw shattered into pieces under her skin.

The woman's excited boasts faded to a quiet groan as her head snapped back sharply her eyes rolling back in her head.

Before she had hit the ground, Creed tensed, his enhanced strength lifting the men who still held onto him from their feet. He swung his arms inward bringing the two men together in a crashing impact that sent them to the wet grass sprawling. He quickly snatched up his dropped revolver firing two rounds into the woman, as well as the two men, sending them to Satan forever.

116

He watched as the two remaining vampire slaves ran in terror across the dark gardens.

He was only slightly winded as he slowly picked up his second revolver and reloaded both weapons. Suddenly the wind shifted and he caught a slight odor. His eyes narrowed in a frown; he had not smelled this scent for a very long time! He scanned the dark wood line trying to see the source of the odor; he could feel the eyes watching him with interest.

Slipping the revolvers back into their holsters, he heard the low warning growl from the nearby trees!

The two vampires moved around their leader, claws extended and mouths opened wide with loud hisses of rage.

"Boy you two have bad breath," Jake adjusted his feet preparing for the rush of the two undead monsters.

They crouched springing at him with all of their inhuman speed, coming low. Jake side stepped the first vampire but was caught by the second around the waist.

"Shit!" he swore as he was knocked off balance falling backwards. He felt his knees hit the windowsill as he went out the window with the demon on top of him.

Out of instinct he turned in the air, rolling the vampire under him, they hit the ground with a thud and the demon below Jake cushioned his fall. He rolled from the demon that was struggling to rise also and recovered his sword.

"Come on," he urged the vampire.

A loud hissing sound from his side and he glanced quickly to the first vampire he had kicked from the window. He turned his body facing both of the hissing things as he twirled his sword easily in his right hand.

"Two on one huh?" he chided. "Not even a challenge."

His bold statement still echoed as from above the third vampire leaped from the window dropping lightly to stand beside his comrades.

Jake raised an eyebrow. "I should have kept my mouth shut," he whispered to himself with a sigh.

From his right the first vampire charged, swinging clawed fingers at Jake's head. With a shriek, metal met claw as Jake swept the demon's attack aside. Dropping to one knee, he reversed his swing driving the sword up into the vampire's stomach with a backhanded stroke.

From behind him, the second nearest vampire attacked as Jake struggled to remove his sword from the chest of the first demon that was rapidly disappearing in smoke!

Something in his mind told the martial arts master he was about to be struck and he reacted with a stiff elbow feeling the solid impact to his rear.

The vampire doubled over above him with a loud wail of inhuman pain while Jake rotated his body delivering a palm heel strike to its throat.

The vampire recoiled as rage filled its blood engorged brain; humans were not supposed to be able to cause him pain! Stepping away he tried to regain his balance while his comrade, the one Jake had landed on, snarled as he too attacked!

Jake tore the pistol on his right side free from its holster pointing it at the charging demon. He pulled the trigger emptying all six rounds into the thing's chest. The vampire stopped in its tracks stunned as smoke appeared from the holes and, with a shudder, the demon felt his insides being pulled apart. With a wail, he dropped to his knees, too weak to stand as the smoke grew and Satan claimed the vampire from the inside out!

The last vampire stood trying to speak through the crushed cartilage that had been his throat.

"You willl die humaan," it croaked out as it stumbled forward raising its claws.

Jake tore the sword from the smoking corpse of the first demon and faced the wounded vampire as they circled each other warily.

The vampire attacked, slowed by its torn throat as it swung a clawed hand. Jake countered with the sword. The ancient blade of the Japanese gods impacted the vampire's wrist cleaving through bone and undead flesh. As the look of disbelief crossed the demon's face, Jake stepped to the side of the demon swinging a reverse stroke that cleanly removed the vampire's head from its torso.

Jake jumped aside as the thick strong smelling smoke of three dying vampires filled the area around him, choking off the fresh air.

"Gotta get back upstairs," he reminded himself as he remembered Selena and the priest were alone with the last monster!

Crandel snarled as he saw the Gypsy Witch sitting on the edge of the girl's bed chanting a spell of protection.

"You cannottt sssave her witch!!" he called out flexing his claws. "I willl tear you from that bed and claim what isss mine!"

He started for Selena who chanted as if he wasn't there at all.

Her indifference enraged Crandel even more and he angrily swung with all of his blood-fueled strength. Shock followed by pain mixed with confusion erupted from his mouth as his claws bounced harmlessly away from the woman's face! He had not even seen what he had hit but could only guess something from her spell protected the bed and its two occupants.

While Crandel stood open mouthed and ranting, Father Joe made his move.

"We the true believers renounce Satan!" He recited the sacred words as he tossed a handful of holy water into the vampire's open eyes.

Crandel tore at his eyes trying to get the burning water out of them. He leaned his head back as his scream filled the room; undaunted Father Joe rushed in tossing the rosary around the vampire's wrists wrapping it with several binds of the beads.

"Surrender demon! The bonds of the one true Lord secure your unholy spirit!" the priest called out as Crandel found himself frozen under the power of the rosary.

"Freeee me, Priest, or I will feeed from your

open belly!" he threatened, trying to intimidate the priest.

Father Joe remained unaffected, obviously beyond the magic of the vampire as he removed the large silver cross from his jacket pocket.

"You will follow my commands unholy demon," he commanded in a strong voice as Bishop Danowski had once instructed him. "I do not bargain with the devil, demon," he answered, holding the cross before himself as he stepped in front of Selena and the sleeping Angela.

"You cannot keeep mee from her priest," Crandel smiled sadistically. "Sheee iss my prize forever!" he chuckled. "You are a foool."

Holding the cross before himself Father Joe addressed his God.

"Hear me Father; restrain this son of Satan, the fallen angel. Save your daughter Angela from his wicked intentions."

Crandel hissed, his breath coming in ragged gasps as from the rosary a foreign power filled his soul.

"Your God will not hear you, priest. He has turned his back on the Roman Catholic Church," he took a deep breath. "We are the new order of this world, one without light and hope, only servitude to the Vampire Lords!" He paused and then added. "There is no room for your God among us.".

Father Joe nodded. "You have not won yet, demon, not while those who remember still draw a breath. We will always come together to battle your unholy kind and to protect the innocents you would taint with your stink!"

121

He held the cross steady over Crandel's forehead. "Now, bow, demon, to the image of the holy Christ!"

The familiar odor he had detected was forgotten as Creed caught sight of the hulking beast that lumbered his way from the small grove of trees. At a distance, it looked like a black bear but with much more defined muscle across its body.

At roughly fifty yards, the creature stopped and rose to its hind legs while the unholy glowing orange eyes fixed themselves on the Gypsy.

Creed, his pistols forgotten drew his silver blades. It had been over five hundred years since he had faced a werewolf but that is exactly what was crossing the lawn right now!

Creed saw the moonlight as it shimmered off his blades. Yes, he could have shot the monster with his silver bullets but the battle with a werewolf was a sacred thing. For a Gypsy, it had to be hand-to-hand, knife against claw.

He stood waiting while the snarling drooling thing closed the gap between them. It too recognized the age old sworn enemy that stood before it. At less then twenty feet the monster charged, its bear like claws and powerful jaws reaching for the Hunter.

Creed ducked the huge paw that had been a human hand at one time, as he caught a glimpse of the eyes that were nothing close to human anymore. The other hand swept across the killing machine's body faster then Creed remembered, catching him flush in the chest. He was tossed like a rag doll a full thirty feet away from the monster where he landed on his back.

Pain from his chest flooded his mind and it was hard to breathe as he stumbled to his feet dimly aware that he still held the silver blades of his clan in his fingers.

"Jesus!" he closed his eyes trying to force the air back into his lungs. He stood on wobbly legs removing the coat as he faced the werewolf again. He tossed the coat aside weighing the protection it offered against the freedom of movement he could gain without it.

He met the orange glowing eyes as they came again his way; this was no werewolf like he had faced before. It was stronger, faster and appeared to be even more demonic. Little or no human characteristics were left in its make up. Someone had gone a long way to delete its human side.

"I don't know who you were," Creed said as the glowing eyes stared at him from three feet away. "But I will free your tormented soul. I ask now for your forgiveness. I know at one time you were a man."

He slid into a combat stance as the creature rose again to its rear feet ready to kill the Gypsy or die.

This would be it, Creed knew. When they joined this time they would only separate when one of them was at death's door.

It was almost as if the monster understood him as it reared its powerful head and howled at the moon as it broke from the clouds.

Jake was almost to the front door of the house when he heard the chilling wolf like howl from across the gardens. He swallowed hard, feeling fear deep down into the secret parts of his soul as he entered the house running for the stairs.

"What is going on? We have heard fighting," Ted Toscanno demanded as he exited the study with his wife and household help following.

"Yes we are worried for the safety of your friends?" the young doctor named Preston added, an excited look on his face.

Jake shrugged. "I got three down smoking on the front lawn. But there is one still upstairs."

"What should we do?" Doctor Benton asked.

Wilfred tossed off his butler jacket. "I don't know what ya'll are going to do," he said, pulling the double barrel shotgun from over the fireplace in the study and popping two slugs into it. "But I didn't run at Khe Sahn and I don't intend to start now!" Shouldering past the doctors and the Toscannos he followed Jake up the stairs!

From the darkness of the trees, a pair of milky white eyes watched with interest as the Gypsy and the werewolf faced off. There would be a death clutch now and in minutes, only one would live.

He shook his head feeling the long silver streaked locks as they brushed over his shoulders.

"For the first time in my existence, Gypsy, I pray to your God that you survive."

Jake, followed by Wilfred, burst into the bedroom to find Father Joe standing over the subdued vampire as a dazed Selena stepped from the bed.

"Don't look into his eyes!" the Gypsy Witch cautioned Wilfred and then repeated the warning as Ted and Amelia crowded behind the butler.

Behind them, Clara nodded her head in agreement. "Don't let him use his power on you," she added with a wink at Selena.

The Gypsy nodded back with a smile as she pulled a powder from her bag.

"I will pull his teeth for a while," she told them as she poured a small amount onto her palm.

Leaning down she blew softly sending the powder into Crandel's face. The vampire recoiled, at first, with a violent shudder until suddenly his shoulders slumped and his eyes glazed over.

"There he will be quite safe for a while," she stated as from outside the broken window an unholy cry of rage echoed through the room.

"Oh my God what was that?" Amelia asked as she gripped her husband's hand tightly.

Father Joe shrugged as Jake held up his hands. "I don't know, either. I heard it before I came into the house."

Selena however turned deathly pale as she went to the window leaning on it weakly.

"I know what it is," she whispered her voice barely audible in the room.

"Are you okay honey?" Clara asked coming to

the younger woman's side in concern.

Selena turned back from the window looking at them. "That sound is the cry of a hunting werewolf," she informed them. "It is preparing for the kill."

She turned back to the window looking out into the darkness.

"What does that mean?" Amelia asked.

Father Joe turned to them. "Creed is out there alone. Selena knows that only one of them will come here alive" His tone was full of dread.

Wilfred grabbed up his shotgun. "I ain't afraid I'll go help him," the butler vowed.

Jake stopped him. "No, it is my job; I will go and help."

He gripped the sword in his hand as Selena turned from the window facing the two brave men.

"Neither of you will leave this room," her soft, but even, voice ordered and for some reason neither man argued.

Ted whispered to Father Joe. "Why wont she let them go and help him?"

Father Joe shook his head. He had no answer for them, as the second horrible roar of the demon shook the room. Selena herself turned to the assembled onlookers.

"Father has no answer for you," she told them her voice trembling with the fear she felt for Creed. "It is an old legend, the story of the Werewolf. Nevertheless, a legend that was proven long ago by many men who hunted them. The story says that the werewolf is the work of a Gypsy Witch, that only the magic of the Gypsies can perform such a ceremony. When a Gypsy Witch of great power was cast aside from her people, it used to be said that she would put the spirit of a man into the body of the wolf, sending it to prey upon her enemies."

Selena paused here, looking at their startled expressions.

"Creed is the only one who can fight the thing down there because only a Gypsy can destroy Gypsy magic."

Jake nodded as from somewhere a memory came to him, memories from his ancestors.

"The curse of the traveling peoples of Europe, of the Gypsies," he murmured meeting her eyes.

She nodded in response before she returned her deep brown eyes to the lawn below.

Creed felt the blood from his body mixing with the animal's blood. He had been clawed over most of his body and his blades were covered in the creature's blood as well.

He stepped back and tore what was left of the cotton shirt from his torso. Under the light of the moon, blood ran freely down his body. The grass around them grew slippery, covered in gore and blood as it mixed under their feet.

Creed steadied himself seeing a haze before his eyes, feeling his strength leaving him.

The werewolf stared at him a deep rasp in each breath as it panted, trying to catch its wind.

Creed knew one of his last knife strikes had penetrated to the lungs.

Their eyes met. Two bloodied weary

combatants who understood only one would survive the outcome of this fight!

The werewolf slightly dipped its head and Creed, standing tall, returned the gesture with a slight bow.

Tensing they charged each other!

From the wooded grove, the onlooker felt his heart sink at the great battle he had witnessed. Once he would have relished the killing, the blood letting. Now, in the early morning light he felt nothing but deep sorrow. Slowly he pulled the dark red robe with the black trim tighter around his shoulders as he let the cowl fall back from his head. Feeling the cool night air in his long locks, he walked over to the battlefield looking down on the body of the dead warrior.

"You fought well," he said with a slight nod.

Next, he moved to the second warrior whose heart still beat in his chest.

Gathering his robes, he knelt down sticking a finger in the blood that seeped from the man's wounds. Raising the finger to his mouth, he licked it.

With a moan of pain, the Gypsy looked up through haze filled eyes.

"Get up Darius Creed," the newcomer ordered. "There is much for you to do yet."

Reaching down he stuffed something into the Gypsy's pocket. "We will talk later."

With a swish of robes, the figure was gone and Creed rolled from his back to his stomach and pushed himself to standing on trembling legs.

EIGHT

His strength almost gone, Creed could make out the mansion door ahead standing open and the three smoking corpses of the slain vampires on the lawn.

He felt immediate relief; Jake had been able to overcome them. He struggled the last few steps before sitting heavily down on the front steps, too weak to proceed for the moment. He released the blood-covered blades from his hand and heard them drop on the polished marble as he sat back against the open door trying to recover his strength.

Closing his eyes, he fought against the burning pain that emanated from the terrible claw wounds.

He had to get inside. His blood ran freely in many places.

Something soft brushed against his arm and he peeked from the corner of one eye seeing Taz, also covered by enemy blood.

The alley cat told him, in the secret language, that it had disposed of the two retreating human slaves.

Creed swallowed. He was growing so thirsty. He looked down and, lifting his left hand weakly, he stroked the cat's ears.

"You did well again, little warrior," he whispered back. "Now go find Jake and Selena. I need their help."

The cat looked up into the battered Gypsy's eyes and with a flash was gone into the house. Creed looked out into the dark gardens barely able to focus beyond the light.

"I know you were there," he whispered. "I sensed you, and I saw you when you spoke to me. Why?" he asked but no one answered except the wind.

He felt his eyes going closed as the sound of running feet filled his ears.

"Oh my God! Creed!" It was Amelia Toscanno's voice.

"He will be okay. Let us get him some place where I can treat him," Selena was there and in control.

He managed to open his eyes as Wilfred and Jake pushed by him.

"Watch the right Wilfred I have the left."

Jake directed and the two men stood guard

around them.

"My Prince can you hear me?" Selena asked kneeling gently at his side.

He took a breath aware only of her perfume filling his senses. He looked up at her, trying to focus on her worried face.

"I will be," he answered and then, lifting one of his knives, he added, "The skin."

Then his head rolled to the side and all he saw was darkness.

Selena looked at the two doctors who had followed them. "Get him up," she commanded. "We will take him to the nearest bedroom."

Ted Toscanno nodded. "I will show you the way; it's on the ground floor."

Doctor Robards and Benton slung the blood-covered Gypsy over their shoulders as they followed Ted into the house.

"Oh my God," Amelia crossed herself. "He is badly cut up."

She looked pale and scared. As the realization hit her, she turned to Father Joe.

"All for my daughter?" she asked.

The priest nodded in reply. "Yes, Amelia, now lets go inside and pray for him shall we?"

As the good Father led Mrs. Toscanno away, Selena picked up Creed's blood covered blades, and walked to where Jake stood watching for more attackers.

"I have much to do to save his life you will have to take care of the beast," she directed, handing one of the silver bladed weapons toward him.

Jake looked down at the knife with a frown. "What?" he asked confused.

She looked up at him while pointing out into the gardens. "The werewolf, it must be skinned so the hide can be used to make more protective clothing for you and Creed."

Jake nodded taking the weapon. "Okay," he answered as Selena disappeared into the house.

Looking at Wilfred, he asked. "Want to come along and help?"

The butler nodded. "Like I said, I never ran from a fight during two years in Nam and I ain't gonna start now. Lead the way, Mr. Jake."

Hefting the shotgun with a determined look, he waited.

Jake smiled. "Good man," he answered and together they started from the porch following the bloody tracks Creed had left in the grass.

"Jesus Christ," Preston Robards exhaled as they placed the Gypsy on the bed and cut away his shirt.

Benton nodded in agreement. "I have seen airplane crash survivors that looked better," he added.

"He will be fine," Selena assured them as she placed her bag on the table removing her vials. "But we need to stitch the wounds tightly so that they heal quickly. Can you two do that?" she asked while pouring some of the mixture into Creed's mouth.

Preston nodded. "Yes we can," he answered. "We should clean the wounds first though."

Selena shook her head. "You cannot; I will have to. The wounds of a werewolf can contain certain wards of protection deadly to the unprotected human system. I will clean the wounds and then you can follow my work with the sutures."

They nodded following her directions.

Jake had been right, Preston thought, he had seen some weird unbelievable stuff here tonight.

"We will listen to her," he told Benton who, for the first time in many years, didn't seem ready to argue either.

They prepared their equipment as they watched the Gypsy woman saturate a cloth with some unknown herb potion.

"This will help clean the wounds of the poison," she said trying to explain her actions as she worked the cloth in the numerous claw tears.

The doctors had to admit the attention that she paid to each wound was incredible, far more thorough then an emergency room nurse would have. As if reading their minds she started to explain as she worked.

"Most of the undead, like the vampire and the werewolf, have poisons in their bodies, mainly because they are the spawn of Satan, but also, in the case of the werewolf, it may be added there by the sorceress that conjured the monster," she dipped her cloth wringing the blood from it.

"It takes special medicines, long forgotten by modern medicine, to treat such poisons."

She glanced up at the doctors. "No offense intended."

To her surprise, it was Benton who waved her

off. "None taken."

He watched in awe, as the simple colored water she was using appeared to cleanse the wounds as well as return the healthy pink color to the skin around them.

"I am amazed at what I am seeing here," he shook his head.

Selena smiled. "It will get more interesting, doctor, believe me," she assured him.

After what felt like an hour, she placed the cloth and potion aside wiping sweat from her forehead.

"The wounds are now clean," she stated as she reached again into her bag removing a tube of thick yellow salve.

"This I will place into the wounds to ward off infection," she told them squeezing some onto her hands.

A terrible smell filled the room.

"What is that stuff made of?" Preston asked wrinkling his nose.

She looked up, an amused look crossing her face. "You don't want to know besides you may not really understand how it all works," she said rubbing the salve deep into the wounds.

"Oh, come now, there are some things us modern doctors do know."

She smiled in an attempt to apologize. "I mean it is not just what is in the mixture that counts but the magic used to meld it all together."

Preston nodded at that statement. "You know, I spend years learning to be a doctor just to have it all destroyed in one night,"

Benton moved a powerful light closer to the

table where the Gypsy lay.

"I believe we are ready to start stitching him up," he remarked.

He looked into the nearest wound full of yellow foul smelling salve.

"The way this looks," he commented, feeling the edges of the wound, "He will be healing before we finish sewing."

Jake and Wilfred followed Taz to where the corpse of the Werewolf lay in the midst of a bloody pool.

"Oh my God on high!" the butler whispered under his breath as he gripped his shotgun.

Jake shook his head whistling. "This must have been one hell of a fight."

He looked around at the torn up grass where boots and paws had slid and fought for traction.

The werewolf was dead, colder then stone, as Jake, holding his sword firmly, poked against the body.

Ten feet away, Taz flopped down on the grass and started to clean himself with his long pink tongue but keeping an eye fixed on the two men.

Wilfred watched the cat. "He doesn't seem to trust us," the butler pointed out.

Jake was sliding out of his own coat and rolling up his shirtsleeves as he nodded in response.

"He only talks to the Gypsies, I guess," he said with a shrug. "They have some kind of secret from the olden days, I don't understand it but it is there."

He picked up Creed's knife stepping towards

the carcass.

"Now I wonder how I do this?" he stated aloud.

Wilfred gave him a shrug in answer and then Jake looked to the cat. "Well?" he asked waiting.

Taz stopped his licking and looked up into the man's eyes.

Jake felt the deep green eyes of the feline burn into his brain as from somewhere a musical voice spoke to him.

"Remember your heritage, Jacob Reid, remember your ancestors."

A bright flash of light that ignited in Jake's mind replaced the voice!

He felt himself spinning, loosing his touch with his own mortal body as he was lifted to another place and another plane of existence. Around him, swirling gray mist filled the air as the sound of dying men and clashing steel echoed across the ages.

He opened his eyes and found himself clad in armor standing in the middle of a great battle. Arrows filled the air and lances penetrated the bodies of men around him.

Turning his head to the side, he saw the grinning face of the warrior from his vision in the chamber of Asmus. The man blocked a vicious sword slash from an enemy soldier.

"Aye, you have come to see me, Jacob," the man said in welcome as he ran his opponent through with his great two-handed broad sword.

"Too bad it is in the middle of this fight with the Roman legions."

Stepping back and breathing hard, the warrior pointed to Jake's hand.

"Better start fighting, boy. You can be killed on this plane if you are not careful."

Jake looked down, his eyes seeing the sword of Takada in his hands, gleaming brightly. With a frown, he looked up as a Roman pike man stabbed at him. Jake slapped the blow aside and retaliated with a cut to the rear of the soldier's thigh. The Roman screamed as Jake reversed a second follow up strike to the back of the man's neck under the leather guard of his helmet.

"Good cut!" the grizzled old warrior smiled, showing yellow stained teeth.

"Like the fight with the vampires, you are learning fast, Jacob Reid."

He sidestepped as a battle hammer swung by his head.

Jake stepped in running the hammer user through with his sword.

"How do you skin a werewolf?" he asked turning back to his ancestor quickly.

The man frowned. "Cut around the joints above the paws and run up each leg with the blade. Then go straight up from the genitals to the neck but be careful to save the head do not ruin it."

He swiped past another enemy sword, beating back the Roman soldier with hammering blows.

Jake nodded, suddenly understanding how the process was to done.

"Hey thanks!" he yelled with a wave.

The warrior smiled as he stabbed his heavy sword into the Roman's stomach.

"But be sure you finish by sun up!" the warrior reminded him. "And next time, come see me when I am in a brothel!"

"Are you awake, Jake sir?"

Jake opened his eyes. He was back on the lawn with Wilfred shaking his arm. Looking around, he remembered where he was and what he was to do.

"Yes, I'm just fine," he answered the butler and then he looked the cat square in the eye.

"You did that to me, didn't you?" he accused.

As if in answer Taz rolled onto his back and started to lick his belly.

Jake walked over to the dead beast; it smelled of dried blood and death.

"Well we had better get started. We have to be done by sun up and that leaves us little time."

Father Joe watched as the vampire began to come around as the drug Selena had given him wore off.

"Are you awake now, demon?" he asked, his cross clutched before him.

The pale white eyes snapped open and Crandel looked up staring with hatred into the priest's face.

"You have done wellll priessst," he hissed in that serpent like speech of the blood drunk vampire.

Looking around at the room they had placed him in Crandel realized that he was no longer in Angela's bedroom.

"Where isss sshe?" he demanded.

Father Joe sat down in the overstuffed chair of the sitting room across from Crandel. "You really don't think that we want you to be the first thing she views this morning, do you?" He raised an eyebrow in a slightly amused gesture.

Crandel smiled back slowly allowing the sharp points of his incisors to show between his parted lips.

"No matttter what you think, priessst, I will have her," he promised. Then the smile faded. "Let me go and I will promise not to kill you later," he said holding up his bound hands.

Father Joe looked at the rosary holding the demon securely as it draped around his wrists.

"I don't think so. Why don't you tell me who is the Lord of your coven, Crandel? Who pulls your strings?"

Crandel shook his head slowly. "The information isss ussselessss to you, human; he isss toooo powerful for your little tricks."

"Then why are you afraid to tell me his name?" Father Joe challenged. "If he is so powerful?"

The question hung in the air between them as the vampire looked into Father Joe's eyes. "Do not provoke me, Priessst!" he warned with a hiss.

Father Joe held up his hands. "I was just pointing out the fact that if this Lord of yours is so powerful, why should you be afraid to tell me his name?"

Crandel gave a snort of derision. "Lord Pakur," the vampire answered staring into the priest's eyes. "The next great Vampire Lord."

Before Father Joe could answer, Ted Toscanno stuck his head into the room.

"Father, Angela is awake. Will you come and

see her?" he asked.

The priest stood. "Don't go anywhere," he told Crandel as he followed Ted from the room.

Crandel watched them go trembling in rage, he had to find a way to remove this damnable rosary and then he would be free!

Amelia Toscanno looked up from her daughter's bedside as the Priest walked in with her husband.

"Look, Father, our Angela has returned to us," she said as the girl smiled weakly.

"Hello Father Joe," she greeted him.

The priest nodded. "It is good to see you getting well, Angela."

He reached down placing his hand over hers. "May God bless you," he added as he made the sign of the Cross over her forehead.

Angela looked up. "Momma says he already has by sending you and some friends to help me get better."

She was still pale but the light of life glowed again in her eyes.

Clara stepped forward from the rear of the room. "Are you hungry, my child?"

Angela nodded. "Yes, for some pancakes."

"I will bring you some."

"Clara, would you mind telling the doctors and the Gypsy woman that she is awake?" Ted asked. "They may want to examine her again."

The old cook nodded as she disappeared into the hall.

"I am so hungry momma," Angela told Amelia.

"You ate a little last night, honey, do you remember?" she asked.

Angela frowned. "Not really. I must have been very sick."

Ted walked to the side of the bed. "You were, dear, but you are going to be fine now."

Angela nodded. "It was Crandel, daddy, he did something to me, didn't he?"

Ted looked at his wife who nodded back; it was time she knew it all. He looked down on his daughter.

"Yes, honey, Crandel is a bad person. He tried to take you from us but Father Joe stopped him."

She looked over at the priest. "You did?" she asked amazement in her voice.

He smiled back. "Yes but I had some very powerful help."

Footsteps from the doorway caught their attention as doctor Benton walked in followed by Selena.

The doctor pulled his stethoscope from his pocket and started to examine her, as the Gypsy sat gently on the bed next to her.

"Hello Angela," she greeted the girl with a soft warm tone of voice. "How do you feel today?"

Angela looked at her curiously. "You are very pretty." She smiled as the scent of wild flowers filled her senses. Something about this woman was very calming.

Selena smiled back at her. "You are also, Angela, and now you will live to allow that beauty to blossom."

Angela smiled at the comment as Selena

reached into her bag and removed a small tea bag that she placed into the glass of water at the bedside.

Doctor Benton removed his stethoscope.

"Amazing," he commented looking at the Toscannos.

"Her lungs have cleared and her heart is back to a strong regular rhythm," He shook his head. "I have never seen the like before."

Selena removed the bag from the water that now looked a slightly rusty color.

"She still has some of the vampire's poison in her system; this will help to dispel most of it."

She offered the glass to Angela who wrinkled her nose.

"What is it?" she asked looking up at the Gypsy in apprehension.

"It is a powdered mixture of herbs with a little cinnamon added for taste," Selena informed her.

Angela took a sip and then smiled. "This is very good."

She beamed up at them.

"Drink it all," Selena urged and then, turning to Amelia, she handed her a bag of the mix. "She will need to drink this three times a day until it is gone."

Taking the bag Amelia nodded. "Thank You."

Selena simply nodded her head in quiet response.

Looking into the Gypsy's tired eyes Amelia asked, "How is Creed?" Genuine worry filled her voice.

Selena took a deep breath. "He will live; he is resting now."

Benton shrugged as he looked at Father Joe. "I can't believe that either," he said. "We hardly were stitching the wounds and it seemed as if the flesh was already scabbing over. I don't know what is in that bag she carries but I wouldn't be surprised if it could cure cancer and the common cold."

Father Joe chuckled. "It has been an amazing night, hasn't it?"

Benton nodded as he yawned deeply in agreement. "One I will not forget in a while. I have to admit my eyes have been opened."

"That man Creed, downstairs, he has a lot of old scars covering his body. He is no stranger to demon fighting, is he?"

Father Joe sighed. "No, he has been doing it for a very long time."

Benton frowned. "He doesn't look much past his mid thirties. He must have started young."

Father Joe chuckled this time. He decided, however, not to tell the good doctor how old Creed really was. The man had seen enough tonight and telling him that the Gypsy was over a thousand years old might be pushing it. "Yes, I guess he has," he answered, leaving it at that.

Crandel opened his eyes sensing he was being watched. Turning his head, he saw the little face framed in dark hair that regarded him.

"Hiii Andrea," he greeted Angela's little sister.

Andrea looked at him with a frown on her young face. "What are you doing, Derrick?" she asked walking slowly into the room. "Are you here

144

to see my sister?"

Crandel nodded. "Yes I am sweetheart, but I have a problem. Can you help me?" he asked trying not to hiss.

Andrea looked at him and nodded. "What is wrong?"

He held up his hands. "Can you untangle me from this rosary, sweetie? I want to give it back to Father Joe."

A smile covered the child's innocent face.

"Were you playing a game?" she asked.

Crandel smiled as innocently as he could under the blood influence in his brain.

"Yes, dear, and he had to go somewhere but he left me like this, could you remove it please?"

He again held up his hands bound in the sacred rosary.

"Of course I can," she stepped forward with a giggle.

Clara had brought the pancakes Angela wanted and the assembled people in the room stood happy just to watch her eat. She was pouring more syrup onto her plate when the scream of the young girl tore through the house!

"Stay with Angela!" Ted directed his wife as he rushed for the hallway followed by Doctor Benton, Father Joe and Selena.

"He is loose," the winemaker yelled in warning as he saw the black clad vampire running down the staircase.

"Daddy, help me!" Andrea cried out from under his arm.

Crandel looked back over his shoulder at them while he ran with the little girl.

"Put her down!" Preston Robards ordered running to cut the demon off from the doorway a scalpel in his hands, he held it up threateningly.

Crandel looked around; he didn't see Creed or the other one with the sword.

"Fooolish mortal, you cannnot ssstop me," he hissed as he struck the doctor with a stiff palm driving Preston back and over an armchair in the hallway.

With a dull thud, the doctor's head bounced off the polished wood floor as, with a gleam, Crandel headed for the mansion door.

"You sure you don't want no help there, Mr. Jake?" Wilfred asked as the martial arts master struggled with the heavy hide of the werewolf.

From somewhere under the pile of fur Jake shook his head.

"No I got it," he responded.

Jake struggled to take each step; even with his enhanced Hunter's strength, the werewolf skin was heavy.

"Is the sun coming up?" Jake asked from under his load.

"Yes sir," Wilfred answered. "Just peeking over the trees."

From under the fur, Jake took a deep breath.

"Good," he said as they reached the sidewalk leading to the mansion.

He dropped the werewolf hide onto the stone. "That is one heavy hide. He must have weighed a lot when he was alive."

He bent over, his hands on his knees, as he tried to catch his breath.

Wilfred agreed with a nod of his head. "Yes sir he was a big monster that is for sure."

Yelling from the house caught their attention and both men looked up to see Crandel running their way with little Andrea Toscanno under his arm.

Jake drew his sword.

"Stop right there, vampire," he ordered as Wilfred raised his shotgun.

Crandel stopped his eyes narrowing as he looked at the two men; the shotgun wouldn't kill him but the enchanted sword sure would. He slid to a stop as from the house Ted and the others burst through the doorway.

"He has Andrea!" Ted called out. "Everyone be careful." There was caution, as well as concern, in his voice.

Crandel watched as the priest and the Gypsy Witch stepped forward.

"Put her down," Father Joe demanded as he stepped forward slowly raising the cross before him.

"Your crosss iss no good priest," he hissed. "You are tooo far awayvy for its power to work."

Turning he also sneered at Wilfred.

"That big guuun will nooot harm me eitherrr."

Jake nodded to the butler. "He's right, Wilfred.

147

Here," he handed the butler Creed's blade; the one they had dressed the werewolf with.

Wilfred grasped it in his hand as he stepped to the side of the demon.

Crandel stood, an arrogant smile playing on his face.

"What willl you dooo?" he asked holding the little girl like a shield before him.

Selena walked away from the others and past Father Joe.

"She is not part of this, vampire; her future is separate from yours," she pointed out, placing herself directly between them and the demon.

Crandel took a long look at the Gypsy Witch. Of them all, she would be the most dangerous.

"Ssstay baack witch!" he cautioned placing a sharp claw against the girl's soft neck. "Or I willl slassh her throat and drink her bloood and you knoow how powerful a bloood fed vampire can be."

"Put her down, Crandel."

All eyes turned to the doorway where Creed stood his wounds still seeping small amounts of blood as he leaned heavily on the marble column.

"Aaaah, Creeeed, you stilll live."

It sounded as if the idea satisfied the vampire. He looked down seeing the revolver in the Hunter's hand.

"You wouldn't shoooot," the demon smiled arrogantly. "You might hit the girl."

Creed raised the weapon with a stern look on his face. "You don't think so?" he asked seriously.

The vampire pushed a sharp claw closer to the pulsing artery in the scared little girl's neck.

"I will drink her blooood as it spurtsss from her Gypsy," he threatened.

Creed cocked the pistol as he maintained his aim on the demon.

"The sun is coming up Crandel you don't have much time to make a decision."

The vampire could feel the heat of the rising sun; he didn't need Creed to tell him about it.

He met the Gypsy's eyes. "I can stand it longer if I feeed now," he said placing more pressure on the girl's neck.

Andrea screamed in pain.

"Please don't!" Ted Toscanno begged.

His sharp claw, close to breaking through the skin of the girl's soft neck, Crandel opened his mouth preparing for his feast of warm blood.

Creed's finger tightened on the trigger hoping for a quick shot to save her life.

It would not be the Gypsy who would save the girl's life as, from a nearby bush, the alley cat sprang to the attack!

Crandel's eyes opened wide as the animal jumped straight into his face, claws and teeth flaying his cheekbones. Crandel released his grip on the child who ran screaming to her father while the demon stumbled to the ground trying to tear the ferocious cat away from its face.

Taz jumped free, evading the razor sharp claws of the vampire, which struggled to its feet. Both of Crandel's milky white eyeballs were missing from their sockets.

The vampire shrieked in pain, a great inhuman wail, as it stumbled about blinded.

Jake made his move ending the demon's agony with one well-placed sword stroke through the heart!

Crandel began the slow smoking death of the undead while around him the humans watched the sun rise on a happier day.

NINE

Creed pushed away his plate, unable to eat another bite as he glanced across the table at Angela.

"You look well," he commented.

She smiled, her face full of happiness and life.

"Yes, I feel..." She took a deep breath as if she had never breathed before this moment.

"...different, as if I never really appreciated things before," she paused with a frown. "Does that sound funny to you?"

He sat back in the kitchen chair, sipping from his coffee cup.

"No, as a matter of fact, it is quite normal for someone who almost died," he explained.

She nodded as she continued to smile while she ate.

Creed sat back, content to watch her, happy and alive.

He had a lot of thinking to do; the woman who had tried to kill him had called the Vampire Lord they served, Pakur. He had talked last night to Father Joe, who confirmed that Crandel had used the name, Pakur, as his Lord.

"Pakur. Is that Hindu?" Selena had asked, as they ate a late supper.

"Persian," Creed had corrected her. "There once was a General by that name who fought in one of the many early holy wars, a particularly cruel and blood thirsty man much like the Count Vlad of Bram Stoker's *Dracula*," he had explained.

The priest and Selena listened with interest as Jake, a frown burying itself deep in his brow, nodded.

"For some reason, don't ask me why, I know that. He was well known for allowing his men to slaughter the innocent non-combatants in the towns and villages he plundered," he added.

Creed nodded, but Selena asked a curious question.

"So, is this Lord the original Pakur or someone who stole the name?"

Jake shrugged and Creed, playing with his wineglass, shook his head.

"That I do not know," he had answered. "But I have an idea who will."

And without expanding he had finished his meal.

Realizing that Angela had spoke, he returned to the present.

"Excuse me," he apologized. "I missed your question."

She placed her glass of juice down on the table.

"I just commented that Derrick was an evil man, wasn't he?" she searched his eyes, as she waited for his comment.

The Gypsy nodded as he sipped more coffee. "He really was not a man anymore, Angela; the process that takes over a human body when the poison of the vampire sets in drains the victim totally of his former self."

Angela nodded. "Father Joe explained some of that to me last night; he also said that there was a good chance that Derrick wasn't really seventeen," she paused. "He said that Derrick might have been much older but to ask you because you would know."

Creed looked up at her and smiled. "What the good Father is referring to Angela is the fact that most vampires, when they are turned from being human, go through an aging process. When the man or woman is bitten and drained to the point of death, a change begins. Now, I am not a doctor so I can't really explain it," he sipped from his coffee mug. "But it begins inside; one of the events in the process is that the thing that evolves from the human being is frozen at his current age."

Angela nodded following him. "That would mean Derrick was bitten as a teenager," she finished his thought.

Creed was amazed at her ability to understand all of the craziness.

"That's right. After he or she is bitten, they basically begin to gain in power. In order to do this, they must consume a certain amount of blood from numerous victims. The more varieties of victims they find and feed upon, the quicker they will grow and develop towards their final goal of becoming a Vampire Lord," he reached for the pot, refilling his mug.

Angela frowned. "Is it good to be a lord?"

Creed nodded. "Of course, it is like being king."

"But how much blood would a vampire have to consume to become a lord?"

Creed shook his head, as he sipped again from his mug. "I really don't know the answer to that. It would seem, though, that it varies from human to human. The one thing I do know is that it takes a lot of blood from many victims. That is why most lords are created during war. Having battlefields full of victims makes it very easy for the young vampire to gain his powers," he paused.

Angela broke off a piece of doughnut, studying it. "What would a lord look like?" she frowned. "Is he different from the others?"

"Yes," Creed nodded. "There are the usual physical traits; milky white eyes, pale translucent skin, and claw like fingernails. But in the case of the lord, he becomes even more demon-like with super human strength and telepathic powers. He can invade your mind and bend you to his will."

Creed shook his head as he took a deep breath.

Angela chewed on her breakfast. "You have been fighting them a long time?"

Creed gave her a slight nod. "Yes for many years," he answered leaving out the words 'over a thousand'.

Selena walked into the kitchen and, leaning over him, whispered into his ear.

"It has been arranged my Prince."

He looked up into her dark brown eyes and answered with a brief nod.

"You are going on a vacation, Angela," he announced. "You and your family."

She met his eyes. "Where are we going, Darius?"

He smiled as Selena sat down taking a cup of coffee. "To my estate in my native Bohemia," he announced.

Standing with his mug, he waved with his hand.

"Let us all go and find your family. We will discuss this in length."

Creed assembled the Toscanno family in the study where they were also joined by the butler, Wilfred, and the maid, Clara. Jake and Father Joe were already there, munching on pastries.

"Good morning," he greeted as he walked in holding Angela's hand.

"What is this about?" Ted Toscanno asked as he turned from the window, a jelly doughnut in his hand.

Creed escorted Angela to the overstuffed sofa where she sat next to her mother.

"Selena and I have discussed this and we feel,

because of the danger to your family, you should take a vacation until after we have destroyed the Vampire Lord and his coven," he explained.

Amelia Toscanno looked at her husband who started to protest.

"I can't just pick up and leave," he argued. "My business is at a crucial point right now. We are working a major merger with two other wineries."

Creed felt his eyes narrow as he regarded the wine maker. He watched as Taz hopped lightly onto the sofa and plopped down in Angela's lap.

"Who would those partners be?" Selena asked sensing her lover's line of thought.

Ted Toscanno shrugged. "Two other wine makers along the valley, long standing families of great power in the business. They have been here for at least one hundred and fifty years."

Selena looked at Creed. "Shall I check the names?"

The Gypsy nodded. "We have to cover all our bases here."

They watched in awe as the beautiful Gypsy woman pulled a round glass ball from a carefully wrapped cloth she had suddenly revealed. Standing gracefully, she walked to the window where the morning sunlight reflected from its polished surface.

Their eyes filled with interest as Selena started to chant in a low melodic voice while she ran her right hand over the ball. Her hand moved in an exotic rhythm seemingly tuned to the song-like chant of her voice and from the center of the ball a light began to grow. From around the intense brightness of light, blue smoke began to emanate until it filled the ball mixing in a savage intensity.

Selena looked at Creed and gave him a slight nod as she continued her chant.

Creed turned to Ted. "The first name of your merger partners, give it to the ball of Asmus."

Ted, his eyes glued to the ball of glass snapped from his delirium. "Randall, Dale Randall is the first name," he said his voice trance-like, his eyes still locked on the ball.

The people in the room watched the swirling blue smoke in the ball, it continued to swirl, unaffected by the utterance of the name.

Selena looked at Creed a second time. "The next name, my Prince?" she asked, her voice singing the request as she continued the chant.

Creed nodded at Ted who revealed the second name.

"Lotelli, Garrett Lotelli; an old Italian family."

They watched, again, as one more time the ball remained the same calm swirling blue color, suddenly Selena broke off the chant as she wiped her hand from the ball.

"No on both accounts," she said as her eyes met Creed's.

The Gypsy nodded sunlight playing on his silver earrings as he turned from the window.

"Have no fear of the merger," he assured Ted Toscanno.

However, this did little to calm the businessman. "Because some old glass ball didn't react to their names, I should trust them?" he shook his head. "I doubt it."

Jake grunted. "Don't mess with Asmus, Ted," he pointed out. "Believe me he isn't someone you want to go and visit."

Ted shrugged again. "I have to stick around. Don't you see, it is the future of my family and business?" Then he shook his head. "If I could read the future, then maybe."

Creed chuckled. "If that is all it takes."

He motioned to Selena who, with a nod, walked to Ted.

"Give me your hand sir," she directed him.

He hesitated a bit.

"Oh, go on daddy," Angela prodded and Amelia agreed.

"Let her see your palm, honey."

Looking from his daughter to his wife Ted extended his palm to the Gypsy Witch.

Selena smiled as she took his hand in her own tracing the lines that lay there. She read the future in those callused-filled lines and, for a second, caught her breath but recovered quickly, the smile returning to her mouth.

"You should not fear. The merger will go through with or without you being physically present."

Ted nodded. "I hope you are right, Selena, because if I leave the country with my family, I would hate to return ruined,"

Selena nodded understanding his fear.

Creed pulled the plane tickets from his coat pocket. "Here you go then, Ted. Your family will go to my native lands in the Elbe River valley. There, you will be protected from any vampire that may pursue Angela and your family.. Gypsy families settled the whole valley, as well as the land around it. They will not allow demons into the area," he assured them.

Ted slowly nodded, giving in. "Okay, we will go, Creed," he looked at Wilfred and Clara. "Start packing. You two will go along also."

The family left the room excited to be going to Europe to visit Creed's old estate.

Creed motioned to Taz. "Go with the girl, cat, protect her," he ordered.

Jumping lightly to his feet Taz followed Angela as Father Joe and Jake stayed behind with the Gypsies.

Creed turned back to the window watching the sun as it hovered in the California sun.

"What did you see?" he asked without turning.

Father Joe and Jake locked eyes both raising their eyebrows; it often became confusing following these two when they conversed.

Selena carefully repacked the ball of Asmus and placed it into her bag.

"The shadow of a spirit was there," she announced without looking up.

Creed nodded but did not answer simply continuing to stare out the window as if concentrating on something in the yard.

Jake frowned. "What do you mean like a poltergeist?"

Selena stopped assembling the contents of her bag and appeared to be in deep thought for a couple of seconds.

"Not really," she began. "Not as you would

define the spirit body, no. Actually, it is more of a premonition of things to come. You see, if a man or woman has something that could possibly occur in their future, many times it is recorded before the event occurs. In the older times, when men and women still believed in the reading of the palm and other signs, such a warning would be heeded and steps taken to protect the victim. It is rarely taken advantage of in modern times though," she shook her head sadly.

Father Joe snapped his fingers. "But if the shadow is there and it is a warning maybe we solved the problem with the death of Crandel. After all, he was the one who would have taken Angela," he reasoned.

Jake nodded, agreeing with the logic. "Yes, that would make sense. We have already destroyed the shadow."

From the window Creed spoke. "Not quite, fellows," he said. "Explain to them, Selena."

With a jingle of her own silver earrings, the witch nodded. "What Darius is referring to is that if the evil that shadows the family were destroyed, the marks I saw would have disappeared. There is no need for the warning to continue if the future has been changed."

Jake rolled his eyes. "Of course, why had we not known that!" He slapped his head sarcastically as he looked at the priest who simply shrugged in reply.

Creed turned slightly. "You are learning, Jacob. That is enough for now," he complimented. "What it does say to us though is that the evil still exists and that the danger is still very real for this family."

He turned completely towards them now.

"So, what is our next step then?" Jake asked from the couch.

Creed removed a blood stained crumpled note from his pocket.

"I need to see someone tonight," he explained holding it up. "Tomorrow I will know better."

Father Joe looked at the note in the Gypsy's hand. "An old friend?" he asked.

Creed looked at the priest a slight smile playing along his lips. "Old he is, Priest, but he has never been a friend," then Creed paused. "But there are times when I have mixed emotions about him; it seems he has been around longer then any friend I ever had," he answered as he walked from the room.

Selena stood following Creed; Father Joe looked at Jake.

"Did that make sense to you?" he asked.

Jake shrugged. "As I said, Father, sometimes it is hard to follow what he says but," the martial arts master shook his head, "sooner or later you *almost* start to understand it all and then it really gets scary."

Father Joe stroked his chin as he thought a minute. "So then the fireworks are not over just yet?"

Again Jake smiled. "That is the second thing you learn around Creed. The excitement never stops."

It was late in the afternoon when the family finally left the house loading their luggage into the car and pulling away.

"They will be okay," Selena assured Creed as she leaned over his broad shoulders, watching them wave as they pulled away.

They were alone in a second story bedroom where they would sleep tonight, or at least she would; Creed had something he had to do.

He took a deep breath. "I know they will be."

He turned from the window and pulled off the werewolf coat, tossing it onto a chair.

"Whoever this Lord Pakur is, he will be unable to pursue them this quickly."

He slipped the weapons from his shoulders, allowing them to fall on top of the coat. "And once they reach the old country, there will be those who can intercede on their behalf, if necessary."

Selena looked at him in her soft seductive way. "They are safer now than they have been for the last three months."

She stepped over to him slowly unbuttoning his shirt and slipping it over his shoulders. "You have healed well my Prince," she whispered, running her hands over the largest of the healing wounds.

He chuckled as he looked into her deep dark eyes. "It is because of you, pretty one, and your talents that I have healed," he answered softly reaching for her chin and pulling her mouth up to his.

They kissed deeply, suspended for an eternity from the battles they had fought recently.

They parted briefly.

"I was afraid the werewolf would kill you," she whispered her voice trembling as she felt her desire rising for him.

He brushed his lips against hers. "I would have spared you that fear," he replied softly. "But you understand, I cannot shrug off the responsibility."

He met her eyes and she nodded.

"Yes, of course, only *you* could have killed the monster in hand to hand combat."

He smelled the perfumed aroma of her hair drawing it deep into his senses while allowing it to intoxicate him.

"Selena." He whispered her name as his strong hands caressed her neck holding her gently but firmly.

She looked up at him through half closed eyelids as her lips reached for his a second time.

They kissed deeply, their tongues entwined, as their passion drove their emotions and controlled their actions. Her soft hands trailed down his hard muscled body finding the clasp of his belt buckle, undoing it with deft practiced movements. She slid them from his hips sending them to the floor where he stepped from them, his lips never leaving hers. They parted slowly as she pushed him back down onto a well-padded armchair. Stepping back, she kept her eyes glued to his as she removed her blouse. Feeling his breath catch in his throat, he looked at her well-formed breasts inside the black lace bra. Next, she started to remove her own leather pants a smile playing on her lips as she slid them over her narrow lips to the floor.

Creed watched her step from them taking notice

of the black silk French cut panties she wore. "My God," he whispered to himself.

Selena, smiling softly, her eyes burning into his, stepped gracefully to the bed where she dropped down to all fours gliding like a panther across the sheets.

"Come to me, Prince of the Gypsies," she seemed to purr. "Make love to me."

Rising slowly from the chair as the blood hammered in his head, Creed reminded himself she was a witch. "But what a witch," he murmured as he dropped onto the bed beside her.

It was ten minutes before midnight when Creed pulled up the stool and sat down at the bar.

He was in a place called The Incinerator, a bar where young leather clad kids with colored hair and pierced tongues gathered.

"What can I get ya there, sir?" A young, big-busted female bartender asked as she snapped her gum.

Creed looked from her fake tits to her orange Mohawk and caught the twinkle of light off of her belly button ring.

"Whiskey and a draft," he ordered, pulling money from his pocket.

She placed the drinks in front of him, waving off his money. "I've never seen you around before."

Creed watched as she leaned closer to him across the bar top, her low cut shirt dropping away enough that he could see her nipples.

He chuckled to himself as he picked up the shot

of bourbon, smelled it and then drained half. "It's my first time," he answered with a half smile and a playful wink.

"These Gothic types scare me," he smiled playfully at her.

She smiled back and a twinkle from inside her mouth confirmed it, she had a pierced tongue.

"I am done in half-hour, handsome, if you're looking for a tour guide, someone to keep you safe," she offered with a flip of her hand.

She stood back leaning into the liquor cabinet, her breasts jutting out as she offered herself.

Creed shrugged. "We will see, later. You never know what may come up."

She raised an eyebrow. "With me, good looking, I know what will come up," She promised, moving down the bar as she waited on other customers but still keeping one eye on the Gypsy.

Creed shook his head; he never did have a problem picking up women, even the wrong ones. He finished the whiskey and started sipping the cold beer; it tasted real good tonight. He looked around at the swirling bodies in this dank little dance club.

They were all young; he guessed early twenties and dressed in combinations of leather and black lace or ripped denim and lace. He could see colored hair and black eyeliner, as well as chains, draped from their bodies. It all made the Gypsy think of how far the newest generation had advanced in their thinking beyond the normal views of society. It was good and bad for a generation that could think on its own could do wondrous things if the energy was properly channeled.

The bartender filled up his empty shot glass and he gave her a little extra wink. She smiled back but still did not take any money from him. He watched her walk away and then lean over an attractive waitress whispering. They both looked his way and he knew where this was heading.

He turned his back to the bar just as a woman led a man past him wearing a dog collar, the lead chain wrapped around her wrist securely.

Over the top of his whiskey, he shook his head thinking of the old medieval castles and their torture chambers. He thought how foolish the master-slave tandem would feel if a real master of pain confronted them.

He remembered the one employed by King Henry the third of England. Arnold Schwarzenegger had nothing on that guy. He was big, cruelly strong and delighted in hearing men and women shriek in pain. Creed felt a tingle run down his spine at the memory.

Suddenly from the crowded dance floor he felt the presence. Turning slowly, he watched as a wisp of dark colored smoke appeared. Creed sipped his drink as the smoke grew to the height of a man and suddenly Rasmere stepped from it!

The Vampire Lord's odor assaulted the Gypsy Hunter's senses, causing him to reel for a second against the bar. Creed regained control of himself and watched as the milky white eyes regarded him from across the dance floor.

With a slight dip of his head, Rasmere walked among the swirling young humans and headed Creed's way.

166

The Gypsy noticed the vampire was dressed head to foot in black leather supplemented with black lace. As he walked closer, Creed noticed the vampire wore his hair long. Falling down around his face and stopping at his waistline, it was heavily tinted in silver streaks that matched the black and silver goatee on his chin. It was the blue centers of the eyes, though, that he found fascinating; the Lord had come far since their last meeting.

"Creed, it is nice to see you," the vampire greeted as he walked to the barstool next to the Gypsy.

Creed nodded back. "I guess I could say the same Rasmere. At least you are the same after all of these years." He responded as he waved about them referring to the bar patrons.

Waving to the bartender, Rasmere turned rolling his eyes at Creed.

"Yes, you are right, Hunter, things have really changed, haven't they?" he asked as the orange Mohawk appeared before them.

"What can I get you?" she asked snapping her gum.

"I would prefer a Bloody Mary," Rasmere answered. "But since your name isn't Mary I will have a brandy."

She started to giggle. "That was funny," and then looking at Creed she raised an eyebrow. "Is he with you handsome?"

Creed shrugged. "I guess so, at least for tonight," he admitted.

"I will have to tell my friend."

She giggled as she hurried away to get Rasmere

his drink.

The vampire shook his head. "Humans, they are so much fun to watch," he commented.

Creed nodded in agreement. "You seem to fit in well tonight, Rasmere, no hissing or clawed hands to give you away?"

The Lord nodded. "I have not fed for over a month Creed, for that reason. I am hungry, yes, but I can hide my traits easier."

The bartender returned placing the drink before the Lord.

"Four bucks," she said holding out her hand.

Creed pushed his money across the bar knowing that Rasmere didn't have any.

She took it and, after running her tongue seductively over her lips, pranced away.

Rasmere turned raising his eyebrow. "She likes you," he pointed out but Creed only shrugged.

"I don't have time tonight," he said and then, looking his long time enemy in the eye, he asked. "What is it, Vampire Lord, that brings you here? After all, I heard you were hiding in Europe in some castle?"

Rasmere shook his head. "I know, I heard that dumb shit, Crandel, say that the other night," he chuckled tasting his drink. "You have chased me enough, Creed, to know better then to listen to rumors as to my whereabouts."

The Gypsy had to agree; Rasmere was never where he was said to be.

"But you know, Creed, it is nice that two men, who have tried to kill each other for over a thousand years, can share a drink."

The Gypsy nodded and the silver earrings caught the low light of the bar, causing Rasmere to shiver.

"Ugh, silver, it makes my skin itch," he admitted.

With narrowed eyes, Creed looked at his drinking partner. "I notice that you are very un-vampirish tonight. The hiss is gone from your voice as well as the other usual signs; hell you look almost human."

A look of mock fear appeared on Rasmere's face.

"Oh no!" he whined in dismay. "Anything but that. After all, I was never turned like these young lords of today. I was born a vampire from a proud line of vampires."

The Gypsy nodded. "Of course, as were the greatest of the Lords, but, as you say, today they are mostly turned-from human to vampire-with little or no real ties to the great demons you once were."

He sipped his drink. "No thanks to you and the other Hunters. You did your jobs too well over the years," Rasmere tossed the remains of his drink down and waved to the bartender.

"Hey, bar wench, give us another!" he ordered motioning to the glasses.

The woman shot him a look of disgust," I hate that word!" she informed him as she went to get the fresh round of drinks.

Rasmere leaned over closer to Creed. "Isn't that the usual title for a woman that slings alcoholic beverages?" he asked, slightly confused.

Creed shrugged slightly. "About five hundred

years ago," he chuckled. "So Rasmere, what is this all about? After all, the other night after my fight with the werewolf, you had me at your mercy. Why do I still live?"

The vampire placed his drink down on the bar top. "Because I need you, Creed."

"You need me?"

Rasmere nodded as from the bar stool next to the lord two drunk young men pushed their way to the bar.

"Get out of the way!" One of them ordered, shoving Rasmere hard enough that the vampire had to step off his seat to keep from falling.

The lord frowned in only the way a two thousand-year-old being could as he regarded the human beside him, demanding a drink loudly.

The kid turned looking at the vampire. "What do you want old man?" he demanded though Rasmere appeared no more then thirty years old. When the vampire didn't answer immediately the kid turned to his equally obnoxious friend. "Hey bud check out this smart-ass over here!" he exclaimed poking his friend as he stuck a thumb at Rasmere.

As a unit, they looked at the lord.

"You don't want to mess with us mister," the one called Bud sneered.

"We will take you outside and kick your ass." The first kid added as he puffed out his chest.

Rasmere turned a frown on his face as he looked at the Gypsy.

"Do you believe this?" he asked Creed who stepped from his barstool and looked closely at the two college age men.

Shaking his head in amazement, he chuckled at Rasmere. "No I don't. This is too funny," he admitted as he motioned to the men. "Here, I will buy you guys a few drinks and do you a very big favor," he explained putting money down on the bar in front of them.

The first loud mouth looked from the cash to Creed. "What do you mean do us a favor?" he asked his voice ringing with contempt. "If we allow you to live, *we* will be doing the favor!" He poked Creed in the chest as he said it.

Rasmere, watching, raised an eyebrow as the Gypsy stared hard into the young man. "Take the cash and have a few drinks," he replied, trying to keep his temper as he turned sitting back down on his stool.

Rasmere also sat picking up his drink.

"Hey we ain't done yet!" Bud said as he gave the lord a sharp shove from behind.

The drink, halfway to Rasmere's mouth, spilled all over the vampire. Rasmere placed the glass back down and, without wiping the spilled liquor from himself, spun on the barstool violently. With the speed and power of his kind, he backhanded the young man.

Shocked by the powerful blow, he didn't see Bud was tossed like a rag doll from his feet out into the midst of the dance floor. The music stopped as the shocked faces of the dancers turned towards the scene of the coming fight.

Rasmere was quickly on his feet his steel like fingers wrapping around the neck of the young human that had started it all. The lord backed the human up to the bar, bending him backwards as he leered down into the man's eyes.

The changes occurred quickly, his teeth growing sharp and pointed as his eyes burned with the unholy blue-white color of a powerful Vampire Lord! He leaned over, mere inches from the man's frightened face baring his fangs as he hissed. "You are a foool human. I have hunted and fed on your kind for thousssands of yearsss and yet you provoke me."

From his side the vampire's free hand appeared and he extended a finger, a razor sharp claw where the nail had been.

"I have nooot fed for ooover two months," he placed the nail against the kids pumping artery. "With a ssslight pussh I could do soo nooow."

Rasmere applied a faint amount of pressure and the now ashen-faced loudmouth passed out!

Rasmere allowed him to drop to the floor and sat back on his chair as three large bouncers approached through the crowd.

"Those two, they were the ones who started it." The bartender said, pointing to the two college kids.

As the bouncers took the kids away, Creed chuckled at the vampire.

"That was cute," he observed.

Rasmere took a bar rag from the orange haired woman. "Thank you miss," he grunted as he wiped himself off. "He has no idea how close he came to being dinner."

Creed sipped from his whiskey. "I was not aware that you could achieve that little trick of switching back and forth like that?"

The vampire waved for a refill on his drink and shrugged. "It has taken me most of my life to master, Gypsy, and as far as I know only the most powerful of Lords can do it."

He sat back down after wiping most of the liquor from his leather trench coat. "Not as exciting as watching you fight that werewolf the other night, but oh well."

He tossed his hands into the air as, with a smile, he looked at Creed.

"I could have told them that you fight werewolves with knives but I am sure it would have been waste of time," he observed.

Creed nodded. "That is why I didn't tell them you were one of the most powerful Vampire Lord's alive, Rasmere; it would have done no good."

They shared a brief chuckle between them.

Rasmere ran his fingers through his silver filled long black hair.

"What I need from you, Gypsy, is your help?"

Creed studied him. "To do what?" he asked his eyes narrowing.

"I want to find Pakur and I need your talents. Who else could find a hiding vampire?" he reasoned.

With a chick of glass on wood, the bartender placed the drink on the bar.

"You are looking for Pakur?" she asked. "I would advise against that," there was caution in her tone.

Rasmere looked at her over the rim of his glass. "Oh really? Why is that?" He asked, amused at the scared look on her face.

"He is a terribly evil man, from what I have heard, no one to mess with," she confided leaning over the bar.

Rasmere pointed to Creed. "Oh my friend here has experience dealing with such men."

She looked at the Gypsy. "Are you a cop?" she asked stepping away from them a bit.

Creed shook his head. "Not quite, but I am looking for this Pakur. Do you know where he can be found?"

"Of course," she answered. "That dump of a club called The Catacombs; he owns it."

Creed tossed back his drink. "A good place to start then," he said stepping off of his stool.

TEN

They took a cab to the neighborhood where The Catacombs was located. As they stood across the street watching the flocks of teenagers walk in and out of the place, Rasmere sniffed the wind.

"The place reeks of vampire," he observed as next to him Creed agreed, feeling the breeze in his long hair.

"And also, the smell of the human slaves desire. This Pakur has a strong hold over them," the Gypsy observed. "Where did he come from Rasmere?"

As a strange look crossed the vampire's face, Creed chuckled.

"Was he yours?" he asked amused.

Rasmere removed his hands from his coat pockets and crossed them in front of himself. "No," he answered seriously. "He was one of Belar's," he answered, his voice hoarse.

Creed wiped the chuckle from his face. "He belonged to your brother?" He frowned, understanding the importance this had in Rasmere's mind.

The Lord nodded slowly, full of feeling, as he sighed.

"Yes my younger brother, a full blood like myself, killed by you in the swamps of Louisiana during the human war of 1812." It was not an accusation but a simple statement of fact. "He was young, but very powerful."

The Gypsy remembered it had been a hard fought battle.

"That would make Pakur fairly young then." He was thinking out loud, as he pondered putting things together. "But what he has done so far with his followers would suggest he is far older and wields great power among his kind," he looked to Rasmere for a suggestion.

The Lord stared at the double doors of the club where two large bouncers stood glaring at the customers from under dark glasses.

"The bouncers are turned vampires," he observed motioning with his head. "And you are right about the fact that Pakur is powerful. He dabbles in strong magic, Creed. Mystical magic, just like my brother, Belar," he paused a second. "Another reason I need your help, Creed. I need someone who understands strange magic, maybe

Gypsy magic."

His earrings shining in the streetlights, the Prince of the Gypsies turned with a shake of his long hair. "But that is not possible," he remarked looking at the vampire who merely shrugged in response.

"Somebody conjured up that werewolf you killed," he pointed out. "At least the last time I checked, even in this crazy age, you still needed a full-fledged Gypsy Witch to pull that off."

With a raised eyebrow, the Lord turned slowly watching for the Gypsy's reaction.

Creed stood thinking, his mind running wild with the possibilities. Rasmere was right, of course, and that is exactly the part that bothered him.

"You know, Rasmere, two hundred years ago it could have been pulled off, but now, with communication as it is, I just have a hard time believing that a witch of my people could switch sides without my knowing."

"Just keep it in mind, Hunter," the vampire warned. "I don't want you hesitating out of surprise later."

This time Creed felt his blood rising. "I have never hesitated in my life," he spat.

The tone of Creed's voice informed the Lord he may have pushed to far. After all, no one said the Gypsy couldn't kill him if he wanted right now. Rasmere uncoiled his hands from his chest and pulled his coat tighter. Lack of blood had caused a shiver down his spine.

Creed, his face serious, waved to the doors of the club.

"Shall we?" he offered.

Rasmere nodded. "Yes, let us go and see Pakur."

If the previous club was dank and dreary, The Catacombs was absolutely down right dinghy, Creed noted, as they passed through the front doors.

The place was crawling with teenagers dressed in various Gothic costumes, their faces painted heavily in white grease paint.

"They emulate the vampire," Rasmere complained as they entered.

Creed nodded as he watched the surprised looks on the faces of the bouncers. As turned vampires, they easily sensed the powerful presence of Lord Rasmere.

"They will tell Pakur we are here," the Lord whispered to him as they approached the bar.

From behind them, a pale white-faced man dressed in a tuxedo placed his hands on their shoulders.

"Please come with me," he offered, waving them to a balcony table.

"What is this?" Rasmere asked the slave.

The man looked startled as he struggled for a reply.

"Such a Lord as you must be treated with much respect," he stammered trying to explain.

Rasmere looked amused," You know who I am?" he raised a suspicious eyebrow at the servant of Pakur.

Looking embarrassed, the slave shrugged. "The

bouncers told me you were an important Lord; they could sense it. They do not, however, know who you are."

"We will have two beers," the Lord told him, whisking him away with a wave of his hand.

"That is the problem with this new crowd of vampires and slaves. They do not attend the meetings with their people and so they do not know who the older Lords are," he shook his head. "No respect anymore."

"It is the sad state of things," Creed replied in agreement.

Rasmere looked over the crowd dancing and huddled about the dark shadow filled club.

"I guess there is no reason to hide anymore," he said as he waved his hand across his face.

Creed watched as the changes slowly took place, the skin turning from pink to translucent white.

From the vampire's jaw line, the incisor teeth grew longer until they protruded from the mouth resting on the lower lip. As the Gypsy watched, the hair of the vampire grew even more silvery and unkempt, almost appearing matted.

Soon the true image of the Lord sat across the table from him, regarding him through milky white eyes that had lost all hint of the blue tint.

Creed smiled from the corner of his mouth. "Now, that's the Lord Rasmere I used to know."

Rasmere placed a clawed hand on the tabletop as the waiter slave of Pakur approached with their drinks. The man paused a bit as he caught sight of the Lord's changed image.

"They were right!" he whispered his hand shaking as he placed each bottle of beer on the table.

With a clawed hand, the Lord reached for his bottle. "On the house, I presume?" he asked looking up at the slave.

The man swallowed hard but managed to nod. "Yes, of course sir. May I ask your name, great Lord?"

Creed looked from Rasmere to the slave wondering if the Lord would give it.

Rasmere slowly looked up at the man. "I am Lord Rasmere, born a True Blood vampire over two thousand years ago in the Swiss Alps."

He paused before adding. "Do not forget it slave," with a flick of his wrist, he ordered. "Now leave us."

The startled waiter slave nodded. "Yes Lord Rasmere," he whispered bowing as he back peddled away.

Creed watched the man hurry back down the steps to the bar-noticing heads turning their way in amazement.

"They seem to be admiring you," he pointed out to Rasmere who sipped from his bottle of beer.

"They are all scheming right now to get on my good side," he explained. "Human slaves are a necessary part of how we survive but they have always disgusted me. I am constantly reminded how really despicable it is that they want to be vampire more then anything else."

This caused Creed to nod in agreement. "I never understood it myself. They will do whatever their master wants just to get on his good side so he gives them the gift of his bite."

He tasted his own beer when Rasmere suddenly turned his head his eyes narrowing.

Following the Lord's suddenly wary gaze, Creed saw three beautiful women climbing the steps to the balcony.

"Be on your guard, Gypsy," he warned, his voice low as his eyes narrowed. "They are vampire."

He turned back to Creed. "We are enjoying a truce but if they sense you are a Hunter, they will attack and those I feel hiding among the crowd, as well as the shadows, will also."

With a clawed finger, he pointed around the room in emphasis.

Creed answered, with a slight bow of his head. "What do they want, Rasmere?" They reached the top of the stairs their eyes seductively fixed on the Gypsy and Vampire Lord.

With a grunt of disdain, Rasmere watched them cross the floor.

"I would guess they want to breed and mother true blood vampire babies," he explained.

Creed chuckled. "What is wrong with that? Don't you like getting laid now and then?"

"It is not that. My mother and father were both true bloods, you know that. If I breed, Gypsy, it will only be with another true blood." He paused again as the female vampires approached the table. "My pride demands no less and these approaching us now are turned underlings of Pakur," he stopped, as they were now close by.

"Lord Rasmere?" the red head spoke first. "May we sit?"

Creed saw the Lord's lip curl in disgust at the boldness of the females and he answered before Rasmere could snap at them.

"Of course, sit with us. The Lord would enjoy it," he invited.

Rasmere shot the Gypsy a look of disgust as the three females sat down leering at them with undisguised need. Creed smiled. He was enjoying this, seeing the Vampire Lord uncomfortable.

From his secret spy hole high up into the dark ceiling shadows, Pakur watched the table below.

He had been feeding on a delightful young female in his secret chamber when the aura of the powerful Lord reached him, ruining his appetite.

He had not been sure at first who the vampire could have been that had invaded his lair but no sooner had he opened the spy hole than the Lords identity swept over him.

"Rassssmere," he hissed the name. "So you are not hiding in some remote castle in the old country."

He watched, seeing first how the scum sucking little leech, Harold, groveled for the Lord as he served them drinks.

Now, much to his disgust, he watched as three of his own turned females flaunted themselves at his table. The muscular male sitting with Rasmere turned a bit and Pakur got a quick view of the figure's face.

"A human?" Pakur asked himself unable to believe that Lord Rasmere would allow one so close to him unless he was draining the man's arteries.

His mind ran with all of the implications of why the most powerful Lord still alive would be here in his club. He licked the drying blood of the teen girl from his lips, thinking.

"Perhaps this is nothing more then a social visit?" he asked himself, but inside he knew better.

Pakur closed the view hole and stepped back. He had turned his back on the council, as had many other young Vampire Lords feeling secure in their powers. Folding his arms in his robes, he walked slowly down the dark corridor that led back to his chambers. He didn't like this, first Crandel and his turned vampires, along with a handful of human slaves, were missing and now, Rasmere was here sitting in his club.

Things had been going really well for him here in California. The drug using teens of this area flocked to his call. He had discovered, back in the mid sixties, how easy it was to invade the mind and control the drug user with their weakened resistance. Pakur had filled the void created by the drugs, giving them a stronger euphoria to pursue, as he introduced them to the blood frenzy. Once they found themselves lost in its orgy-like sensations, they spread the word, bringing legions of human prey to his doorstep.

During the years he had turned many, feeding on them until they surrendered to his bite, their deaths added to his power. Now he was as powerful as many of the older lords save for maybe a dozen or so such as Rasmere.

Ten years ago, he decided that he didn't need the council or anyone else telling him how to run his little kingdom and he turned his back on them.

Now, he reasoned, they must be upset and had sent Rasmere to speak with him. It made sense, of course, since Rasmere was the brother of his original master who had also been a very powerful Lord.

Pakur stopped a second in front of the heavy door to his chamber. He debated going back and talking to the Lord.

"No," he decided. "If he is here for me, he will find me."

He pushed through into his chamber where the still barely alive girl sprawled on his feeding couch.

"Just in case this is a coincidence, I will wait," he told himself as he knelt down over her and resumed his feast.

Creed felt the hidden eyes regarding him from somewhere above them and he turned looking about. He didn't want to give the impression that he knew he was being watched but at the same time, he wanted a look at Pakur.

The three female vampires were all ignoring him anyway content to drape themselves over Rasmere trying to out do each other impressing him.

The Lord looked over the blonde female's shoulder.

"Let's get out of here," he suggested with a

bored look on his face.

Creed nodded in agreement. "Yes we have seen what we wanted to, correct?"

The vampire drained his glass. "I think so."

He shook off the three females as he stood heading for the door.

As they were about to leave, the waiter rushed up red faced and visibly upset. "What is wrong, Lord Rasmere?" he lisped in a huff. "Is there something special you wish?"

The man was making a fool of himself, whimpering at the Lord's feet.

Creed stepped past him shaking his head as the little man attempted to block the Lord's way.

"Please, Lord Rasmere!" he begged. "Lord Pakur wanted to meet with you," he whined.

Rasmere raised an eyebrow. "Nonsense, human. If your master wanted to meet with us, he wouldn't have hid in the dark and spied on us," he accused.

Creed grunted. Rasmere had realized that the Lord had been watching them also.

The little waiter stuttered. "But Lord Rasmere," he begged. "Please do not look down on the rest of us because Lord Pakur is busy tonight!"

Rasmere looked down at the little man, meeting his eyes. In his complete vampire form, the Lord was an intimidating sight.

"Pakur is not busy, human; he is afraid."

With that, the Lord followed Creed out of the club pushing aside startled teenagers who waited to get in.

As they stepped from the curb into the street, Rasmere turned to the Gypsy.

"Did we find out what you wanted to know?" he asked.

Creed walked with his hands folded behind his back. "I think so. Number one, and foremost, Pakur is in there."

He paused his hair blowing in the early morning air as he took a deep breath.

"But there is something else?" Rasmere asked before Creed could finish.

The Gypsy nodded slightly. "Yes, a very evil presence, old and powerful and while I can sense it is there, I can't explain it."

The look on his face matched his words. "It is an evil I do not know how to explain," he paused. "I smelled it on the werewolf also."

They walked a bit in silence with only the tapping of their boots on the concrete filling the air.

Still in vampire form, Rasmere scratched his chin with his clawed finger.

"Yes, we have long suspected that Pakur is in bed with an impure form of evil," he admitted with a nod of his head.

Creed grunted. Impure evil to the vampire was any kind of magic other than their own and it scared them.

"So whom is he plotting with?" he asked.

The Lord shrugged. "I do not know but as we have witnessed the unknown partner has the ability to conjure a werewolf."

"So you would guess that the magic user was a Gypsy of great power then?" He wondered out loud.

Rasmere paused. "Who else could do such a thing, Creed? You of all people would know?"

The Gypsy Prince searched his mind. He could feel the answer out there eluding him but he couldn't pin it down.

"I am not sure," he answered truthfully. "But there is a way to find out."

Stopping mid-step Rasmere turned regarding him. "You want to come back tomorrow?" the Lord asked.

Creed met his look. "Yes, when the sun is up," he answered. "Want to come along?" he offered.

Rasmere stroked his chin with the long claws of his right hand. "I think I will Hunter."

Pakur, his belly filled with the still bubbling oxygen filled blood of the young woman felt intoxicated as he hurried to another secret chamber. He was deep below the club in the old caverns where he had constructed sleeping chambers for his turned followers so they could slumber away in the daytime safely.

His head swimming with the blood he had just consumed, he rounded the corners of the narrow tunnel unaware of the dampness in the rock. Stopping in front of a red colored door, he tapped softly.

"Come in Lord Pakur," an old but strong voice invited.

The vampire swept through the doorway his robes flowing around his thin frame. At the far side of the chamber, staring into the fire in the fireplace, sat the witch, Semma. She turned, looking at him as he removed the cowl from his head.

With a shake of his white hair, he glared into her with his pale blue eyes.

"Rasssmere wasss here," Pakur hissed reeling from his blood intoxicated mind.

The old woman narrowed her eyes. "The Lord Rasmere, powerful member of the council?" she asked disbelief in her voice.

Pakur nodded. "Yesss Lord Rassssmere, witch," he confirmed a bit impatient with her.

He sat heavily in a chair across the room from her.

"Heee had a humannnn with himmm alssso," he added. "But I did nooot knoow hiiimmm," he admitted still bothered by the human.

Semma picked up a small amount of powder from the side of the fireplace.

As the Lord watched she tossed it into the fire causing a cracking and spitting sound as from the spot where the powder landed, a blue flame appeared.

Pakur watched it quickly fade, disappearing before the Lord could see anything. The woman sat back quickly as if trying to escape from the image she had seen in the blue flame. Slowly, her face ashen in color, she looked at her lord and master.

"You do not know who the human was?" she asked as if unable to believe him.

His eyes narrowed in a frown. "I have never seen him before, witch," he replied with conviction.

She shook her head. "It makes no sense," she whispered.

With a glare, she looked at Pakur again. "Are you sure Rasmere and this human were together?"

You are really beginning to upset me, Lord
Pakur thought. *No one, not even you, witch, should
ever challenge me.*

"Yesss of courssse I am sssure," he answered
growing short-tempered at the worried look
plastered on her face. He narrowed his eyes in
question.

"What isss it, witch, what have you seeeen in
your fire?" he demanded.

Semma took a deep breath as she slowly met his
gaze. "The human with Rasmere was the Gypsy
Prince Darius Creed, the legendary Hunter and
slayer of the vampire." She explained slowly giving
it time to sink into Pakur's blood soaked mind.

He raised an eyebrow almost ready to answer
but she stopped him with a wave of her hand.

"There is an aura about the Gypsy," she warned.
"He has killed the werewolf I conjured."

This statement caused the Lord to look up in
surprise.

"The abominaaation isss dead?" he asked
amazed.

The witch nodded in silence and Pakur stroked
his chin with a taloned hand.

"That would also explain why Crandel has not
returned," he reasoned.

Semma shook her head. "I do not know about
him,"

Pakur shot her a dirty look. "If you were a
Gypsy Witch instead of a voodoo priestess you
would know," he accused.

Semma shook her head with a slight shrug. "I
serve you as best I can, do I not?" she asked,

bowing slightly.

His anger receding a bit, Pakur grunted. "Yes, you do," he agreed and then, changing his tone, he gave her an order.

"Summon my underling vampires as well as all of my human slaves," he said. "There is a battle coming for the very survival of this coven and I have a feeling I will need them all."

Rasmere walked along the deserted city streets alone having sent Creed back to the house and his friends by taxi.

In a way he had to envy the Gypsy; the man had found friends again after all of the years of solitude. Rasmere sighed, as a Lord he could not afford friends in the deadly in-fighting world of the vampire. How many, he wondered as the cool air ran about his long hair and pulled at his long leather coat, had trusted an underling only to be betrayed in the following power struggle?

He shook his head with disgust as he thought about humans. They come to you wanting the gift of your bite giving them power and everlasting life. Then it seemed they would wait as they grew in power until one day they would unite with other underlings and rise up, often times slaying the Lord who had turned them. It made him wonder about the human animal and sometimes he pondered if it was easier to understand the Hunters like Creed.

The Hunter had a clear vision of his destiny, to hunt and destroy the enemies of man; Rasmere could understand and even admire that. What he did not understand, though, was a human who sought you out, begged and pleaded to be turned and then rebelled against you. Most vampires had a certain sense of loyalty for their masters or at least a small amount of respect for the Lords. But these current day human-turned-vampire beings had nothing but a desire to become the masters themselves no matter who they had to step on.

Rasmere hissed, knowing it was a bad thing when tradition and structure were left behind for personal gain.

"At least with Creed," he thought to himself. "I know he is coming to kill me when he shows up, not like some underling who bears gifts only to later plunge a knife in my back."

The Lord decided that it was a bad thing when your enemies are the ones you can count on to be honest.

Deep in thought and studying the concrete sidewalk, he did not sense the three dark shapes that followed him down the street slowly coming closer. When the scrape of shoe leather snapped him from his reverie, he turned to see three black youths dressed in colorful outfits approach him. A frown formed and grew on his face as he watched them step boldly into his personal space.

"You are on our turf!" the biggest one spat as he stood menacingly facing the Lord.

Rasmere didn't answer as a second black youth snapped a switchblade knife from his pocket.

"You have to pay to use our sidewalks," the big kid added.

Rasmere raised an eyebrow in question.

"Is that so?" Rasmere asked a hint of defiance in his voice.

"Yes," the third kid answered stepping from the shadows as he pulled a chain from his pocket allowing it to swing menacingly.

"So I am to be afraid now?" Rasmere asked searching their faces.

The big kid frowned. "Hey man, don't you get it?" he asked as a smile crossed his face.

"Get what?" Rasmere asked shrugging both arms wide.

The kid with the knife stepped forward. "Just give us the money, man!"

Rasmere snarled like a caged animal.

He swiveled his head slowly regarding the weapon, open contempt on his face.

"I would advise you children to leave now," he replied slowly his voice full of warning.

The three would be muggers shared a look.

"This honkie ain't getting it, is he?" the one with the chain asked.

The big kid, who Rasmere figure was the leader, chuckled. "No he ain't, Stoogy," he answered. "Guess we will have to brighten him up some."

As if on command, they began to circle the Lord who stood unmoving.

Rasmere watched them, unworried and certainly unafraid, as the kid with the knife off to his right lunged driving his blade into the Lord's kidney!

In seconds what had appeared as just another victim to the gang members whirled in a blur, his face growing longer and paler as teeth protruded from his lips!

The gang member looked up in growing fear as he tried to retrieve his blade from the victim's ribs seeing instead a clawed hand that tore his hand from his wrist.

Rasmere, now reverted to vampire form, backhanded the kid who had stabbed him, thirty feet across the street. He turned as he was struck from behind with the chain; it wrapped around his upper torso trying to enclose him in its links.

The gang member screamed in triumph seeing his weapon coil about his victim's body.

Rasmere however simply frowned as he looked down at the stainless steel chain. In his natural form, he felt the power flooding into him as he flexed his muscles against the chain. With a roar of anger, he raised his arms tearing through the steel links as if they were made of paper!

Pieces of chain flew from him and he wheeled on his heels grabbing the black kid by the back of his neck, pulling him forward. With a lightning fast swipe of his razor sharp claws, the Lord tore open the kid's neck and lapped at the blood as it flew skyward.

Like a starving man, he languished in the warm thick liquid that filled the back of his throat running into his stomach. It fed him, bringing the blood lust of the feeding vampire to a blood red frenzy as he drank.

The spasms of the dying kid ended as Rasmere dropped his appetizer on the sidewalk drained of blood. He turned wiping the fresh blood from his face as he looked upon the last gang member.

"What the fuck!" the kid screamed as he pulled

a handgun from under his coat and pointed it at the Lord.

"I don't know what you are, mister," the black kid shuddered in terror. "But if you take one goddamn step I will blow you away!"

With the fresh blood flooding his system for the first time in over a month Rasmere barely realized the man was there before him; he only saw the main course of his meal.

Pointing a clawed finger dripping with fresh blood at the wide-eyed gang leader, he smiled slowly showing his incisor teeth.

"Thattt willll dooo you noooo goood humannnn," Rasmere hissed all restraint now gone from him.

A determined look on his face the kid raised the gun and started to fire!

The Lord advanced absorbing the bullets as if they were no more then gnat bites as his clawed hands came up flexing.

"I warned you," Rasmere hissed as he suddenly reached out clasping the kid's neck and pulled him close.

Bending the screaming human's head backward, he exposed the pumping artery swollen with fear filled blood. Rasmere could no longer reason, feeling the blood filled vein below him within easy reach. With a powerful jerk, he stretched the neck of the kid even farther as he lowered his hungry mouth filling it with human flesh.

The Lord bit hard feeling the sudden spurt of blood fill his mouth as his lapping tongue swam in its warmth. The thick salty liquid poured down his throat with each swallow filling his stomach and surging into his veins.

Under the light of the moon, the satiated Lord dropped the now drained body and stood breathing deeply.

"Damn! I neeeeded thaaattt!" he whispered under his panting breath as he wiped blood from his face, smearing it onto his leather coat.

With three dead corpses in his wake, the Vampire Lord walked away on intoxicated feet looking for somewhere dark to sleep before the sun came up.

ELEVEN

After Lord Pakur left her chamber, the old woman called Semma stood and walked to the jars above the fireplace.

She had been a full-fledged practicing voodoo priestess since she was old enough to bounce on her granny's knee in Haiti. She kept many secrets buried in her deepest memories and one of them came to mind now as she puzzled at Lord Pakur's fear of these strangers.

Her power had grown over the last years until now, at fifty-three years of age, she easily surpassed the greatest of the Voodoo Queens. But the magic demanded and received a heavy price from her;

physically she appeared at least eighty.

"There is no reason for you to fret, Vampire Lord," she whispered to herself, reaching for the small orange clay jar and removing the cover.

"I will secure the needed knowledge and power to defeat the Lord Rasmere and his companion, the Gypsy Prince Darius Creed," she promised.

From inside the jar she scooped a small amount of clear crystal powder holding it in her palm. Closing her eyes, she pictured the soul chaser she wanted to contact. Once it was firmly in her mind, she opened her eyes. With a toss of her hand, the powder flew up into the air and she took a quick step allowing it to rain down over her. She was covered in the white crystal and, taking a deep breath, felt it enter her system.

Immediately, Semma felt herself float above the floor, weightless, and she felt herself beginning to drift out of the room.

"Weillia ollat cojer," she recited the words of the summons.

Almost before the words were out of her mouth she felt her feet sink slowly into the soft sand of a distant beach. Salt-filled air flooded her nostrils as the sound of crashing waves assured her of the sea. The sun was just setting in this secret place she had entered, a lifetime from her small chamber in Pakur's stronghold.

The strong odor of wood smoke mixed with the salty air as she felt a light breeze in her hair. Semma turned away from the setting sun and the open sea glancing up the beach where a small fire burned brightly, its flames dancing in the growing darkness. With a slight smile, she saw the small figure of the dark skinned man who added twigs slowly to the flames.

She began walking down the beach to where the Voodoo spirit sat. He had finished feeding the fire and was now braiding dried palm leaves into a sleeping mat. Studying his face she could see it was painted with the thick white ceremonial cream of the Voodoo Priest, as in the basic tradition his eyes and mouth were outlined with black paint. He had painted stripes of red, orange and yellow across his chest, colors that signified hate and revenge.

She stopped before the fire and slid slowly down to her knees searching his eyes for a sign of recognition. He looked up at her continuing his work on the mat.

"Semma," he said in greeting as he nodded his head slightly.

She felt his eyes regarding her as his fingers continued to work.

"Nuate," she answered, using his name of power, allowing it to roll easily from her tongue.

The spirit smiled showing stained teeth as he chuckled. "So is this business or pleasure?" he asked with a teasing look.

Semma felt the coolness of the beach sand on her knees. "I need your strength, Nuate," she told him. "There is a battle I must fight soon and I worry my own power will not be enough." She watched his fingers as they deftly formed the palms.

"Who would cause you such concern?" he asked without expression. "You are the most powerful of the Voodoo Queens. Even here, I can feel it exuding from you. Only a very powerful witch can accomplish such a feat in my realm."

She nodded, "A Vampire Lord named Rasmere has joined forces with a legendary Shadow Hunter called Darius Creed, a human well known for his exploits against the Nosferatu. They are united in a campaign against my Lord."

With a puzzling shake of his head, Nuate placed his palm mat down on the sand beside his fire. He picked up a hollow gourd filled with strong smelling liquor and took a drink. "Your Lord Pakur finds strong enemies." He sighed placing the gourd back down gently. "Rasmere is so powerful he is beyond your efforts. Creed, on the other hand, has been endowed with a long lifeline and has strong contacts with magic users. Together they are a tremendous team and, quite possibly, indestructible," he met her gaze.

Semma felt her eyes narrow. "I could destroy them," she said. "With your help."

Nuate picked his almost finished mat up and folded the leaves obviously deep in thought. Semma watched his face twist and contort as he worked it over in his mind.

"If Creed fights back, and he will, you will be facing Gypsy magic, Semma. You are a voodoo priestess, and even if the witch he recruits to fight you is weak, it will be a great risk."

He was shaking his head, uncertain about her request.

"I can win if you help me," she stated again more firmly.

The spirit chewed his lower lip. "Rasmere can

199

not be defeated by your spells. What will happen if he gets his hands on you? He will tear you apart."

Semma smiled slightly. "He will bite me and kill me, Nuate, and I will gain the power Pakur has held from me for so long."

The idea made her smile grow wider in pleasure.

The spirit shook his head, taking a sip from his gourd again. "No, Semma, he will not. As an enemy, he will tear your heart and throat out but will not give you his bite. It will not be the gift you will receive, only death," he held the gourd this time not setting it down.

The priestess pursed her lips. "He will not be able to resist the desire to feed," she stated flatly in her own defense.

This caused the spirit to chuckle deeply. "Rasmere has been alive too long. He has gained in power to the point that he can resist the temptation of the blood feed. If he is after your Lord, and you get in the way, he will deal with you as a hostile enemy. He will simply kill you."

He said it in a sorrow filled voice, sipping again from his gourd.

Semma frowned at his reluctance to help her; but she had one card left. "I wish to request the rite of Kadahl," she said as firmly as possible.

The spirit looked up at her quickly as a smile crossed his face.

"Is that right, Priestess?" he asked, amused. "You realize what that means, what you are asking for and what you will have to do?"

The Voodoo Priestess nodded, her face full of

resolve. "Yes I do."

The spirit jumped to his feet spilling some of the contents of his gourd.

"Come with me, Semma. We will see the demon Kadahl."

With a mix of fear and excitement, she stood following him into the darkness of the woods.

Creed returned to the Toscanno estate just as the sun began to peek above the horizon. He stepped out of his borrowed car and could see Selena watching him from the second story window.

He waved to her with a smile crossing his lips and hurried to the bedroom where she waited for him.

He entered the room closing the door quietly behind him.

"Good morning."

She greeted him sprawled on the bed her thin nightgown doing little to conceal the voluptuous body underneath.

Creed looked her over seeing her taunt nipples under the fabric.

"Good morning to you," he answered slipping his old coat from his shoulders.

"You have met Rasmere?" she asked as she brushed several strands of hair back from her face.

Creed marveled how her every move seemed to have a seductive lure to it.

"Yes I have talked to him; we also went to the place where this Lord Pakur has assembled his coven of followers."

He removed the silver blades from behind his back undoing the cotton shirt from his muscled upper torso.

"The vampire has been building himself quite a little army out here in the sunny state of California."

He sat down in a chair across from her pulling his heavy boots from his feet.

She rolled to her side propping her head onto an elbow as she regarded him.

"He must have done a good job to avoid detection for this long," she pointed out.

With a nod, Creed slipped out of his leather pants and allowed himself to fall heavily to her side on the bed.

"Yes and it puzzles me that he has been able to do so; some one should have detected him," Creed said, more exhausted than he had been for years. His midnight foray had been too soon after his injuries at the hands of the werewolf.

"Yes, unless he is protected by magic," Selena offered as a strange look crossed her face. "But then someone conjured that werewolf for him. Maybe that person also provides him with spells of protection."

The Gypsy Prince rolled onto his stomach feeling himself relax as Selena moved closer and began massaging his back.

"Do you think he has retained the services of one of our own people?" she asked curious.

Creed shrugged his shoulders lightly as she began to work on his muscular trapezes.

"I don't know," he answered half asleep. "Rasmere seems to think so but I wonder if it could

202

be another type of magic user."

He rolled over looking up into her eyes as her long hair fell about his chest.

Selena frowned slightly. "But only a Gypsy Witch can conjure the werewolf. No other magic user has that ability."

Creed played with her soft hair. "You're right, at least no other spell caster has been able to up to this point, warlocks, witches, wizards, druids none of them."

He paused shaking his head.

Selena looked up at him. "Tell me the story of the werewolf curse on the Gypsy people, please?"

Creed frowned. "You don't know it?"

He frowned, amazed her grandmother had not told the story to her.

She shook her head. "I have heard bits and pieces but Grandma Lela never told me the whole thing."

With one hand back under his head and the other still in her silky hair he took a deep breath.

"Okay I will tell it for you," he allowed his mind to wander back over the passages of time.

"I was still a teenager when it happened; there was a small band of traveling Gypsies who appeared one early morning at the entrance of our valley. They told us they were Rolti, an ancient word even in that time. They were a special group of Romani dedicated to the pursuit of magic. As they came into our midst and set up camp, the rumors started to spread among the valleys inhabitants of how the Rolti were said to speak with demons and spirits seeking to gain their help in securing greater powers. Well it so happened that among the Rolti was a very beautiful young woman named Deni who caught the eye of a young adventurer from our valley.

He was a handsome Gypsy mercenary named Pallo who fell smitten with this enchanting Rolti witch. As summer moved on slowly and as the nights grew warmer, the Rolti did not seem inclined to leave our safe warm little valley, which suited the young lovers well. Pallo was only a few years older then me and we hung around together when he was home between wars. One night he told me he was going to ask Deni to marry him.

Well, he did and she said yes so together they planned a fall wedding like the area had never seen before. A week before the blessed day was to take place, a huge man-killing wolf appeared in the lower valley killing shepherds without disturbing their flocks. The elders of the village were soon aware they had a man-eater on their hands so they called the fighting men together to track and kill the monster.

The first two nights passed without a sign of the animal but each morning more bodies of helpless victims were found. On the third night, I went with my father to a hillside where we sat watching the sleeping valley below. Pallo had ventured with two other men to scout the river bottoms.

The next morning only one man in his group returned with the horrible story of what had occurred.

They had been on patrol when Pallo, his incredible senses warning him of danger, stopped

204

suddenly pulling his sword. The surviving man
explained to the growing horror of the crowd how a
wolf lunged from the darkness with large glowing
eyes and saliva coated fangs! It leaped on the first
man killing him instantly before it turned on Pallo,
its green eyes studying the valiant fighter who stood
sword in one hand dagger in the other.

The man told how Pallo had ordered him to run
for help as he lunged at the great beast slashing with
his weapons. The poor fellow had tried to run but
found he was transfixed as he watched the inhuman
struggle of man and beast. He watched in numb
shock as steel tore fur and razor sharp claws
rendered human flesh. Before he knew it, the wolf,
as well as Pallo, lay bleeding and gasping on the
forest floor.

Willing himself to walk forward, the young man
made it to the mercenary's side. What had once
been a great warrior now was little more then flayed
meat as Pallo struggled to lift himself from the
ground. The man had tried to give the warrior water
but he was already dead laying feet from the wolf
that had killed him.

We all followed the man back to the scene of
the fight finding a grizzly bloody scene of death.
Deni had followed also crying in horror over Pallo's
body.

Members of the Rolti helped her remove the
body of her beloved to a place high up on the
mountainside where she built a huge fire. Night and
day, she kept the fire blazing as she chanted secret
spells and worked the fabled Rolti magic. The
evening that was to be her wedding day, the body of

Pallo sat up, brought back to life by her powers.

I remember as the sun went down she led him back into our village, the superstitious Gypsy people whispering all the time that he was an abomination of evil. Deni, however, was happy to have her lover back and disregarded their warnings. I have to admit even her own people, the Rolti, appeared to be unsettled by the appearance of the walking dead man.

Exclaiming to all that they would be married the next day the couple retired to Pallo's small cottage to spend the night. I still remember the way Deni screamed that night. You see, just after midnight, something started to happen to Pallo; he started to turn into a monster as he lay next to her in bed.

Of course, Deni realized that something had gone wrong with her spell. Instead of her beloved, the thing that now stood before her was a mingling of the wolf and human blood. You see, what she had over looked in her grief was that Pallo had been covered in the animal's blood and it had entered his body through the terrible wounds he had sustained. It lay dormant until night when the moon reached its full zenith in the night sky.. The chemical reaction that took place turned the valiant Pallo into the monster before her. Deni tried to talk to him but she could see from his eyes that the wolf had fully taken control. The beast let out a roar of frustration before it leapt through the bedroom window fleeing down the valley past the frightened stares of the Gypsy men who had come to the aid of Deni upon hearing her screams.

The beast Pallo had become fled the valley

never to return. Over time, stories drifted in about a man-wolf that terrorized over all the northern European hills and valleys. The day after Pallo fled the Gypsy clan of the valley drove the Rolti out, afraid that the beast Deni had created would return seeking its creator. Harsh words were spoken from both sides until finally Deni stepped forward, a long bladed knife in her hands. She pointed at my people with an accusing finger saying that it was our fault that Pallo was dead and that he should have had more help tracking the wolf.

From the crowd stepped a very old, very wise woman, a Gypsy Witch of very great power. She shook her cane at Deni saying that her own selfishness had brought this plague to the world of men. In answer, Dani placed the knife to her breast and, before plunging it in deeply, she recited the curse: 'I Damn the Gypsy people,' she said. 'This thing I have created was brought forth out of love but from this day on, it will wreak unholy horror!' And then she took her life.

The Rolti loaded up the body of the woman and carried her away, disappearing into the wilderness of Europe."

At this point, Creed stood up from the bed and Selena could feel the change in her lover.

"What happened next?" She asked, instinctively aware that this was not the end of this story.

Creed watched the rising sun, feeling its warmth through the window.

"It was about ten years or so later when I became a Shadow Hunter. One day I received an urgent message to return home to my valley. When

I rode in, on a horse barely alive after the all night ride, my father told me of the man wolf creature that had returned, killing anyone it could find after dark. In my heart, I knew very well that it was my old friend, Pallo the Mercenary, and I decided on a plan to meet him alone.

The next night I had the entire valley lock themselves behind their thick doors with instructions not to come out until dawn no matter what they might hear.

That evening I built a large fire and sat down with bread, cheese and roasted venison to eat while I waited. As the darkness settled in, I felt his presence around me and started to carve the venison. He walked slowly out of the dark and sat down across from me at the fire just as young and handsome as the day he left to hunt the wolf.

Without speaking, I handed him the wine bottle but he waved it off. Then I speared a huge chunk of roast and handed it to him but, again, he waved it off.

He smiled slowly then and chuckled 'No Darius,' he said. 'I no longer crave animal flesh or wine. Only human flesh will satisfy the hunger I have now.' He looked up at me as he said it.

I nodded as I chewed on bread and cheese allowing him to continue.

'I see you are older and have grown in your powers.' He motioned to the twin silver blades that lay by my side in their leather sheaths. 'You have become a Hunter,' he observed, his smile growing larger as inside of him something was satisfied by the knowledge.

'I was called.' I answered and he nodded.

'As only a true Hunter of the Shadows can be.' Then he rolled back and looked to the sky. 'Soon we must fight, for the moon will change me,' he said.

In my youth, I thought I had the best plan.

'Go away, Pallo, I don't want to fight you.'

His smile didn't fade, though, as he shook his head sadly. 'Soon you will not have a choice, my old friend.' He sighed, as above the moon rose higher.

But still I tried. 'Go away and never come back. I will tell them we made a bargain.'

Pallo stood stretching. 'You have to understand, Darius; soon I will change and then I will not recognize you anymore. Like it or not, I will kill you.'

He clasp his hands behind his back. 'Besides, as much as I appreciate the offer, you know as well as I that no matter where I go, some day a Hunter will come for me.' He shrugged then. 'It may as well be you, old friend.'"

Creed turned back from the window.

"What happened?" Selena asked. "Did you fight?"

Creed nodded. "I killed my friend. No matter what he had become, I killed him," he sat back down on the bed next to her. "It was one of the first hard decisions I have had to make."

Selena frowned. "So as I understand it, it is Deni's curse that enables the Gypsy Witch to conjure the werewolf. Then, as you have said before, only a Gypsy could accomplish the act."

Creed nodded. "As only a Gypsy of true blood can kill one," he added.

Rolling over to her back, she ran her fingernails lightly down his back.

"Someone out there conjured that being you killed the other night," she said. "Sooner or later they will appear."

Lying back and closing his eyes Creed agreed. "Yes they will and I really hope it isn't one of our own people. I would hate to think that a Gypsy Witch was working with a vampire to help build his legions of the undead."

Without answering, Selena rolled on top of him and kissed him lightly on the lips.

Nuate stood poised, his thin arms raised over his head. Semma looked around at the smooth stone sides of the cavern where they stood ankle deep in seawater.

The old Voodoo Queen felt the dampness of the cave settle into her very soul; the taint of the stone around her stank of evil. Nuate called out in a voice stronger then the old woman thought possible from the frail looking spirit.

"Kadahl!" he summoned.

"Kadahl, Lord of the Netherworld, of fire and stone. I call you forward demon, I order you to respond!"

Semma stood shivering from the dampness watching as nothing happened around them.

"Where is he?" she hissed to the spirit.

The spirit turned facing her. "Be patient; he is

near," Nuate reassured her with a wave of his finger.

Semma shot him a glare. "I don't feel him near."

The spirit ignored her, returning to his summoning. "Lord Kadahl, first of the demons in the Netherworld, I ask for your audience!"

His voice echoed loudly in the cavern.

As Semma watched, a glow began in the far rock wall, growing in intensity until it appeared as if the wall itself was on fire! Semma stepped back shielding her face as a hot blast swept through the cavern followed by the heavy smell of smoke.

"He comes now, Priestess!" Nuate yelled stepping back closer to where Semma herself stood.

The orange spot on the stone wall of the cave appeared to pool as if it was turning to liquid before their eyes.

"He will come through that liquid rock," the spirit told her, pointing.

As the voodoo priestess and the spirit watched wide-eyed, a muscular leg came through the wall followed by a massive torso. The demon materialized before them and Semma caught her first glimpse of the Lord Kadahl in the flesh.

He was tall, almost seven human feet and built massively, muscular and bulky. His head was that of a bull, huge pointed horns protruding from his head.

"Who calls the Demon Lord Kadahl?" the thing asked, flexing its massive hands the muscle of its chest rippling with inhuman power.

Nuate stepped forward standing before the huge

lord.

"I do, Lord Kadahl, Nuate, spirit of the Haitian people and your humble servant," the little man announced with a slight bow.

The great head of the Lord slowly regarded the little spirit. "Yes Nuate I have relished your servitude over the years."

He turned and then, with a finger, pointed at Semma and asked, "Who is this you have brought here to my sanctuary?"

Semma was a product of modern day Earth and she stepped forward ready to speak for herself but Nuate stopped her.

"Hold your tongue," he warned. "You are a human female and must not speak until spoken to first."

Semma shook her head; this was not the place to argue about equal rights.

Nuate turned back to the Demon Lord.

"This is Semma, your Lordship, a servant of the voodoo ways and a priestess in the world of humans," he explained.

Kadahl looked at the black woman before him.

"She is old," he observed to Nuate. "I wonder what she looked like when she was young?"

The Lord waved his hand and suddenly Semma felt as if a warm wave had passed over her.

She opened her eyes finding herself on her knees before the great lord. Looking down, however, she realized she appeared as she had when she was twenty years old.

"That is much better," Kadahl smiled undisguised lust in his eyes.

Nuate couldn't believe the transformed woman who stood before him either.

"Wow," he said quietly under his breath.

"So, woman, what do you want with Lord Kadahl?" The demon asked breathing heavily.

Semma looked from her subtle firm breasts to the Lord who had given them to her. "I need special powers," she announced bravely. "I request the rite of Kadahl," she added, resolve in her voice.

The demon looked down at her. "You understand the consequences of your request?" he asked with a smile on his horse's face.

Staring him in the eye she nodded. "Perfectly."

Nuate was dismissed as the Lord walked around behind Semma.

"So you want the power I can give you, priestess?" he asked as his large hands slid around her young supple waist.

She nodded. "Yes, my Lord, whatever the price."

"That is good, woman," he answered his breath hot on her shoulder as she was pulled roughly back into him. "I will take my pleasure, Voodoo Queen, but you will get your power," he said as Semma felt the thin dress she wore torn from her body.

Surprisingly she felt herself becoming aroused with the Lord's large powerful body against hers. She looked down at her young firm body amazed that her dark nipples were erect as passion grew inside of her and the insides of her thighs grew moist at his touch.

"Ooo."

She moaned softly feeling his strong hands

parting her buttocks and his stiff member push against her from behind.

With a cry of passion, Kadahl pushed into her, his erection so hard it felt like a log had been shoved between her legs.

"Ooooo yes!" she called out pushing back into him.

TWELVE

Jacob Reid followed Father Joe down the sidewalk to the rectory of the church. The priest wanted to get a few things and prepare for the battle both men guessed would be coming. Creed and Selena had retired to their bedroom with little or no word to either the priest or their fellow Hunter.

Father Joe unlocked the door to the church. He wanted to collect more holy water, as well as a very old Bible, which was said to have been blessed by the Pope years ago. They were strong wards against evil and something made the priest feel he may need them soon.

"Come on, Jacob, follow me," he motioned to

the back of the church crossing himself as he walked past the statue of Christ.

Jake followed Father Joe, pausing a bit. He was puzzled as he felt a cold breeze run through him.

"Must be getting nervous," he mumbled to himself with a shake of the head.

With a second glance about the empty shadow-filled church, the Hunter turned and ducked into the room he had seen the priest enter. At his side, the sword of Takada seemed to glimmer as if a strange light had caught it from somewhere.

"What the hell?" Jake frowned; something was going on here. At the back of the room, he could see the priest rummaging through a drawer.

"Found it," he said holding up an old key.

"Come on."

As Jake looked on, Father Joe inserted the key in the closet door, turning it slowly. The door swung open revealing a small room.

"What is this?" Jake asked. He could see a small dark room filled with shelves containing various church artifacts.

Father Joe led the way in.

"Over the years the church has collected certain things, oddities if you will, in case they would ever be needed. Most people have never been told about these secrets because, frankly, the church has always felt they would not understand." He placed his hand on an old thick book.

"The prophecies of Rasputin," he explained before pointing to another object. "Sacred wood from the groves of ancient English druids."

He held up a plain-looking willow branch.

"Even the age-old writings of a man called Merlin," Father Joe held up a wrapped scroll of frail paper.

This comment stopped Jake in his tracks and he latched a strong hand on the priest. "Are you telling me that Merlin of the King Arthur stories existed?"

The priest wiggled his eyebrows and shrugged.

Jake nodded to himself. "Of course," he answered his own question. "But then why would someone who has seen what I have over the last few days ask such a stupid question?" he sighed. "I will learn some day."

Father Joe chuckled to himself. "Others are usually much more upset when they learn that the Catholic Church has been hiding these things."

Jake agreed. "Kind of like the things the FBI under Hoover hid from the citizens of this country."

The priest nodded. "Yes, a lot like that. See that big black box over there?" he asked pointing.

"Yup why?"

"That is what the church knows about Hoover and his cover up of the Jack Kennedy-Marilyn Monroe controversy."

Jake felt his fingers start to itch. "Boy I would like to read that," he exclaimed looking at Father Joe. "Ever read it?"

The priest shrugged as he stepped into a far corner of the closet.

"I can't tell you specifics but you know it all would have worked out if Jack would have had Teddy drive her home."

He gave the Hunter a quick wink.

Jake started to laugh in spite of himself. "I heard

217

that before."

Father Joe snapped his fingers. "There you are!" he cried out excited as he pulled forth a dust covered and badly scarred leather satchel.

Jake squinted in the dark corner. "What did you find back there?" he asked curious.

The priest held up the satchel giving the Hunter a better look. "This has been worn and used by the greatest vampire hunting priests of the church," he explained. "It is filled with all the tools I will need to be a productive part of this endeavor."

He opened the bag looking in. "Special holy water," he said, holding up a green flask of liquid. "Blessed by St. Paul himself."

Next, he pulled wooden stakes, blowing dust from them. "These were made from the sacred wood of the cross our Lord died upon; no demon can survive their sacred powers."

Rummaging around some more he removed an old Bible, its pages yellow from age.

"The sacred Old Testament Bible carried by King Richard the Lionhearted during his most famous Crusades."

He blew more dust from its ancient leather cover. His eyes shining, he moved his hand softly over the book. "This is great power Jake," he whispered in awe.

The Hunter, however, looked at the articles around him littering the room.

"How is it that these even exist?" he asked. "I mean, why has the church hid them all this time allowing the myths of their existence to circulate?"

Father Joe placed the Bible back into the

satchel, rummaging around making a mental list of the contents. Pausing he looked up meeting Jake's questioning glance.

"It is like always; the powers of the church do not, nor have they ever, trusted the ability of the common man to understand such things. They feel it best to hide such pieces of knowledge until the day when they may be needed again."

"Okay, but where is the Loch Ness monster hidden then?"

The cocky look on the Hunter's face faded as Father Joe shook his head.

"Not here. I believe the manuscript explaining that phenomena has never left Scotland."

Jake was about to reply when a strong cool breeze penetrated his leather coat and soaked slowly deep into his very soul. Raising an eyebrow, he turned toward the closet door.

"Did you feel that?" he asked suspiciously, feeling he should be aware of something bad.

Father Joe swung the strap of the satchel over his shoulder. "What are you talking about Jake?" Again a cold wind blew through the small closet, this time icy cold and smelling of great evil.

The priest shivered despite himself. "I felt that!" he announced as from outside the closet they plainly heard the loud slamming of a door.

"That was in the main church," Father Joe answered Jake's questioning glance.

The Hunter nodded. "Someone has come to visit us Priest, let's go out there carefully I smell a trap," he cautioned.

With a nod, they walked from the closet and

through the empty offices of the church staff. Jake paused, placing his fingers on the reassuring grip of his sword before they walked out into the church.

The taint of evil filled the air as the two men stepped from behind the altar seeing a tall thin form standing under the statue of Mary holding the baby Jesus.

Jake felt his eyes wandering the room reflexively looking for trouble as Father Joe stepped past him.

"May I help you?" he asked walking towards the stranger.

The newcomer sighed loudly placing his hands behind his back as he turned, regarding the Priest, a strange twinkle in his pale blue eyes.

"Hellooo Father Jossseph," the being hissed.

Father Joe stopped as if he had slammed into a wall.

The stranger, Jake could plainly see, was a vampire. He was tall about six foot two and rail thin. His face and skin were so pale they appeared translucent, his eyes pale blue and his long hair pure white. He smiled showing long pointed incisor teeth over lips so red they appeared to have been painted.

The pale blue eyes flashed to Jake.

"Soooo a Hunterrr isss here alssssooo," the demon chuckled. "Thisss promisssesss to be a gooood dayyy," He hissed.

Jake felt his ears lay back against his head. "Are you the one they call Pakur or one of his flunkies?" he asked stepping closer to the priest as his fingers tightened on the sword of Takada.

The demon held up a clawed finger picking at

his teeth.

"You willl addressss me asss Lord Pakur, humannnn," he insisted.

Jake noticed the arrogant look that crossed the Lord's face and it reminded him of the way the wealthy looked down on the poor.

"Yeah, sure, shithead," he sneered. "I don't call blood sucking parasites Lord or anything else but what they are."

Father Joe turned to Jake. "Relax a minute. Remember, this is a house of God."

Jake nodded. "I know that, but why is he here then, Father? I thought vampires could not enter holy ground?"

He looked at the priest in question.

Father Joe turned and looked at Pakur. "I was wondering that myself, Lord Pakur. How do you come to be standing in my church?"

Pakur shrugged. "I have special powers and powerful friends," he snapped his clawed fingers and from the shadows stepped a dark skinned woman.

Jake frowned. He had not been aware she was there.

The woman spoke, "I have allowed him to enter, Priest," she announced, her head held high in the same arrogant manner of the vampire.

Father Joe met her gaze. "Explain that to me miss-what did you say your name is?"

"I am Semma, Voodoo Queen and worshipper of Kadahl," she informed them.

"Voodoo Queen?" Jake mocked. "What in the hell does that have to do with this?" he demanded.

221

Semma stepped farther into the light. "Do not mock me!" she warned raising her finger at the Hunter.

Jake could see her face better now, she was young and beautiful but someone had beaten her recently and the bruises still showed on her face.

"Who put the ugly stick to you?" he asked. "A disgruntled zombie?"

His sarcasm was not lost on the woman.

"I have paid dues to be Kadahl's favorite," she tossed back her head. "It is a great honor."

Looking over the puffy eyes and healing lips, the Hunter could only roll his eyes in agreement. "I guess he has a strange way of treating his favorite," he observed.

The Voodoo Queen shot him a look of pure venom. "We will see who is what soon, Jacob Reid."

Father Joe raised his hand. "That does not explain how you can enter this holy church of Jesus Christ though. Everyone knows that a vampire, even a Lord, cannot come into a scared place," he persisted.

Pakur smiled showing his white fangs. "I caaan doooo whatever I want Priesssst," he hissed. "I have grooown to the point innn my pooower that nooo one caaan touch meee. Your sssimple rulesss mean nothing to meeee," he chuckled. "The point howevvvver isss nooot that I am here, bbbut whyyy?" Pakur pointed out with a smile playing on his face.

Jake met the Lord's gaze. "What are you babbling about?" he demanded a look of disdain on

222

his face.

Pakur raised his arms. "I ammm nooot here for yyyou Hunterrr, not thissss dayyy. SSSoooon enough for thatttt."

"Come on," Jake exclaimed," Quit playing games and get serious here."

It was a challenge and the Hunter's tone was not lost on the Vampire Lord.

Pakur chuckled as he suddenly lowered his arms, dark gray smoke rose from the floor behind him covering the back half of the church. The vampire waved his right arm and suddenly the smoke began to vanish revealing a dozen human slaves dressed in their master's colors.

A smile played on Jake's lips as he slowly pulled the sword of Takada from his jacket.

"About time we got down to it," he sneered at Pakur. "I am tired of your pussy little games."

He squared off as the acolytes of the vampire walked slowly down the aisle.

"It isss nooot you thaaat wee want," he said. "It isss the priessst!"

Swinging the sword over his head Jake jumped in front of the priest.

"Run for it!" he called out over his shoulder as he placed himself between the vampire's minions and the priest.

Father Joe to his credit did not falter as he reached into his bag.

"Do not worry about me," he called out. "I will meet you back at the mansion later if we get separated."

Jake answered with a nod of his head.

"Good luck!" he said as he turned to face the first of the slaves who reached out with black gloved hands.

"Here we go."

The Hunter tensed, his fingers locked on the handle of the ancient sword, as he stood prepared to deliver the first deadly blow!

Above the Hunter and the priest a pair of green eyes observed the scene unfold below. As the breath came to him in pants of excitement, he watched the outnumbered forces of good face off with evil incarnate.

Quietly he padded to the far corner of the choir loft studying the vampire that stood in the swirling clouds of smoke below him.

Thousands of years ago, others of his kind had made their pledge, along with the dog, to protect man against all evil. The dog taking the vow of daylight, promising to keep the frail humans alive during the hours the sun walked the sky. The cat, however, had chosen the night, a time of stealth and dark shadows.

Over two thousand years previously, the feline's ancestors had watched over the Pharaohs as they slept, when the first vampires walked the earth, cast from Hell at the whim of Satan. The fallen angel had been banished from the side of his creator for trying to imitate him by creating his own beings. Satan had not equaled his God's creation of man; instead, he created the evil vampire, a race destined to feed off the life essence of God's children.

Taz had followed the human Jacob Reid here sensing as the sun rose this morning that the Hunter was in danger from evil forces. So now as the twelve minions of the Vampire Lord closed in below him the warrior feline named Taz, descended from a legendary line of defenders, leaped!

Jake swung the enchanted sword as a pale hand reached for him; a mighty down stroke severed the limb leaving the slave screaming as blood poured forth. Recoiling Jake reversed his grip delivering a deadly powerful slash to the wounded humans mid section. From one knee Jake watched as the open mouthed human slave died on his feet. He spun aware that there were more of the hissing creeping creatures coming his way.

"Oh for God's sakes! You shitbirds ain't vampires yet so cut the hissing!" he told them, disgusted in their little act.

Hatred registered on the faces of every single acolyte as they raised their fingers in perfect imitation of the way a real vampire would do it.

"Hey? Do you guys spend all day practicing that in the mirror?" Jake taunted as his grip tightened on the sword in his hands.

Their hissing grew to the point where Jake knew he had pissed them off and he readied himself; they would pounce soon. He checked over his shoulder making sure that Father Joe had escaped; he could not see the priest and felt confident the man was safe.

"Come on boys lets tango!" He challenged in

glee. Suddenly growing tired of waiting for them, he jumped into their midst!

Father Joe ran from the back of the church and down the narrow alley to the street, praying that Jake would make it out alive. He really didn't fear for the man, knowing how the Hunters could fight. He had heard the stories from the others of how men like Darius Creed had at one time or another defeated numerous demons in hand to hand combat.

He rounded the corner of the alley vaguely aware that there was a lack of other people in the area. When he looked down the street he froze, three pale men, their skin hidden under robes and sunglasses stood watching him. He felt fear crawl slowly up his spine

"Vampires!" his mind yelled in warning even though he was not quite sure how he knew it.

He felt the bag at his side seem to tingle as if it was alive; it could sense the evil in front of them too. His hand pulled out the old wooden cross from the satchel. It carried great power.

"Stay back!" he ordered pointing the talisman at them.

They hesitated throwing up their hands in fear as shields.

"Puttt ittt doooown Father Jossseph."

A low hissing voice ordered from behind him.

He turned, seeing Pakur standing almost on top of him.

"What-how-did you-"

He almost finished the question before the

vampire struck; the backhanded blow was incredibly fast driving the cross from his hand.

Father Joe tried to duck the next swing, a closed fist that impacted the side of his head sending him twenty feet across the sidewalk. He tried to lift his head as hard heels tapped on concrete, approaching him.

The cross, made from the wood used to kill his Lord, was tore from his grasp and flung somewhere far from him. As he rolled to his back he tried to focus his eyes upward; the sun and the clouds swam before his dazed senses.

Suddenly the face of Pakur surrounded by the other vampires filled his blurred vision.

"Yesss Priessst, I havvve you noooow," the Lord grinned.

Father Joe tried to answer but he felt like puking instead, as his head spun around in a million circles.

The vampire snorted looking at his comrades. "We finalllly haaave whaat weee neeeeed," he drooled as he said it. "A young virgin priest whooo carriesss the sssatchel of the churchesss cooonencealed sssecretsss."

As his head spun in circles Father Joe wondered how in the heck Pakur knew anything about him.

"Take him," the Lord ordered with a wave of his hands.

"Semma?"

"Yes my Lord?" she stepped forward bowing to his power.

Pakur nodded to the church. "Letss retuuurn I waaaant to be ssssure the huuuunter diesss."

Jake was in their midst his blade a whirling gleam of silver as he struck at the human slaves of Lord Pakur. He spun, delivering a deep and deadly slash to the midsection of one to his right, when he felt strong arms and sharp claws at his neck. Reaching back, he was able to slip the monster-human off of him delivering a swift powerful kick to the side of the man's head.

"Take that!" he cursed.

Two of the acolytes closed from his left and Jake realized he couldn't get his sword around in time to stop them.

"Shit, where is the Calvary when you need them?" he swore. As if in answer, from above a blur responded to his curse.

Taz the warrior cat was quickly atop the two attacking slaves, his teeth and claws rending their flesh with each swipe!

Jake shook his head in silent tribute to the animal he was beginning to admire. He had little time for reflection, however, as from behind he was grabbed roughly. Jake fought to regain his footing but he was pulled back off balance by a strong arm around his throat.

"Damn!" he swore through half breaths as his wind was slowly cut off. Dropping his center, he allowed the arm to suspend his full weight as he reversed the sword in his hand.

"Aiiaa!" he let go with a martial arts kiup as he drove the inverted razor sharp blade backwards.

A cry of pain and the loosening of the arm at his

throat were his reward. Pulling away, he kicked backward hard feeling his heel impact squarely on someone's shinbone.

"Take that asshole," he shouted while meeting more attackers closing in from the front of him.

They had been sure that their comrade, who had tried the strangle, would be successful. When the martial arts master broke free, he caught them in their attack; they had no choice but to continue, as they could not retreat.

The katana sang as it drove through the human flesh rendering skin from bone. Jake, his face locked in the grim visage of death and his heart full of battle rage, fought as if possessed.

Only feet away in the aisles of the church cries of the injured vampire slaves mixed with the angry hissing of Taz, the warrior feline.

Jake could see the cat springing about from one enemy attacker to the next leaving them with gouged eyes or shredded faces. A slave jumped, vaulting towards him and Jake swung the sword like a ball bat striking the vampire minion in the midsection. The blow bit deep sending blood showering down on Jake who soon found himself covered and sticky.

"Oh just great!" He shook his head in disgust as the sticky substance began to dry.

His eyes strayed to the spasming slave who was quickly dying on the church floor. Jake looked down suddenly feeling sorry for the man who looked up meeting the Hunter's stare, a look of fright on his face.

Closing his eyes Jake shook the feelings from

his guts and surveyed the room searching for the next attack.

There was no one left to attack him; the human slaves laid sprawled across the church their blood seeping into the neutral colored carpet. Jake felt his breathing start to relax as the adrenaline started to drain from him.

Before he could enjoy it though, the side doors of the church burst open as if caught in a great gust of wind and Pakur, followed by the voodoo witch, stepped in.

"So you came back?" Jake smiled raising an eyebrow as he met the Lord's eye.

Pakur chuckled slowly as if amused. "You arre quiiite arrooogant, Hunter," he pointed out, raising a clawed finger. "You ssshould not presssuuuume soo much. You are nooot the Gypsssy Prince."

Jake felt his palms sweating on the grip of the sword. "What does that have to do with anything? I am still a Hunter."

Pakur shook his head as he began to laugh, a loud mocking sound that echoed in the empty church.

"Yessss you are stillll a huuunter," he answered, his chest heaving in mirth.

"But Dariusss Creeeed isss more then thattt, he wasss the firssst of the great onesss!" He stopped laughing and met Jake's defiant glare.

"Dooo you knooow, young hunttter, what thaaat meansss?" he challenged, his eyes alight with fire.

Jake shook his head. "I know he is way out there," he agreed. "But I don't know what the hell this Great One crap is all about?"

To the Lord's side the Voodoo Queen stepped forward.

"Enough of this!" she hissed. "Let's end it."

Her words were filled with silent urging.

Pakur held up his hand. "Be quiet, woooman," he cautioned. "He should knooow thessse thingsss before he diesss and joinsss my legionsss." He explained with the same sadistic smile on his face.

Jake frowned. "There ain't no way I am joining you," he vowed through clenched teeth.

Pakur sighed. "Oh yesss you willll, Jacob Reid. You sssee, I am going to biiite you and bring you into the glooory of Sataaan."

He waved to the dead slaves around them.

"These wretched specimensss all want that gift but I denied themmm. For you, though, I will give it freeeely."

Jake raised an eyebrow. "Why is that, shitbird? I ain't submitting to no neck munching by you."

"You cannnot fight meee," the vampire whispered. "Listen tooo meee, Jacob Reid. Become my ssservant; leave the gypsssy. He cannot give you what I can."

He let the offer dangle until Jake asked.

"And what in the hell is that?"

Pakur, his eyes glinting in the low light hissed an answer.

"Everlasssting life huuuman, everlassting life."

While the Vampire Lord tried to persuade Jake of his destiny, back at the Toscanno mansion, Creed rolled over. Deep in sleep, he felt something was wrong.

"You've got it all backward," Jake defended. "I will never go willingly vampire; I have met Asmus."

This time Semma chuckled. "That old fool has no power," she scoffed. "He is nothing compared to Kadahl." She added, a nod of her head lending credence to her statement.

Jake tensed. "Enough of this!" he yelled leaping forward.

"Time to die, Pakur!"

He swung the sword aiming for the Lord's head.

The razor sharp blade covered in blood sliced through empty air as the vampire disappeared!

Jake spun meeting the eyes of the witch. "Addira sul molla," she chanted pointing a finger his way.

Jake felt the impact as he was struck in the chest and faintly realized he was flying back over the rows of pews. He landed with a heavy thud striking his head against something unyielding. With a groan, he passed out.

Semma smiled, satisfied with the power her bargain with Kadahl had yielded.

"Thaaat wasss impressssive," Pakur hissed as he reappeared in the same spot the Hunter had charged to.

"Letting thaaat aaanimal Kadahl sssodomizzze you was a ssstroke of geniusss. He is usssually far more stingy with his pooowersss," the vampire met her gaze.

Semma took a deep breath and did not flinch

from him. "I think so," she agreed. "It was a small price to pay for what I gained."

Rolling his eyes, Pakur chuckled as he stepped towards the spot where Jake lay barely breathing.

"It isss time to bring him tooo our world."

Semma agreed. "Let's do it then, my Lord. Fulfill the prophecy and be the first to bring a Hunter into your fold."

Her eyes were bursting with excitement as she followed him to where the Hunter lay.

Pakur felt the excitement flood his system. A Hunter was about to feed him and the Vampire Lord had not accomplished that for a very long time.

Of course, Takada had been the victim of Rasmere but the ceremony had been ruined by the interference of Creed. No, there had been few Lords who could claim they had turned a Hunter. Pakur knew the power that this would give him, elevating him beyond the remaining members of the council.

Drawing up his arms, he extended his claws as he watched the pumping artery in the side of the unconscious humans neck. Semma, standing at his side, cheered him on.

"Do it my Lord!" she whispered.

His incisor teeth growing in anticipation of the coming feast, Pakur slowly began to kneel next to the Hunter's side.

"Thisss wiiilll puuut meee at the right haaand ssside of Satan himssself."

The vampire clenched his clawed hands reaching forward. One slice of his razor sharp claws and the artery in the human's neck would geyser forth the blood that would fulfill his dreams. Pakur

233

paused a second, glowing in his moment of triumph. The prophecy of Kadahl, as told to Semma, was about to be realized.

It was when he opened his mouth ready to taste the human's blood that the animal made its move.

Taz, leaped from his hiding spot, landed on Jake's chest, his teeth bared and claws extended in his upraised paw.

"Whaaat?" the Lord exclaimed, stunned.

"Geet awaaayyy beast!" he ordered, raising his arm to swipe the cat away.

"No!" Semma shouted in warning, grasping the Lord's hand and stopping the blow.

"Hooww dare you womaaann!" The enraged Lord turned on her, rising to his feet. "Yoouu daaare to stop meee?" he spat, his eyes narrowed in anger.

She pointed to the cat. "Look, my Lord. Don't you see who that animal is?"

His frown deepening, Pakur turned looking for the first time into the green eyes of the feline blocking his way.

A strong gasp of surprise burst from the vampire.

"You!" he blurted out, his anger rising again. "Whaaat are you doooing here?"

His eyes glowed as he raised a clawed finger, pointing it accusingly at Taz.

The cat met the glares of the Lord and the Voodoo Queen remaining defiantly on top of the Hunter's chest protecting him.

Semma, her eyes narrowed, tugged on Pakur's sleeves. "Let this be for now, my Lord. Stay away from Shach Meril."

Her voice was filled with alarm mixing with panic.

Pakur felt himself starting to shake. "Hooow diiid you coome tooo be here?" he demanded of the cat.

Taz sat back on his haunches his front legs stiff in readiness while the hair on his neck stood on end.

"I want to know?" Pakur demanded. "Whaat isss itt that bringsss the King of the Trillii to thisss place?"

Semma watched in fear as the green eyes of the feline glared back at the Vampire Lord in a look of hatred thousands of years old.

She didn't like this. Why was the King of the Trillii, the great Shach Meril, here facing Pakur at the moment of the Lord's greatest triumph?

She studied the feline noting its regal bearing. Maybe she could cast a quick spell, she thought until the cat turned meeting her glance.

"Do not begin to think you are my equal," a strong voice purred into her mind.

Semma shrunk in fear as the cat turned its gaze back to Pakur and the voice left the Voodoo Queen's mind.

Pakur clenched and unclenched his claws. "I want that human, Shach Meril. Leave him to me."

Semma turned towards the vampire hearing the tone of his voice. It sounded like begging.

The cat did not move, instead the strong purring voice filled the air around them in the church.

"You cannot have him today, demon," the voice said, disgust thick in the tone. "Leave here. This is a house of God; your voodoo witch will not be able to continue the spell that allows you to remain here."

The echo of the majestic voice slowly faded in the church and Pakur reluctantly nodded slowly.

He did not dare to tempt the fates against this warrior.

"All right, King of the Trillii; we will go for now, but you will see us soon and he will be mine!"

With a flick of his wrist, the vampire and the Voodoo Queen were gone.

Taz studied the spot where they had stood. He counted on the fact that they would meet again; there were debts that had to be paid!

THIRTEEN

They reappeared back at the car where the three vampires were loading the unconscious priest into the dark windowed van.

Pakur spun on Semma.

"Whaaatt wasss that alll about?" he asked hissing in anger as he glared into her eyes.

She felt a shiver pass down her spine, a cold chill of evil as the vampire's foul breath pierced into her. She shook her head.

"I do not know?" she admitted searching for the answer.

Pakur climbed into the van.

"Go back to Kadahl and tell that fool I want to

know everything!"

He slammed the door as they sped away leaving her alone with her thoughts and fears.

Jake felt the swimming of his mind and tensed, here it came the bright flash of the separation.

Soon he was flying upward to a different place and time, a place where his great warrior ancestors lived.

Suddenly he was seated in a great hall full of feasting warriors who sang tales of adventure as they swilled strong ale from their drinking horns. He looked about feeling the warmth from the blazing fire in the great fireplace as servant girls hustled to keep up the pace.

"Hey you've come back, young one!"

He heard the great booming voice as he was roughly punched in the shoulder.

Looking up he met the eyes of the great warrior he had talked to before.

"Don't ask me why; I never know why I show up here," Jake answered with a shrug reaching for the closest drinking horn.

The ancient heavily muscled warrior frowned as he shoved another man aside and squeezed in next to Jake.

"Well last time you needed guidance. I wonder what the reason is this time?" he commented.

As if on impulse he waved to an old stooped man who stood in the corner near the fire.

"Old one, come here!" he demanded with a wave of his brawny arm. "My ancestor needs a reading."

There appeared a slight nod of the head under the frayed cloak as the old man turned and came their way.

Jake wondered if the cloaked figure had the strength to make it to them as he shuffled across the floor.

"Sit down and tell my ancestor what he is doing here, soothsayer," the warrior invited with a wave of two gold coins. "I will pay well for the information."

He held the money close to the old man.

Jake raised an eyebrow in surprise as the coins disappeared quickly and deftly into a fold of the robes. Another hand removed a bowl from somewhere under those same robes holding it in front of Jake.

"Spit," an old voice commanded from under the hood as he held the bowl under Jake's chin.

"Go on," the warrior urged. "He may have strange ways but his babbling always come true." He winked.

Jake leaned forward a bit and spit a stream of saliva into the bowl.

The old man shook the bowel and removing small-carved figures from a leather bag added them to the bowel with the spit. Next, the old man picked up an ale horn adding some of the strong beverage to the bowel also.

Jake watched as the soothsayer vigorously shook the contents of the wooden bowel dumping the figures onto the table.

"What do they say?" The warrior asked but the

old man held up his hand stopping him.

"Do not talk just yet," he ordered as he peered down on the design the figures had created.

He looked up slowly, his old wizened eyes meeting Jake's as he removed the hood from his head.

"You have powerful enemies," the old man said with a shake of his head. "But you also have very powerful allies."

He moved one of the figures across the table with his finger.

"I see the Gypsy Prince, Darius Creed, is with you," he paused. "And the King of the Trillii, Shach Meril, fights by your side."

Jake grabbed the old man's arm. "Who?" he asked puzzled.

"The cat you call Taz," the soothsayer explained. "An animal of truly great powers as you will see. He is the one who sent you here."

This caused Jake to frown. "What are you talking about, old man?"

The soothsayer fingered a second figure. "Shach Meril sent you here to keep you out of the clutches of the Demon Lord, Pakur. He knew that once you were gone from your body, the demon could not claim you."

He raised an eyebrow. "Whatever the danger is I sense it is over he will be calling you back soon."

Jake nodded. "Okay I will take your word for it," He answered as he sipped ale from the horn he held. "But tell me, what is a Shach Meril?"

The old man leaned heavily on a walking stick as he swept the figures from the table into the pouch.

"Shach Meril is not an 'it,' stranger, but a 'he,'" the man answered sitting down next to them.

"You see, he is the four hundred and thirty seventh King of the Trillii, the legendary warrior guards of Egyptian temples."

Jake felt his head starting to swim on him. "Oh no! I wanted to hear this," he exclaimed in frustration as suddenly the flash of lightning struck and he was driven back to the present.

Nuate sat across the fire from the Voodoo Queen, smoking from a long stemmed pipe.

"So you are sure it was Shach Meril?" he asked between puffs.

Semma nodded seriously. "Yes, it was the King himself, spirit; there can be no mistake about it. He stood there defiantly blocking Pakur from achieving his glory and claiming the Hunter as his slave."

The eyes of the scrawny spirit opened and closed as he shook his head.

"It is hard to believe that this would be the time of his reappearance," he wondered out loud.

Semma nodded. "That is why I must see Kadahl again. I need to know what is going on here."

Nuate chuckled drawing smoke from the pipe up into his nose. "You cannot, he never grants two audiences to one woman, even one who has satisfied him as you did," he answered a slight amused smile on his lips.

Semma remained firm in her resolve.

"My Lord demands that I gain the knowledge to

help him in this quest. Please make the presentation to Kadahl?"

The little spirit looked up at her, aware he would not win this argument. He reached into a small bag of powder at his side and withdrew a small handful. As if it didn't matter, he tossed the powder into the fire at their feet.

There was a sizzling sound followed by a quick bright flash and with a shake of his head, Nuate pointed to the cave.

"Go, he awaits you inside," he directed her over his shoulder.

Bowing to the little spirit, Semma stood.

"You may not survive this time," Nuate added as she walked by him.

She didn't answer but walked bravely to the cave entrance.

"Come in little one," a deep voice beckoned her. "I had hoped you might return."

A hot wind caressed her face and with a deep breath, she walked in.

Creed rolled from bed as the sun began to set in the western skies. He was well rested and felt much better, his wounds from the werewolf fight almost completely healed. He looked down on Selena who moaned softly as she rolled over, still asleep. With a smile on his face, Creed walked into the bathroom. He wanted a shower and a shave, deciding they would have to get some kind of battle plan put together before they joined Rasmere on the assault of Pakur's stronghold.

He looked at his reflection in the mirror as steam began to build in the bathroom; the new scars from his last fight covered other older wounds. He pulled the silver earrings from his ears washing them with soapy water and setting them aside to be put back in after his shower.

Stepping past the curtain, he entered the shower feeling the first wave of hot water covering him. It felt like Heaven and Creed was sure one of the things he liked about this century was the running hot water.

From the soap dish he reached for a green bar of perfumed soap thinking it was almost feminine in odor. With a shrug, he used it anyway.

He rolled it all over in his mind; Pakur was rapidly gaining in power as well as stature in the vampire infrastructure. He could understand why Rasmere and the older traditional Lords hated the way these newcomers, especially the American ones, turned their noses going their own ways.

It seemed to have happened a lot lately in every step of life. Young people just didn't care to follow the older ones who had come along first. It made Creed chuckle to think that the same frustrations faced by modern adults also plagued the vampire species. But Creed also wondered why it would be such a shock to Rasmere and the other Lords. After all, the struggle for power was not a new concept.

Up to this point Pakur had been smart though, shielding his little empire from the rest of the world while still hunting and feeding his growing brood. Creed had met many smart vampires in his time and right now it looked like Pakur was right up there with the best of them.

As he washed the soap from the thick muscles of his upper body, he took a minute to reflect on the old ways. The lords never used to hide so well. When a lord moved his brood or family into an area, he killed and created havoc until it reached the attention of a Hunter who dealt with the problem.

Now it seemed that lords, like Pakur, moved in quietly, using legitimate businesses to get heir victims to come to them.

Creed thought the idea of a vampire like Pakur owning a club for folks who pursued the Gothic lifestyle was ingenious. Reaching for a bottle of shampoo, he also realized that it made it much harder to track the slaves of the lord. In a club setting on a given night, maybe a thousand people could go through the doors. Who knew how many of those were human slaves waiting to be gifted by their lord? In the old days, a wary Hunter would survey the domain of the lord and count the possible slaves as they entered or left; it was so easy then.

How does one sit outside a club and count among the throngs of young folk, how many were slaves or innocent club goers?

He shook his head as he lathered up, there would be no counting ahead of time.

Rinsing off, he allowed the water to run over him a few minutes more before he stepped from the tub into the steam filled room.

Jake snapped awake finding himself laying on the floor in the church surrounded by the bodies of the dead human slaves he had killed. Sitting several feet from him, he looked into the green eyes of the cat.

"Where is the vampire and the witch?" he asked trying to struggle to his feet but feeling dizzy from his head wound.

The cat didn't answer but simply regarded him through those deep eyes; Jake paused meeting that knowing gaze.

"Oh I suppose I should have said, Your Majesty," he added rubbing the large lump under his hairline.

"That is not necessary," a purring melodic voice answered from somewhere in the church.

Jake almost jumped out of his boots. "What the hell," he looked wide-eyed at the cat. "You can talk?"

Taz sat back on his haunches. "Of course," the voice answered as the cat tilted his head slightly.

The expression on the animal's face reminded Jake of an arrogant young child reprimanding his parents.

"Well, now you tell me, Shach Meril, or whatever they call you in the cat world."

He grunted sitting heavily in the nearest bench.

"It is pronounced Shach Merrill," the voice corrected putting more of a rolling sound to the name.

Jake waved his hand in the air. "That must really piss off the lions. Ain't they supposed to be the King of the Beasts?"

The cat regarded him questioningly and Jake continued. "I mean, to have an alley cat as the King,

245

that must really bite?" he pointed out with a shrug of his shoulders.

Taz licked his paw. "We tried that one time, electing the Lion to the regency. It didn't work though; they are all brawn and violence. They lack the cunning and stealth to be a leader of the feline people."

Jake nodded; it made sense to him. "Hey, does Creed know who you are?" He asked rising to his feet.

Taz paused a minute as he dropped from the church bench to the carpeted floor.

"I do not know?" he answered. "We have not spoke of it. He knows I am Trillii, that is certain. I do not know though if he realizes my identity."

Jake snapped his fingers. "Don't tell him, let me. For once, it would be nice to know something he doesn't."

He sheathed the sword as Taz headed for the doors.

"If you want, Jacob Reid, I will do that."

Together the Hunter and the Trillii warrior left the church.

Semma walked slowly into the cave feeling the water at her ankles getting warmer. Her lord, the great Kadahl, was close by. A great fire burned, as if by magic, on the far stone ledge and she approached it, lost in its hypnotic effect.

"It is good to see you have returned to me." The low growling voice whispered close to her left ear.

Semma almost jumped as the two sweaty hands

covered her arms reaching around to her breasts and delivering a good squeeze to each.

"I admit," the demon drooled. "That I have thought about you may times in the last few hours."

Semma allowed herself to be handled feeling somewhat aroused and soiled at the same time.

"I need some answers, my lord."

His huge hands ripped her dress away allowing her large round breasts to fall free. She felt his hot drool as it dropped from his tongue on her shoulder.

"You will have all answers you wish, sweet one," he promised as he ran his tongue along her throat and up into her ear.

"But first you will pleasure me," he ordered forcing her down to her knees and turning her to face his groin.

"Do not disappoint me," he warned as he pulled aside his loincloth.

Semma ran her hands slowly up his massive thighs; seductively, she trailed her nails on his hot flesh.

"I will not fail, my Lord," she promised as she placed her hands lovingly around his penis, stroking it lightly.

"Oh yes my Lord."

She sighed as she opened her mouth and lowered her head.

Freshly shaven, Creed was toweling off his long hair as he stepped back into the bedroom.

Selena lay on the top of the comforter, awake and stretching, looking up at him

"Good evening, my Prince," she greeted him.

Creed watched her, unable to tear his eyes from the thin fabric of her gown as it stretched across her taut nipples.

"Good evening," he answered. Feeling lust flooding his brain, he tried to refocus his mind.

"I was having a dream," she said pulling the quilt to her. "A dream of a green meadow that rolled along softly next to a river and bordering a mountain range."

Creed sat down next to her. "Oh really? Please go on."

She allowed her mind to wander recalling the dream in living color.

"A powerfully built handsome young man rode a beautiful roan colored horse, a jeweled rapier at his side and a bow of strong Yew wood in his hands. He rode the horse as if born to it, studying the woods ahead as he hunted for game. It had just rained and he studied the muddy ground below him."

She paused and Creed asked, "Then what happens?"

He listened amused as he lay back on an elbow.

She looked at him. "The man kills a wild stag, one shot through the heart at twenty paces after a long stalk in the heavy woods. He dresses the animal and, draping it over the horse, heads back to a cabin where wood smoke from the chimney invites him home. I get a feeling he makes it just in time, as rain again threatens the countryside from the surrounding mountains. The Hunter drops the Stag from his horse and takes the animal into a nearby barn stabling it. Then he returns, cutting the loins from the slaughtered stag. As he picks up the choicest cuts of the animal and washes them in a nearby pail full of fresh well water, a woman emerges from the cottage. I see her, the clearest of them all, dressed in tanned leather pants, knee-high soft leather boots, a white cotton shirt and a leather vest. At her right side is a handsome Scottish Claymore; on her left rests a large but sharp looking dagger. She hurries out, her long red hair trailing behind her as she launches herself into the young man's arms. They kiss passionately."

At this point Selena paused looking up into his eyes. "The man was you," she said her eyes on his in question.

Creed nodded. "Her name was Marisa and she was beautiful; I won't deny that," he answered shaking his head at the memory.

"And I loved her a very long time ago back in Scotland. She was a Highlander and as great a warrior as any of the men of that era."

He paused remembering her in silent tribute.

Selena scanned his face as she propped herself up on the bed.

"What happened to her, Darius, I sense tragedy in the dream?"

She searched his eyes knowing she could see what lie there as if reading a book.

He hesitated, as the painful memory flooded back.

"She was killed," he said. "By Rasmere."

As the words came out of his mouth, he realized the same Vampire Lord he had shared drinks with last night had killed her. It struck him suddenly that all the while he had sat next to Rasmere not once had Marisa's death come to mind.

He looked up into Selena's eyes meeting her intent gaze.

"When a Gypsy Witch dreams, there is always three things with that dream: a warning of the future, an omen or prophecy or a message from the other world."

She nodded agreeing with him.

Creed felt his eyes narrow. "So which one was it?" he asked.

Selena watched the look that passed over her lover's face and couldn't help but feel the cold chill passing along her spine. She held herself steady, though, as she answered.

"There was something said on that day, the one from the dream, something she promised and you laughed at. Tell me, Darius, what was that thing Marisa said that you mocked, making fun of her?"

Just as he had over a thousand years ago, Creed chuckled.

"She promised that no matter what, if I ever needed her and asked for her, she would come back to me," he answered shaking his head. "But that is foolhardy."

Selena shook her hair allowing it to fall over her shoulders.

"You, of all people; it is funny that you would scoff at such a statement."

He turned away from her stepping over to the side of the bed and starting to dress.

"What do you mean by that?" he asked in a

neutral tone while standing to pull on the scarred leather pants.

She rolled back on the bed. "You know people can come back to life. Why would it so strange? Why even in such heathen practices as voodoo... oh my God!" she cried out sitting straight up in the bed. "Voodoo!"

Her alarmed cry was mixed with an alarmed look on her pretty face.

Creed spun, searching the room by instinct, with his eyes. "What are you saying?" he asked, seeing no immediate threat.

Selena slapped the palm of her hand to her forehead. "What if the werewolf you fought was not a true werewolf of Gypsy magic? What if it was a creation of voodoo?" she asked.

Creed spun meeting her eyes. "In God's name," he whispered. "What is going on here?"

Semma fell to her knees in the hot water of the cave. Kadahl was done with her and laid breathing heavily against a mighty rock outcropping.

"So, Voodoo Queen, what brings you back to me?" he asked a sadistic smile on his face.

Semma looked down at herself, her breasts were larger, rounder and even firmer; her whole body, she noticed, appeared even younger then before. If she had not been so completely spent she would have been excited by the prospect of growing younger. Screwing a god obviously had its advantages.

She sat down heavily in the how water its

251

soothing warmth feeling good on her aching privates.

"I need more knowledge," she said looking upon him. "Something else has happened, something that I was not aware of earlier, and the Lord Pakur requires more guidance."

She splashed water over her large supple breasts, the hell with plastic surgery she thought to herself.

Kadahl sat up flexing his massive structure.

"What would be so troubling to you, young one?" he asked. "I gave you the power to overcome the effects of holy ground and it worked, did it not?" he demanded.

She nodded. "Yes, Lord, it did, however a second problem has arisen since then and we are confused about how to deal with it?" She met his eyes as she made a deliberate act of washing her swollen privates.

Kadahl tore his eyes from her actions, trying to act concerned about her question even as his desire began to rise again.

"What is the problem, my little Voodoo Queen?" he asked drool falling from his mouth into the water. "Tell Kadahl. There is nothing I cannot fix for my favorite followers."

He started to move towards her. As he spoke, more hot drool foamed from his half open mouth.

She smiled at him invitingly. "We had the Hunter, the one called Jacob Reid. Pakur was about to honor him with the bite, giving him immortality while giving my Lord great power among his peers. From somewhere out of the dark came Shach Meril;

he placed himself on the human's chest blocking our chance at the man's blood," she looked down pouring more water from her cupped hand over herself.

She glanced up, a seductive smile on her lips expecting to see her God and lover almost upon her. Instead, she saw him frozen in mid-step a look of dread on his face.

He was ashen in color his mouth locked open in awe.

"What did you just say?"

Before she could continue, he shook his massive head.

"The King of the Trillii was there, protecting the human?"

It was as if the information was too much and Kadahl staggered slightly almost falling before he caught himself on a rock.

Alarmed and confused, Semma watched him. "Yes my Lord it was Shach Meril," she confirmed starting to become worried at his reaction.

Kadahl sat heavily placing his head in his hands, shaking it back and forth as if he had a great pain there.

"You must leave here," he said to her, looking up slowly. "Do not come back until this is over," he instructed with a look of disappointment.

Semma could feel something was wrong here. "What is wrong, my Lord?" she asked reaching for him.

Kadahl looked up but pulled his hand back from hers. "Do not touch me," he growled sharply.

She recoiled sharply. "What is it, my Lord; tell

me please!" she begged, startled at his reaction.

Kadahl smirked at her. "You don't know, do you little Voodoo Queen?" he asked.

She shook her head. "Know what?"

The demon god sat back on his rock.

Kadahl shook his head sadly. "You young magic users these days, you know so little outside of your own little world," He sighed heavily.

Semma held her hands up. "Know what, my Lord?" she asked filled with dread at this reaction.

He sat back. "Sit, young queen, and learn from what I tell you. Shach Meril is the current king of the Trillii; that you know and thank Lord Satan, you at least recognized him. Now the Trillii are old; I mean, they go back over the centuries to the great Pharaohs of Egypt."

She nodded understanding and he chuckled.

"It is good that you know at least that much of the tradition," he jibed to her startled look.

He continued before she could respond. "A Warrior King of the Trillii has exceptional powers, powers you couldn't begin to fathom. Tell me, did he say anything that sticks out in your mind?"

Semma nodded. "He told me-or threatened me. He said 'Don't begin to think you are my equal,'" she waited for the Lord to answer.

Deep in his chest, Kadahl chuckled again. "He warned you. That is strange. You are lucky that you were not turned to dust."

He shook his head.

Semma curled her brow, she was getting more confused by the minute.

"I know he is not to be trifled with, but what

frightens such a great Lord as you?"

Kadahl looked deep into her eyes. "The Trillii are very old; they know things and have access to magic you have never dreamed of. A Trillii King has the power to kill a vampire with its very touch."

Semma nodded slowly. "So that is why Pakur backed off so quickly."

The demon god nodded. "The vampire is the ultimate predator but when faced by the one thing that can kill it, it will instinctively retreat. Even the Hunters do not have that power; they must rely on silver and other enchanted objects."

Semma nodded. "I see, but what is it that makes the Trillii so magical?"

Kadahl shrugged. "I do not know for sure. The rumor, or legend, if you will, has it that a child had need of their protection. A special child born in a manger," he paused glancing at her.

Semma bowed her head. She knew the name could not be spoken in this world without grave consequences.

"I know the one," she answered.

Kadahl chuckled. "Satan sent a serpent to give the new baby a special birthday kiss, but as the snake made its approach, it was attacked by the King of the Trillii and several of his greatest warriors.

"I believe the name of that King was Velloh, or something like that; well no mind, they killed the messenger of Satan and gained the blessing of the child. Since then the King of the Trillii has been the most powerful creature to stand against evil in any realm."

255

Semma was still puzzled. "But how did the Trillii know about the attack of the serpent?"

The demon laughed out loud this time rolling his head backwards.

"Woman, do not be foolish! Of course, they knew. It is the sworn oath of each Trillii to protect man from evil and in that instance they protected the savior of man!" he rolled back onto the rock laughing hard.

Semma watched him starting to feel very foolish and very used!

FOURTEEN

They dressed quickly. "I wish there was a way to tell?" Selena wondered out loud, as she buttoned her shirt.

Creed pulled on his boots. "I think we can."

He walked to where his weapons hung on the chair arm and reached for one of the Colt Python revolver's pulling it from its holster.

"I would be ready to bet that if the animal was conjured as part of a voodoo spell instead of the original Gypsy curse, the coat will not have the usual wards of protection."

He opened the cylinder dropping the six silver bullets from the weapon. Reaching into a coat pocket, he replaced them with normal lead rounds.

"And I know how to find out," he motioned with his head. "The skin is still hanging in the garage?"

She nodded. "Yes we have not moved it; it is very heavy wet."

He strode from the bedroom thrusting the revolver in his waistband and tossing his sheathed knives over his shoulder.

"Never leave home without them," he answered her questioning glance.

They made their way through the large house walking out into the attached garage filled with expensive cars. Near the far wall strung up from large utility hooks, was the great hide. Creed opened the overhead doors.

"It is getting ripe already," he wrinkled his nose.

Selena nodded agreeing. "We will have to get it tanned quickly if it turns out to be authentic."

With only a slight nod in answer, Creed pulled the revolver from his waistband and aimed at the hide.

"Here goes." He warned and Selena plugged her ears as he cocked the hammer on the Colt.

The report from the big gun shook the garage as the Gypsy fired three quick rounds. He lowered the smoking weapon slowly his eyebrows curled in a heavy frown.

"It is not authentic," he said. "No need to tan this."

She stepped close by him staring at the round holes in the hide.

"So we are probably right about the voodoo connection," she shook her head. "Now to find out why?" she raised an eyebrow. "Quite a little mystery we are building, isn't it?"

At her side, Creed nodded with a deep breath. "Such a good job of creating a werewolf, though."

He felt the hide again for the first time since the

battle he had survived.

She watched him run the fur through his fingers. "It is a realistic rendition?"

Creed nodded. "Yes," he reflected a bit. "The smell, the feel of the fur, the sharpness of the claws and teeth and the great strength it battered me with. Whoever did this has personal knowledge of the werewolf or had some help from someone who did. My question is why? It would have to be a lot of trouble to go through such an immense conjuring."

Selena had an idea. "Let's ask someone who knows?" she suggested pulling the ball of Asmus from her bag.

Creed watched her; it was a good idea.

She placed the ball on the worktable removing its protective cloth covering. Moving her hands over the balls clear surface she began to chant, closing her eyes, Creed watched, amazed at the lack of visible energy she used.

He had seen powerful witches who would shake and tremble calling Asmus from his netherworld slumber. He realized that Selena was indeed a very powerful Gypsy Witch. Watching close, he could see the gray hazy smoke filling the inside of the ball. Selena's chant grew, summoning the great Gypsy teacher Asmus.

It took seconds as quickly the face of the old warrior appeared looking out from the ball, his soft and kind face greeting them.

"Creed and Selena, good to see you both together."

The old man smiled at them.

Creed bowed his head in reverence to his

ancestor. "It is good to see you also, Asmus, it has been a long time."

Asmus chuckled slightly. "I would say that over four hundred years is a long time. Say, how is young Jacob Reid getting along?"

Creed shrugged. "I think he is doing okay. He has been blooded and so far seems to be learning everyday; he was a wise choice."

In the ball, Asmus nodded. "He has had many things to digest quickly and he is going to need them all; you have a great battle coming with the undead."

Selena nodded. "That is why we have called you forth master," she explained.

The old man turned to her. "What is going on my child? Tell Asmus your question."

Selena looked to Creed who nodded his consent. She took a deep breath before beginning.

"We were originally summoned here at the request of Bishop Danowski, an old acquaintance of Darius," she paused and Asmus nodded.

"I know him, Selena. He was once a powerful warrior against the vampire broods."

The Gypsy Witch nodded and continued with the story. She listed all that had happened since arriving in this place to find the young girl who had been bitten by a vampire. She told of meeting Father Joseph, a trained student of the Bishop, and of his joining the fight against the vampire.

When she told Asmus about the vampire returning with a large retinue of vampire slaves, Asmus became visibly excited. "There was a battle?"

Selena answered with a nod. "Yes, and the vampires, as well as, the human minions were killed in the fight. Something strange occurred, though, and that is the reason we have summoned you. Along with the vampire and his brood, there was a werewolf."

She allowed this sink in before she continued.

Asmus looked at Creed as a deep frown curled across his features. "The spawn of the curse?" He looked directly at Creed. "One of the damned souls of the Rolti witch, Deni?"

Creed placed his hands behind his back as he nodded. "Yes, at first I believed so, a werewolf conjured by a Gypsy Witch."

"At first?" Asmus asked slightly curious as he waited for the Prince of the Gypsies to continue.

Creed went on. "It looked like a werewolf, smelled like one and fought like one but it was not a true creation of the Rolti. It was, we believe, a creation of another form of magic user, possibly a voodoo follower."

"Voodoo?" Asmus wondered out loud. "A voodoo user in league with the Vampire Lords?"

He paused considering the possibilities.

"That is quite interesting since there has never been ties between the two factions in the remembered past."

Creed gestured with open palms. "This is America, Asmus, things are different here."

Biting his lower lip, the old Gypsy mulled the information over in his head.

"There is one more thing," Creed added. "Rasmere is here and he has asked me for my help against this upstart Lord they call Pakur."

Asmus turned slowly focusing an intense look onto the Gypsy.

"Rasmere?" he said as disbelief crossed his face. He turned his look back to Selena and then again to Creed.

"What is going on here?" he whispered.

Before anyone could answer, screeching tires tore their attention to the driveway of the mansion.

The red Corvette from Ted Toscanno's collection sped up the driveway, a wild-eyed Jacob Reid at the wheel. It slid to a stop in front of the open garage doors where the martial arts master burst out of the car, followed by the cat, Taz.

As they walked quickly into the garage Jake was already shaking his head in excitement.

"They have kidnapped Father Joe!" he blurted out. "We had a hell of a battle with them in the church," he stopped seeing the face of Asmus watching him through the crystal ball. "I am sorry Asmus; did I interrupt something?" he asked with a slight bow to the old man.

Asmus returned his bow before his eyes snapped to the cat that followed with his tail twitching.

"It has been a long time since I have been in the presence of Trillii royalty," Asmus greeted and Taz stared back intently at the man in the crystal ball.

"Yes, Asmus, legendary trainer of the Vampire Hunters, it has," the purr like voice answered.

Both Selena and Creed turned regarding the animal.

"Trillii?" Creed asked scratching his chin in

question.

Taz turned to Creed. "Yes, Darius Creed, I am Shach Meril," the cat answered. "I am sorry for not telling you sooner but I had to be careful. My mission here is very important."

Creed smiled slightly. "There is no need to explain, King of the Trillii," he answered. "It is an honor that we have one so great in our humble presence."

Sitting back on his haunches the cat appeared to reply with a dip of its head.

"I am the one honored. This is a great selection of warriors to fight beside," Shach Meril answered with a wave of his tail.

Asmus, from inside the ball, regarded all of them. "There is something happening here," he observed. "I feel it."

Creed agreed. "Yes, I have never had so many powerful figures involved in a situation before."

He was scratching his jaw trying to sift through it in his mind.

Selena looked over to Jake. "What did you say about the church and Father Joe?" she asked and all eyes turned his way.

The Hunter shook his head as a look of bewildered excitement crossed his face.

"Well, we went there to get these old artifacts of the church. Father Joe said they were powerful weapons against vampires. As we were collecting them, some very unwelcome guests showed up."

He paused, scratching his head. "Actually I should say they kind of popped out of no where. Well anyway, this vampire, Pakur, puffs out of a cloud of smoke with some voodoo bitch and he has some human minions with him. I yelled at Father Joe, telling him to run for it, as I dove into them, joined by Taz here."

He jerked his thumb at Shach Meril who nodded in agreement.

"Well, as we are putting the big slice job on the human slaves, Pakur and this voodoo babe leave, when they come back I get bowled over and almost gutted by the asshole before the cat saved me," he motioned a second time to the King of the Trillii.

"To make it short, they captured Father Joe and would have killed me too if it wasn't for Taz here scaring the beejeezus out of them."

Creed looked from Jake to the cat. "Of course, as powerful as you are, combined with the fact that you were on holy ground, your very touch would have been deadly to the demon."

In the garage around them, the purr like voice answered. "Yes, Gypsy Prince, it was the gift the baby Jesus gave us the night in the stable when the Vampire Lord appeared to take his blood."

Creed and Asmus nodded; they knew the tale well. Selena, however, frowned.

"I never heard how that came about?" she commented. "Would you please tell it for us?"

Creed nodded to the cat. "Yes please tell them. Jake and Selena should both hear it from someone like you, a king of the Trillii," he urged.

Shach Meril nodded. "You are right, Darius Creed. It is always better that way."

The cat looked at them all, a serious look on its face.

"As you all know, it was in Bethlehem in a small stable where the baby called Jesus, the true Son of God and savior of the human race, was born. The stories tell of the three wise men from the east who came to visit the baby and of shepherds from the nearby fields. However, it forgets about how Satan sent a vampire in the shape of a serpent to attack the child, barely hours old, when it was vulnerable to the kiss of the Devil. They have also forgotten of the brave Trillii King, Belo, not Velloh as some pronounce it, who traveled from the great Egyptian kingdoms to that small desolate town with three of his finest warriors.

"They arrived on the night of the child's birth hiding in the stable's loft. After midnight, the serpent made his move, slithering along the cold stable floor as the parents slept. From the loft, Belo watched, waiting for the exact moment to make his move. The great king knew he would only have one shot at the serpent's unprotected neck.

"One by one the animals in the stable backed away from the deadly serpent. No matter how they loved the child before them, none would give its life for him.

"The serpent backed them off until suddenly one did step forward from behind the manger, a mixed breed yellow haired dog. As the others watched, the serpent issued an angry call of battle towards the short-legged mutt. The serpent coiled ready to kill the foolish animal before it that dared to challenge his power.

"It was as the serpent rose, ready to strike, that Belo and his warriors attacked, springing from the loft onto the great serpent's back. A tremendous battle erupted and two of the warrior cats of the Trillii gave their lives defending the child. But in the end, the dog, with Belo and his surviving fighter, stood panting as the serpent died.

"Knowing he had been saved from the fallen one, Satan, the child raised its head in the manger where it lay, calling them forth. With his touch and blessing, the dog became protector of man in the day and the cat became protector of man in the night," Shach Meril paused. "It was a proud time for our people."

Creed nodded in approval. "It should have been a very proud time for you," he agreed.

Selena gasped as the full impact of the story hit her, and even Jake stood open mouthed. Asmus, however, chuckled.

"Thank the Lord that you were successful, my friend," he told the cat who nodded with a slight bow.

"Yes," the purring voice agreed.

Creed took a deep breath. "It would seem, though, we have one missing in action," he turned to Jake. "So the vampire and his minions took Father Joe?"

The martial artist sighed. "Yes, there was nothing I could do."

He held out his hands in apology.

Creed looked his way with a shrug; he realized that the Hunter had his hands full.

"You were manipulated, Jake, that is obvious. Pakur, it would seem, is suddenly one step ahead of us."

Selena wasn't satisfied as she turned to the crystal ball. "So Asmus tell us why has this Vampire Lord turned to a Voodoo Queen and how is it she has given him these powers? Jacob says she was in the church with the Lord, but no Lord can stand on holy ground."

Asmus seemed to consider the facts before him. "I will find out," he said and in a swirl of mists, he was gone.

After his mentor and teacher left Creed turned to the rest of the warriors with him.

"It doesn't really matter what allows Pakur to enter a church like a mortal, we need to get ready. Tonight we meet Rasmere and we will enter Pakur's lair," he looked around at them. "The battle will be great and bloody; prepare yourselves."

It came out as a warning.

Jake nodded his head. "We will all be ready," he assured the Gypsy Prince.

With a toss of his long hair and the sunlight glancing off his silver earrings, the Gypsy turned, heading for the house.

After he had gone, Jake looked at Selena.

"He sure got damn serious all of a sudden," he observed.

The Gypsy Witch watched the broad back of her beloved as he strode away; she turned back to Jake and the cat Shach Meril.

"He is worried about this battle," she said, feeling something was making her Prince upset.

Jake was about to answer when the voice of the cat broke the air.

"He knows something of great power is

267

wrapped up in all of this; he can read the signs," Shach Meril answered.

The cat waved a furry paw around the garage. "Darius Creed has fought many battles for many years. He can feel the significance of this one in his blood."

Selena bowed slightly at the King of the feline warrior race.

"You are right, great one. We will all be ready."

Across the garage, Jake nodded as his fingers nervously played with the great sword in the worn leather sheath.

"I will be," he assured with a nod of his head.

As the humans walked from the garage following Creed, Shach Meril licked his feet. Battle was coming and in his animal soul, only one outcome would be acceptable!

Asmus walked through the wall of smoke, which allowed him access from one realm to the other. So Creed wanted to know what was at play, huh? He stepped through three separate realms until he came to the hot humid sticky atmosphere of the one called Kadahl, the lord of the Voodoo world.

Asmus was respected and feared by almost all of the ghouls of the dark realms; hell he had sent most of them there at one time or the other, and many shrank as he walked past.

Asmus was at least two thousand years old and he had walked the earth when all of these dark minions of Satan had been on the loose. It made him smile now as they shriveled from his arrival,

hiding in their dark shadows where the servants of
Satan always hid from the light.

He wanted to find Kadahl; if anyone could
speak for a Voodoo Queen, it would be that
oversexed pervert. Asmus could smell the odor of
the damned lord of voodoo close by and started to
look into the various rooms carved out of the
molten rock that was Kadahl's lair.

"Come bastard, show yourself to me," he called
through pursed lips.

The one thing about Asmus that had never
changed was the simple fact that he watched over,
not only the Gypsy people, but also those that wore
the mantle of Hunter as well. Right now the very
idea that some voodoo bitch had helped a Vampire
Lord kidnap a priest who was a future Hunter made
his blood boil!

He swiped a stained curtain aside and stepped
into the room where the smell of the demon he
searched for hung like a stench of the grave.

"Kadahl!"

He called out to the Demon Lord, who was in
the act of sodomizing a young voodoo witch.

At first, the demon did not hear him intent on
completing the sexual act with the young initiate.

Asmus shook his head; after so many great men
had been killed when they also were so enthralled in
sex, you would think a demon like Kadahl would be
smarter. The Gypsy walked over to where the sweat
soaked monster knelt ramming the young woman's
ass with all the fury in his soul. Asmus stood his
arms folded in front of him looking down over the
two rutting figures waiting.

269

Suddenly, as he sensed someone above him, Kadahl opened his eyes

"Hello Kadahl," Asmus greeted as he delivered a high hard roundhouse kick that caught the demon under the chin and tossed him back across the hard stone floor.

The human voodoo witch looked up at the old Gypsy as Asmus tossed her a sheet from the bed.

"Leave here," he ordered as she looked up at him with scared haunted eyes.

Nodding her head, she tore her gaze from him scrambling towards the door of the chamber and ducking out.

With a grunt, Asmus walked over to the prostrate form of Kadahl. He shook his head; the demon never could take a good punch.

The old Gypsy picked up a dipper of water and tossed it over the demon's head.

"What the hell!" Kadahl snapped up, sputtering and spitting water from his mouth.

He looked up into the Gypsy's icy glare.

"Asmus what in the hell was that for?" he asked bewildered and surprised.

Without answering, Asmus walked over to the nearby table and sniffed at the contents of a large pitcher.

"Wine?" he asked, looking to Kadahl.

The demon nodded. "From the island of Crete itself, squeezed by the toes of a thousand Greek virgins." He sputtered as he stood.

Asmus poured a goblet of the liquid for himself. Kadahl watched, as the old Gypsy legend tasted the drink.

"Not bad."

He smacked his lips at the demon sitting down and reclining in the chair at the table.

Kadahl felt his eyes narrowing as he watched the old human.

"So what brings the famous Asmus to my humble realm?" he asked, snatching up a towel and drying himself.

Asmus sat back sipping from the goblet. "I agree this is not bad, demon," he smiled as he drained the vessel.

"You Gypsies always did like the wine a little too much," he grumbled under his breath.

Asmus placed the goblet on the nearby table. "And you have always been a sex-starved fool," he answered, his gaze locking on the demon.

A questioning frown came over the demon's face. "So since when does that concern you?"

Asmus crossed his hands on his lap as he regarded the demon.

"You are involved with several of my people. It would seem this little Voodoo Queen, who is working with a Vampire Lord, may threaten some of them."

"Don't threaten me!" he warned raising a clawed finger. "This is none of your concern."

Asmus shot him a look and then slowly refilled the wine goblet from the pitcher.

"Oh, I think it is, demon. You see, Creed is involved, as well as Shach Meril. I would say that makes it my business."

He lifted the goblet to his lips, drinking as he watched the Demon Lord.

Kadahl sat down heavily on the messy bed. "Stay out of it, Asmus; let them fight it out. We can do nothing this time, you know it as well as I do."

Asmus stopped drinking. "So you feel that this is the Dolmage, the fight talked about from before the dawn of men?" he asked with a playful gleam in his eye.

Kadahl nodded seriously. "Yes I do, and you know as well as I do that we cannot interfere in the Dolmage. It will happen with or without us," He shook his head in sorrow. "To bad too; that Semma is a good little servant," he added playfully.

Asmus, the glass of wine to his lips, chuckled. "I bet she was, demon, but I have not come here about the Dolmage, that would be pointless. What I want to know is why you gave the Voodoo Queen the power to conjure a werewolf and also to allow a Vampire Lord to cross the threshold of a Catholic Church?"

He paused and then continued. "To mess with the curse of the Rolti is one thing, but to mess with God himself?"

The Gypsy shook his head taking a long drink. "You have more guts then brains." He swallowed the wine from the goblet.

Kadahl frowned. "Why? I mean, whatever we do is always up to the mortals to straighten out isn't it?"

Asmus looked at him, rolled his eyes and wiped imagined sweat from his baldhead.

"Oh, wake up, Kadahl," he jibed. "Humans act *through* us, not because of us. Someday, even you will have to answer for what you have done."

He left it at that, smiling, as a sadistic look crossed his face.

Kadahl scratched his head, wondering what the old man was getting at.

"I am not quite sure I follow you?" the demon said, puzzled.

"It is really simple, demon. Some day you will have to explain to Saint Peter, and the rest of heaven, why you crossed over the line, allowing a vampire to enter the sacred house of God."

Asmus drank, keeping his eyes on Kadahl, wondering if the message was getting into that thick ugly skull.

"But I did not really allow that, Asmus. Semma did-the Voodoo Queen-she is the one who will be at fault, not me."

Asmus started to chuckle and almost spilled his goblet. "You fool! That won't wash. You gave her the power, idiot; what she does with it is still your responsibility."

He wiped wine from the sides of his mouth.

Kadahl glared at the Gypsy. "So, do you agree with me? Is this the Dolmage?" he asked.

Asmus shrugged as he stood. "Could be; the signs appear to be right for it I guess."

He walked to the doorway of the chamber.

"If I were you though, I would be careful whom I give too many powers to; it may be hard to explain later."

With that, he stepped from the chamber leaving the Demon Lord to ponder his fate.

It was hard for Kadahl to siphon the meaning of that old bastard's words; Asmus preferred to speak in riddles when he could. Kadahl stood, walking over to the bookcase hewn from the rock wall of his chamber; it was time to look something up. He ran his finger down the line of the old books that rested there

"Let's see; where are you?" he mumbled to himself as his eyes caught the glare of the blood red book, *'Fallen Angels'*.

He pulled the book, bound in the skin of Satan's Angels who died in the battle for heaven, and thumbed through it slowly.

In seconds, he came to the section describing the Dolmage in ancient script of a forgotten time. Quickly he skimmed the information listed on the yellowed pages grimly aware that all of the elements needed for the prophecy were now present. For some reason he read a little further than usual into text he had never cared for in the past.

He trembled as he saw the words before him: *'Unwittingly, the Demon Lord will grant powers to bring the events closer to their deadly climax.'*

His hands shaking, he leaned against the rock chamber walls; it didn't predict the fate of the demon!

Selena pulled the ball of Asmus from her bag when she felt the tingling inside; the old man was summoning them. She placed the globe onto the polished table in the Toscanno study where Creed, Jake and Shach Meril looked on.

The face of the Gypsy Hunter-trainer appeared before them.

"The demon, Kadahl, gave the Voodoo Queen the power she has been using," he announced to them.

"Why?" Creed asked crossing his powerful arms over his chest.

Asmus shook his head. "The why is not as important as the who, Gypsy Prince, because when one knows his enemies the actions of that enemy become insignificant."

Creed's eyes narrowed as he regarded the information. "That is true, Asmus, but I was concerned as to why this demon would become involved at all. I thought most demons hated the vampire?"

"I thought the same?" Selena added. "I thought they hated vampires because they were the chosen of Satan allowed to walk among men and feed off them on Earth, unlike the demons who may only have their souls?"

Asmus nodded in answer. "To a point, you are right but this Kadahl is a demon who thinks about his own lust-filled pleasures first. He no doubt granted the woman the power after he had his way with her with no regard to how she was about to use the power. He is a rather dense demon. He also thinks this is the beginning of the Dolmage and he has no alternative but to go along with it all."

Creed looked at Selena with a frown but she could only shrug back in answer; it was Shach Meril who nodded his head.

"This is not the Dolmage," he countered. "It is a

275

significant happening, but it is not that terrible time of man against undead Lord."

"It may be one of the events that could hasten the Dolmage," he added as an afterthought.

The cat glanced at Asmus who agreed.

"It would seem to me that you are right, King of the Trillii."

Creed looked at them both. "What is this Dolmage; I have never heard of it?" he asked them.

"A very old story," Asmus explained. "More of a prediction actually told since the beginning of time by soothsayers of doom and destruction. It tells about the rise of Satan who, along with his chosen, the vampire, will attempt to assault the gates of Heaven one more time. The battle, it is foretold, will begin on Earth as the favorites of Satan destroy the favorites of God; vampire versus man. The battle will then climb the heavens until it comes to the sacred realm of God himself and the Angels of the Lord will battle the fallen Angels of Satan."

Asmus paused as Creed absorbed this information.

Shack Meril continued. "It is said that thirteen signs of evil will preclude the Dolmage and only as each sign is fulfilled can the chain progress."

Selena frowned at the cat. "What does that have to do with us?" she asked.

"If this is not the Dolmage?"

Asmus answered from inside the globe. "More then you know, Selena. You see, the first sign is the growth of the Vampire Lords ranks to the number one hundred. This has been hard for them to do because of men like Creed and Jacob who have been successful in slaying them."

This time Jake cleared his throat. "Why is this Rasmere involved with us against the other Lord then? You would think that it would be to his advantage to allow Pakur to keep making vampires who, some day, will become Lords, right?" he looked around at his friends who nodded.

"I was wondering that also." Creed agreed.

Asmus smiled slightly. "Unless someone like Rasmere wants the fabled one hundred to be True Blood vampires only," he pointed out.

At this Creed grunted and Jake nodded. "That would make sense," he agreed.

"So, in a way you are actually doing Rasmere a favor by wiping out Pakur and his brood," Shach Meril added.

Selena was still puzzled. "Rasmere would put off the Dolmage by killing the Lords who are not true bloods, which is devious even for a vampire?"

At her side, Creed slowly turned towards her.

"He is capable of it, believe me."

Asmus raised an eyebrow at them. "Rest today for the battle tonight, Hunters. Father Joe must be saved."

With a puff of smoke in the globe, he was gone.

Lost in their own thoughts they filed from the room to ready themselves for the coming fight.

FIFTEEN

The dark blue clouds rolled overhead as the cooling breeze blew the Gypsy's hair from his shoulders. Creed stood studying the lair of the Vampire Lord Pakur from across the street.

He was under a street lamp but at this point, he didn't care; they would already know he was coming. Creed had been here for over two hours watching as the crowd slowly weaved its way from the club breaking off into individuals or couples as they disappeared down the street.

A man and a woman walked by arm in arm trying to stay warm in the quickly cooling breeze.

"Damn weather," The man cursed, pulling the

lapels of his trench coat closer around his head.

The Gypsy looked at the couple, a deep frown on his face as he rolled his eyes at the clouds overhead.

"This is not weather," he said in a flat tone to the young man. "Weather is a natural phenomena, while this…" he motioned with his head to the sky. "…is brought on by evil."

The couple stopped, a look of disdain on the face of the young man as he clutched the woman closely.

"What are you, some damn whacko?" he asked as he turned to face the Gypsy.

Creed lifted an eyebrow regarding the man before him.

"Do yourself a favor, take the lady home and stay there. You will be safe inside your house. Stay there until morning," he warned.

A funny look crossed the man's face. "Get away from us, asshole, I have a gun."

"It would do you no good against this man."

A higher pitched voice sounded from the shadows.

Together Creed and the young man turned as Rasmere suddenly appeared from the darkness. "Besides he is making good sense," the Lord agreed as he stepped close to the couple towering over them.

"Take her home," Rasmere directed with his hypnotic milky white eyes. "Tomorrow the sun will shine on a new day."

The young man opened his mouth as if to answer until he became entranced in the Lord's eyes.

"I… I think I will," he stammered reaching for the woman's hand. "Come on, Judy, let us be on our way."

He hustled her away as the vampire stepped over to the Gypsy Prince.

"Some humans are far too arrogant for their own good," he observed.

The wind blowing his long hair, Creed turned regarding his old enemy.

"It is our way, I guess," the Gypsy grunted. "Men forget that they are not the supreme Hunters in this world."

Rasmere answered with his own grunt and a nod of his head.

"The majority of humans are great fools," he agreed and then without turning he added. "But no matter how this night goes, Gypsy, know one thing."

He paused and Creed turned slightly his eyes on the vampire as the Lord continued.

"You have always been the best. Regardless of the pain you have caused me, I have never been let down by you." With that statement, Rasmere returned Creed's look.

The Gypsy nodded slowly. "There is an old saying, Lord Rasmere, that the greatness of a man is judged by the greatness of his enemies. I would say, in our case, we are equally at fault for each other's reputation."

Rasmere frowned. "Why do you say that, Gypsy Prince?"

Creed spit onto the dirty sidewalk. "Because,

Rasmere, as much as I hate to say it, without you I would have never come to be," he turned his gaze back to the club owned by Pakur.

Rasmere thought a second. "You know, Creed, I think you are right." Suddenly the vampire erupted in deep laughter and Creed turned, regarding him.

"What is wrong with you?" he asked, confused by this show of mirth from the Lord.

Rasmere wiped his eyes as tears ran down his cheeks from the laughter.

"I was just thinking how the True Blood vampire babies are told that if they do not behave or go to bed on time, the Hunter, Darius Creed, will come and get them," He was almost rolling now and his knees grew weak as he continued to laugh.

Creed smiled despite himself. "You know, Rasmere, it is to bad that Stoker wrote that book, *Dracula*, because you are twice the demon that Count Vlad was."

He shook his head as the kneeling vampire recovered from his laughter enough to stand.

"Do not bring that up, I beseech you," he looked up through watery eyes at Creed. "I hated that damn book." He took a deep breath finally getting hold of himself.

The vampire wiped tears from his face with the sleeves of his leather trench coat while Creed had a thought.

"Tell me, Rasmere, why is it so important to you that this Lord Pakur be destroyed? After all, if he were a True Blood you would die trying to protect him."

Rasmere took a deep breath. "Because these

turned Lords are all bastards," he answered as he clasped his hands behind his back.

"I do not believe, as the council does not believe, that Satan ever intended to give the gift of immortality to humans. Tell me, Hunter, in your years of battling my kind, which do you consider more bloodthirsty, a True Blood or a Turned vampire?"

His eyes bore into Creed as he waited for the answer.

Creed tilted his head a bit, thinking it over, before he decided on the issue.

"Well, I suppose that would depend on your definition of blood thirst. I would say the Lords generally drain more of one victim's blood consistent with a feeding animal," he paused picking his words.

"But the Turned vampire has more of a tendency to take multiple victims when he feeds, more like a bloodlust. I believe it was the Lord called Barchone who illustrated it well, feeding only partially from over twenty victims in a single night. That was in southern Texas, if I remember right, about 1871A.D. He left bodies everywhere," Creed shook his head and Rasmere nodded.

"Yes a Turned bastard Lord," he spat the words out as if they caused his tongue to curl. "I do not know if it is their human nature, at least the small amount of it that remains after the change, or some whim of Satan, but the Turned do not feed, they butcher."

Creed raised an eyebrow as he regarded the very old vampire before him.

"I find that an interesting thought from one who also kills human victims to survive," he observed.

The Lord shrugged. "Does not man butcher cattle to eat and yet abhor the large-scale slaughter of buffalo and other animals simply for hides or tusks?" he asked forcing Creed to agree.

"Yes, but I am not sure how that is considered the same thing?"

"Humans feel the butcher in the meat shop is a necessary thing," the vampire stated. "But they do not accept the man who shoots the elephant for the tusks to make jewelry."

Creed grunted. "So is it their human side that causes that?" he wondered out loud. "Does it make them kill for the joy of it?"

He paused and the vampire gave a slight shrug.

"The human race is homicidal, the only animal on Earth who openly preys upon each other. When that kind of animal is given powers and the ability to inflict great harm on its species, it becomes uncontrollable." The Lord rolled his neck as if trying to loosen the muscles there.

"They have no right as Lords and should remain as underlings for the remainder of their existence."

He motioned with his head to the club across the street. "Looks like it is closing," he pointed and Creed agreed.

"They are locking the doors and turning down the lights. I can smell the vampires inside and there are many."

Rasmere grunted deeply. "They are ready to protect their bastard Lord and his power hungry beliefs; this is going to be a very nasty fight Darius

284

Creed."

The Gypsy Hunter stretched. "If there was another way, we would take it, but we have to retrieve the priest if he is still alive and for that, we cannot wait for an invitation."

They walked in silence to the bus stop where the others waited. They looked up as the Gypsy, with the Lord in tow, arrived.

Selena stood. She was dressed in black leather pants and jacket with knee high soft leather boots. Creed could see two knives at her waist.

Jake was stalking about, to wired to sit. "Well it's about time," he commented as they arrived.

Creed motioned to the Lord. "This is Lord Rasmere of the House of Haeth," he announced. "Second highest seat in the Council of Vampire."

Rasmere bowed his head reverently.

Creed pointed to Selena. "Rasmere this is Selena, a Gypsy Witch and Hunter."

She returned a slight nod of the head acknowledging the Lord.

"Exquisite," the vampire responded quietly.

Before the Gypsy could go on, Jake stepped up thrusting his hand at the Lord's chest.

"Hi, I am Jake Reid, Vampire Hunter, slayer and generally all around bad dude," he announced with an edge in his tone.

This brought a chuckle from somewhere inside the Lord's chest.

"Of course, you carry the sword of Takada. It was mine once."

He reached forward taking the bold Hunter's hand.

"Ya, well, I have it now, vampire and I don't think it will so easily leave my hands."

Rasmere raised an eyebrow. "Oh," he asked amused. "And why not?"

Jake pushed back his coat revealing the ivory handled weapon in his belt.

"Because you will have to pry my cold dead fingers from around it," he answered.

Rasmere looked into Jake's eyes, a slight smile forming in the corner of his mouth.

"How do you think I obtained it the last time?"

It was an unspoken challenge as man and vampire stared into each other's eyes. The spell was quickly broken by a purr-like voice.

"There was no Trillii warrior present, Vampire Lord, or you would have never fouled the sword's enchanted handle."

Rasmere turned his narrowing eyes as he saw Shach Meril sitting easily on the bus stop bench.

"Are you sure, King of the Trillii, that it would not have been your blood sacrificed that night?" the Lord asked.

With what could best be described as a noble bearing the cat stiffened, meeting the milky white eyes of the Lord.

"You will not scare me, vampire; I am a Warrior King of the Trillii. I was bred and raised for battle. It is my destiny to defend the human race against the legions of the undead, vampire or other. If my life is to be forfeited, so be it," the cat responded.

Rasmere dipped his head, a slight bow of

reverence to the feline warrior.

"Well met, Shach Meril," he admitted.

Creed adjusted his weapons under his coat as he looked around at the small band.

"We are going into a Vampire Lord's lair," he explained simply. "Rasmere knows what that means, of course, as do I. I have been there many times before. We will need to divide up, after we enter, to search for the priest. It is going to be very dangerous and you will have to be on your guard at all times."

Rasmere pointed around to the others. "They should stay together, Gypsy Prince, for their own safety," he interjected.

Creed chewed his lower lip weighing the idea. "It will slow the search," he pointed out. "And regardless of how I hate the idea they need to learn. Sticking together will teach them nothing."

It was a cold statement, even for the vampire to swallow, but Rasmere nodded.

"Okay, we do this your way." he pulled his trench closer, resigned to Creed's plan.

At three a.m. in the morning they walked across the quiet dimly lit street to the front of the club, now deserted by the bustling crowds of young folk. They stopped down the block a safe distance as Selena reached into her bag.

"Here," she handed Creed and Jake a vial of colored liquid.

"It is a special mix of the strength potion; it will make you stronger, quicker and raise your senses even higher. I think we will need it in the dark rooms inside."

Without question, the men drank their portions.

"That tastes like shit," Jake made a face. "But hell, if it doesn't kill us it sure may help us. All I have to do is breath on them now."

Selena smiled. "Unfortunately, it is not made for the taste, Jacob, but it will come in handy when you need the extra boost."

While Creed studied the club's doorway, Rasmere turned to the others.

"Remember, we are dealing with a Lord here as well as a Voodoo Queen. Things may not be what they appear to be and there will be traps and secret surprises at every turn."

They understood, nodding seriously.

"There is also one other thing," he added. "I cannot fight or kill any vampires, it is against the code. I will handle the human minions or anything else that gets in the way, however."

At this Creed spun looking at him his eyes narrowing.

"I figured as much," he snorted and with a motion of his head, he asked.

"Can you tell how many are in there? I can smell a lot of vampires but as far as humans…" he only shrugged.

Rasmere shook his head slowly as his eyes looked at the darkened club windows. "There are many," he assured them.

Creed turned back to the front door. "Okay follow me and be careful."

They crept to the heavy steel door and Creed stepped up next to it carefully running his hands over its smooth exterior. Rasmere stepped next to him, his eyes scanning the door also.

"There are no wards," he whispered as if puzzled.

Stepping back, Creed reached for the handle turning it easily. He looked back at the Vampire Lord.

"I guess they knew we were coming," he whispered back over his shoulder.

Rasmere only shrugged as Shach Meril brushed by his booted feet tensing near Creed.

"They are waiting," his feline-like voice confirmed.

Jake grunted. "Let's get it done with," he said under his breath, confrontation thick in his voice.

Looking at him Selena nodded nervously. "Yes, if they knew we were coming, let us do this thing," she added.

Even Rasmere had to agree meeting the Gypsy Prince's eyes.

"I agree Creed lets go in and start the party," he urged.

With a deep breath, Creed nodded and as he allowed the air to escape from his lungs, he shoved the door wide open!

They walked in, aware of the dim lights that caused shadows throughout the barroom.

"Damn!" Jake swore under his breath as his senses were assailed by the stench of evil.

Creed stepped from the entryway into the open room of the club his hands tensing in anticipation as his senses searched the darkness. Rasmere was behind him allowing the human image to fade away from his features and he appeared, as he truly was, a full-fledged Vampire Lord!

Shach Meril on padded feet rushed by them into the dark searching for his age-old enemies and the battle his senses cried for.

Jake pushed Selena ahead of him content to be the rear guard of the group when a rustle from the coat checkroom drew his attention. He spun on his heels as from the dark room a female vampire, her fangs bared and claws reaching for him, sprang!

Creed had taught the martial arts master well so instead of stopping her charge, he spun dropping to a knee while he draped the protective coat over his head. The female demon hissed in rage as she flew at him faster than humanly possible. She couldn't stop as she sped at him, her own ferocious attack carrying her over the top of Jake as he knelt under the protection of the enchanted coat.

Jake heard her razor sharp claws rake across the leather and her loud hiss of anger when she could not find his skin. He jumped to his feet as she sprang back off of the wall like a billiard ball again speeding his way.

"Aiiiii!" She came at him, claws outstretched and hungry for his blood. Jake whipped the left side of his coat open gripping the enchanted sword of Takada and drawing it, she was almost on him when he reacted snapping a hard stiff legged front kick that caught her under the bosom.

A second time the vampire was tossed into the far wall his enhanced strength superior to hers.

"Take that you foul smelly bitch!" he cried out as she rebounded falling hard to the polished floor of the club. Like a rubber ball off of a brick wall, she was coming at him again, her incisor teeth dripping with drool. Jake jerked the sword free of his coat bringing the polished blade up over his head in a shiny arc of destruction. As the she-demon rushed his way, he lashed out with the sword like a major league slugger aiming for the center field wall. Enchanted blade met vampire skin and bit deep, striking the hissing head from the charging body below it. Reminding Jake of a headless chicken, the body flopped about on the entryway floor.

"Good night sweetheart," he commented as he stepped over it and followed the rest into the dark club.

Creed was halfway across the club, almost to the ring of tables around the dance floor, when the three vampires dropped from the dark ceiling! He whipped out the enchanted silver blades blocking razor sharp claws as they rushed at his face.

"We are attacked!" he cried out a warning to the others as dark forms appeared all around the small group.

A dozen human minions rushed from the shadows swarming over the form, Lord Rasmere, who raged as he was attacked.

"How dare human servants of a Lord attack one

who is greater then your bastard Master!" he called out in anger his razor sharp claws slicing through human skin and rendered throats.

Rasmere stood, his claws clenching and unclenching, while he trembled in unrestrained fury.

The humans paused as they started to consider for the first time what it was they were doing, attacking a great Lord like the one before them would do little to gain them the precious gift of a vampire's bite.

They stood thinking; Pakur promised them he would give anyone who fought the intruders his gift.

As they eyed the great Lord before them, however, the promise of Pakur seemed to dim greatly. They circled warily as from the other side of the tables the Hunter faced three of their vampire masters.

With a smile full of challenge the Gypsy bounced lightly on the balls of his feet as he weaved an arc of promised death with his silver blades.

"Come on then," he invited them as the earrings in his ears glimmered in the half-light.

The monsters didn't flinch as they poised for the attack; Creed waited loose and relaxed as the left one sprang!

In a large circle his silver blades cut the air sinking deeply into the first demon and cutting halfway through the monsters chest. As the Gypsy turned his back following through with the first strike a second vampire sprang for his back.

Creed sensed him closing and reacted with a backstroke of the second blade, it drove deeply into the vampire's throat, wasting little time Creed twisted the weapon tearing it free. From the right the third swiped at the Gypsy with its claws, which bounced harmlessly off of the shoulder of the werewolf skin coat. Creed spun thrusting his right foot out into a powerful back kick that connected squarely into the attacker's chest.

The skinny emaciated demon was flung back over a table and two chairs where it clawed itself up from the floor hatred in its bluish eyes.

At Creed's feet the two dead vampires were already turning to smoke!

Across the bar he could see Rasmere now completely reverted to his vampire form in among a dozen human servants of Pakur as he battled.

He had little time to worry about his old enemy though as the third vampire climbed to a table and sprang across the room!

Creed snatched up a heavy wooden chair throwing it into the air straight into the creature's path. The vampire crashed into the heavy wooden object and fell to the floor rolling about stunned. The demon managed to roll onto a knee and rise slowly as the Gypsy stepped forward with a hard front kick that caught the thing up under the chin and spun it over backwards. Dropping to a knee Creed slashed the demon's throat as it writhed about on the polished floor.

As the third demon disappeared in smoke Creed watched as four more dark robed figures appeared before him on the dance floor.

"Cooome, Dariusss Creeeed," the tallest beckoned. "Weee awaaiit you Huunterrrr."

Creed stood from where he knelt readjusting his grip on his silver blades. Stepping lightly over the tipped furniture strewn across the floor he nodded.

"I am here for all of you demons." He stepped among them. "Tonight Satan's halls will be full of your kind," he promised, flexing his fingers across the weapons handles feeling their old and familiar grips.

The vampire's stepped back forming a circle, which the Gypsy stepped into, his head up and his eyes bright in his unspoken answer to their challenge. He stood relaxed and ready to fight as they started to circle around him their claws shining in the dim light of the club dance floor.

Rasmere released the throat of a human minion whose heart he had torn from the unlucky man's chest. This had caused the others to step back, pausing their attack as they stared at the bloody Lord who met their gaze; he lifted the blood soaked organ in his hand and placed it in his mouth drinking the foamy liquid.

Rasmere felt the oxygen rich blood filling his stomach sending greater strength to his inhuman body as the blood lust took over inside of him.

"We have been ordered to slay you," a woman said as she pulled a long bladed knife from under her jacket.

"Yes, our lord will reward us all," a male agreed.

Rasmere smiled as the last faint human traits he had assumed left him completely. "Cooome humaansss and fight Lord Rassmere, seeee the power of a True Bloood Lorrrd."

He challenged them; the blood-drunk state he was in taking over. "I willl drink froom allll of you but none willll seeee immortality!" he promised.

Creeping closer, they were too foolish to realize the power of the vampire before them, intent only on serving their master.

As a unit, they jumped, flinging themselves onto the blood drunk Lord their knives slashing at his body. Rasmere was driven to the floor overcome by the weight of their sheer numbers as sharp knives slashed through his leather trench coat and tore at his skin.

Pain from the blades registered in the back of the vampire's mind as it cut through his blood drunk haze. It was no more then an inconvenience, though; the human knives could cut him but never kill him.

He was able to get his arms under him as a heavy boot kicked him in the side of the head. This was starting to really piss him off! He needed to get back to his feet where he could use his claws and strength to his advantage, he needed to feed, to drink more blood and grow even stronger!

From somewhere above him a loud battle cry rang out cutting through the sounds of the humans covering his body as the one named Jacob Reid rushed into the fray, the sword of Takada swinging wildly.

"Aiii!"

The Hunter shouted as he swung the sword slashing the head from the shoulders of a nearby human minion. A second human was foolish enough to attack the Hunter, swinging his knife at Jake's kidneys. Sidestepping the attack, Jake slapped the sword aside with his open left palm as he reversed the grip on his sword, swinging a vicious upstroke that opened the human from belly to sternum. The wound was lethal. While his guts seeped from a wide open belly, the human stared in horror as he stumbled, his eyes glazing over. He fell to the floor dying in a growing pool of blood.

From the pile of arms and legs that swarmed over Rasmere, Jake kicked another human, a woman who screamed as the Hunter's boot caught her under the chin, tossing her away from the fight. To his side, someone thrust a knife blade into his back but it skidded off of the enchanted trench coat he wore.

"Nice try!" Jake yelled as he spun, swinging the sword down across the arm holding the knife, the hand fell flopping to the carpet.

As the human howled in pain, Jake kicked the ugly faced attacker with a roundhouse to the stomach, it doubled the human over allowing Jake to follow up with a crushing punch to the unprotected side of the minion's head. Jake looked about searching for the next attacker as a roar of anger echoed through his ears.

To his side, Rasmere stood, shedding the remaining human minions, which he tossed aside like rag dolls. With a wild animal look of the feasting vampire, Rasmere snatched the nearest human, a stocky muscular woman; staring into her frightened eyes, he bared his incisors.

While Jake watched he pulled the woman close to his fangs and clamped his mouth over her pumping jugular. With a snap, the Lord drank deeply of the woman's lifeblood. As quickly as he had bit her, the Lord tossed the woman aside, his gaze swiveling to Jake and the two locked eyes.

"Beee careful Huuunter," the Lord warned. "Theyvy are nuuumerous and are everyyywhere in thisss dark building."

Jake nodded his head as his eyes scanned the Lord's blood covered body; his leather trench coat, as well as the clothes underneath, were rent with slashes from the minions blades. Rasmere's hands and face were also covered in deep knife slashes that were already healing as the Lord fed and recovered his strength.

"I will be, Rasmere," Jake answered surprising himself by the respectful tone in his own voice.

Around them on the floor lay the littered bodies of the dead humans, as across the room another fight was about to begin. Jake was about to head for the dance floor where Creed stood in the center of four vampires but before he could make his move a door flew open. He turned as three more hissing demons rushed his way.

They flew at him five feet from the floor skimming over tables and chairs. Jake crouched as he raised the sword in front of him. He was grateful for the potion Selena had given him because these things were fast!

Rasmere stepped from the human bodies at his feet, blood running down the sides of his mouth after he had gorged himself. He watched the Hunter spin to face the oncoming attack. True to his vows, Rasmere kept his own clawed hands at his sides unwilling to fight his own people. It was a strong effort on the Lord's part but even with the best of intentions, it was not to be as the first of the three spotted the powerful Lord and hissed a challenge!

A deep frown crossed Rasmere's dark brow as the Turned vampire landed in a battle crouch mere feet from him.

"I willll killll you Looord Rasssmere, traitor whooo aligns himssself with humansssss!" it was an accusation.

This caused the Lord to raise an eyebrow as he regarded the younger bastard vampire.

"The tenets dooo nooot allllow for usss tooo fight each other," he explained folding his arms in front of him. "Nooot even Pakuuur can chaaange thaat simple fact," he pointed out.

The young vampire raised an accusing hand pointing a clawed finger.

"Pakur hasss prooolaimed you traitor, asss wellll as outlaw; you should never have left Europe. Thisss iss a new country ruuuled by the young and nooot the old vampires of the council who have grooown ignorant and long in the faaang!"

This comment caused Rasmere to flare his nostrils. "You insssolent little puppp!" he replied his voice full of disgust.

"You wooould staaand here befooore a True Blood Lord and ssspeak like thisss?"

The young vampire's answer came as he sprung for Rasmere's throat!

SIXTEEN

The first vampire came at Creed from his right side. Creed's enhanced speed and reflexes took over as his right hand swung a vicious backstroke with the silver blade. The enchanted weapon bit deeply, cleaving across the forehead of the demon almost completely scalping him.

The vampire fell to the ground in its death throes as the next demon rushed from Creed's front side. Seeing the rush of black coming his way, Creed swiveled his hips and kicked the rushing attacker flush in the chest.

The blow swept the demon from his feet sending him back over the railing that bordered the dance floor. He landed heavily on an upturned table leg; it punched through the vampire's chest holding him there. Creed spun, searching for the two remaining attackers; he was immediately grabbed hard by the left shoulder as one of the demons tried to knock him off balance. Creed wrapped his left arm up over the top of the demons extended limb holding it securely in a joint lock. The vampire's eyes shot wide open in surprise, as for the first time, it realized the humans strength was equal to its own.

As it struggled in panic to get away, Creed held it in place; swiveling his hips, the blade in his right hand whipped between them. Coldly, the Hunter glared into the vampire's eyes as he drew the blade across its throat! The monster fell to the floor already starting to smoke.

"Say hello to Satan," Creed grunted as he saw the fourth vampire disappear into a hidden hallway.

Sprinting with inhuman speed Creed slipped into the chamber just as the trap door slid shut behind him!

The vampire's hand struck Rasmere across the left cheekbone, snapping his head back and causing the Lord to stumble backwards tripping over one of the human corpses. He rolled to his hands and knees feeling unspoken rage burning through him.

He could not believe a Turned bastard vampire had attacked a Lord!

"I willll killll you Looord Rassssssmere," the youth promised. "I willll beee given a sssseat at the right haaand of myyyy Lord, Pakur."

He was smiling as he stalked forward almost on top of the great Lord.

Rasmere tried to rise, stumbling again in the human blood that greased the polished club floor. He struggled to stand; the youth could kill him if he didn't get back to his feet soon. He rolled forward over the body of the knife-wielding woman, planning to gain his feet. Shock filled his mind instead as the heels of his boots slipped and he fell again his head striking the hard floor.

Rasmere winced at the sudden pain he felt from the impact; he would not be able to get up fast enough.

"I haaave you nooww," the youth cried out in glee as he flew into the air landing directly over the struggling Lord.

Rasmere felt vulnerable, still sliding about and unable to get a defensive position. Above him, with a cry of victory, the youth was about to strike a deadly blow to the Lord's unprotected neck.

As the young vampire wound up preparing to drive Rasmere back to Hades, through the hard floor there came a violent inhuman battle cry! From his place on the blood covered slippery floor Rasmere looked up in time to see the fur covered warrior as he launched himself from the bar.

With teeth and claws flashing Shach Meril flew into the young vampire's upturned face. Howls of rage mixed with the cries of pain as Warrior King battled demon.

Rasmere finally made it to his feet in time to see the Trillii warrior jump free of the vampire. What had once been a face was now little more then destroyed flesh.

Shach Meril landed on a nearby table and joined Rasmere in watching the dying vampire who stumbled left to right like a drunkard before finally tumbling over onto a human corpse. The youth's body spasmed slightly before it began to smoke, the powers of the Trillii warrior's claws killing it quickly.

"I did not knooow," Rasmere gasped breathing hard. "Thaaat you would helllp out a vampire, Lord Shach Meril?"

The cat, its green eyes looking for other attackers, turned quickly regarding the Lord.

"Today you fight with Creed, vampire, and so I am bound to protect you also, but do not forget this warning. After this fight, we will be enemies again!" The cat vaulted from the table heading out of sight leaving Rasmere alone among the carnage.

With a slight bow of his head, Rasmere gave the cat a silent thank you.

Jake had easily dispatched the two vampires that attacked him turning to see Rasmere in certain trouble as the third hovered over the fallen Lord. Before Jake could move to help, he watched the warrior cat attack, flinging himself from the bar. Jake watched amazed at how much damage the cat did in such little time and how quickly the vampire died. Just as fast, the warrior cat disappeared again into the dark shadows.

Jake looked across to where Rasmere stood looking quite ragged for a powerful Lord.

"That was close, hey?" he asked across the floor.

Rasmere nodded pulling himself to his full height. "Yesss it wasss toooo clossse."

Jake jumped over the railing between the two areas of the club as Rasmere pointed to the still open doorway the attackers had sprang from.

"Shaaalll weee?" He invited.

Jake nodded his head. "Yup, lets get the rest of this brood of jackals."

With a nod, the Lord agreed. "I willl lead the wayyy," he headed for the door.

As Jake followed, he had the distinct feeling that Rasmere had just learned a valuable lesson about life. "I guess you never get too old to be surprised," he whispered to himself slipping into the dark staircase.

Selena was cut off from the rest following a hallway that pointed to the restroom area. She could sense great evil coming from down the hall, evil tainted with the smell of magic!

Clutching her knife in one hand and a secret vial of magic powder in the other she padded slowly on the heels of her soft leather boots. She made her way to a door marked maintenance; from inside, the smell of evil filled her senses telling her she had found it. Turning the door handle slowly, she tensed ready to attack with knife or vial as she opened the old door seeing nothing inside but darkness.

With her left hand she reached in running the back of it along the wall finding the switch; with a flip she turned it on. She stepped halfway in looking about the small cramped empty room when from behind, the door flew closed hitting her squarely in the back and shoving her forward.

Selena fell forward feeling the knife as well as the vial torn from her grasp as she hit the floor.

"Come to me, pretty one!" a deep voice ordered and with a rush of hot air, Selena felt herself falling!

She landed hard, several stories below. She could sense she was still in the same building but deep underground.

"The Voodoo Queen was right, you are very beautiful," a deep harsh voice sounded and she turned, looking into the lust filled eyes of the demon Kadahl!

He was tall and muscled far beyond what a human frame could carry but it was the Demon Lord's eyes that caused a chill in Selena's spine.

"Who are you?" she asked warily trying to get to her feet. She hurt badly from the fall she had suffered.

Kadahl looking down at her from the rock on which he perched and chuckled.

"I have made a little bargain with Pakur and that delicious little voodoo witch, Semma. They were afraid of you, Gypsy Witch, and in return for dealing with you myself, they have given you to me for my pleasure," he took a deep breath smiling at her as his eyes devoured her sensuous body.

"I will enjoy every inch of your, Gypsy beauty," he promised stepping slowly from his rock.

Selena could see a huge erection from under his loincloth; there was something grotesque about it.

She met his eyes defiantly. "You will never have me, Demon Lord," she told him. "I am the promised of Darius Creed. No one can change that."

Kadahl continued to chuckle, his massive chest shaking.

"The Gypsy Prince is not here, little beauty, and even if he was, he could not help you. I am a great Demon Lord, answerable to Satan himself, not some Gypsy." He laughed loudly.

He stepped close to her as she finally made it to her feet. "You will never touch me, you ugly beast!"

She pulled the enchanted dagger from her boot and swung. It struck Kadahl across the meaty part of his forearm, biting deeply. The demon jerked his arm back, grasping it as pain flooded into his brain.

"Enchanted steel!" he roared, as intense rage overtook him.

Out of pain and anger, the demon reacted lashing out with his razor sharp claws.

They tore across Selena, ripping her leather coat and the soft cotton shirt underneath as the force of the blow tossed her across the chamber. She fell away from the hard rock wall looking down at her blood-covered hand that had reflexively clutched her mid section.

"Oh no, look what you have made me do!" Kadahl roared in anger. "I wanted you whole and in one piece!"

He swung a huge fist knocking a row of vials from the nearby table.

"Oh, never matter," he yelled tearing his loincloth from his body revealing his erection. "I will use you quickly as you die!"

He took two menacing steps forward as Selena winced in pain and blood continued to flow freely from her wounds.

She clawed her way back from his advance reaching for her bag with a blood-covered hand.

"I don't think so," Kadahl laughed at her, as he pinned the bag to the stone floor with a foot. "There is nothing in there that can help you now." He reached down and jerked the bag from her weakening fingers.

For the first time in her young life, Selena felt helplessly doomed; there was little she would be able to do soon unless she could stop the bleeding.

With a second sadistic laugh, Kadahl tossed the bag over his shoulder into the far wall where it rebounded to the floor spilling its contents over the cold stone.

Kadahl was so intent on Selena that he didn't bother to turn to see what had slipped from the bag. It would be a mistake, as from under the flap of the leather case rolled the ball of Asmus and it was unwrapped!

Kadahl stretched his massive frame allowing his unbridled lust to flow through his body. It would soon be satisfied and by such a beauty.

He was feeling proud of himself when the furry figure slipped past his feet and planted itself in front of the wounded woman.

"You!" the Demon Lord called out his eyebrows rising in anger.

"How dare you interfere!"

With undaunted courage, Shach Meril looked defiantly up into the demon's eyes.

"You cannot have her," his purr-like voice sounded in the rock chamber as his green eyes settled on the Demon Lord.

"I cannot!" Kadahl roared in laughter. "You do not have the power to stop me!"

Shach Meril dipped his head. "That is true, I cannot. You have been summoned and a bargain struck. It is not for me to interfere."

However, he did not move from in front of the injured woman.

Kadahl noted the swelled chest of the defiant cat, as well as the confident look.

"Then get out of my way," he ordered looking through lust filled eyes.

Shach Meril shook his head. "I cannot. I have agreed to come here and keep her safe for another who cannot travel as fast as I," he answered.

Kadahl frowned, his patience growing thin. "Then why are you in my way, cat; you know as well as I that you cannot harm me here."

The king of the Trillii dipped his head agreeing.

"No, I cannot kill you, Demon Lord, not under these circumstances. But I could battle you to keep you away from her until help came."

"Then why get in my way, cat? You know I could kill you."

Shach Meril looked up at him again resolve shining in those deep green eyes.

"And I would gladly give my life for that of a human, Kadahl. It is my solemn oath as a warrior of the Trillii. However, I will not have to do so." He sat back on his haunches.

Kadahl met the animal's calm gaze.

"And why not cat?" he demanded, flexing the razor sharp claws of his hands.

"Because I am now here, demon."

Kadahl turned, knowing too well the voice behind him.

The rush of lust turned to fear as the Demon Lord turned, meeting the snarling face of Asmus!

The balding Gypsy protector let loose with a battle cry that froze the blood of the Lord's veins as his right palm shot out and struck Kadahl straight into the sternum!

Creed stopped to catch his breath as he peered down the dark corridor cut from solid stone. He looked down at his blood-covered weapons and sighed, breathing deeply.

This maze of underground tunnels was full of the Lord's vampires, as well as human minions that he had been feeding on.

Creed had put an end to at least a dozen lost souls so far and expected more to pop up from the rock. He had to admire Pakur; if he had been ignored for much longer, he would've had a huge coven of followers under him.

From behind him came the shuffling of booted feet and a familiar, age-old odor.

"Rasmere," he called out into the dark gloom. "I am here."

He could hear the boots change direction,

coming closer his way, until Jake's familiar face met his in the gloom.

"Hey, Creed, nice seeing ya," he greeted cheerfully even as the sweat streaking down his face.

The blood covered sword told Creed his partner had been busy.

Rasmere soon appeared peering over the Hunter's shoulder.

"Theyyy are thick Creeeed," he said.

The Gypsy nodded agreeing. "Your bastard vampire was doing one hell of a job," he admitted.

Rasmere grunted. "Hee haas done mooore then thaaat Creeeed. Hee haaass taught theeemm to haaate their owwwnn," the Lord spat.

Creed felt his eyes narrowing. "What do you mean?"

Jake motioned with his head back to the Lord. "He was decked by one of his own boys tonight."

Creed raised an eyebrow, an amused look on his face. "Their human side Rasmere?"

Rasmere nodded, a look of disgust mixed with a deep frown.

"Yesss, the bastardization processss, I am sssure," he answered shaking his head in disgust. "Nooothing, Gypsssy, isss asss it wasss. I long for the older easssier timesss."

Creed grunted with a nod of his head and even Jake had to agree.

"It must be a real shocker at times, the way things have become," he added.

From down the hall, Creed pointed to a faint glowing red light that seamed to flicker in strength.

310

"Pakur has another surprise for us down there I bet."

Jake raised the enchanted sword of Takada. "We'd better not keep him waiting then," he looked at the vampire and the Gypsy prince raising an eyebrow in question. "Should we?"

His expression grim in the dark hallway Rasmere scraped his claws against the rock as anger continued to build in his lithe frame.

"I want to see this bastard-breeding Vampire Lord shudder in fear," he pointed to Creed as he looked at Jake. "You watch this man-boy before he kills Pakur. He will show him his humility and break him before he ends the bastard's life."

Creed rolled his eyes but Rasmere added.

"I have seen it happen before," and with a wisp of his long leather coat he nodded ahead of them. "But you are right, Jacob Reid, we should be on our way."

The Gypsy Prince turned down the rock cavern. "Yes let us get this over with."

His broad back began to fade in the half-lit shadows.

Rasmere held out his hand. "After you Jacob," he offered and the martial arts master returned a slight mock bow.

"Thank you sir."

Together they followed the Gypsy.

They crouched near the source of the red flickering light.

"A room," Creed whispered grasping his blades.

"Probably more of the coven awaits."

Jake nodded with a tense but determined look on his face. "Let's do it then," he answered.

Before the Gypsy could decide exactly how he wanted to enter the possible trap, a strong voice from within called out.

"Cooome innn Dariusss Creeed. We have beeen waiting for you."

As the words faded from his ears, Creed turned, looking to his companions. Jake answered with a nod and Rasmere whispered.

"I aam ready, Gypsssy, for whatever maaay wait inssside."

"Okay," Creed stood holding his blades tightly as he stepped into the cavern followed by Jake and Rasmere.

The picture that met his gaze made him stand up straight, drawing air sharply into his lungs, as behind him both Jake and Rasmere stiffened.

In front of them sat twelve Vampire Lords reclining in throne-like chairs several feet in the air above them.

"It isss a great pleasssuuure thaaat the famousss Dariusss Creeeed comesss tooo visit us." The demon to the right of the empty center chair greeted them. Had that chair been filled there would have been thirteen vampires.

Rasmere stepped forward before Creed could answer.

"What isss thisss?" he demanded his rage growing.

The Gypsy looked at the Lord wondering what was under his saddle this time.

Above them, the vampire that had spoken first, stood matching the Lord's stare.

"Rasmere wee honor you alssso, great Lord and memberrr of the Old World council," the vampire dipped his cloaked head in reverence but it did little to soothe the Lord.

"Whaaat did you juuust sssay tooo me?" Rasmere asked his anger barely in check.

Creed looked at the Lord wondering where this was headed.

The vampire in the purple robes slowly raised his hands flipping back his hood. From where Creed stood, he could see the milky eyes and the lightly silver tinted hair of a young Lord.

"I welcooome you Lorrd Rassmere," he repeated folding his arms in the wide sleeves of his cloak as he regarded Rasmere.

The centuries old Lord was starting to fume and Creed could sense it.

"What is going on?" he asked from the side of his mouth.

Rasmere exhaled so loudly it sounded like a bull preparing to charge.

"There isss something under the table here, Gypsssy," he explained through pursed teeth.

Creed frowned. "What are you talking about?" he asked.

He was feeling uncertain. If something made a great Vampire Lord like Rasmere uneasy, it was worth being afraid of.

Rasmere looked up at the young vampire.

"Dooo you waaant tooo tell him or should I?" he asked hatred in his voice.

The vampire flinched as if stung by the words of the great Lord.

"There isss nooo reasooon to beee ruuude, Lord Rasmere."

It was the same tone one would use on a young child. Turning to Creed, he continued.

"I am caaalled Golgath and I aaam the chooosen of the Master Pakuuur. You see, Gypssy Huuunter, Rasmere and the ooold Lords of the councccil would like to seeee all of ussss gooone. You seeee weee are the future, the council of the newww world and weee are ready to chaaaallenge for our place among them."

He pointed a clawed hand at Rasmere who stood shaking in uncontrolled rage!

The Gypsy struck Kadahl so hard in the solar plexus that he felt the air pushed from his massive chest as he was blasted from his feet! He struck the far rock wall as Asmus, that little balding human, slowly took off his cloak, a sadistic smile playing across his face.

"I have waited for this, Kadahl, for a thousand or so years, and now you will pay for your sins!"

Kadahl scrambled to find his feet while Asmus lay his cloak softly over Selena.

"How is she?" he asked Shach Meril who was monitoring her.

The Warrior King looked up sadness in his green eyes.

"She is not good, Asmus. You must end this quickly so I can go for help or both of our missions will be forfeited."

Asmus nodded, a look of determination on his face.

"Do not worry brave one," he assured the cat. "This will be over soon."

"Ready yourself, Kadahl, for you are about to meet Satan himself," the old man warned.

The massive demon laughed as he rocked back on his heels.

"You, little man?" he asked. "How dare you come here challenging me?"

The Demon Lord stuck a finger in his chest full of self-confidence.

Standing relaxed, the legendary warrior named Asmus lifted an eyebrow in mirth.

"So, come on then, Kadahl. Lets get this out of the way so I can go about my business."

The demon flared his nostrils. "So you think it will be so easy?"

He took a step forward flexing his muscles.

Asmus shrugged. "I think I have defeated bigger monsters then you before breakfast."

This caused Kadahl to lower his head and charge with a tremendous roar of anger. He was intent on hooking the old man on his horns and tossing him about the room until the stone walls and ceiling turned him to pulp.

It was not to be, however, as quickly, Asmus stepped away and dropped to a knee delivering a blinding fast foot sweep. It caught the demon in mid stride and sent him off balance. Roaring, Kadahl flew into the far stone wall!

Asmus stood as Kadahl, his bull like nose

streaming blood, stood with murder in his eyes.

"I am going to kill you slow!" the demon promised, as again he charged the old warrior.

Asmus dropped to a knee firing a hard straight fist into the demon's midsection; it brought Kadahl to his knees gasping for air.

The mighty bull-man tried to breathe on one knee as Asmus stood.

"Good-bye, Kadahl; give my regards to Satan!" and he reached around the massive neck using a technique taught by years of practice.

The old Gypsy clamped his arms hard around the chin and forehead of the demon and with a twist of his upper body, he snapped Kadahl's massive neck.

As the demon fell lifeless to the hard rock floor, Asmus looked to Shach Meril.

"Go," the Gypsy ordered. "Find Creed and tell him about Selena!"

As the cat disappeared from the room, Asmus walked over to the woman who could barely keep her eyes open.

He leaned down next to her, listening to her whispered words.

"Yes," he agreed with a nod as he met her eyes. "I will see to it."

As if satisfied, the Gypsy Witch closed her eyes and lay back against the stone.

Asmus put his hand against her stomach laying his palm there as he prayed. He could feel the blood of her wounds running over his callused hands.

Creed looked to Rasmere. "Are they saying what I think they are?"

The Lord nodded, his icy glare burning a hole through Golgath.

"I think theyyy are sayyying thaaat theeyy are the newww council," he answered, with a voice full of hatred. "A council of Tuuurned Bassstard vampiresss."

From behind them, Jake grunted.

"I am getting it now," he said. "The Turned vampires are sick of being second rate so now they have made their own council with their own rules."

He nodded to himself, understanding as Creed's eyes narrowing looked upon Golgath and the rest of Pakur's chosen.

Placing his enchanted blades in his belt he held out his open palms.

"Is Pakur, as well as the rest of you, aware that to become a Lord and to sit on the council is a very long complicated process?" he asked. "You just can't make one up."

Jake agreed stepping forward. "Ya, you just can't buy some black robes, make up a secret handshake and decide to become the World Vampire council."

Seething at their side Rasmere raised an eyebrow.

"Where isss Looordd Pakuuurrr?" he demanded crossing his arms in front of him.

Golgath stepped away from his chair placing his body directly in front of the throne.

"Heee hasss gooone to the oold country," he answered. "To continue thisss processs."

Creed frowned. "What process and where in the old country?"

Golgath looked back to his fellow council members who all gave him a nod. He turned back to the Gypsy. "There isss nooo reassson nooot to tellll you Creeeed," shifting his eyes to Rasmere, he added. "Weee are nooot afraid of the ooold one or the Gypsssy Huntersss."

At Creed's side, Rasmere took a step ahead.

"Oold oone?" he blurted out flexing his claws. "Weee willl seee about thaaat, and ressspect for the Huntersss is what has allooowed me to become oold!"

Creed stopped him in mid stride. "Not yet," he cautioned as he turned to Golgath. "So tell me then, vampire, what is Pakur up to?"

Golgath looked at the poised Rasmere a taunting look on his young face. With a blink of his eyes, he switched his gaze to Creed.

"It is simple, Gypsy, Lord Pakur goes to your estate to locate the Toscanno girl; she is still needed." For Creed, it didn't take long for the information to sink in.

"Why?" Creed asked in a dry serious tone.

Golgath cocked his head slightly. "The legeeend of Broshmer," he answered with a slight smile.

Creed's frown deepened. "What?"

To the Gypsy's side, howeve,r Rasmere roared in unrestrained anger.

"Tooo saayyy thaaat naaame in huuuman company isss sacriligousss!" he shouted. "Noo vampire thaaat values his soulll would dare!" the Lord was trembling with rage as he pointed to

318

Golgath. "You willll paaay for being soo arrogant," he promised.

Golgath's smile grew as he raised his arms. "You willll live to tellll nooo one, old man."

He sneered openly, as behind him the rest of the chosen council of Pakur stood, tossing off their robes!

"They are going to attack!" Creed yelled in warning as he pulled his blades.

"I want Golgath!" Rasmere called out and he launched himself across the chamber.

In a flurry of robes, the older Lord struck the younger vampire throwing them both backward over the throne chairs.

"Looks like they will never get along, doesn't it?" Jake chuckled as he swung, the sword of Takada spinning it in his hand.

Creed, a serious look on his face watched the rest of the chosen walk slowly down off the throne.

"Get ready Jake this is going to be nasty," he warned as they were circled by the hungry eyed demons.

Jake nodded back as he started to concentrate on his side of the room. "No time for rest here," he agreed as in front of him two vampires made their move!

Jake reacted, the Gypsy potion in his system allowing him to move faster than thought. He kicked the first vampire hard enough to knock the demon onto his back fifteen feet away.

The second one jumped at him, flying into the air and swinging his deadly sharp claws. Jake used his left hand to swat the clawed hands aside as he spun, swinging the sword in a vicious backstroke.

The razor sharp blade rendered the vampire's head from its shoulders as another unseen attacker raked its claws down Jake's back.

The Hunter spun as the demon froze looking from its claws to the coat, which remained unharmed. Jake didn't give the demon time to get his wits as he plunged the sword through the vampire's dead heart!

"If you screw around, pretty soon you won't be around!" Jake yelled as he kicked the corpse from his blade.

Only feet away, Jake watched as Creed stopped a rushing vampire by clutching his throat and forcing the monster to his knees. The martial arts master shook his head in wonder. No matter how many times he saw Creed fight, he was amazed at the man's abilities.

As Creed held the first vampire pinned to his knees, he side kicked a second demon, knocking the thing back into several others, stopping their rush. With a quick thrust of his knife, Creed sent the demon at his feet to Satan as the others regained their feet, ready for a second attack.

As they started to come at him, he looked quickly to the spot where Rasmere had tumbled over the throne room chairs, his hands locked securely around Golgath's neck!

SEVENTEEN

Rasmere felt the anger inside him burst forth unchecked as he strangled Golgath below him on the hard rock floor.

"Sooo you think you are myyy eeequal, you insssolent pup!" Rasmere yelled loudly while he pounded the younger Lord unmercifully into the stone.

Golgath tried to tear away Rasmere's talons but could not. He was beginning to turn a dark red as the air was being kept from flowing into his lungs.

In his rage, Rasmere rose up above his enemy ready to deliver a killing blow. Golgath saw his chance. He drove his knee up hard into the older vampire's groin.

Reacting in pain and surprise, Rasmere fell off the youth rolling over onto his back on the floor as he grasped his privates. His breathing came in gasps and he could feel blinding pain in front of his eyes as he wondered if he would ever sire a True Blood baby again! He struggled to his knees, still gasping for air, as beside him he was aware that Golgath had struggled to a chair and was pulling himself up also.

Trying to get air in his body Rasmere stood on wobbly knees his groin still on fire from the blow. He saw that Golgath was almost upright already.

"Nooot thaaat easssy." He sneered through clenched teeth as he kicked the younger demon behind the left knee sending him shooting back to the rock floor.

Golgath rolled as Rasmere jumped over him taking a swing with his right hand. The razor sharp claws tore through the youth's clothing, causing deep wounds to the skin underneath. Demon blood ran freely, soaking the black cloth of Golgath's shirt as he climbed to his feet, meeting Rasmere's eyes.

"I willl kill you ooold ooone!" he repeated his earlier threat as he forced himself to stand extending his claws.

Rasmere gave him a short curt nod. "You are iiinviiited tooo start aaat any time."

Golgath took the first strike, his clawed hand shooting at Rasmere's face. With tremendous speed, the powerful Lord blocked the blow and turned it aside. In a flash of moving leather, Rasmere spun counter, attacking with a sharp back fist that impacted the side of the youth's head.

Again, Golgath fell to the floor but quickly shot back to his feet whipping up a heavy throne chair. He caught Rasmere coming in too quickly and crashed the chair down onto the Lord's head. The furniture splintered pushing a stunned Rasmere back into the far wall. With a piece of chair leg in his clawed hand, Golgath charged trying to plunge it into the older vampire's chest. Rasmere saw him in time to roll sideways avoiding being impaled. The chair leg struck hard stone instead of unholy flesh and Golgath grew angrier, swinging a sideways blow that caught Rasmere in the middle of the back.

Caught by the flat side of the wood, he was thrown down to the floor where he rolled and in one motion he was back up on his feet. With a roar, he lunged back at Golgath his claws raking the younger vampire's face and neck.

Pain and anger mixed in the young demon's scream as he fell back against the rock, dropping the chair leg. Blood spurted from the wounds covering Rasmere as he stepped closer to Golgath delivering two swift strikes. The claws of the great Lord did terrible damage as they tore across Golgath's face twice rendering skin and tearing an eyeball from its socket.

Badly wounded, the young Lord staggered forward unable to see and barely able to take a breath. Rasmere stepped behind the youth grasping the head and neck of the bastard Lord and pulling him back into his chest.

Rasmere leaned his mouth close to the wounded Lord's ear.

"I ammm Looorrd Rasmere of The House of Haeth. I aammm oooover twoo thousssand yearsss old. Whennn the young learrrn tooo ressspect what the ooold have toooo say, then and ooonly then will theyvy hope tooo gain powwwer!"

The words came out filled with anger as Rasmere drew the sharp claw of his right forefinger along Golgath's neck.

It took less then ten seconds for the young Lord to die and as his knees gave out Rasmere did nothing to keep his body from hitting the cold rock floor.

"I seeee the caussse of Pakur's madnessss nooow." The older Lord said, looking at the corpse on the floor at his blood covered boots. "But Creeed willl stooop himmm," he added as he walked from beyond the throne area to where the battle still raged in the chamber!

Creed pulled a blade from the chest of a dying vampire while he kicked another away from him. As the demon stumbled backward, Jake appeared. With a flash, the blade of the katana slashed through the vampire's neck sending its head flying across the chamber.

With a smile, Jake gave the Gypsy the thumbs up as he elbowed another demon off his back. Creed himself was again under attack as a shape rushed from the dark corner of the chamber. He sidestepped and the vampire lost his balance shooting past, stumbling.

The demon struck the chamber wall and used it

to turn around, coming back at Creed with tremendous speed and power. The Gypsy Prince dropped to one knee just under the sharp claws as he allowed the vampire to impale himself on his outstretched blade.

Looking around quickly Creed could see that the fight was almost over as Jake drove his sword through the last of Pakur's chosen few.

He stood covered in vampire blood, feeling wet and sticky from it. With a grunt he pushed the corpse from his blade-it was already starting to smoke-and saw a very battered looking Rasmere stalk from behind the throne chairs, which now were strewn about the rear of the chamber.

"Golgath?" he asked.

"Tryyying tooo explain hisss crimesss to Satan right about nooow," the Lord answered.

Jake wiped the katana on a curtain in the chamber.

"Well he ain't alone in that one," he commented. "But what in the hell was he talking about, what is the legend of Broshmer?"

Creed frowned. "I am curious about that too; I have never heard the name before?"

Rasmere took a deep breath, his coat hung on him like ribbons of leather, he was battered, bruised and his balls hurt like someone was driving a nail through them.

He pulled up a chair from among the smoking corpses, his released breath sounding like a deep sigh.

"Ittt isss a naaame that no mortal isss ever supposed tooo hear," he began. "The verrry fact

Golgaaath sssaid it in front of you showssss hisss arrogance," he paused and Creed, sheathing his blades, crossed his arms in front of him.

"What is this all about Rasmere? We need to know. The Toscanno family is at great risk now."

Rasmere looked up at his age-old enemy. "He wasss one of the firssst, Creeeed," the Lord explained.

Creed's eyes narrowed immediately.

"One of the nameless?"

Rasmere nodded. "Yesss, ooone of Satansss favorite fallen angelssss."

Jake shook his head. "Wow! You mean one of the very first vampires?"

Rasmere nodded again. "Broshmer wasss the third tooo leave the Dark Angelsss ssside and coming to Earth so long ago," he appeared sad as he looked at the floor. "Heee wasss alssssooo my sssire," he said quietly.

Jake stopped cleaning the sword as he studied the Vampire Lord sitting humbly on the chair, Creed nodded slowly.

"And that also has something to do with all of this, doesn't it?"

Rasmere looked up, his face unreadable but his eyes blazing.

"Yesss, Gypsssy Prince, sssit and I willll tellll you thisss tale," he motioned to a pair of chairs.

Jake and Creed both sat as invited waiting patiently for the Lord to begin. Rasmere sat forward, his elbows on his knees as he began.

"A long time agooo a young woman wasss bitten by a vampire in a sssmall villllage deeep in

326

the Russsain Steppesss. She was nooot killed by the bite and the next dayyy her woundsss were dissscovered by her family. Well, you remember, Creeeed, how many of the people haaad powersss back then when they ssstill believed."

Creed nodded; he remembered well.

"The ooold man desssigned great wardsss of pooower that kept the vampire away and fed the young girrrl powerful herbsss that eventually healed her completely. The vampire wasss Broshmer, my sssire. He wasss the mosst powerful of the original chosssen of Satan and a great Lord of the firssst council. Asss I have said, the girrrlll wasss able to recover from hisss bite but there wasss one thing that Broshmer had dooone that could not be cleansssed from her system. He haaad given her a drooop of his unhooooly blooood. It hasss been a long time but asss far asss I can trace the lineage of young Angela Toscanno, she isss a descendant of my sssire and carries his blooood. It toook thiss long but over the centuriesss a child was born whooo hasss the same exact blooood asss Broshmer. She is not vampire but she isss of hisss line, and in fact she is of mine alssso," at this point he stopped.

"Oh shit," Creed whispered sitting back.

Rasmere nodded. "It isss why Pakur wantsss her."

From where he sat, Jake frowned.

"What does it all mean?" he asked feeling the other two knew something he didn't.

Rasmere looked at the Hunter. "Pakur isss a turned vampire but very hungry for power. He knowsss that if he can drink the blooood of such a legendary vampire, he would becooome the first of all of usss still on Earth; then he would be able to taaake ooover the council. His bite would give great powersss to his followers, they would become as powerful, maybe more so, then True Bloods."

This caused Jake to whistle softly. "Like this Dolmage thing then, he could create the one hundred powerful Lords he needed to become a Supreme Being and return to Hell sitting next to Satan himself."

Creed turned looking wide eyed at his fellow Hunter and Rasmere himself shot Jake a look.

"What?" he asked.

Creed stood. "I had not even considered such a thing," he admitted.

Rasmere was soon standing also. "Nor had I. Well dooone, Jacob Reid," he slapped Jake on the shoulder with a blood-covered hand.

Jake smiled. "Well of course I knew I would catch on pretty soon to all of this," the Hunter joined them standing.

"But what do we do now?" he asked them.

Before anyone could voice an opinion, Shach Meril burst through the chamber door.

"Come quickly, Gypsy Prince. Selena has been badly injured!"

As a unit the three bloody fighters ran down the tunnels following the King of the Trillii!

"What happened?" Creed asked bursting into the chamber where Selena lay.

Asmus looked up. "She was attacked by the

voodoo demon, Kadahl," The old Gypsy explained, pointing to the piled up corpse of the Demon Lord.

As Creed kneeled gently next to her side Selena was barely able to put her hand into his. She tried to speak, but could barely whisper. Creed tore open her shirt seeing the terrible slash wounds that bled badly.

"Oh Jesus," Jake said over his shoulder.

Asmus nodded grimly. "She is fading, Darius, she needs medical attention quickly or she will surely die. There is too much bleeding."

Creed looked from her gentle face to the wounds; he knew what Asmus was saying was correct.

"We are too far away from the hospital," he said through pursed lips without looking up at them. "There is no way we can get her there soon enough."

Jake knelt at his side. "What if we bind her up tightly and then call for a ambulance to meet us upstairs?"

Creed looked at him and to Asmus, the old man shook his head.

"She will not be able to hold on that long."

Jake looked at the sad eyes of the Gypsy Prince. "So you are telling me there is nothing humanly possible we can do to save her life?"

Creed turned back to Selena who was now completely unconscious and held her hand as Asmus turned from the couple, fighting back tears of his own.

Across the chamber, Rasmere had been studying the dead Demon Lord and listening. Suddenly, he stood and walked over to Creed. The Lord had switched to his human form and now placed a hand gently on his shoulder.

"You are right," he said softly. "There is nothing a human can do, but I can."

"I am the most powerful Lord alive, Creed. I can take her to a hospital in seconds and you can follow later."

The Gypsy looked up at the vampire, his face unreadable.

Both Jake and Asmus also turned regarding the Lord as Shach Meril walked softly next to the Gypsy placing a padded foot on Creed's boot.

"Allow him to help," the cat said in a soft but firm tone, a tone that allowed no argument.

Creed swallowed hard as he gently placed his arms under his lover and picked her up, before he handed her to Rasmere he paused meeting the Lord's eyes.

"I have lost everyone I have ever loved in this world at one time or another," he said his voice almost breaking. "But if you do this for me, Lord Rasmere, I will return the gift a hundred fold."

Rasmere reached over taking the badly wounded Gypsy Witch into his arms.

"You have already done much for me, Gypsy Prince," he said. "I do this out of respect, respect earned by you over the last thousand years or so."

And as he shifted her once in his thin but strong arms the Vampire Lord closed his eyes and lowered his head. Suddenly, they were gone!

☐

Creed stood taking a deep breath. "Good luck,

Vampire Lord."

Asmus walked over to Creed. "It will be okay." He tried to sound reassuring. Then with a serious look on his old face Asmus asked, "Where is the priest; was he in here?"

Creed shook his head.

"No, we failed to find him," he admitted, concern for his beloved still in his mind.

Jake however had no problem explaining the story. "Well, from what we can tell, this Pakur idiot has tracked down the living ancestor of one well known vampire, Lord Broshmer, who also happens to be Rasmere's old man, or something like that, in vampire talk. This ancestor, it appears, is the young woman, Angela Toscanno, who we have saved once from the clutches of Pakur. Well, anyway we now have found out that maybe this guy is looking to put the bite on Angela and get to be the super dude of vampires, so he can go back to Satan and be a bigwig down under." Jake paused. "I am getting it right, ain't I?" he asked Creed.

The Gypsy nodded. "Yes, with an interesting twist on it all but you are right," he agreed.

Jake smiled. "I figured I was close. Well anyway, the only thing we can't figure is the role Father Joe has in it all."

Asmus rubbed his baldhead as he looked at Shach Meril. "I don't know," he admitted to them with a shrug.

The cat, however, twisted its head a minute in thought.

"It is an old story," Shach Meril started, as he looked at them with green eyes. "But there has been rumors over the years of a time when the vampire could once again rule over man. It tells of a wedding performed by a virgin Catholic Priest joining a great Lord of the Nosferatu and a young woman who carries the blood of the ages. Until now, we never understood what that meant. Now it would seem, we are finding the answers to the mysteries of the ages."

They all nodded, agreeing on these points.

"And he goes back to the Elbe River valley for the ceremony," Creed whispered. "We are going to my home, Jacob, to fight the good fight," as the Gypsy walked from the chamber Jake scratched his chin.

"Cool," he told himself.

As he walked past the figure of the dead Kadahl, Jake stopped. Looking down on the demon he took two steps back and then kicked the corpse as hard as he could.

"That was for Selena," he said as he also left the room.

The emergency charge nurse looked up over her half glasses as for the second time tonight a group of blood covered men walked in.

"Don't tell me; you are the second half of the gang war?" she asked sarcastically.

She watched expressionless as the broad shouldered serious looking one walked to her desk and stopped.

"A woman was brought in here by a man in a badly shredded leather coat. Could you tell us where they are now?" he asked, his tone hard and short as his eyes scanned the emergency room.

The old nurse stood; she had seen them all in her times and no one scared her anymore.

"Listen, Mister, sit down and I will call you when they are ready to be seen."

She pushed the glasses back on her face about to sit down when from out of nowhere an iron-like hand grabbed her arm.

She looked up into the stranger's dark eyes. "Do not put me off, woman," the suddenly cold voice demanded. "You would not like me upset."

The nurse felt her voice freeze in her throat as the security guard jumped up from his desk, reaching for his weapon.

Quickly Jake was at the man's side holding the wrist down on the weapon in its holster.

"Believe me, buddy, you don't want to do that. That man is just worried about his wife and he is not the kind of man you want to push."

The guard looked up into Jake's eyes as the Hunter nodded, adding weight to his words.

Just then, Asmus strolled in with Shach Meril riding his shoulder, a wide grin on his face as he walked over to the counter and handed the nurse a flower.

"Please, young lady, help us out," he asked, his voice full of charm.

The nurse looked at the old Gypsy as Creed released her arm.

"Do not be talking nice to me," she snapped. "I am old enough to see through an old pervert like you."

Asmus recoiled in mock surprise and shock. "I am far from a pervert, madam." He extended the hand with the flower in it.

She looked at him suspiciously, but finally took the single rose, smelling it.

"Well, thank you," she said. "But the filthy animal has to go," she added pointing to the Warrior King.

Asmus made a face as he scratched his chin and looked at her. "I wish you wouldn't have said that." He shook his head.

From the old Gypsy's shoulder, Shach Meril stood regarding the nurse with his green eyes.

"Tell this insolent old woman that she has no idea who she insults with that statement," the cat's voice rang out.

The charge nurse looked wide-eyed at the cat. "Did that cat just talk?" she asked.

Asmus nodded. "You are the one who asked for it. A Warrior King of the Trillii does not accept such comments. His people were protecting ours since King Tut was a gleam in his daddy's eye."

The nurse was about to answer, when Doctor Preston Robards walked down the hall.

"Darius, Jake and, yes of course, Taz," he greeted them extending his hand to Asmus. "I do not know you, sir, but you travel in good company."

Asmus took the offered hand. "I know who you are, doctor, I am never far from the Gypsies."

Doctor Robards nodded as he walked quickly to Creed taking the Hunter by the arm.

"She is here," he said quietly as he led him from the emergency room. Creed nodded as the doctor went on. "We have sewn her up and given her blood. I won't be foolish enough to ask how she was slashed so badly or who that is with her," the young doctor shook his head. "He came in here yelling for help and threatening the staff. Good thing I was just leaving after an emergency call in. I recognized Selena and took her under my care. He is still with her," Robards said.

Creed nodded. "Rasmere stayed by her?"

"He said he would kill the man who tried to remove him and I don't know about you, Creed, but I wasn't going to try."

The Gypsy chuckled. "Wise choice, doc, believe me," and he allowed the doctor to lead him down the hallway.

Rasmere whirled, tensing as they came through the door of the hospital room; he relaxed as he saw Creed led by the doctor.

"You made it," he observed clasping his hands behind his back and stepping back from the bed Selena lay in.

"Your Gypsy Witch lives," he added with a slight bow of his head.

Creed walked away from the doctor and over to the vampire's side. He clamped a firm hand on Rasmere's shoulder.

"As I vowed," he repeated. "One hundred fold."

Rasmere actually chuckled. "Don't make promises, Gypsy," he replied.

"Only those I can keep," Creed assured him.

Asmus walked to the Gypsy's side. "She will be

okay warrior," he said putting his hand on Creed's shoulder. "You have business in Europe."

Creed nodded. "You are right, old one; we must go at once and head off the fate Pakur would seal for the Toscanno family."

Asmus shook his head sadly. "No, Darius, I cannot make this journey with you."

Creed frowned but he knew better then to question Asmus about such things.

"Okay," he answered. "Go with God, old friend. Jake and I will-"

Before he could finish Asmus repeated the same sad look

"No he cannot," the old Gypsy again answered, and this time even Jake had a bewildered look.

"Sure I can," he tried to defend himself but Asmus shot him a look that shut him down.

Creed studied the old man. "What is it going to take?"

Shach Meril jumped from the old man's shoulder and landed lightly on the bed walking over to Selena and laying by her side.

Creed frowned. "What? You are staying here too?"

The cat looked up at him. "Prince of the Gypsies," the soft voice rang in the room. "I lied a bit when I said I came here to watch over Jacob Reid," he paused looking to Asmus who nodded.

"Tell him."

The King of the Trillii returned his eyes to Creed.

"I was sent here on a mission, a mission much like the one Belo once departed from home to accomplish. I was sent here to protect a special child. I was asked by Asmus to protect the life of the unborn Gypsy Prince growing inside Selena."

Shach Meril paused as he looked at the assembled faces in the room.

"What a baby it will be!" the cat added. "Saved by a Vampire Lord and guarded by a King of the Trillii. Some things do tend to surprise us after all," He lay back against Selena, quiet for the moment.

Asmus however looked at Jake. "That is why you must stay here, young Hunter. Creed and Rasmere must go to Europe and stop Pakur, but you will have to stay and, in the father's absence, guard the unborn baby as if your own. It is not just a child you watch, Jacob Reid, but the next Prince of the Gypsy people."

Jake stood, his mouth open. For the first time in his life, he had nothing to say.

After saying their good-byes, Asmus followed Creed and Rasmere from the hospital room.

"Do not worry about her or us," the old man said, clasping his hand. "We will be okay. After all, Shach Meril watches over all of us."

Creed nodded, returning the handshake. "We will stop Pakur," he assured the old man.

Asmus nodded. "I know you will, old friend, but don't forget you will need help with the Voodoo Queen. Powerful help."

Creed chuckled. "I already have that worked out," and with a wave he walked down the hall to where Rasmere stood looking into the rising sun; he turned as Creed approached. "I am glad to hear that you will soon have a son," the vampire said.

"There is something romantic about it all."

At his side Creed chuckled. "Yes, I think, Rasmere, that you are right," And with a turn they walked for the exit of the hospital, enemies for centuries, allies for a few days.

EIGHTEEN

Creed stepped from the rented car taking a good long look at the Inn where he had arranged to meet Joel, the caretaker of his estate and the Toscanno family's butler Wilfred. As he slammed the door on the little car, Rasmere unfolded himself from the passenger seat, grumbling for the hundredth time that the car had not been designed to fit someone with his long frame.

With a chuckle and a shake of his head, Creed stepped to the Inn door.

"Remember," he cautioned the Lord. "The people of this village are Gypsy and very superstitious. If they have the slightest notion that you are a vampire, they will have you strung up and burning by lunch time."

Rasmere nodded in response. "I realize that, Creed. I will stay in my human disguise and behave. I have no intention of messing this up while we are so close to Pakur."

They walked through the door eyes, immediately scanning the dozen or so locals who sipped their coffee or ate their breakfast over the local newspaper.

They stopped in the entryway, looking for a suitable table for their little meeting when a crash of plates and cups caused Creed to snap his gaze across the restaurant.

"Oh my God!" an old woman cried out, as she came stumbling across the floor, her hands outstretched.

"Prince Darius, you have returned!" She cried out in a voice filled with love and respect.

The people in the restaurant turned their eyes, looking over the newcomers, their faces dropping in awe.

"What is it, Momma?"

An old man stepped from the kitchen looking from the smashed dishes on the floor to his wife, as he wiped his hands on his apron.

"Come, Julius," she cried out. "He is back. Our Prince Darius has returned."

The old man began to tremble as he walked across the floor.

Noticing the confused looks on the patrons in his inn, the old man stopped, turning on them in anger.

"All of you, take off your hats and get on a knee. Don't you young people recognize your Prince?"

Creed was about to tell them it was all right just as the old woman, her name was Sophia, he remembered, knelt before him bowing her head.

She grasped his hands, her grip surprisingly strong for an old woman. He knew they were hands tempered by hard work.

Julius was quickly by his wife's side. "I have to apologize for the young ones," he blurted out waving among the room behind him. "Most of them have never met you but they have heard the stories of our great Prince."

Behind Creed, Rasmere grunted. "It would appear the young seem to be forgetful everywhere these days," he whispered into the Gypsy's ear.

Creed shot him a look over his shoulder. "Maybe if I had not been so busy chasing you all these years they would know me better."

Rasmere shrugged. "True," he agreed.

Creed looked back over the assembled village folk who sat among the tables in the Inn openly staring at him now as he helped Sophia back to her feet.

"Stand, there is no need to kneel before me," he said gently.

She stood, a look of wonderment on her face while she clutched her husband's arm.

"It is a good sign that you have come back," she said. "Things are so strange these days with the young people in this village. Maybe the return of our prince will help give them something to structure their own lives after," She looked up at her husband with a nod.

Julius turned to Creed. "There has been word that strangers are staying in your estate; Americans, and the rumor has been that you were dead and they had bought the lands of your family," he explained.

Creed chuckled. "As you can see I am still alive and healthy and the family at my estate are guests. They are being hidden there from vampires," he admitted to them.

The old couple nodded, it had been the mission of the Gypsy people to defend others from the demons of the night.

"I should have realized it would be something like that," Julius said.

"Now come, you must be tired and hungry from your trip."

He took the Prince by the elbow and opened a palm to Rasmere waving them to a private table in the corner.

"Thank you," Creed said as they sat and a bottle of fine red wine was placed before them. The old woman hurried to bring them something to eat.

Soon, Creed was eating a thick stew of venison and munching fresh bread as Rasmere enjoyed the wine. Even in his human disguise, food did not agree with him.

"This is very good," the Lord observed, looking into the glass as he swirled it around. "Deep red color, rich, yet light to the taste. Who was it that said wine should not appeal only to the tongue but to the eye as well."

The Gypsy nodded. "My people have long

understood the importance of rich food and drink," he motioned to the stew. "For instance, the meat in this stew has been marinated in a secret recipe of spices. You do not find that type of cooking in many places anymore," he bit off a piece of bread as he spoke.

The vampire nodded and was about to say something when the inn door opened, drawing their attention. Creed sat back sipping from the wine as he watched six angry faced young men walk into the restaurant.

They drew wary glances from the rest of the patrons who stopped eating or drinking as the young men pushed their way across the floor.

"Friends of yours?" Rasmere asked, an amused look on his face as he refilled his wineglass.

Creed shook his head as he extended his glass for the vampire to fill.

"Darius Creed?" One of the young men asked with a demanding tone as he stood in front of their table.

Rasmere raised an eyebrow as Creed sat relaxed in his chair taking a drink of the wine.

"Want me to negotiate with them?" the Lord asked across the table as he barely contained the smile playing at his mouth.

Creed didn't look at the Lord. He kept his gaze on the young man wondering where this was going.

"I am," he answered. "Is there something I can help you with?"

He waited patiently for the answer.

Julius rushed from the kitchen, a look of worry covering his face. "What are you doing Raoul?" he demanded. "Are trying to shame us?"

The youth shot him a defiant look. "Leave me alone, Papa."

"If this is the Gypsy Prince you have told me about it is my right to ask him?"

The youngster's tone was demanding but far from belligerent.

Julius turned looking down to Creed and Rasmere.

"Please, Prince Darius," his tone respectful as well as apologetic. "He is young and full of crazy ideas."

Creed frowned as he looked from Rasmere, who shrugged, back to the young Raoul.

"It will be fine, Julius. Allow him to speak his mind."

Raoul took a deep breath calming his nerves as behind him his friends whispered words of encouragement.

Creed looked him in the eyes and asked. "So what is it that I can do for you, Raoul?"

Across the table the Vampire Lord mumbled. "Be careful what you offer, Gypsy." If Creed heard him he didn't react.

"We would like to become Hunters like our great Gypsy ancestors," he announced proudly.

Behind him throughout the inn there were murmurs mixed with chuckles as across the table Rasmere laughed openly out loud.

A stern look from Creed caused the vampire to stop, loudly clearing his throat, as with a toss of his long hair he took a sip of wine.

Raoul didn't flinch as he ignored the chuckles of

the folks behind them.

"We are serious," he went on. "We want to be your students. We remember the old ways and would join you in the war against the undead."

His tone was so serious Rasmere stopped his chuckling looking up into the young man's eyes. "Do not be so ready to throw away your life," he told them. "You do not know what it takes, the sacrifices you must make, to be a Hunter."

This time it was Creed who raised an eyebrow but Raoul did not back down.

"Tell us what it takes then?" he demanded.

Creed, amused at the Lord, chuckled. "Yes, tell them what it takes to be a Hunter," and then under his breath he added. "I want to hear this."

Waiting he poured more wine sitting back.

The youths behind Raoul stepped closer wanting to hear what the companion of the legendary prince had to say.

"Well, it takes great skill and courage," Rasmere began and at least as far as Creed could tell, sounding sincere.

"You have to be able to put your whole life on hold in the pursuit of one single burning objective."

"What?"

"To seek out-no more then that-to hunt out, find and destroy your mortal enemies whether they are vampire, werewolf or any of the other so called undead of this world," the Lord looked deep into his glass. "Before any of you youngsters ask to go down this path, make sure, make *damn* sure, that you know what it is you are asking to get into. I will be outside if you want me."

He said to Creed as he stood draining his glass and placing it on the tabletop. "Good wine," he nodded as with a flourish of his leather trench coat he walked from the inn.

Raoul watched him leave.

"Who was that," he asked. "A great Hunter companion of yours, Prince Darius?"

The eyes of the young men burned with desire as they looked at him waiting for his answer.

Slightly confused, but utterly amazed, Creed called Julius over to the table.

"Would you please bring glasses for my young friends here, old friend?"

Julius, with a look of relief on his face, nodded. "Yes, my Prince."

"We will have a drink," he told the young men as they sat waiting for the glasses.

Looking at each other, they smiled, satisfied to be sharing a table with the Prince. Creed, however, chuckled at them.

"That gentleman?" he asked with an amused look on his scarred face.

They nodded in unison. "Yes, who was he?" Raoul asked.

This caused the Gypsy prince to laugh out loud. "What if I told you he is a very powerful Vampire Lord and one of the most dangerous enemies a Hunter could have?" he asked looking into their young faces.

They glanced at each other wide-eyed and then as if they thought he was joking them.

Raoul smiled back at him. "Ya, right," he chuckled. "No Vampire Lord would be sitting here drinking wine with Darius Creed," He observed.

Creed just shrugged as he sipped from his glass and Julius placed both fresh glasses, as well as a new bottle, on their table.

The Gypsy prince passed out the glasses.

"Fill them."

He handed the bottle to Raoul, who nodded and passed the bottle to his friends.

It was at this time that Creed took a chance on these young men.

"Are you serious about becoming Hunters?" he asked.

As a unit they nodded and several said. "Yes, we are."

Creed took a deep breath as he looked at them. "Okay, I do have work for you, but it will take a great amount of secrecy for you to pull it off."

They all shared a look and then they nodded at him. "We are ready, Prince Darius," a short but stocky youth assured him.

Creed lifted his glass. "Then join me, young ones, in a toast to Lord Rasmere of Haeth, a warrior, a gentleman and, whether he likes it or not, the most honorable man I have met in centuries."

With frowns on their faces they lifted their glasses and all drank to Rasmere of Haeth!

After the bottle was empty they left the inn following Creed outside to where Rasmere stood wearing his heavily tinted sunglasses.

"I see you have brought friends," the Lord observed as they exited the inn.

Creed nodded with a chuckle. "Yes, I have, I think, if the feeling I get is right, they will help with the human minions I am sure Pakur has brought along."

Rasmere appeared to think about this.

"You may be right," he agreed with a nod. "I am not sure what the bastard has in mind but he may well need humans to pull it off."

Creed nodded as he saw his truck from the estate pull up and Joel, accompanied by Wilfred, climb out.

"Good, we are all here," he said. "Let's go somewhere less occupied," And as he waved his arm they all followed him down the street.

The Boars Head tavern was just down the block and when Creed led his small procession into the dark bar room, only a few heads lifted long enough to notice.

"This is perfect," he said, taking them to the far corner where a booth sat empty.

"Let us sit," he offered as he waved to the bartender.

"A round of beer," he called out and from behind the bar the bored looking man nodded.

"What, no more wine?" Rasmere asked appearing disappointed.

Creed shook his head, whispering over his shoulder. "Not in this place."

Rasmere nodded. "I see."

Two of the young Gypsies had to sit separately pulling up chairs and sliding over a small table but they didn't seem to mind. Creed looked over to Joel and Wilfred.

"It is good to see you both," he smiled, as the bartender arrived with two pitchers of beer and a round of glasses.

"Let me pay," Raoul offered, reaching for his pocket but the man waved him off.

"There will be no charge today," he began bowing his head slightly to Creed. "I know very well the Prince of my people without being reminded of it by you, Raoul."

He said it as if offended before returning to his cleaning behind the bar.

Creed chuckled, despite himself. "I see that Cyrus is as happy to be alive as ever," he said looking to Joel.

The old caretaker nodded. "He has always hated this world, Darius. Who knows why."

Rasmere tasted his beer. "Too many humans are in such a hurry to leave. Don't they know what awaits them?" he shook his head looking into his glass.

"What do you mean?" asked one of the young Gypsies.

Rasmere looked up at the young interested faces. "The vampire sits at the right hand of Satan, so for him, Hell is not such a bad place, but the human is the lowest of life forms in Hell and they do not have such a good time in Satan's care."

For some reason this made perfect sense to the younger men and they all nodded, sitting back.

Creed raised an eyebrow wondering if they would have been so secure knowing Rasmere truly was a Vampire Lord.

Joel was talking to him. "We did as you asked, sir. The Toscanno family has been moved to a new place of safety."

Creed looked at Wilfred. "You should have gone with them."

The black man shook his head. "No sir, Mr. Creed, I ain't gonna miss this fight and don't tell me that there ain't one coming either. Like I said back in the States, I didn't run at Khe Sahn and I ain't gonna run from this. The Toscannos are like my family and when this vampire decided to attack them, he also attacked me."

There was a deep resolve in the man and it was hard for Creed not to smile at him.

"Okay," he relented. "So we have more help then even I bargained for; this is nice for once."

Before he could go on with his plans a second group of serious looking young men walked into the tavern.

"Oh, Jesus," Raoul whispered under his breath as he slumped in his chair.

It seemed as if all of the young men with him did the same, growing quite nervous as a grinning young man walked across the floor.

"Well, if it isn't Raoul and his little band of legend believers," he mocked stepping towards them.

Raoul slumped forward embarrassed by the other youth.

"Not now, Chaz," he said from under his arm.

The teenager started to laugh, a loud sarcastic chuckle, as he stepped around the chairs to where the rest sat in their booth.

"The dreamer, Raoul, who believes in stories and wants to be a Vampire Hunter," he mocked. "You are such a fool."

Looking up from his glass, Rasmere frowned, a questioning look on his face.

"Why does that make him a fool?" he asked the newcomer named Chaz.

The kid looked into Rasmere's gaze too foolish to realize what he was seeing there.

Chaz chuckled as he looked at the Lord. "Listen, old man," he said pointing to the Lord. "Anyone with half a brain knows there is no such thing as vampires."

He turned shaking his head as he said to the youths with him.

"Dumb old bastard."

Rasmere was halfway to his feet when Creed stopped him.

"Let this play out," he said across the table.

Chaz had better ears then the Gypsy prince gave him credit for because he turned looking at Creed.

"Yes, stay out of it, because kicking the hell out of one old man doesn't bother me," he pointed at Rasmere again. "But two is a bit too much even for us."

This time Rasmere stopped Creed as he began to rise from his seat.

"As you said, Gypsy Prince, leave it alone."

Before he could answer, Chaz looked at Creed, his eyes narrowing.

"So that is why Raoul is here!" he laughed over his shoulder. "This is Darius Creed, the so-called

Prince of the Gypsies!" he yelled out squaring his shoulders in challenge.

Creed looked up at the youth. There were seven others with him, all arrogant and full of themselves.

Creed was about to answer the challenge when Joel rose from his seat. "You little pup!" he exclaimed. "This is Darius Creed, the last of the royal Gypsy line. Do not dare to talk down on him!"

His finger was close to Chaz's face and the young man, with a look of defiance, simply shook his head. "Get away from me," he ordered as he pushed Joel back into the booth.

The elderly yard keeper fell back into Wilfred.

The two-tour Vietnam vet had seen enough, he lunged punching Chaz hard across the chin knocking the kid to one knee.

Chaz wiped blood from his lips as he stood looking Wilfred in the eye.

"I am going to hurt you, old man!" he promised as he balled his fists.

"Bring it on then," the Silver Star winner invited. "I'll show you how we used to do it in Saigon!"

Chaz stepped forward but Raoul blocked his way. "No, this is between us. We will come outside and finish this once and for all."

The other kid nodded in agreement. "Fine, let us do it outside!"

And he turned leading his boys out.

Raoul looked at Creed. "This has been long overdo," he said. "Don't worry about us."

Creed shook his head. "I wont," he answered looking to Rasmere. "If they want to join us what better way to get a look at them in action?"

The vampire picked up the pitcher of beer. "You do have a point there, Gypsy Prince," he agreed with a nod.

They walked from the tavern, Rasmere carrying the pitcher that he was drinking from and neglecting the glass entirely. In front of the tavern the young men faced off.

"Okay," Chaz challenged, rolling up his shirtsleeves.

Before Raoul could step in to face him, Creed cleared his throat. "I have an idea," he said, suddenly catching the attention of the two groups.

They turned facing him.

"What are you talking about?" Raoul asked as he frowned in question.

Chaz also stepped forward. "Yes, what are you getting at?"

Creed stepped among them as Rasmere, Wilfred and the yard keeper, Joel all watched on from the sidelines.

The Gypsy prince looked at the young men.

"I have a better way to settle this. We are here to save a young family from an evil Vampire Lord. Now if you want to be Hunters," he pointed at Raoul and his group. "You will come and help us. The vampire will have human minions and someone will need to keep them off our backs while we deal with the Lord. So, what do you say? Instead of wasting your energy on each other and the made up hatred of youth, will you combine to battle the true enemies of man?"

The challenge was thick in his voice as he turned and pointed to Chaz and his crew.

"And as far as you young men are concerned, it is the perfect chance for you to prove that we are all fools; that vampires do not exist. That is, if you have the guts to do so?"

Creed left it hang there between them, an open challenge for each.

Chaz and Raoul fixed their eyes on the Prince.

"Of course, we will do it," Raoul answered. "We have waited for our chance to prove our worth."

Beside him Chaz nodded. "We will come along also Prince of the Gypsies, I want to see this for myself."

"Shake on it?" Raoul asked the other youth.

Chaz extended his hand. "For tonight then, we are allies."

Several feet away Rasmere let out a loud burp as he chugged the pitcher of beer.

"Good idea, Creed," he added with a shake of his long hair.

"We are growing in number all the time," And tossing back his head he drained the remains of the beverage. "You know I am starting to like hanging around with you," He burped louder as Creed walked back over by him.

The Gypsy simply looked at him with a chuckle as he shook his head.

"After tonight we will see Lord Rasmere, we

will see."

NINETEEN

The emergency room of the hospital was a holy terror at three p.m. as nurses and doctors shuffled about trying to contend with another busy day of gun wounds and traffic accidents.

While the frantic screams of injured men mixed with arguing gang members the automatic doors swung open silently and from the hot afternoon sun stepped a frail-looking old woman walking heavily on a cane.

She was dressed in a multi colored skirt that matched curiously with the deep red-dyed blouse. On her head, bundling up the long gray hair, she wore a red scarf-deep red like the blouse-and over her shoulder hung a worn leather bag.

Walking among the chaos of the emergency room, she exuded a calm unlike those around her. Without an expression on her face, she walked to the elevators punching the keypad.

The doors opened and she stepped in, right in front of two large muscular young black men who took in the old woman with the large leather bag.

One of them towered over her by a good sixteen inches.

"What's in the bag?" he asked, hovering over

her shoulder.

The old woman turned, a smile on her face as she met his eyes.

"Things that would make you wet your pants," she answered amused.

The twinkle in her eyes almost reflected the mirth in her voice.

"Hey," the kid tensed. "Don't be giving me any lip, you old bitch," he warned in a low growling tone.

"You really want to look in this bag?"

He nodded. "Yeah, we want to know. If you show us, we wont take it by force."

Of course it was a threat but the old woman didn't seam to be worried.

"I have warned you," she insisted.

He reached for the old bag trying to tear it from her shoulder. He gave it a vicious jerk, surprised when neither the strap broke or the old lady so much as moved.

"Young man," she said in a quiet soothing voice. "There are things in this bag that you do not want to be involved with. I'm warning you."

He met her eyes, something there warned him, sending chills down his spine as the door slid open.

"The hell with her," he jabbed his buddy by the arm. "Let's get going," And quickly they were out of the elevator.

She kept the smile to herself as they hurried down the hallway away from her. They really wouldn't have liked what was in her bag.

Leaning heavily on her cane she made her way slowly down the hallway towards the room she was looking for. No one noticed her; just another old woman.

Hearing voices she stepped quickly into the room next to the one she was looking for. No one needed to know she was here just yet.

As she waited in the open doorway, the old one called Asmus walked past followed by the young Hunter, Jacob Reid.

"Let's get something to eat," Asmus suggested. "This may be a long night."

The younger man nodded in agreement and soon they were gone, their boot heels echoing off of the sterile floor.

The woman smiled, now she could go in.

Looking suddenly younger, she stood straighter and slipped the cane under her elbow as she pushed the room door open and stepped inside.

On the bed, propped up with pillows, the young Gypsy Witch slept but at her side, a pair of green eyes studied the newcomer.

"You have come," Shach Meril purred across the room as he rolled to his side and then stood.

She nodded. "Yes, I had too," she answered in a voice stronger than one would expect from a frail old woman.

The Warrior King bowed his head slightly, giving the due respect to the woman in his presence.

"It has been a long time, Lela."

He greeted her before pointing a paw to Selena. "As you can see, your granddaughter sleeps; she is resting and regaining her strength."

Lela nodded as she placed both her bag and the old cane down in an empty chair.

"It honors our family that the great Shach Meril watches over her as she recovers from her wounds."

She stepped over to her granddaughter's side and felt her forehead.

"There was no effect from Kadahl's attack?"

She raised an eyebrow as she questioned the cat.

Shach Meril looked from the young woman's face to Lela's.

"Asmus treated her immediately," he replied. "Just in case."

Lela smiled softly. "It was fortunate that he was there," she ran her hands over the younger woman before, stopping at her belly.

"The baby is fine."

She whispered more to herself than to anyone else.

Shach Meril turned his green eyes on her. "Asmus felt there was a cloud of danger following her; that is why he asked that I keep an eye on her."

Lela nodded as she removed a small bag of herbs from the folds of her skirt.

"He was always very wise," She agreed, rubbing the mixture between her hands and creating a powder.

As the cat watched, she began to rub it onto the exposed skin.

"This will help her recover more quickly," she explained to the cat. "And it will also give her a little protection against what is coming."

Shach Meril looked at her with a confused expression. "The danger continues?" he asked.

Lela nodded. "Creed contacted me. He asked me to trace a Voodoo Queen named Semma. He thought she was headed across the ocean to the old country, but she was not. She never left the states."

As she explained, Lela poured a small amount of red elixir from a vial into Selena's open mouth.

"She is coming here?" The cat asked with a wary look. He wanted a shot at the Voodoo Queen himself.

Lela took a deep breath. "Yes, I would venture that she is, especially if she knows that Selena carries the unborn heir to the Gypsy crown."

Shach Meril agreed. "To kill the next great Hunter before he is born, that would be a mighty stroke for the forces of darkness," with a twist of his head he asked. "Do you know when she will come?"

Lela nodded. "Tonight, near the hour of the witch. When her power is the greatest, even though Selena is badly injured, this Voodoo Queen knows she is no match for Gypsy magic. She will want to be at her strongest."

They shared a look; both knew that the hour of midnight was the time a Voodoo Queen would be in her zenith, her powers the greatest.

"I will be ready," Shach Meril vowed.

Lela reached down running her hand over the cat's ears scratching them a little.

"Creed told me about your valiant efforts in this battle. You give pride to the line of the Trillii."

Before the cat could answer, the room door popped open and in stepped Jacob Reid.

"Hey, what is going on in here?" he asked reaching for his sword.

"Hold your hand," Asmus warned, stepping past

him, his eyes meeting those of the old witch.

"You would never get the sword free of its case."

At this Jake grunted. "Why? Who is this old woman?"

Asmus extended his hand towards Lela. "This is Lela, goddaughter of Darius Creed, a Hunter and powerful Gypsy Witch. She is Selena's grandmother."

Jake rolled his eyes. "Oh geez, I'm sorry." He stepped forward extending his hand. "I didn't know."

Lela simply smiled. "It is quite all right, "But we have much work to do. Tonight, the Voodoo Queen and servants of the Vampire Lord will come here. Their aim will be to slay the next Prince of the Gypsies."

At this announcement, Jake shook his head. "Over my dead body," he vowed.

Lela looked up meeting his intense gaze. "I hope you mean it, Hunter, because that may be the case before this night is over."

Jake looked about at the figures assembled in this small hospital room.

"What can I say?" he replied. "It's a good night to die."

Asmus grunted a sort of reply while Shach Meril flashed the Hunter a strange look.

"What?" Jake tossed up his hands as he glanced at the cat. "Don't give me no looks," he teased.

The Trillii warrior simply licked its front paws. "I would not attempt it, Jacob Reid," the voice rang through the room. "I am getting used to your sense of the dramatic."

Jake looked at Asmus. "What did he just say to me?"

Asmus smiled as he plopped down in an unused chair. "I think he said he likes you, now sit down and rest. We are going to need it." The old Gypsy lay his head back and quickly went to sleep.

Lela allowed a soft chuckle to escape her chest. "He always could sleep in the middle of an emergency."

She walked over placing a blanket gently across the old Gypsy Warrior.

"What would you have us do?" Shach Meril purred in the room.

Lela took a deep breath. "Across the ocean, Creed fights the vampire legions of the Lord Pakur; here we will defeat a very large part of his plan."

"What part is that?" Jake asked adjusting his jacket over his shoulders.

Lela removed a bottle of ointment from her bag and rubbed it into her hands. As she began to apply it to Selena she looked up at them. "His plan to eliminate the Prince and future Hunter. Just think how powerful Pakur would be if he did not have a Gypsy Prince to worry about?" she allowed her question to hang in the air.

Shach Meril gave her a slight nod. "He would be very hard to stop without such a powerful Hunter."

Jake looked at them. "What about me?" he protested. "I am going to be pretty powerful someday."

Lela looked up at him. "Yes, you will, if you

survive this night," she sighed.

"I am sure Pakur has made arrangements that no one will."

Jake stiffened. "Then we will just have to see that we ruin his plans."

In the corner, Asmus snored loudly as he turned in the chair and pulled the blanket higher over his shoulders.

Jake looked at the old man. "We could always place him in front of the door. They would fall over him as they came and then we could jump them," he thought he had made a joke.

The disapproving glances he received from both Lela and Shach Meril told him they didn't find it funny.

"Oh forget about it then," he stalked from the room.

"He is a funny fellow, isn't he?" The old woman asked looking to the cat.

Shach Meril stretched himself on Selena's bed.

"Very strange for a Hunter, but he grows on you eventually."

Flustered and feeling left out, Jake stalked down to the bar located a block from the hospital.

Hell, it was not his fault that he really didn't understand these strange people. After all, he was new to this vampire fighting crap. Tossing the door open he stepped into the smoke filled dreary tavern. Aware of the suspicious stares of the patrons, he walked to an empty stool and sat down.

"What do you need, stranger?"

The thin nervous-looking bartender tossed a dirty bar rag over his shoulder and stood chewing a toothpick.

Jake looked over the bottles on the back shelf. "Whiskey."

The bartender nodded and hurried away.

Behind him, Jake felt the eyes of the assembled locals watching him; there was very little love in this room. He turned slowly looking over the room. The men averted their eyes, pretending they had not been watching the stranger in the worn leather coat.

"Friendly place you have here," Jake commented to the bartender as the man placed a tumbled of whiskey in front of him.

The rat faced little man nodded. "They don't like strangers much," he explained. "If I were you I would drink up and leave, I don't need anymore trouble in here."

Jake smiled as he tasted the liquor. Allowing it to slowly roll down his throat, he relished its burning taste.

"If there is any trouble in here tonight, someone else will start it," he assured the bartender.

The man gave him an enthusiastic look and turned back to polishing glasses until someone ordered another pitcher of beer from across the bar.

Jake sat sipping his drink and relishing the feeling of the liquor as it spread through his body.

"I needed this after the last few days I've had," he told himself taking another drink.

Across the street from the tavern, a dark skinned beauty watched from under the cowl of her leather trench coat.

"How lucky it is that we observed him enter the bar," she whispered to the vampires behind her.

They nodded in agreement, their milky white eyes glaring at the bar from under their dark hoods.

"We willll driiink his bloood and fulfiiillll the Lord'sss wish," a tall vampire whispered behind Semma's back.

She nodded her eyes peering into the windows of the bar across the street. Using her unholy powers she could see through the building and watch the Hunter as he swilled liquor.

"He is getting drunk," she said her partners. "Soon we will make our move."

She formulated a quick plan of attack.

"Roellick, Walet and McMall," she said over her shoulder. The three vampires stepped forward, and awaited her decision. "You three are the most able of us all," she began. "Wait here and kill the Hunter when he leaves the bar staggering drunk."

She pointed to the rest as she turned looking into their eyes. "The rest of us will proceed to the Gypsy Witch and kill her. He is her only chance, so do not fail."

They bowed their heads to her; they knew how important it was that they succeed.

Semma turned back to the bar, staring again at the Hunter who sat on the barstool pouring down drink after drink.

"I have looked ahead to the witch's room. She is all alone now that Jacob Reid has left her," she allowed a smile to play across her lips. "She will be alone and defenseless."

Asmus turned from the window and regarded the witch "The Voodoo Queen is near; I can smell her." He wrinkled his nose in disgust.

Lela returned a short nod as she rocked in the corner of the hospital room.

"She has a small army with her; she has already probed the room."

"She made a mental probe?" he asked turning back to the window and peering out.

Lela smiled as she reached for a glass of water at her side. "Yes she tried it about an hour ago," she took a sip. "But I only allowed her to see Selena."

"You are greasing the trap," he concluded. "She will be unable to resist."

A soft chuckle escaped from the old woman's throat.

"Yes she will come tonight and then this will be over. After this night it will be up to Creed to finish."

"The bitch thinks she will gain favor from her Lord by slaying a Gypsy Witch and offering him her powers. To bad she doesn't know that Kadahl met Lord Satan already."

Asmus sneered as he said it and Lela could tell killing the Demon Lord had pleased him.

Shach Meril rolled over onto his stomach and nestled into Selena's side.

"These are close quarters for combat."

Lela nodded. "Yes, that is why I will wait here for this Voodoo Queen alone."

Asmus turned from the window. "Oh really?" he

365

asked waiting for her to explain.

She chuckled again softly. "She will not share the moment of her victory; she will enter this room alone."

Jake waved his empty glass at the bartender.

"Another?" the man asked with an amused look on his face. The stranger had just finished his second bottle of whiskey; he had to fall over soon.

Jake nodded after checking his watch. "I have time for a few more," he smiled.

The bartender shook his head. For someone who had consumed two quarts of whiskey, the man sure did not look drunk.

"Here you go," he refilled the stranger's glass.

Jake had the glass halfway to his mouth when he caught the scent, the stench of the vampire!

Seconds later three large men in leather trench coats entered the room, dark glasses covering their eyes.

He smiled, he knew who they were and he also knew they were here for him. He drained the glass feeling the whiskey slide down his throat; it was one of the nice effects of the Gypsy given powers. Alcohol did not affect him like it would a normal human. In fact, it appeared to enhance his senses. Creed had explained that the potions did things like that, enhance your senses and change the way your body handled outside influences.

He slid his sleeve back a bit rechecking his watch, 11:45 pm. He would need to be getting back soon. Glancing at the three demons that now sat across the room, he wondered when they would hit him.

Under his coat he felt the reassuring handle of his sword.

"Come get some boys," he whispered to himself as he finished his drink and tossed a handful of bills on the bar.

"See you some other time," he said as he headed for the door.

"Anytime," he answered. As he watched the three leather-clad figures stand and follow the man out the door. "What in the hell is going on now?" he wondered out loud as he wiped down the bar.

Jake walked slowly down the dark street; he felt the breeze pick up, a cool unholy breeze. Their smell assailed his senses and he reached for the sword under his coat allowing his fingers to caress it possessively.

From the dark a figure hurried towards him.

"Hey, mister!" Jake spun almost pulling the sword from its sheath.

"Hey, there buddy!"

It was the bartender his hands up in warning.

"What do you want?" Jake asked looking about them. "Take my advice and run while you can," he warned feeling the demons were very close now.

The bartender looked at Jake as if he was losing his mind.

"What are you talking about, dude, I know you drank a lot of booze but come on?" he paused and then continued. "I just came to warn you that three ugly looking dudes were following you; they looked like Mafia or something."

"Or something," Jake grunted, their demon aura growing even stronger.

"Hey, don't worry." The bartender smiled as he pulled a handgun from his jacket. "I always travel with some heat."

Jake looked at the nine millimeter; he was about to tell the guy to put it away when the attack came.

With his hyper senses he saw the vampire as he rushed them. Fangs bared, he flew their way about waist high.

"Get back!" Jake warned reaching forward and tossing the bartender aside like a rag doll.

There was no time to pull his sword and the martial artist used his training instead. In a blur, he sidestepped, allowing the speeding vampire to fly by, barely missing him with raking claws.

The demon disappeared briefly into the night but almost before Jake could free the sword of Takada from his coat, the monster flew at him again.

This time Jake was ready and the flashing sword blade met with the demon's chest. A loud scream of death tore through the darkened night as the vampire was cut completely in half.

"What in the hell is going on?" the bartender cried out in shock as he rolled away from the smoking upper half the thing that had rushed them from the dark.

"Vampires," Jake warned under his breath as he pivoted on his left foot, his enhanced vision and smell searching the night for the remaining demons.

"Bullshit," the bartender snorted. "There ain't no such damn thing as vampires."

Before his words died the next demon dropped from the dark!

The demon crouched in front of Jake his claws flexing and his fangs dripping saliva in anticipation of the kill.

Jake readied himself as the leather-clad killer began to stalk him, moving slowly while circling to his right.

"Hurry up, I don't have all night," Jake invited him.

TWENTY

Semma strode proudly into the hospital and through the trauma center followed by a dozen black-clad followers of Lord Pakur.

"You can't come in here like this!" the admission nurse warned standing from behind her desk.

"Sit down, bitch," The Voodoo Queen pointed a finger.

Suddenly the nurse fell to the floor clutching her chest, her heart had stopped beating, killed by the witch's spell.

Semma proceeded right through the middle of the trauma center as tired doctors and nurses mixed

370

with police officers and paramedics.

"What are you doing in here?" a young intern challenged.

A longhaired vampire paused to look at the young man.

"Looooking for bloooood!" he hissed, sticking his right forefinger into the bloody wound of a dead gang member.

Horror stricken, the young intern watched as the monster before him slowly raised the blood-covered digit to his mouth. With a wide smile, the demon placed the finger into his mouth and licked the wet sticky substance from it.

"Yesssss we neeeeed bloood," he added.

Turning white the young doctor fell to the floor.

"Enough of this," Semma cautioned over her shoulder. "We have a job to do, get serious, all of you."

Falling in behind her they filed down the sterile smelling corridor closing in on the room of their prey!

"Room 208, this is it."

The voodoo witch came to a closed door in the center of the hallway.

"Half of you to the right and the others to the left."

She spun on them her gloved hand coming up in their faces.

"Remember, no matter what, I am not to be disturbed. Anyone who shows up here is yours to do what you will."

This brought smiles from their pale faces.

"We cannot fail," she added before pointing to two female vampires.

"You two will come with me just in case."

With looks of excitement they stepped closer to her. They knew to please her was to please the Lord Pakur.

"Okay, here we go. To the future and a newer greater race of vampire."

With that statement she opened the door quietly and stepped into the room followed by the two young demons.

"Wake up Gypsy Witch," Semma ordered. "I have come for you."

There was no response from the young woman who lay resting peacefully under the covers on the bed.

"I said, wake up, witch!"

Her voice boomed into the room as she raised her gloved hand.

"She cannot hear you."

Semma looked about the room, her eyes narrowing.

She knew that soft purr-like voice.

"Where are you?" she demanded, her fists curling in anger.

From the far side of the bed Shach Meril stepped over the young Gypsy woman's body and lay down on the bed at her side.

Hatred burning in her eyes, the Voodoo Queen stared into the dark green eyes of the King of the

Trillii.

"You are not supposed to be here," she hissed in an accusing tone.

The cat simply regarded her as his tail twitched slowly back and forth.

"I have not completed my mission," he informed her patiently.

"And what would that be, cat?"

"To protect the unborn future Prince of the Gypsies."

She allowed a small smile to form slowly on her face.

"You cannot fight all three of us," Semma pointed out and, as if on cue, the female demons stepped from behind her.

As they spread out, they bared their fangs and razor sharp claws.

"I have plenty more warriors in the hallway," she pointed out.

Shach Meril returned a slight nod of his head. "I will handle these two," he said as if disinterested. "You are not for me to deal with."

This forced a frown from the witch.

"Then there is nothing to stop me, is there cat?"

Before Shach Meril could answer there came a blinding flash from the corner of the room!

With flashing fangs the vampire sprang!

Jake spun, allowing the razor sharp claws to rake harmlessly across his werewolf skin coat. Stunned the vampire tried to halt his charge so he could turn, getting a second shot at the human.

Jake was already in position, his left foot shooting out as left hand caught the demon in a powerful grip. With a well-timed foot sweep, Jake put the vampire to the sidewalk. The streetlight shone brightly off the enchanted blade as it rose above the Hunter's head. With a twist of the wrist, Jake reversed the sword and drove downwards. The sword of Takada shot through the demon's chest and into the concrete a full seven inches.

"Holy Jesus!" the bartender crawled to his feet as he watched the vampire began to smoke.

"I ain't never seen somebody take out two dudes that fast before; and believe me, I have seen a lot of bar fights."

"Get down again; there is another!" Jake hissed sensing a strong aura coming closer.

From the dark shadows of the streetlight he walked, tall and broad shouldered. He did not look like most of the vampires Jake had seen so far. Instead of thin and sickly, this one was built something like Arnold Schwarzenegger.

He looked at the smoking remains of his two companions and then raised his hands clapping them together.

"Bravoooo, Jacooob Reid," he met the Hunter's eyes and smiled a bit.

"For sssomeone ssso new to the gaaaame you have respectable skillsssss. Creed still choosesss his alliesss well, I ssssee."

Jake felt his eyes narrow reflexively at the Gypsy's name.

"What do you know of Creed?" he asked his palms sweaty on the handle of the sword.

The Vampire folded his arms in front of him. "I know him wellll, Jacob Reid. My name is Roellick and I haaaavvve battled Creeeed many timesss."

"I thought that all of Pakur's little band were turned vampires and relatively young. So how or when would you have found the time to mix it up with Creed?"

Roellick had been studying the bartender who was trying to hide behind the water fountain along the sidewalk. He turned his milky white gaze towards Jake.

"I was born full blood," he explained with a slight nod of his silver white hair while his speech cleared.

"Long ago, I was a follower of Rasmere; his equal if you will. A few years back I came to America and discovered the small coven Pakur was building. It was simple to join up. The human minions were more than happy to have a true full blood among them. Pakur is on a collision course with his destiny. If he survives his meeting with the Gypsy Hunter, he will grow very powerful," The vampire named Roellick shrugged his heavily muscled shoulders.

"Maybe even more powerful than Lord Rasmere, I don't know. What I do know is that you had better get back to the Gypsy Witch; that voodoo bitch is going to try and kill her."

Jake allowed his own smile to play over his lips. "It will be okay; she is well protected."

He twirled the sword in his hand gripping it in a

two handed combat grip.

"You and I have something to settle, however," Jake invited.

Roellick looked at the Hunter and slowly shook his head. "No, Jacob Reid, I will not fight you tonight. As a True Blood, I have no desire to be involved in this plan of Pakur."

He spun lightly on his boot heel. "Tell Rasmere that I will see him soon," he said over his shoulder as he strode towards the dark night.

"Wait a minute," Jake called out.

The leather-clad vampire paused turning partly back towards him. "Yes Jacob Reid?"

Jake sheathed his sword. "How did you say you knew Rasmere?"

Roellick cocked his head. "He is my brother, Jacob Reid."

And with that he spun away and was quickly gone.

The bartender struggled to get to his feet on his weak knees. "That was a vampire?" he asked incredulous.

Jake nodded as he watched the spot where the big demon had disappeared.

"Yes, he was buddy."

Before the man could respond the Hunter was also gone, sprinting down the street towards the hospital.

The female vampires hissed, flexing their clawed hands while Semma stood watching the white smoke. From its center stepped an old woman.

"So you are the Voodoo Witch?" The old woman asked as she placed her cane in front of her.

Semma raised an eyebrow. "Who are you, old woman?"

"My name is Lela, adopted daughter of Darius Creed, grandmother of Selena."

"In my day, I was the strongest of all Gypsy magic users and under my careful instruction, my granddaughter will share the power of our line."

Semma shook her head as she replied with a grunt.

"She will not live to see another sunrise." Stepping forward, she raised a gloved finger. "I will see to that."

A spell of destruction sped from her outstretched finger and into the sleeping woman.

Semma watched her look of confidence turning to dismay as nothing happened.

"What?" she gasped, turning to face the old woman.

On the bed Shach Meril raised a front paw. "Do you think we would allow such a precious warrior to lay here under your nose?" his soft voice asked.

"Lela and I," he nodded to the old Gypsy. "We have fought your kind before. Do not think us foolish."

Semma stared at the animal. "You are starting to get to me, cat," she said through clenched teeth.

"I will call upon my Lord, the great Kadahl; he will handle you Trillii."

Shach Meril shook his head. "Your Lord is dead," he informed her. "Slain by the mighty

377

Asmus. He will not answer your call."

"Yes, it is between you and I," Lela challenged from the corner of the room.

Semma looked from the cat to the old witch. "We will see. Get them!" Stepping back she pushed her female companions in front of her.

They sprang across the room straight at the old woman.

From the bed, Shach Meril sprang. Striking the first vampire, he drove her off course and into the far wall. They impacted hard and fell to the floor. The vampire screamed as it flailed the air with its claws trying to tear away the hissing and spitting feline. The Warrior King of the Trillii shredded her face and neck with his own sharp claws. Avoiding her assault he jumped from her shoulders to the nearby table and turned watching as she struggled from the floor. One eye swung from the socket and the other was terribly slashed.

Checking over his shoulder he watched the old woman bounce the second vampire from the wall. As the demon crashed to the floor Lela stepped ahead driving her enchanted dagger into the thing's chest.

"I must go after the witch," she called out to the cat.

Shach Meril nodded. "Go, I will finish this one," he assured her.

She nodded grimly as she clutched her bag in her hand.

"The witch is fleeing I think; she must not escape this building."

With a second flash of white smoke Lela was

gone!

Shach Meril turned his attention back to the stumbling vampire. Tensing he sprung back onto her head, avoiding her claws again as he drew his sharp claws along her throat. His enchanted weapons severed her head from her shoulders. As he jumped away, she was already smoking on the floor.

Jake ran through the crowded hospital trauma center and vaulted the body of an unconscious young doctor. He wondered briefly what had happened to the young man but with the strong smell of many vampires flooding his senses, he hurried on.

Rounding the corner of the hallway leading to Selena's room he slid to a stop. Down the length of the corridor there were at least a dozen leather clad demons and they were staring at him with bloodlust in their eyes!

"Oh boy," he exclaimed as he drew his sword. "I should have known you wimps would come in a pack."

He watched as they spread out in the hall starting to slowly stalk his way.

He tensed feeling his hyperactive muscles bunching under his skin.

"Well, no one ever said life was fair, did they?" he whispered under his breath as they slowly began to close the distance in the hallway.

"What is wrong Jake, afraid?"

Jake turned raising the sword; he froze as he

recognized Asmus.

The Gypsy legend had changed into leathers and a great coat of werewolf skin. He stood to Jake's side, a silver-coated short sword in each hand.

"What?" he asked at the questioning look on the Hunter's face. "You did not think I would miss this, did you?"

Jake felt a smile growing on his face. "No, I guess not. I am very honored to fight at your side."

Asmus chuckled. "Don't give me that crap, Jake. Now, as they say in these modern times, let's show them how we do it downtown!"

The two Hunters stepped forward meeting the approaching vampires!

Semma looked upward as the Moon broke free from the cloud cover. It was a good sign. If the old Gypsy Witch pursued her, she could call on the Moon's power.

She felt the breeze blow lightly against her face, caressing it. How had she not detected the old woman and the cat this afternoon?

She shook her head. "Details like this have a way of ruining my night," she said under her breath as she tried to decide what to do next.

She could return to battle the old woman; even without Kadahl, she may still beat the Gypsy. Or, she reminded herself, she could flee and go to Europe to find Lord Pakur; he would be unhappy with her but what else could she do?

She felt the arrival of the old woman before she heard the faint tapping of the cane on the stone covered roof.

"So you followed?"

Stepping out of the darkness, Lela nodded as she stopped ten feet from Semma's back.

"Yes, Voodoo Witch, we have unsettled business, you and I."

"What would that be, old one?" she asked turning to regard the woman.

"You fight for the Vampire Lord, for the undead enemies of man. As a Gypsy, I have taken an oath to confront and defeat your kind, to defend humans from you and those like you. You have crossed the line, Voodoo Queen; when you fight at the side of the undead, you are lost forever."

This brought a grunt from Semma. "Old woman, I am a Voodoo Sorceress. I have been lost since I chose that path."

Lela nodded almost as if sad for the woman. "I realize that. I know the unholy allegiances to your Lord you must make."

"Lord Pakur will show me power unheard of. I will be unstoppable."

Lela returned her challenging glare.

"This young Lord, the one you call Pakur, he will not defeat Creed," she assured the voodoo witch.

"He will," Semma replied. "To bad you will not be there to find out." With a slight movement of her lips she threw up her finger and sent a spell across the hospital roof.

Lela raised her cane, whispering her own secret words.

When the enchanted wood of the cane was

struck by the force of the Voodoo spell it instantly absorbed it!

Surprised, Semma did not hesitate as she pulled a small talisman from inside her coat. It was a small figurine of a woman and, motioning to Lela, she raised the doll.

"Selact con ool," she directed the spirit of the talisman.

Lela watched as a faint green glow began to emanate from the figurine. It grew in intensity rising up above the Voodoo Queen's head. It hovered there and Lela felt as if she was being sized up.

"This is the empty doll," Semma told her through pursed lips. "Unlike the dolls we use to control others this doll has no essence. It is an empty void looking for a soul to occupy. Ready yourself, old woman, it comes for yours."

Lela watched it hover across the rooftop. Like a green fog it continued from the doll trailing towards her.

"Your demon spawn magic cannot harm me," Lela said, reaching into her bag.

The Gypsy Witch pulled out a vial and removed the top. She held the glass container up over her head.

"Come to me," she whispered.

"You cannot control the power of the doll," Semma blurted out but before her disbelieving eyes the fog headed for the open vial.

As she continued to watch, growing more dismayed by the second, Semma felt annoyed as the power of the doll was sucked into the Gypsy's glass vial.

Lela corked it, trapping the soul stealer within the magical container.

"You think your magic is strong because you have conversed with demons?" she asked looking at the disgruntled Voodoo Queen. "I have inherited mine, passed down through centuries, and transferred through blood. Gypsy Witches are born not made."

Semma reached inside her leather trench a second time.

"Fine, then, forget magic. I will kill you the old fashioned way!"

Her arm flashed from her coat and Lela could see a wicked curved blade in her dark hand.

Slowly Lela dipped her head. "If that is the way you want it," she consented, removing her own silver tipped dagger.

Crouching, Semma started to close in on the older woman feeling she would be able to finish this quickly. She was much younger and stronger, thanks to Kadahl and his magic. This frail looking old woman would be an easy victim.

She lunged taking a wide swipe with her blade.

Steel met steel as the blade of the Gypsy met hers and turned it aside.

The Voodoo Queen sidestepped kicking hard for the old woman's knees. Lela however was not there and her strike contacted nothing but empty air.

Semma spun looking for her opponent, the old woman was standing a few feet away to her left. Unsure how she had avoided the strike, Semma faced her again.

"Let us try that again," Lela invited as she stepped forward driving her own blade at Semma.

There was a sudden sound of ripping cloth and torn leather as the Voodoo Queen felt the blade pass along her left hip.

"Ugh," she let out a groan as the Gypsy whirled and struck a second time, her enchanted blade burning across Semma's right shoulder.

She felt the fire in her waist as she realized her grip was weakening on the blade in her hand. Slowly, willing her fingers to work she tossed the weapon into her left hand. Brushing her hair back from around her face she looked for the old woman. How had she moved so fast and with such grace?

She had little time to wonder as a strong blow struck her in the kidneys and she was driven into the rough tar and stones of the rooftop.

Rolling to her back she stared up at the Gypsy.

"Give this up," the old woman offered. "Renounce your unholy allegiance to the undead, to Lord Pakur. I will heal your wounds and allow you to go away."

"No!" Semma snarled as she rose wobbly to her feet raising the blade before her.

"I will never forsake the Lord Pakur or my God, Satan," she spat out.

Lela raised her own weapon. "I understand."

They squared off again. Semma tensed; she would be faster this time, she would not make the mistake of underestimating this woman again.

She drove forward sending her blade at the old woman's eyes. With a flash, her blade was turned again and she redirected the attack trying for the inside of the Gypsy's thigh.

For the second time steel met steel and her weapon was tossed away before it could bite into flesh. She swung again trying for the old woman's throat.

Lela ducked the blow and blocked it; Semma's strike sailed harmlessly wild, deflected over her head. She drove upwards her enchanted weapon sinking deep into the Voodoo Queen just below her heart!

Semma let out a startled gasp as she felt the blade cutting into her.

"No!" she gasped.

Lela stepped away, quickly pulling the blade from the dying woman.

"Voodoo Witch, I was born with a blade in my hand," she explained wiping her weapon with a cloth. "It is instilled deep into my Gypsy heritage."

Semma clenched her teeth as her insides curled and pain shot through her.

Lela shook her head sadly. "I offered you the chance to leave here; you should have taken it."

From the rough stones of the roof Semma looked up at the old woman and suddenly she knew the awesome truth, they could not defeat the Gypsies. These people had been playing this game far to long; they were ready for the fight!

Jake dove into the approaching demons cleaving left and right with the sword of Takada. Close by his side, Asmus also drew Vampire blood. A loud shrieking of inhuman pain drew his attention across

the hall to the door of the hospital room. He caught
sight of Shach Meril as his deadly claws shredded
the screaming demon.

Spurred on by the little warrior, Jake tore into
three snarling vampire who swiped at him with their
claws. He side kicked one away, slamming the thing
into the near wall. Dropping to a knee he slashed
with the sword, driving it down across the body of
the next closer one.

It sunk to the floor, baring fangs, and turned to
smoke after the stroke of the enchanted weapon.

"Go back to Satan!" Jake yelled Creed's
favorite battle cry.

Asmus had just pulled his short swords free of a
smoking corpse. He saw the attack coming and
screamed a warning.

"Jake behind you!"

Jake turned and the motion kept him from being
decapitated. The attacking demon's claws tore
across his trench coat, but were turned aside by the
werewolf skin. Jake twisted trying to bring his
sword into play against the monster. At the last
moment his coat flapped open. The monster swept
again with its razor sharp claws tearing across the
unprotected chest of the Hunter.

Jake winced as the hook like claws dug deep
into his skin. In reflex Jake shot his sword upward.
The blade tore into the vampire up to its abdomen.
His eyes blurred with pain and tears. Jake drove the
blade in as deep as he could before he felt himself
fall to one knee.

Jake felt his vision blurring as a raging fire
spread through his veins. Selena had explained to

386

him the poisons of the vampire's claws. He gasped for breath vaguely aware of the pair of boots that ran at him from his left. Before he could react he was wounded again. Another set of claws raked the left side of his face and head. He was tossed backward hard into the wall, barely aware of slipping down to the floor. In a growing fog he looked down at the floor tile, it was quickly becoming sticky with blood-his blood!

His ears felt as if they were stuffed with cotton. He heard Asmus yell something to someone as the boots came at him again. His sword was gone; he did not know where it was, maybe still in the vampire that had wounded him. From above him he heard another unholy scream of pain and suddenly the boots were gone from his blurry vision. Struggling to raise his head he could make out Shach Meril, as the warrior cat slashed wickedly at the vampire's face.

The screaming in front of him ended as he slumped down to the floor lying in his own blood.

"You are injured badly," the soft purr-like voice sounded in his mind.

Asmus spoke from somewhere above him. "There are three that escaped; we will let them go. Jacob is much more important right now."

The cat's voice again. "He is hurt badly, old one. Creed could survive this; he has the wisdom and the experience but Jake is too young and too new to this business."

"I realize this," Asmus grunted. "We have to do something; he is a Hunter."

There was a pause above him before the feline

voice spoke again.

"I will send him away, separate the mind from the poisoned body. It is his only chance. In the meantime, pray the old woman returns quickly. She is the only one who can save him now."

There was that familiar flash of light and Jake found himself crossing through to that secret plane!

TWENTY-ONE

Jake found himself in a room filled with soft pillows and strong perfume. Looking down he could see his wounds were gone; in this realm he was whole and uninjured.

"Well, Ancestor!"

His head snapped to the far side of the room where the giant warrior of his previous trips sat. He was waist deep in a huge tub of steaming water waving a jeweled goblet at Jake.

"Be a good boy and refill me, will you."

He motioned to the large bottle of wine that was placed on a nearby table.

Jake smiled as he crossed the room to the bottle.

"How did the battle go?" he asked.

The giant frowned for a minute. "Battle?" he asked. "Which one?"

"The one with the Romans. How did it go? Did you win?"

The giant warrior smiled widely. "Yes we did, hundreds of those bastards decorated the poles that night," he waved again at the wine. "Hurry I am very parched right now. After all, I have pleasured three women tonight. I must rebuild my strength before the next arrives."

Jake felt the smile break his face. "Four women; in one night?"

The warrior shrugged. "It is my way, Ancestor. I fight; I eat and drink and I screw," he chuckled a little. "What else is there?"

Jake picked up the wine bottle and stepped across the room refilling the giant's goblet.

"Nothing I guess," he had to admit.

The warrior winked back. "I should say not."

He drank deeply from his goblet before looking up at Jake.

"So what have you done now?" he asked pausing. "Why are you here this time?"

He leaned forward in the tub examining the face of the young Hunter.

"I was in a battle with a large number of vampires," Jake began. "I reacted too slowly, I guess, and was wounded badly."

The warrior raised an eyebrow. "A large number of them?" he paused.

"How many two or three hundred?"

Jake felt his face flush under the warrior's gaze.

389

"No, more like a dozen," he admitted.

Sitting back in the tub the big man drank from his goblet with a loud sigh.

"That is not a large number," he said shaking his head. "But you are young and new to this; you will get better with age."

He swallowed more wine and met Jake's eyes. "How were you wounded?"

"I was clawed across the chest and face, at least I think so. I was starting to pass out about that time."

The warrior grunted as he reached for the bottle again. "You will learn to battle the effects of the vampire's poison," He pointed out, filling his goblet.

Jake reached for the empty cup on the table near the tub. "I hope so. I feel bad that I left Shach Meril and Asmus alone, because I was wounded."

The giant chuckled throwing back his head. "You do not have to worry about those two, Jacob Reid. They are more than capable of taking care of a few demons."

Lela suddenly appeared at their side.

"What happened?" she asked, looking down on the ashen face of the Hunter.

Asmus took a deep breath as he stood. "He is wounded badly. Shach Meril has separated his mind and body for now. We were praying you would return soon."

She reached into her bag.

"I will be able to cure him." She removed vials

of powerful Gypsy potions.

They watched as she separated the various vials, setting them out before her. Most were strange colored powders.

"We must hurry," Shach Meril advised as he monitored Jake's breathing. "He is starting to fade."

Lela reached forward running her hand over the Hunter's forehead, withdrawing it she shook her head.

"He is far from dead, King of the Trillii; but you are right. Time is of the essence here."

With Asmus and the cat watching for possible surprises, Lela went to work opening and mixing her vials. She removed a bowl from her bag placing it next to the open vials.

"Sacred water," she said to them as she produced a small wineskin.

She continued with her work, filling the bowl with the malodorous liquid.

"Wow," Asmus commented, wrinkling his face. "Smell that."

"It is strong magic," the cat agreed his eyes glued to witch. Lela was casting a spell as she mixed various powders into the water.

The water in the bowl hissed and turned various colors as the powerful ingredients were added while the old woman murmured above them.

"Solre dolac medzal."

With her right forefinger she stirred the mixture, which gave off a stronger but more pleasant smell as it combined.

Lela had her eyes closed starting to sway from the waist up while she whispered the spell over and over repeating it in a rhythmic chant. She continued to stir the mixture with her finger while Jake lay barely breathing at her side.

"He gets worse," Shach Meril purred looking into the face of the woman.

Lela opened her eyes stopping her chant.

"It is okay. I have completed the spell; we can apply the salve to the wounds now. Slowly it will drive the poison of the vampire's claws from his system."

She dipped her hands into the yellowish mix. "Hold him still while I administer it."

With a nod Asmus knelt beside her taking Jake's hands.

"Well of course they are."

The big man said stepping from the tub and reaching for a large rough looking towel. "They have fought many vampire before," he added.

Jake frowned. "I know that Asmus is old, but the cat, how many could he have fought in his time? Cats don't live that long."

The warrior looked over his shoulder as he ran the towel across his hard, well-muscled body.

"Shach Meril lives much longer than your average feline," he pointed out. "I believe the original Warrior King lived for one hundred of our human years."

Jake nodded as the scarred hand of this giant fighter picked up the bottle again, refilling his goblet. He realized the man's whole body was covered in old scars, much like Creed's. He also realized his body would be scarred also if he continued to be wounded like he was now.

"That cat never fails to amaze me," he admitted filling his own mug.

The giant sat, his towel wrapped about his waist. He walked across the room to the fireplace where he tossed in more wood.

"Shach Meril, as the Trillii Kings before him, is a tremendous warrior and deeply devoted to the war against the undead. You will find that having such an ally can be a tremendous help to you. Trillii warriors have a way of showing up when you need them the most."

"Do you know Asmus very well?"

The giant sat back, the chair groaning under his weight.

"Ahh, yes, Ancestor, I know him very well. We have fought many battles side by side over the span of time. I was quite happy when he told me another of my line had been chosen."

With a smile he regarded Jake closely. "In these current times it is not so easy to find those who can be Hunters."

Jake raised an eyebrow. "What do you mean?"

With a wave of his hand the warrior went on.

"To be a Hunter you must be chosen, preferably from a long line of warriors, men who have fought the undead from the beginning of time. My line, your family tree if you will, has that honor. We have fought the monsters of Satan since long before recorded history. Of course, we are not of the Gypsy blood like Creed or Asmus but we are special in our own way."

"What makes the Gypsies so special?" Jake wondered. "No one has ever explained that to me."

The giant looked from his wine. "They are not *special*, so to speak; it is their heritage that is. You see when the world moved on men forgot some of the old ways, how to communicate with the animals, how to read the moon and the winds, how to become one with the forces of nature, using them to their advantage," he burped loudly. "In your time, Ancestor, they are simply superior when it comes to hunting the undead."

Jake had to agree on that point. He had watched Creed in action enough to realize that. "Creed has seen a lot of battles."

"More than that," the warrior added. "He has lived a very long time with one burning desire, to hunt and destroy the enemies of human kind."

He was about to drink again, but stopped, a far away look coming into his hard eyes.

"I will never forget the first time I met him." He smiled with a shake of his head.

"I would like to hear the story."

The big man shifted in his chair. "Very good."

"It was a very, very long time ago. My village was located deep into the mountains, an area in the central Alps. In your time, it is best described as near Lake Constance, located where the borders of Germany, Austria and Switzerland meet. It's a beautiful area, even more so in those days, where you could ride for weeks between villages. In my village, there was a small tavern where we would meet to drink and discuss matters of the area. It was there on a dark rainy day, that he appeared.

"I was sitting by the door watching the heavy dark blue clouds full of rain above the mountain peaks when I saw him. He appeared as if from the very fog itself, riding from the thick woods that surrounded our little settlement. Behind him rode a very beautiful woman with fiery red hair and deep green eyes. The rain was drizzling down slowly on the two, who appeared to have been in the saddle for a long time. They were completely drenched and their horses moved stiffly as they navigated the mud.

"I was puzzled and curious at the same time as these two strangers rode into our camp from the wilderness. You see, very few men would travel alone with a woman through the woods and mountains. There being numerous thieves and highwaymen, not to mention dangerous animals that would eat a man. Of course, after I got to know Creed and Marisa, it became quite clear that they were in no danger from anyone or thing."

"Marisa, the first love of Creed's life," Jake murmured.

The giant nodded. "Yes, and what a woman she was. Stunning good looks mixed with great skill and ability with the sword. She was his soul mate. I have never seen a man and woman so well matched," he smiled softly as he peered into his wine goblet.

"They dismounted and walked into our little tavern. Creed led the way, looking about, studying our faces before he allowed her to enter. Despite her being a warrior, he was always strangely protective of Marisa.

'Food and wine.' He said as several men stood, allowing them the table nearest the fire. He removed the dark coat of werewolf hide revealing his arsenal of weapons that had been concealed from our eyes.

'I will return,' he told the woman before walking back outside to their horses where he removed a large well-wrapped bundle from each. We watched, curious as he came back to the table and unwrapped the first package. It was a finely made Scottish Claymore. Of course, at the time, I didn't know that; he would tell me later. He handed it to her and she slid it over her shoulder like she had been born with it there. This was amazing to us because women did not fight in the way of men in our culture.

"Next he unwrapped the second bundle revealing a strong looking sword with a long narrow blade. This he placed over his own well-muscled shoulder.

"Food was brought and wine, and as they ate, Creed looked about the room.

"'Who is the leader here in this village?' He asked.

"I stepped forward, explaining that I was the village chieftain. He invited me to sit and then proceeded to tell me that we were all in grave danger.

"'Danger?' I snorted.' We are safe enough here in our village. Our enemies have been defeated and we have agreements with most of the surrounding villages.'

"I remember he allowed a deep burp to rise

396

from his chest and then looked at me, his deep dark
eyes burning into my soul.

"'These are not human enemies.'

"He then went on to explain to me what kind of
new danger lurked in our surrounding forest.
Aghast, I listened as this stranger relayed to me
story after story of the vampire. Of course, I thought
this longhaired stranger had lost his mind. I mean, it
all sounded so strange and bizarre. I knew how to
fight men, but I had never fought such beasts. He
smiled at that, this Gypsy Warrior. He explained
that only the Hunters could stand a chance against
the demons.

"It was not very long before he recruited me,
just as he recruited you to be a Hunter. After that
time in my life I was never quite the same again."

At this the huge warrior shrugged at the memory
and allowed a slow smile to creep across his face.

"We had quite the battle with that coven of
demons in my forest, but in the end, Creed killed
them all."

Jake grunted, he could imagine the scene as the
Gypsy Hunter drove through his enemies like a hot
knife through butter.

A low knock on the door drew his attention
away from the warrior who also looked to the door.

"Enter," the warrior invited.

The door to the room opened slowly and a
round face framed in soft blonde hair peeked in.

The warrior waved with a scarred right hand.

"Come in missy, I have been waiting for ya."

Jake felt his eyes run over the plump body that
followed the face. She was young and well

developed, her large right breast lying outside of her
garments. Jake felt strangely aroused by her.

"If you would excuse me," the warrior waved
towards the door

"I have an account downstairs with the Lord of
the house. Whatever you want he will take care of
for you. For now, my young ancestor, please allow
me to slake my thirst."

Jake stood draining the glass in his hand.

"It has been a pleasure, as always," he addressed
the warrior before turning to the door. "I will see
you when I see you."

With that he walked out into the hallway and
made his way down the steep steps into a smoky
room filled with wild-eyed warriors.

There was a bar at one end and a roaring fire at
the other. Jake felt the eyes of several scantily clad
females upon him.

Across the floor he locked eyes with a very
beautiful red head; her green eyes were surveying
him with undisguised hunger.

He smiled back and nodded pointing to his drink
and to her; he would be glad to buy her one. She
was making her way across the floor her eyes
locked to his when he started to feel the familiar
feeling. He was being summoned back to the world.

"Not now!" He cried out in vain as his form
slowly started to drift away.

"He will live to spout more foolish babble,"
Lela nodded in satisfaction.

"We should get him into a soft bed; he will need

to rest," Asmus reached down and tossed Jake over his shoulder with a show of strength peculiar in a man of his age.

Groaning Jake tried to raise his head. "Where am I now?"

Asmus dropped him lightly into a bed next to Selena and Lela moved to his side.

"You were wounded," Lela explained, pouring some powder into her hand. "But you are going to be fine. You only need to rest for now."

She leaned down softly and blew the powder into his face.

"Hey, what was that?" he asked weakly.

Before she answered he felt himself drifting away to a deep sleep.

"He will sleep for a day or so now," Lela informed Asmus and Shach Meril. "When he wakes, he will be completely healed, thanks to the magic herbs in his system."

The old Gypsy Hunter looked at the witch, concern in his experienced eyes.

"Something worries you though," he observed. "Will there be more trouble tonight?"

She stepped to the large window staring out over the restless city. Fingering the talisman at her neck she shook her head, her earrings shining in the low light of the room.

"No; I do not worry for us," she whispered as if afraid someone might hear. "There are strange things at work here. When Darius called me, he spoke of The Dolmage."

"We don't believe this is it, however," Asmus interrupted.

Lela nodded. "Darius does not believe so either. But I was doing some reading on one of his hunches, an old memory he had heard around a campfire over four hundred years ago."

She paused and even Shach Meril watched her intently waiting for her next words.

"Darius told me about a priest he once met, a man very much like Nostradamus, but wiser because he kept his visions to himself, except for one night while they shared a fire in the Dutch countryside. He said they were sitting there after a large dinner of roasted venison when this man suddenly looked at him with a strange expression. Knowing they had consumed most of their wine, my uncle thought at first he was simply drunk. But soon he began to babble and draw strange figures in the sand. Next thing Creed knew, this man stood and pointing the smoldering end of a branch at him, whispered the words 'espresse do latte'."

Asmus frowned. "The language is above me. It's not Latin, though. It sounds very much like the older version."

"That is because it is not," Shach Meril purred as he met the gaze of the witch. "Unless I miss my guess, it's much older than Latin."

Lela nodded as she turned from the window. "As a king of the Trillii you remember the source of such speech," she dipped her head in a reverent bow.

"What are you talking about?" Asmus asked becoming impatient.

Lela cleared her throat. "They were the words of Satan predicting, not a Dolmage, but a great shift in the world of the vampire itself. A time when human survival would not be challenged but the survival of the race of vampire itself."

"Of course," the cat dipped its head. "The shift in power that would allow the Dolmage to become possible. The story is of the powers that could stop such a nightmare-a Gypsy and a vampire fighting side by side. Natural enemies who would ally themselves for a higher cause."

Asmus shook his head. "But that would mean Rasmere would welcome the coming of Pakur and his followers, not fight them tooth and nail. I don't know about you but I think that Rasmere really hates this Pakur."

Lela nodded at his reasoning. "This is what worries me. I cannot see what Darius is heading into or what Rasmere truly feels. As far as I know, it may be a trap."

Asmus snorted. "I should be there then, standing next to Creed and helping to stop this thing."

Lela smiled as she pointed to the cat. "And so should he," she announced.

"We had best leave at once, then," Asmus spun on his boot heel.

"He does not understand," Lela said to the cat.

Shach Meril lay down on the bed licking a blood-covered paw. "It is not for us to do, Asmus," he explained. "Creed must face this on his own, win or lose."

Lela nodded grimly agreeing with the sacred animal on the bed.

401

Asmus looked from one to the next. "Now is a fine time to tell me all of this."

Lela chuckled slightly. "If you had known you would have gone with him no matter what," she explained. "And it was already written that you would stay here and protect the unborn Prince. You see, fate chose you and Shach Meril along with Jake over there, for the job."

Asmus raised an eyebrow. "Why?" he asked dryly.

Lela allowed her smile to widen. "Because someone somewhere knew you would succeed."

In a huff, Asmus jerked open the room door and burst into the hall.

"Witches!" he exclaimed as he slammed the door behind him.

Lela looked from the door to the cat. "Are you ready?" she asked reaching out her hands.

Shach Meril stood shaking himself. "Yes, Gypsy Witch, it is time for me to go." He looked at the door to the room. "He will explode when he finds I have gone."

Lela took the cat in her hands rubbing it lovingly between the ears.

"But you are the only one that can stop the minion of Satan long enough if the ceremony works."

Shach Meril gave her a brief look. "It is the honor of my kind, even as my ancestor fought off the serpent once before."

The witch felt a tear form in the corner of her eye. "Be careful, great king," she whispered. "The one Satan sends will be powerful."

Again the steady gaze of the cat met hers. "I only have to make him pause long enough for the priest to send him back and close the door or Creed kills him. It is my solemn vow to give my life if it becomes necessary."

At his words Lela reached down and kissed him lightly on the nose.

"Good journey, brave one."

With a flick of her hands, he was gone!

TWENTY-TWO

Creed sat at the small table outside one of his favorite taverns, drinking a well-preserved red wine while feasting on venison, fresh bread and cheese. He sighed; it was like the old days-days of riding the open meadows of the world with Marisa. A Scottish highlander and the daughter of a noble clan, she had caught his eye one day during some local festival, as he happened to be passing through.

"Hmmm Marisa."

He spoke to himself in quiet private tones as he pictured her on a beautiful roan stallion galloping across the woods of her homeland, her red hair flying wildly behind her.

Of course her favorite Claymore bounced at her side and at least two pistols were in her belt.

He shook his head as he wondered if the days he had spent since the day she had died were as fulfilled as he could have made them. A picture of Selena shot into his mind and he nodded to himself; he had found true love again and now, possibly after this was over, he could find peace.

At the thought, he peered at the top of the mansion that peaked over the hills on the far side of the valley, his family's home for more years than he could count. Tonight its halls would be filled with the hated vampire and as this thought made his skin crawl, the image of their unholy blood running down its halls seemed fitting.

"Tonight, Father, I make you proud," he whispered to the memory of the man who had given him life.

"What?"

The voice broke him from his thoughts as Rasmere sat down heavily in the chair across from him.

Creed had to admit that he could have been friends with the man in front of him had it not been for the monster inside of the man.

"Lord Rasmere."

The vampire smiled sarcastically. "I would prefer you did not call me that while I am in human form, and we are friends," he rolled his eyes. "Save it for when we are trying to kill each other again."

"Do you think it will be so easy the next time?" Creed asked filling the glass in front of the vampire from his wine bottle.

Rasmere sat back with an audible groan. "I do not think; I know," he explained. "After this is over we can never be friends."

Creed chuckled and picked up his wineglass. "Answer me a question then so I have a good reason to kill you."

Raising an eyebrow Rasmere allowed a slight smile to play across his lips.

"Yes, Creed? I am curious, go ahead."

The Gypsy ran his hands back through his hair before raising his eyes to meet the Lord's.

"Marisa," he said. "She was my love and you killed her, the only woman I loved."

Rasmere sipped from his glass of wine and stopped meeting the heat of the Gypsy's gaze.

"Yes I did," he admitted. "But now you have a new love and I have saved her life."

He paused and then pointed at Creed's chest. "You owe me one."

"Yes I do," Creed admitted. "But I have a damn good idea you will reclaim that debt tonight."

Rasmere snorted. "You are very good, better than they have always claimed. You smell or sense them, don't you?"

This time Creed snorted. "Of course, and you knew they were here also, or at least should have by now."

"I knew," the Lord admitted.

They sat a few minutes, each drinking their

wine as they stared at the top of the home of the Gypsy Prince.

"A beautiful place," the vampire admitted. "I have never had a home. Even a man like you, who is rarely there, must appreciate the comfort of one."

Creed plucked a piece of cheese into his mouth and savored the taste of the homemade fare.

"I love it here; I always have. I am sure it is the one true place on Earth where I feel peace."

"Is it because of the Gypsy magic that guards the valley?" Rasmere asked trying a piece of cheese before spitting it out. "How can you eat that crap?"

The Gypsy Prince simply shook his head as he watched the piece of cheese bounce along the cobblestones of the sidewalk.

"No, it is because it has always been my home no matter where I travel. I have seen some of the most beautiful places on the face of this planet. But here," he paused waving a scarred hand at the village. "I am simply at rest in this valley."

Rasmere nodded in agreement. "I think I can identify with you a little on that one. The area where I was raised is dear to me also."

"It has always been a place of solitude, a place where I could rest and heal but now the vampire enters this valley and I must fight him here."

Above them heavy clouds of angry blue and black rolled across the far end of the valley. Rasmere sniffed the air before his eyes locked with Creed's.

"They are here."

The Gypsy nodded with a heavy sigh. "Yes, I can smell them also. A lot of them."

406

His hand froze, the wine glass halfway back to the tabletop, as Rasmere shot to his feet with a menacing snarl.

"Do you sense that, Hunter?" the Lord snapped, his tone short and his milky blue eyes searching the skies.

Creed stood slowly, his hands going to the silver knives in his belt.

"Yes," He looked about at the growing storm. "Pakur has brought along some powerful friends."

Rasmere whirled his long trench coat flowing about his waist as he clenched his hands into tight fists.

"Not just powerful friends, Creed, members of the council!" his voice resonated the anger that was growing in the Vampire Lord's chest.

"They dare to involve themselves with a bastard like Pakur!" his voice was growing louder and Creed could see the stares of nearby townsfolk.

"Come on, let's get out of here," he suggested, pulling the Lord by the elbow. "Save that anger for tonight you will need it in the coming battle."

"I swear to Satan himself," the vampire roared to the growing storm. "I will tear this turned bastard's heart from his chest myself!"

As they watched the Prince drag the screaming stranger away the townsfolk whispered to themselves as they also kept an eye on the fast building clouds.

"Devils work!" an old woman yelled over the street before she pulled her shutters closed and threw the bolt. "Thank the Lord that Darius Creed, the Prince of our people, is here!"

Hurrying away the villagers did not notice the small flash of light that died quickly behind the restaurant's garbage pile.

From the slowly rising smoke stepped a cat. The animal was wearing a rich looking cloth cape upon its back. It was red and tinged in gold tassel with the ancient emblem of the Trillii warriors emblazoned upon it. Around the neck of the proud feline, there was suspended a finely crafted silver chain, while matching silver earrings dangled from his ears.

It padded from the alleyway, its sharp nose picking up the scent of both Creed and the Vampire Lord Rasmere of Haeth. With a turn of its head, it also took note of the growing clouds in the valley skies, an unnatural magic-conjured storm. Shach Meril knew what this meant; the enemy was here and in full force.

He pointed himself in the direction of Creed's scent and padded down the cobblestones.

Turning the corner at the end of the block, he heard a low angry growl from across the street. His eyes narrowed as he studied the large yellow dog that trotted at him past several young men.

The growl grew deeper and more menacing. The dog stopped five feet away and tensed, preparing to leap at the foolish cat that had allowed him to get so close.

Meeting the watery eyes, Shach Meril shook his head, the earrings glittering in the fading light.

"Do not be so foolish," he warned.

At this the dog froze.

"You are a Trillii warrior?" it asked in the rough language of the canine.

Shach Meril nodded in answer.

The dog stepped back warily; it was not wise to battle one of the Trillii, especially one wearing the sacred cloak of battle.

"Forgive me, I was foolish," it explained with a slight bow of its large head.

The cat accepted the apology. "I am here on a mission to battle the unholy vampire. I know that in this sacred valley of the Gypsy there are a small number of my warriors. I need you to put out the word. Shach Meril calls them to battle."

At this a tremor passed through the body of the canine. "You are Shach Meril?" it asked, stepping back even more. "It shall be done Warrior King. I will pass the word."

Shach Meril answered with a nod. "Tell them to find me tonight; we have a war to fight!"

With that he was gone down the street on his way to find Creed.

"Something bothers me."

Rasmere looked at the Gypsy. "What?" he asked before turning back to the coming storm.

"They do not have the Toscanno girl. I thought she was a very important part of all of this?"

Rasmere frowned. "Yes, or at least her blood was."

Down the valley the winds began to pick up and they could feel the warm breeze as it swept upon them.

It was infested with the stench of the vampire.

"Why would the Council be here?" he asked watching his estate through the blowing tree limbs.

They stood in the grove below his lands in the farthest corner where the grave of the vampire he had killed saving Lela was located.

"Something is going on here and I do not like it." Rasmere folded his arms over his chest. "They do not belong here and certainly do not belong near that bastard, Pakur. The Council I remember, would never have given a turned vampire the time of day, much less appear to them. I do not like it at all."

"What would the priest be to them?" Creed asked trying to work out the angles in his mind.

Rasmere shook his head again. "I don't know. There are stories and legends even older than I. I could only guess that it has something to do with the Dolmage or an event much like it. Pakur is after power and that is what motivates him. Whatever it is, there is a great reward involved, of that I am sure."

"It is much more than that," a purr-like voice sounded from the trees.

"Join us," Creed invited.

The cat dropped from the tree limb and the Gypsy noted the battle dress of the animal. Trillii warriors only wore their cloaks when they knew the battle was going to be important.

Rasmere watched the cat as it came to their side.

"What do you know, cat?" the vampire demanded his tone short, but respectful, towards the enemy warrior before him.

"An old legend that warns of a restructuring of

410

the entire Vampire race.

"The fall of the True Bloods and the rise of a newer stronger breed of demon blessed by the powers of Satan and poised to spring upon the human race. This new form of vampire will feed and gorge itself until it destroys all of mankind. In the end Satan will realize all of his dreams; he will have destroyed God's children while placing the vampire above all others on the face of the Earth."

"What?" Rasmere scoffed. "That is nonsense, I have never heard of such a thing."

The cat met his gaze. "It was a very old legend, as I have explained. I believe an Egyptian smoke seer originally forecast it in the time of the Pharaoh Rameses."

"They were all crazy babbling idiots," Rasmere countered. "I would not believe anything one said."

Shach Meril returned a brief nod. "There are signs," he explained.

They turned regarding the feline closely as he explained.

"The legend calls for the blood of a powerful Lord, Broshmer of course, carried by a young woman and allowed to grow in power while it feeds off her essence."

Creed and Rasmere shared a look.

"We have already discussed this possibility," Rasmere agreed.

Creed grunted. "Even though the girl herself is safe."

The cat met his gaze. "Yes, Hunter, I would guess that Pakur has her blood and enough of it to continue with the ceremony. The priest, of course, will have to recite the sacred words that will allow Satan himself to step into our world. If that happens, Pakur will be granted absolute power from the Dark Prince. My next guess would be that he would set up his own council and sit at its head as the most powerful vampire of all."

"The bastard!" Rasmere fumed his eyes turning to the building storm over Creed's estate. "He would destroy all that we have built over the thousands of years we have hunted on this world."

Ignoring the vampire, Creed looked at the top of his home. "How many will there be? Members of the council, I mean."

Rasmere's eyes narrowed. "Normally it would be a death warrant to discuss such things with you. But with the way things have been going," he paused. "There will be a full twelve."

"Twelve?" Creed raised an eyebrow. "I was not aware that the council was back to full strength."

Rasmere replied with a nod, his anger subsiding a bit. "Of course it was done quietly and in great secrecy, we did not want you to know, of course."

At this the Gypsy chuckled. "I guess I cannot blame you. But how long has it been since you have talked to your kinship? Surely you would have been told of these plans sooner. I cannot believe that the council would make such a move without one of its most powerful members?"

There was a strange sound in the Gypsy's tone and the Lord turned to Creed.

"If you think I have knowledge of this, you are wrong. They know I would never settle for a turned bastard vampire sitting in the high seat."

There was a pause between them before Rasmere continued, a growl low in his throat. "Lord Dahm, on the other hand, has grown old and senile. I believe it is he who has allowed this."

"Dahm," Creed asked. "He is still sitting in the high seat?"

Rasmere replied with a short nod. "Yes, for over seven hundred years now."

Before they could continue the sound of men filled the wind whipped grove.

Filing in next to them appeared the young men of the village, Wilfred and Joel. They were carrying the ancient weapons of battle and were adorned in numerous knives, swords, pikes and other odd pieces of armor.

"We are ready," Raoul announced as they met the Gypsy and the Lord.

"I hope you are," Creed remarked looking at the assembled teenagers. "This is not a game we will play in a few short hours." He motioned to the growing clouds and the coming storm. "The magic of the vampire at work."

They followed his finger and several gasped softly in awe.

"Tonight, there will be very powerful vampires in my estate. With them will be a great number of human minions who want to be slaves. The humans are yours and you will leave the undead to us," he motioned to Rasmere and himself.

"I will be there also," Shach Meril purred, his soft voice entering the grove.

"Of course," Creed agreed. "And we are grateful to have the help of the Trillii."

The cat dipped its head in response to the Prince of the Gypsies.

"I must stress to you the importance of staying away from the vampires. The weapons you have are enchanted and will kill them if it becomes necessary in self-defense. I suggest you team up two on one if it becomes necessary. One on one, you cannot match their strength or speed."

"But you can?" Chaz asked a tone of disbelief in his voice.

"I have been trained and also possess powers from the secret Gypsy Witches."

"Don't forget to point out the vast experience you have in killing them," Rasmere interjected, a serious look on his face.

Creed ignored the Lord and continued.

"You keep the humans off our back; that is your job. We will pursue and battle the demons. No matter what happens, do not follow us if they lead us inside of the main buildings," he caught their eyes. "Is that understood?"

Each stated in a clear voice that they did indeed understand.

"I want to split you into two groups; Joel will lead one and Wilfred the second."

"Me?" the butler asked as he stepped forward adorned in two ancient Hindu swords. "I do not think that is a good idea."

Raoul and Chaz both shook their heads.

"We lead our own groups," Chaz argued.

Creed's eyes narrowed as he regarded the two young men.

"Have either of you ever been in real battle?" he

asked the young men, to which they shook their heads no.

"Joel, here, has been fighting the undead for a very long time, and Wilfred," He gave the butler another tap on the shoulder. "Is a Vietnam vet."

He met the Butler's gaze. "Khe Sahn right?"

"Yes," the butler admitted.

"So, they will lead the groups tonight and if you young men want to survive, do what they tell you."

Disappointed, the two younger men relented, stepping back into the group.

"Now lets talk about how I want to do this."

Taking the two men and Rasmere aside he started drawing with a stick in the soft ground.

TWENTY-THREE

The angry clouds swirled overhead blotting out
the moon as the wind whipped across the courtyard
of Creed's estate.

His long werewolfskin coat slapped about his
leather-clad thighs as the Gypsy walked into the
empty courtyard with the Vampire Lord at his side.

"I smell them," Rasmere snarled as his milky
blue eyes scanned the shadows among the gardens.
"Lots of them, human and vampire mixed."

Creed nodded, he could sense them also and his
fists tightened on the knives at his waist.

They continued on, the hard stones of the square
slapping against their leather soled boot heels, but

416

barely audible over the howling wind outside of the stone walls.

"Remember to stay cool," Creed reminded the hotheaded vampire at his side. "I want Pakur to reveal his plan before we attack."

"Just stay out of my way when the time comes," Rasmere snarled at his side.

They were under the great lights in the center of the square when the sound of running feet and rushing bodies filled the night.

"Here they come," Rasmere whispered.

Out of the night appeared the human minions their hands filled with weapons or torches.

"Halt!" one ordered stepping forward.

"On whose authority?" Creed asked feeling the growing numbers as they were quickly circled.

"Miiiine!"

From behind the humans Pakur stepped forward followed by eleven hooded shapes. "I ammm master of thisss house toniiiight Creeed," he continued.

"And after thisss isss ooover I may remain here. It isss quiiite beautiful and wellll maintained. It mussst haaave taken yearsss toooo put togetherrr."

With a flick he tossed back his hood and stared directly at Rasmere.

"Sooo the traitor shoowsss himself," he stated in an accusing tone. "The lord whooo prefers the company of a Gypsssy Hunterrr."

Behind him the eleven hooded shapes nodded in unison.

At Creed's side Rasmere fumed and the Gypsy noticed when he raised a fist in answer, it was in his true form.

417

"You bassstard," the Lord responded pointing a clawed hand his way. "You woullld daaare toooo accuse meee?"

Pakur smiled flashing blood stained incisor teeth. "I dooo, ooold man." There was challenge in his tone and his eyes.

Rasmere looked over the younger Lord's shoulder. "And the ressst of you. To ssstand with himmm?"

"It isss of nooo concern tooo you nowww," a hooded voice spoke in answer.

Rasmere's eyes narrowed. "Dahm, you daaare tooo speak to meee while standing at hisss baaack?"

The high Lord of the vampire council simply nodded back.

"I daaare."

Rasmere took a step forward but soon a dozen spears pointed at his chest.

"Noot yettt!" Pakur stopped his minions. "But sooon enough."

Turning to the Gypsy, Pakur smiled. "You haave coome alooone Creeed?" he asked, a smile playing about his lips. "You muust be groowing foolish, Hunter."

"I am not alone," Creed answered before whistling over his shoulder.

From the dark there shot the young men from town, their weapons bristling in the yard lights and directed at the minions of the vampire.

"Very good," Pakur smiled. "Someone to keeep myyy men busssy."

He spun on his heel followed by the eleven lords of the council.

"Allow the Gypsy and the traitor to follow, kill the rest," he ordered over his shoulder before they disappeared into the main house.

"Here we go," Creed warned as he drew his knives.

"I will gut that bastard child," Rasmere vowed at his side as they hurried to the house. Behind them, the clash of weapons and yelling men drowned out the crashing thunder of the storm overhead.

They entered the main house and Creed drew his enchanted knives feeling their reassuring grip in his scarred fists.

"They will be in the main hall; I would bet on that," he whispered over his shoulder.

Rasmere nodded. "Lead on, Gypsy Prince, this is your home, after all."

They slipped down the entryway into the hallway of the mansion. Rasmere marveled at the highly polished wood that lined the hall; it was expensive and rare. The Gypsy had good taste, which was apparent.

As they came to the end of the hall, he raised an eyebrow. Two great doors appeared that had been hidden before, detailed into the wood itself.

"Impressive," the Lord reminded himself.

"Ready?" Creed asked back over his shoulder.

"Yesss," the vampire answered. "Let's get thisss ooover with."

With a deep breath the Gypsy threw open the doors.

"Come in, Creeeed and bring the traitorrr with you," Pakur's voice sounded loudly from across the

419

hall.

Rasmere bristled in anger. "I ssswear I wiiill riiip hiiis heart out."

"Come on," Creed motioned with his head.

They stepped into the immense hall and Rasmere could see the eleven council members with Pakur seated in high-backed chairs, replicas of the original council furniture. In the middle a full two feet higher from the rest sat Pakur, his hood thrown back and a smile on his feral face.

"Loook."

He pointed with a claw to their right, trussed up on an inverted cross was the priest. He was pale and drawn but he looked their way and appeared to hold himself higher when he saw Creed.

"A mockery of the crucifixion of Christ. How nice," Creed said across the hall to Pakur.

"Before thisss isss over heee will regret dying for your sinsss, human," Dahm, to the right side of Pakur, said.

"We will see," Creed replied stepping forward.

Several of the council members stood as if to block his way.

"You are alooone, Gypsy Hunterrr," Pakur warned raising a finger toward them. "The traitor weee will deal with later but you willl die right nowww. Noooot even the legendary Dariusss Creeeed can stop eleven of the pooowerful council members."

"You would sacrifice them to kill me?" Creed asked gripping his knives and feeling the excitement of a coming fight.

"Dooo nooot worry, Gypsssy. We will tell them

420

allll how bravely you died."

This time a chuckle escaped from the Gypsy's lips. "I am not dead yet," he reminded them.

"You sooon will be," Dahm warned stepping forward. Three others followed.

"Step back, Rasssmere of Haeth; stay out ooof thisss and we will have leniency on you later."

"After whaaat I haaave seen, I prefer tooo fight with the Gypsssy," he replied, stepping next to Creed.

"Have ittt your wayyy," Dahm snickered while motioning three more vampires to join them in encircling the pair.

Seven vampires, powerful blood gorged Lords, flexed their claws preparing to attack and rip the Gypsy and their vampire brother to pieces.

"Whaaat would you like to ssssay before weee killll you, Creeeed?" Pakur asked a look of glee radiating from his dead eyes.

"Only one thing," the Gypsy answered watching the shuffling boots of the vampires around him. "Now."

"Now?" Pakur asked in confusion.

"We are here, Gypsy Prince, at your command."

Pakur's jaw dropped as the soft purr-like voice rang out into the great hall. He looked up as the Warrior King peered down upon them from the balcony above the hall.

"Shach Merilllll," the vampire hissed. "Not even you are enough tooo even the odds toniiight. I have plannnned welll."

With a slight shake of his head the King of the Trillii settled back on his haunches and thumped his hind leg twice on the polished rail.

Immediately, on each side of the Warrior King appeared twenty Trillii warriors, forty in all. Upon their backs they wore the red cloaks of their proud heritage and around each neck sparkled the shiny silver chain of the Trillii elite guard.

"The odds grow even," Shach Meril purred through the hall. Turning toward Creed, the cat bowed his head. "We are your servants, Gypsy Prince."

Pakur looked from the Trillii elite guard to the members of the council, they were staring at the warriors above them while backing slowly away from Creed and Rasmere.

"Doo nooot fear themmm!" Pakur ordered. "Our looord willl come to usss. Just keep them busssy until I can get tooo the priest!"

Their eyes shot to him and he could see they were weighing their chances. Forty Trillii warriors and a Gypsy Hunter, not to mention, Rasmere of Haeth; it was a dangerous challenge.

"I willl cast the spelllsss," he called out to them. "Killl the Gypsy and the traitor and every ooone of those foul beastsss," he pointed to the champions of the human race.

"For Satan!" he urged them while running to the spot where Father Joe hung suspended, hands tied over his head on the upside down cross.

"For Satan!"

They cried out in unison and poised to attack!

Creed watched Pakur run madly across the hall

as Shach Meril led the warriors of the Trillii from the balcony above. They were met by snarling Vampire Lords whose claws raked the air searching for their bodies.

At his side, he was aware that Rasmere was now in full vampire form and snarled in answer to his kinship while the three circled and waited for an opening to attack.

"Remember, Creed, when I need you, you owe me!" he yelled without the hissing speech of the vampire. It must have taken great strength to restrain the demon speech of his true form.

Creed had little time to reflect upon this as he was rushed from the left. With the flat of his blade he turned aside the claws that raked for his flesh and spun, driving a pounding back kick into the chest of a second attacker. Crying out in pain, the vampire was tossed backward into the high backed chairs as Creed turned his attention back to the first demon.

"I will eat your heart!" the Lord promised as he rushed in claws punching for the Gypsy's face.

With a quick flip Creed reversed the blade in his right hand holding it cutting edge down and away from him. Without using the blade in his left he elbowed the creature hard across the chin driving the vampire to a knee. With all of his enhanced strength, Creed spun again bringing the blade in his right hand up and into the kneeling demon's neck.

Enchanted silver met with cursed flesh and in the blink of an eye the head separated from the neck and the body crumpled to the floor starting to smoke.

Claws raked down the back of his werewolf coat

and he whirled into the charge of yet another demon. His hyper reflexes responding to the unseen attack, he took hold of a vampire cape and swept the monster from its feet, driving it down onto the floor hard enough to steal the demon's air.

In two quick thrusts of his blades the Hunter sent another vampire back to Satan.

Dropping to one knee he caught sight of Rasmere holding his own against the three attackers while all about the hall Trillii warriors battled against any demon foolish enough to come near them.

Several of the brave animals lay dead or dying but they continued to fight sending at least two more vampires to Hell.

Charging again, Creed reacted, sending the form of Dahm crashing onto the floor before him.

"Get up, High Vampire of the Council. Finally we meet in combat!"

His knives flashed as he steadied himself into a combat stance and allowed the three thousand-year-old Lord to regain his feet.

"You are a foool to seeek mee out," Dahm spat flexing his claws. "I am the strongest oof our kind, Hunter. Cooome and try to killll me, asss you have the others."

Creed simply nodded as he waited for the demon to attack.

Dahm smiled a sadistic blood crazed smile as he tensed to rush the Hunter.

He flew from his feet coming at Creed his claws out and flailing at inhuman speed as they tried to find the Hunter's soft skin.

Turning in a blur Creed allowed the claws to rake along the shoulder of his coat as he spun following through with flashing blades. He missed the vampire by mere inches as Dahm shot past.

Turning in mid air the vampire's feet shot out and Creed was kicked backward colliding with one of the wooden pillars in his own hall. He saw stars and felt blood run down his neck soaking his shirt, the blow would have killed an average man but it barely dazed the Gypsy.

The impact did leave a spot of blood on the column though and as Creed rolled away from Dahm's next attack, the vampire paused running his fingers through the blood.

"Gypsy blooood," he moaned as he ran his bloody finger over his tongue.

"Finally I taste the bloood of Dariuss Creeed."

"Enjoy it monster," Creed responded. "It is the last you will ever taste."

He brought his knives up ready to finish the Vampire Lord.

Dahm smiled his lips encrusted with the fresh blood.

He lowered his head and rushed in again.

Creed met him his knives flashing as they thrust aside the demon's claws.

He pushed the Lord back gaining some space and was instantly rushed from the side. He kicked backward feeling a solid impact and the grunt of an inhuman voice. Creed paused long enough to see the demon he had kicked pounced on by several of the Trillii.

By the time he turned Dahm was coming his

way again and the Gypsy could see by the way the vampire was holding his claws their last encounter had been a painful one.

The vampire jumped forward and swung a vicious strike, his claws barely missing the ducking Gypsy. Creed came up and under the attack driving his knives into the soft spot of the Lord's stomach. The enchanted blades sunk deep and as Creed met Dahm's eyes, he was already beginning to smoke.

Creed pulled his blades free and stepped back feeling the adrenaline of his enchanted system running freely into his brain.

The hall of his home was complete carnage as several Trillii warriors finished off the last of the vampires in a far corner. To the near side, Rasmere leaned heavily against a stone pillar, three dead vampires at his boots.

He looked up, his glassy gaze settling on Creed as he wiped blood from his mouth.

"Pakur?" he asked as he struggled for air.

Creed spun glancing about the hall. The turned Lord was kneeling on the floor under the suspended figure of Father Joe who appeared to be glassy eyed and incoherent.

"He has been hypnotized," the Gypsy realized as he took a step toward the kneeling vampire.

Seeing the Hunter coming, Pakur stood, a chalice of blood in his hands.

"You are tooo late, Gypsssy. The ceremony hasss begun." He pointed on the polished wood floor of the hall.

"The voodoo witch taught meee the correct symbolsss to conjure and now that I am within the

426

circle I cannot be touched."

He chuckled loudly and Creed realized he was right; he was within a protective magic pentagram.

"We mussst ssstop him," Rasmere panted stepping to Pakur's far-left side.

"He is right," Creed observed with a glint in his eyes. "We cannot reach him now that he has begun the spell."

With an arrogant smile Pakur turned his back to them lifting the chalice.

"I callll you, my Lord Sataaan, with the blood of your greatest ssson Broshmer." He lifted the chalice in emphasis. "Preserved and feeed byyy the soul of a young womaaan, the descendant of the woman the great Vampire Lord loved."

He paused and poured a small amount of the blood onto the sacred symbols at his feet.

"With a virgin priessst, the ssservaaant of God, your bitter enemy. He willll call you forth and alllow you your firsst tassste of blood once you have made the transssition to thisss realm."

Now he raised the chalice and drank from its salty contents.

"I am your ssservant, Lord Satan. Hear my callll aasss I bring you forth into the world of the humansss you so despissse."

Upon the cross Father Joe called out loudly in a strange voice that echoed throughout the hall.

"Untum milia doe sertia ulum!"

The words sent a chill down the back of Creed as he watched the scene unfold in his home.

Off to the side of the cross a section of the air began to blur as a portal appeared and began to

427

grow. It started as the size of a baseball and quickly grew to larger-than-human proportions.

"Coome to meee, myy Lord!" Pakur cried out holding the chalice high above his head.

"Loook!" Rasmere pointed a clawed finger as a figure appeared in the watery image of the portal.

Creed felt his breath catch as he made out a figure, a tall figure with strikingly silver hair and milk white-eyes. He was tall and wore a strange coat of some unknown animal as he strode out of the portal and stood defiantly looking about.

"Broshmer!" Rasmere gasped in surprise as he recognized the dark angel and one of the very first of the vampire breed.

The figure turned his gaze to the Lord and regarded him briefly before nodding its head slowly.

"Rasssmere my sssonnn." Broshmer's voice was low and powerful and reverberated across the hall.

Creed shot a glance at Rasmere. He was standing as if frozen, his eyes fixed on the powerful vampire standing there before them.

They stood a moment in silence as sire and offspring met each other for the first time in a thousand years.

Slowly Broshmer broke eye contact and locked his milk white eyes onto the Gypsy Prince.

"Dariusss Creeed," a smile played across his blood red lips. "I have heard so much about you. Finally we meet."

"Enchanted, I'm sure," Creed answered his eyes remaining locked to those of the ancient demon.

Standing in his circle Pakur lowered the chalice

and stood amazed at the figure before him.

"Broshmer, where is Lord Satan?" he demanded his tone full of confusion.

The vampire regarded the much younger Lord.

"Sataaan?" he asked raising an eyebrow. "Did you really believe thaaat myyy bloood would bring foorth the very Loord of Hellll, the creator himself?" he shook his head. "You are nooot only arrooogant, Turned Bassstard, but alssso very foolish. The surviving esssence of my bloood will only summon meee back from the pitsss of Hell."

Then, as if thinking of something, he added with a chuckle. "Saaataan would noot cooome to a turned bassstard like you anyway."

At this the chalice dropped from Pakur's hands as he began to shake in unrestrained rage.

"But the old text explains that it would," he whispered anger filling his voice.

Broshmer leaned back and laughed loudly. "As I meant it too," he roared.

"I trusted that some day a power hungry Lord would resurrect me and call me back to this realm. I did not dream it would be a lowly bastard, however. I always thought it would be a proud True Blood."

"You dare call me a bastard?" Pakur stepped from the protective circle his claws flexing at his side. "I will send you back to Hell myself!"

With a scream of anger he sprang at the form of the mighty vampire, his claws raking for Broshmer's face.

In a blur of motion Broshmer caught Pakur in mid air, his massive claws closing about the younger Lord's neck. A loud crack echoed across the hall as Broshmer snarled and thrust his teeth deeply into Pakur's jugular!

The vampire's powerful jaws tore a huge chuck of the younger demon's neck away and he tossed the lifeless Pakur to the polished floor spitting the neck flesh from his mouth. Wiping away the excess blood that ran down his jaw and onto his chest Broshmer let out a loud growl.

"I have not fed for eons!" he roared feeling the power of the younger Lord's blood feed his system.

"Now that I am back, I will start my own world order, my own council and the beginning of the Dolmage!"

He roared even louder scanning about the hall until his eyes settled on Rasmere.

"Ahh, my son, the traitor who walks next to the Gypsy Hunter."

He stalked across the circle of Pakur kicking aside the chalice that the Lord had used to call him back.

"Unfortunately, you will have to die. After I have taken the blood of the Priest, I will be more powerful than any vampire in our legends."

As he approached, his claws flexing, Rasmere still remained as if frozen, caught in the spell of the return of the great Lord.

"Give Satan my regards," Broshmer wound up and unleashed a tremendous blow that caught Rasmere flush in the chest.

He was thrown across the hall. He crashed into the ancient statues of the Greek gods. He pulled himself up from the broken marble pieces and his eyes met Creed's.

"You owe me," he whispered before he collapsed, gasping for air onto the hard polished floor.

Broshmer stalked onto the open floor his eyes meeting Creed's, the Hunter was in the way and he wanted to finish Rasmere before his son had a chance to get up and shake off his shock.

"Step aside Gypsy," the Lord commanded. "Allow me to finish this so I can get on with building my empire. Our time will come soon enough."

His knuckles white on the handles of his blades, Creed shook his head. "No, Lord Broshmer, my mission is to hunt and destroy the forces of evil, to exterminate those who would live among the shadows and prey upon humans. Rasmere may be a Vampire Lord and he may be my greatest enemy, but I believe that you are far more dangerous. I am pretty sure you are insane."

This angered the Lord and he dove forward hitting Creed with a speed the Gypsy had not been prepared for. He flew across the polished floor on his back striking one of the tipped over high backed chairs of Pakur's council.

He struck with a thud and felt the blades fly free from his hands as he ricocheted towards a marble column where he stopped, trying to get his breath back. The vampire was strong, stronger than any he had ever faced and now he strode across the hall heading for the injured Rasmere, his claws flexing for the kill.

Creed struggled to his feet and reached for his weapons, afraid he would be too late to stop

Broshmer!

As the Lord stepped over the crumpled form of his son he paused, fixing his predator's gaze on the thumping artery of Rasmere's neck.

"There is no room for you in my new empire," he hissed as he prepared to tear the artery free and drink his blood.

As he reared back to strike something leaped to his neck and Broshmer heard a hissing sound as sharp claws dug into his back and shoulder. He glanced back seeing the gold trimmed red cloak and silver chain of the King of the Trillii!

"Get off me, cat!" he screamed, trying to tear the snarling beast from his back.

Around him the room suddenly came to life as more of the surviving warriors joined their king in the attack. They leaped upon him, throwing the Lord off balance and stumbling backwards as sharp claws tore at his eyes and face. He tripped upon the smoking skeleton of one of the dead vampires and fell rolling to the floor. The Trillii jumped for safety as the Lord tumbled and rolled about trying to regain his balance. Brushing the last one away he made it to one knee, wiping blood from his torn flesh.

"Shach Meril!" he roared in anger and pain from his torn face and shoulders. "You willll payyy for thisss!"

His vow rippled across the hall and he looked about trying to catch a glimpse of the feline warriors. Instead he looked up into the dark eyes of the Gypsy Prince!

"Come Broshmer," Creed invited his silver

blades shining in his scarred fists. "It is time for you to return to Satan."

Broshmer snarled as he climbed to his feet. "Thisss coat I wear isss made from the skinsss of my humaaan victims Gypsssy, I will add yours to it."

He shot forward swinging a powerful swipe towards the Gypsy's head.

This time Creed was prepared. He slapped the blow aside with the flat of his left-hand blade. In response, he whirled, slashing a backstroke with the right knife that narrowly missed the vampire's neck.

"Goood ooone. You are very fassst, Gypsssy," Broshmer grunted as he slashed upward with a taloned hand.

It raked across Creed's werewolf coat and one of the claws caught in the Gypsy's right front pocket. In a blur Creed slashed down and severed the taloned hand from Broshmer's arm.

The vampire stepped back and screamed in pain as it watched the hand fall to the floor.

Creed, too, paused, the silver blades usually killed a vampire on contact no matter where they struck. It became apparent that Broshmer was stronger than even the silver of his blades.

He jumped forward launching himself towards the reeling Lord, spinning in the air his boot shot out and he kicked Broshmer hard across the face. The vampire was tossed from his feet and crashed to the floor landing with a thud.

Snarling, he rolled and managed to get back to his feet.

He rose keeping his hate filled eyes on the

dangerous human before him.

"I thiiink I will leave fooor now, Gypsssy," he announced. "The hand I cannn grow back after I haaave fed well. We will meeeet again."

He spun to flee from the doors of the hall but suddenly there was the sound of padded feet and a purr-like voice sounded in the hall.

"We will not allow that," Shach Meril vowed as he appeared with the remainder of his warriors blocking Broshmer's escape route to the doors.

The vampire glared at the red-cloaked animals, many bloody from their own wounds. With a snarl of frustration he spun facing the Gypsy.

"I willl killll you allll!" he promised charging toward his human enemy.

He kicked forward but Creed blocked it with his left forearm while slashing viciously towards the vampire's waistline.

A second time Broshmer screamed in pain as more blood appeared, soaking through his unholy clothes. He hesitated a second too long and the Gypsy took advantage of the opening.

With every ounce of his enhanced strength the Hunter drove the blade in his right hand up under the demon's rib cage. It bit deep until the handle grew sticky with demon blood. With a back handed stroke Creed slashed with his left-handed blade across the vampire's neck. Again the blade bit deeply and Creed reversed the weapon in his hand. This time with a forward stroke he completely severed Broshmer's head from his shoulders, it fell to the floor with a dull thud.

Creed pulled his blade free from the vampire's

torso. Already the body was beginning to smoke.

"Send my greetings to Satan," Creed whispered. "Tell him I am still here waiting."

Rasmere stumbled on weak knees as Creed helped him from the hall and out into the dark of the night. The Gypsy looked upon the scene of the mighty fight that had occurred in the gardens and the square.

At the ancient fountain, Joel and Wilfred sat while many of the young Gypsy men lay about them exhausted or bandaging their wounds.

Creed gave them a short nod and they returned it. The battle had been won.

Shach Meril led his warriors past the Gypsy and to the fountain where they drank or washed themselves cleansing the demon blood from their coats.

Creed placed Rasmere down gently on one of the stone benches before he walked to the fountain and knelt beside the courageous felines.

"We owe you a mighty debt," he said, meeting Shach Meril's gaze.

The cat rested on the cool stone of the fountain rim.

"No, you do not," he purred back. "It is our duty as it is yours, Prince of the Gypsies, and we do it freely and without regret."

His tail whipped about as he looked from his bloodied surviving warriors back to Creed.

"Through time, it has always been the Gypsy Hunters who form the catalyst and hold us all together. We exist to serve you and as long as the line of the Gypsy Hunters exist, we will always be here."

Creed nodded, there was little to add to the statement.

"You have a habit of showing up when needed," he placed his hand gently on the cat's neck. "Thank You."

Shach Meril simply dipped his head accepting the praise.

Creed stood rolling his muscular shoulders before he turned to check on Rasmere, the stone bench was empty.

He chuckled to himself. The Vampire Lord was gone!

EPILOGUE

Creed reclined as he felt the warm evening air of mid summer blow over his beautiful valley. He was sitting in the grove resting in the marble chair he had hauled down here last year after the birth of his son.

The child had turned one today and he had brought him here to give Selena a rest, at least that is what he had used as an excuse. The truth was that he enjoyed these moments alone with the boy and he allowed a smile to cross his face as he watched the child and the kitten play on the blanket next to him.

The kitten had mysteriously appeared this morning, sleeping on the child's blanket next to him in the crib. Neither Creed nor Selena had heard anyone enter their room during the night. At first they were concerned but when they lifted the child and the yawning kitten from the crib, the answer had become clear as a small red cloak and silver chain appeared from the folds of the cloth.

"A Trillii warrior?" Selena had raised an eyebrow. "You are a lucky baby."

She kissed the child as she took him into the bathroom for a tub.

Creed looked at the kitten that slowly opened one eye and stared back at him. With a grunt, he placed the kitten back in the crib lightly and watched the animal snuggle as it slipped back to sleep. Picking up the red cloak he noticed the gold trim.

"Not just a Trillii warrior," he whispered to himself. "One of the royal family."

A strong aroma on the wind caught his attention and he stood slowly picking up the antique flintlock pistol loaded with a silver ball.

"There is no need for that."

Creed searched for the source of the voice and soon the form of Rasmere appeared from the trees. "I have only come by to see the young Prince."

Creed lowered the weapon but remained alert. He had not heard a whisper of Rasmere's name in the last year.

"After all, I did save him and his mother," the vampire chuckled as he stepped over to the blanket and gazed upon the child. From beside the baby the kitten stood raising its front paw and hissing at the Lord.

Spying the kitten Rasmere sniffed stepping back. "A Trillii?" he snorted. "The young Prince is well guarded already."

Creed shrugged. "He appeared this morning."

Rasmere folded his hands behind his back, he was in human disguise and he even smiled a bit.

"I would like to give the boy a gift, a small thing that I have had over the years. I will never have a son, at least in the way you humans do. Would you mind if I passed it on to him?"

Creed felt his eyes narrow. He did not like the idea of Rasmere being so close to the boy.

"Yes, but do nothing foolish," he cautioned.

Rasmere shot him a half smile. "I assure you that is not my intention, Gypsy King."

Folding his coat about him he knelt taking the infants hand in his. Slowly reaching into his coat he removed an object wrapped in cloth and carefully placed it into the boy's hand.

The child looked at it and allowed it to drop, dangling from its finely crafted chain.

Creed saw it and frowned; it was a finely made cross of pure silver.

"How did you?"

Rasmere stood looking from the boy to Creed. "The cloth allows me to handle the metal without adverse effects. That cross at one time belonged to the woman warrior, Joan of Arc. How I obtained it is of no matter but I felt the need to pass it on to someone. I guess that since I helped save his life, I felt he should have it," he smiled down upon the infant. "Some day I may live to regret that act of mercy."

Creed had to nod with a smile. "It is very possible."

Meeting the Lord's eyes he held out his hand. "It is a nice present; thank you.'

Rasmere looked at the offered hand and shook his head. "Let's not, Gypsy."

He stepped to the end of the grove knowing he had already stayed too long. He unfolded his arms ready to mouth the spell that would allow him to vanish into the winds.

He paused looking back over his shoulder.

"What is his name, Creed? What is the name of the next great Hunter of the Shadows?"

"Asmus," Creed answered. "Asmus Rasmere Creed."

Tossing his head back Rasmere let out a mighty roar of laughter.

"I like it!" he replied before he whispered the words of the spell and was gone.

Creed sat back down relaxing in the chair as he watched the baby drift off to sleep the cross still in his tiny fist.

"Wait until Father Joe hears about this," he chuckled deep in his chest.

"This has been a strange day, my son," he whispered. "To have been visited by both the King of the Trillii and the new head Lord of the Council. I shudder to think what the future will hold."

The End.

ABOUT THE AUTHOR

Mark Haeuser was born and raised in the beautiful
farm country surrounding Fountain City Wisconsin.

A graduate from C-FC High School in 1983, he
attended WWTC in La Crosse and graduated with a
two-year associate degree in Police Science.

After working ten years in law enforcement he
decided to pursue other interests. Mark began
writing in 1997 when he grew frustrated with what
he felt was a lack of realistic action books available.
As a former police officer, SWAT team member,
SWAT sniper and a recognized expert in tactics and
firearms he decided he would try to write his own
stories. Using over twenty years of martial arts
training and his police experience he set out to write
the first book, which grew into Battleground USA
"The Beginning"

Mark intends to write twelve to fifteen books in this exciting action packed series. He has currently published two of the books with Iuniverse and plans another for the spring of 2002. He has five of the books completed and plans for number six is in the works. He also writes fantasy and his current book with Iuniverse is *"The Second Coming Trilogy"*. This is the first book in the trilogy titled *"The Protectors"*

Mark can be seen on such web sites as Zinos.com and Authorsden.com. His new series of short stories *"Memoirs of a Rogue"* is highly popular on the Authorsden site. He is also involved in co-authoring a book with the romance novelist, Kristie Leigh Maguire.

Mark currently lives in La Crosse and is working on more Battleground USA books as well as a western titled *"Deacon Cade,"* and a crime story titled *"Black OPS."* He plans on putting together his *"Memoirs of a Rogue"* for publishing in the near future.